I GUESS
I LIVE
HERE
NOW

I GUESS I LIVE HERE NOW

Claire Ahn

Viking

VIKING
An imprint of Penguin Random House LLC, New York

First published in the United States of America by Viking,
an imprint of Penguin Random House LLC, 2022.

Visit us online at penguinrandomhouse.com

Library of Congress Cataloging-in-Publication Data is available.

Book manufactured in Canada

ISBN 9780593403198

10   9   8   7   6   5   4   3   2   1

FRI

Design by Kate Renner
Text set in Celeste Pro

FOR 엄마. FOR TEACHING ME TO DREAM.
사랑해요

ONE

*n*ew Yorkers throw things away too easily. Sitting on the soccer field on 52nd Street and 11th Avenue, I'm painting patterns on a small wooden stool I snagged from the block my mom and I live on, a few avenues east of here, and the turf makes the underside of my thighs feel prickly. I'm wiping sweat from my forehead every few seconds so it doesn't drip onto the wet paint. My favorite oversized yellow sunflower-print dress is potentially ruined, with multiple smears of blue paint now dotting the hem.

"Boo!" Sophia pushes me lightly on the shoulders, causing me to almost knock my stool over.

I grip my stool in surprise. "Soph! You can't scare someone who's already so nervous."

"You'll live. Here," my best friend says, handing me a slice of pizza half falling off a paper plate. She looks especially cute today—her curly black hair tied up in massive space buns and dressed in a bright blue crop top with high-waisted white jeans. "I got the goods," she says mischievously.

I inhale the cheesy aroma of 99 Cent Express Pizza and gratefully take the plate from her. "Thanks," I say between bites. "Soph, I'm sweating." I lift up my pizza-holding arm and fan my armpit with my free hand.

"You're sweating because it's the end of August," she replies. "Cool stool. Another street find?"

I ignore her question because I can't stop thinking about what we're about to do. "Are you sure this is a good idea? What if we get caught? Can you go to jail for this?" The thought of my mom bailing me out raises goose bumps on my skin despite the beating sun. We have perfect records both in school and, well, criminally, as in zero offenses, and I'm not sure junior year is the time to taint them.

Soph massages my shoulder like she's giving me a pep talk. "Mel, if you walk down Tenth Avenue, all you smell is weed. No one gives. It'll be fine, trust me," she says confidently. "We said we'd try to be a little bit more badass this year, right?"

"Yeah, like a sip of alcohol, Soph, not potentially getting thrown in jail," I whisper, so no undercover cops hear us.

Soph raises her eyebrows at me and shrugs. "If you've changed your mind, say the word and I won't force you. But mind you, it was *your* idea to be 'rebellious,'" she says in air quotes.

I sigh and look at her for a long time. "Fine, but not here." I stand up, wrestling the dry part of my stool into my tote bag.

As we walk an avenue west, toward 12th, I feel sweat dripping down my neck and tie my hair up in a big bun with my favorite scrunchie. "We're going to be *juniors*." I feel sentimental just stating that. In just two years, we're going to be in colleges possibly outside of New York, although I can't imagine living anywhere but here.

"I feel so old," Soph says. "Oh yeah, what were you saying about your parents yesterday? On the phone, something about your dad not coming this month. You hung up so quickly."

"Sorry, I freaked out thinking my mom might've heard me." I shrug. "Something feels off. My parents talk maybe once a month, if that, but these past two weeks, she's been on the phone with him almost every day. And she closes her door then comes out all tense afterward. Maybe it's all in my head, but I doubt it."

"I think I'm more impressed they can talk that often from opposite ends of the world."

I shrug. Maybe it's strange to other people, but I've never known another living situation. My dad lives in Seoul, and while I've only been there once, he visits us in New York City exactly three times a year—no more, no less. To me, Korea is what I see on TV during my mom's Korean-drama marathons: boys with over-the-top romantic gestures who really need to stop grabbing girls' arms, and girls who never sweat no matter how fast they run.

"Why don't you just ask?"

I chew on my lip in thought. "I don't know. Feels weird."

"Well, are you sad your dad didn't come this month?" she adds.

"No, not really. My mom said he's busy right now in Seoul. Maybe he'll come visit in September." When my dad comes, he's usually here for just one week, so after sixteen years, I still don't fully feel comfortable around him, the way I do with my mom; he's the most formal and stern person I know, the quintessential Strict Asian Parent, a real-life K-drama figure.

When we reach 12th Avenue, we find a secluded corner and

Sophia carefully draws a small white paper stick from her pocket. "You ready?" she asks me. She lifts it up to show me. "My cousin rolled it up for us already."

My phone vibrates in the pocket of my tote bag and I jump about a foot, making my stool fall out.

"God, Mel, you need to calm down. You're going to get us caught," Soph chides me.

I open my phone and it's my mom.

UMMA
taco bell for dinner tonight?

My thumbs nervously text back a thumbs-up emoji, and I put my phone away. My mom has her Scary Mother side but is usually a very chill person and my other best friend. Not every daughter has a mom that loves getting Taco Bell takeout as much as she does, and I know I'm lucky. I feel a twinge of guilt and give Soph a concerned look, which she reads instantly.

"You're not backing out now, right?"

"No, I'm not." We exchange grins and she pulls out a lighter—also from her cousin. I look at her trying to light the joint and stifle my laughter.

"Struggling there?"

She pulls a face at me. "Shut up, I need to focus." Sweat beads on her forehead as she concentrates on the lighter, applying the flame very carefully to only the edge of the joint. "Then you have to rotate it around slowly, so it burns evenly."

"Look who's a pro."

"My cousin taught me, and Google and YouTube. Apparently, if it's burnt unevenly, might as well not even smoke it." She holds up her finished product. "Ta-da! A work of art," Soph says, pointing to the tip of the burning joint.

"What happens if it burns unevenly?" I ask, leaning in to take a closer look.

"I dunno."

At the ripe age of sixteen, we have yet to be interested in what our more precocious classmates have already indulged in over the last school year: drinking, late-night partying, smoking, sex. But it's time to catch up. Drugs first, apparently, thanks to Soph's cousin's connection.

"Okay," she says steadily, bringing it to her lips. "Here goes." I don't realize I'm holding my breath until she bursts into a fit of coughs and I'm hitting her back rhythmically because I don't know what else to do. Between coughs, she hands me the joint. "Your turn."

"You barely smoked it!" I say accusingly.

"Well, I need a break. You try."

"Wait, do you feel anything?"

"No, not yet. My cousin said it takes twenty minutes or so."

"Well, you probably have to actually inhale it, not cough it all out." I take a deep breath and repeat Sophia's motions, daintily holding the joint between my fingers. I take my first hit and try to keep it down but also end up in a coughing fit. We're ready to try for the second time, but before we can really start to enjoy our little act of rebellion, a voice calls out from behind us.

"You girls look a little young to be doing that."

We whip our heads around and my body tenses immediately. I drop the joint and step on it as smoothly as I can, but I know the police officer's already seen it. And smelled it.

I shake my head and put on the most innocent, casual smile

my facial muscles will allow me to form. My words tumble out in a mess that rivals the blue paint splatters on my dress. "Oh, we're not. Koreans have very youthful genes. You should see my mom, she's in her forties but could pass as my older sister. Or a young aunt. Or an older cousin. And my friend is Ethiopian." I pause. "Good young genes there, too."

Sophia nudges me. "Stop talking," she says between clenched jaws.

"We're twenty-three," I add, my mouth unable to comply with this basic cue.

"Mel, for the love of—"

The police officer cuts her off. "IDs?"

Oh God. I am *toast*. My mom will definitely not be my best friend today.

Less than twenty minutes later, we're back on Ninth Avenue, and my building's front door is taunting me as I wait with the officer for my mom to come downstairs after he spoke with her through the intercom.

"I have the key, you know," I mutter, but he just stands there, impassive and cold like a statue.

When my mom sees me with the officer upon opening the door, her brows are furrowed with concern. Studying her more closely, I realize she looks tired, like she hasn't been sleeping well. Then, as he explains why he brought me home, her concerned face changes, contorted with anger.

"I dropped off the other young girl, um, Sophia Taye," he says, like he's trying to remember her name, "and now I'm dropping this one off with you. It's a warning," he says, turning to me, "but don't let it happen again."

I stare at the ground while my mom nods multiple times

like she's grateful for the warning and nothing more. "Thank you, Officer." She closes the big brown door and says nothing while angrily stalking up the flights of stairs to our apartment. When we get inside, I keep a good distance from my mom, or as much of a distance as I can. Right now our tiny kitchen looks suffocating instead of cozy, and the apartment feels too small for the tension that's breaking through the low white ceiling. I stare past her at our sink, which is too narrow to fit more than a few pots at a time, wishing it could swallow me whole right now.

"*Lee Solmi,*" she says angrily, whipping around to face me. "What were you thinking? Smoking *weed*?" Her face is red and her eyes are glaring coldly. It doesn't help that they're twice the size of mine. "Well?"

My voice comes out small. "It was just one small puff. I don't feel anything. It wasn't even a real drag because I barely smoked it. I promise I'm not high. I coughed it all out." I stare at the burnt-orange wood floor. "It was for . . . future memories."

"Future memories?" She's looking at me like I just said something really stupid, which is probably true. It certainly feels stupid hearing her say it back to me.

"You know . . ." I say, shifting my body, "something we can laugh about in the future."

My mom presses her fingers to her forehead and shuts her eyes. I steal a glance at her while keeping my head bowed. She's wearing a faded green tie-dyed tee. I remember the day we tie-dyed it together years ago, back when I was in elementary school. I hated how my green one turned out and cried about it, so she gave me her purple one. "Melody, you could have been arrested, you know that? And we're lucky the officer didn't fine us. What are you thinking, to risk throwing away your future like that?"

I look again at her green tee and can't remember the last time we did something fun like tie-dyeing together. "I'm sorry," I mumble. "I didn't think it was that big of a deal."

I know that was the wrong thing to say because right after I say it, her face gets redder and I can see the outlines of her veins. Without a word, my mom goes into her room and shuts her door loudly. I feel a little bit at a loss of what to do or say because she's rarely this mad. Things blow over relatively fast in this household. I guess I could follow her and apologize profusely, but really, deep down, I don't think that what I've done warrants so much anger from her. I'm a top student, only second to Sophia in school, and I never get in trouble. It was *one* time and not even a real puff.

I go into my room and quietly close the door behind me. Four missed calls from Sophia.

"Soph?" I say when she picks up.

"Is your mom mad?"

I nod even though she can't see me. "With the rage of a thousand wronged girlfriends."

Sophia lets out a sigh. "I guess we deserve it. My dad grounded me for a month from all screens, except my phone, for one hour a day. I'm sorry, Mel. I really didn't think we'd get caught."

"It's not your fault. Those youthful genes of mine probably got us caught," I say, feigning lightness. "I'm sure it'll blow over by tomorrow," I assure her, willing myself to believe my own words.

After we hang up, I ignore the gurgling sound in my stomach.

There are tacos on the table, but I'm too scared to leave my room right now. I change out of my clothes, which smell very faintly of weed, and sit cross-legged on my floor, pulling my sketchbook out from under my bed. When I open my portfolio—the one I'll be submitting to Maison & Saito Interiors' summer internship program—I let the familiar soothing feeling that comes from looking at art wash over me as I comb through drawings and designs. I can only hope my drawings are good enough to be considered for the coveted internship position at one of the top interior design firms in the world. But I don't think about that tonight. Tonight, I stare at my art longer than usual, wishing I was inside a fake home I've drawn for myself, one with high vaulted ceilings and colorful Moroccan poufs. I never traveled much, but my drawings allow me to capture the places I dream of going or images from movies or memories I hold on to in my head so I don't forget.

WHEN I WAKE THE NEXT MORNING, I CAN HEAR MY mom humming from her bedroom. The tension in my chest releases. She must be in a better mood. My mom sings a lot but *always* when she's in a good, relaxed mood, the way most of us would play a Spotify "Café Vibes" playlist. Our apartment is a one-bedroom flex, so the fake wall in my room is thin enough that I can hear when my mom moves around. I hear her humming "Sweet Caroline," except for the "ba ba ba" part, which she sings loudly. My mom has the best singing voice I've ever heard, besides actual professional singers, although she's probably better than a lot of them, too. Her voice makes our apartment feel lively, even though it's just the two of us. And today, her singing nearly makes me forget about last night. Usually, I'll chime in with her singing, and she'll disagree when I sulk and say my voice is nothing like hers. Instead, she'll usually harmonize once I join in with the melody, and we'll sing until we forget the lyrics, usually halfway through.

I leave my bedroom, and when she meets my eye, I offer a tentative smile. "I like today's song," I say as I head to the bathroom to remove yesterday's winged eyeliner off my face, now smudged in multiple places. I look like a sad raccoon.

I can see her staring at me in the bathroom mirror. "There's kimchi jjigae on the table. I have to talk to your father for a few minutes. After that, we're visiting Halmoni today. Be ready to leave in fifteen minutes."

I mumble an okay and my curiosity nudges me to ask why we're going today, but she shuts her door before I can get a word out. We usually visit on Sundays once a month. Today is Saturday and we just visited two weekends ago, not that I'm complaining. I love my halmoni.

I'm praying my mom doesn't tell my dad about last night. He's a lot more conservative than my mom and me. He's like a well-mannered Korean dictator who's always immaculately dressed in outfits that scream "I am an Important Man at a fancy law firm" and is constantly wishing for a daughter he can teach his ways. Too bad that daughter will never be me. Every time he visits us from Seoul, he's always telling me I need to stop wasting my time and take myself more seriously, whatever that means. When I was younger, I remember being really sad that he lived so far away, but he told me that a lot of Important

Business Families live separately, so I didn't bring it up again. Mostly because he told me to stop asking stupid questions. Once, in second grade, I cried because a classmate, Toby Yang, told me my parents must be divorced if they don't live together and don't talk often and that they're just probably keeping it a secret from me. I soon learned that my parents' situation is different, and that living separately is common in Korea and other parts of Asia, like Singapore and Hong Kong. There's even a name for it—a "gireogi appa" is a father who lives in Korea while his family lives in an English-speaking country for a better education for the kids.

Toby Yang is a jerk.

I dig into my food, sating my hunger from yesterday with big spoonfuls of brown rice today. The spicy kimchi stew warms my stomach, and while I eat my breakfast, I try to empty my mind of the cold-shoulder treatment from my mom and the conversation happening behind her closed door. I wish I could hold on to this feeling of satisfaction longer, but I know life has a way of ruining dreams when you least expect it.

TWO

*T*he subway ride on the 7 train to Flushing is awkward and tense. My mom and I sit next to each other but don't say a word. We weave through the crowded streets of Flushing, dodging street vendors and aggressive middle-aged women with their shopping bags. My mouth waters at the varied aromas of stir-fried vegetables and beef and fish balls mixing in the air. Eventually we arrive at Hanguk Flushing Home, and I see my grandma outside in the main garden area. I rush toward her and wrap her in a bear hug. "Missed you, Halmoni." The retirement home is catered toward elderly Koreans, and soon a swarm of other ladies—my grandma's friends who have seen me visit every so often for the last ten years or so—surround me, pinching my cheeks and telling me to enjoy my baby-butt-like skin while it lasts. My halmoni comes to my rescue and waves them off, and I insa to the other grandmas as we follow her into her apartment, politely promising in my elementary Korean to say goodbye before I leave.

Inside, my grandma walks slowly toward the small kitchen

table and hands me a plump persimmon. I always get a little sad when I see her because I can tell she's aging fast. The persimmon is soft and mushy and ready to eat. "Eat," she says, handing me a plate and spoon. In Korean, she tells me she and my mom need to talk in private and that I should sit and wait in the kitchen.

"About what?" I turn to my mom, expecting an answer, but they don't respond.

A part of me wants to eavesdrop, but the persimmon is so juicy and soft and reminiscent of warm summer days with my halmoni that I let the happy memories of my elementary school years keep me distracted on the sofa. Between bites, I strain to hear their conversation, but their voices are so quiet that even if I pressed my ear against the door, I don't think I'd hear anything anyway. Instead I continue to enjoy my fruit and pull out my book, turning to an unfinished chapter of *An Ember in the Ashes.*

After their mysterious mother-daughter talk, we visit a Chinese restaurant together for lunch, where I promptly inhale a whole basket of steaming soup dumplings. Even in eighty-four-degree weather, I can think of nothing more satisfying than the hot fatty soup that gushes out of a xiao long bao as I bite into it. Inevitably, I burn my tongue but finish slurping the rest of the soup from my last dumpling carefully so that it doesn't splatter onto the plate. My halmoni compliments me on how well I eat while also telling me not to overeat in case I lose my slim figure. I nod obediently as I stuff my mouth with bok choy. Leave it to a Korean grandma to remind you that metabolism won't last forever. Pretty soon our meal is over, and we are back at the nursing home, where we part ways. I hate saying bye to my grandma because she loves when we visit. I determine to visit her more often this school year as we wave goodbye.

It's late afternoon by the time we come back home. On the subway I dared to ask my mom what she and Halmoni talked about, but she just stared out the window across from us. I can't tell if she's still mad at me or if something else is wrong. For a moment I panic and wonder if my halmoni is sick. If she is, she didn't show it. I'm about to ask when my mom turns to me.

"I have to run some errands. Be home by eight." She talks with a stoicism I'm not used to.

"I was just going to stay home."

"I need the house to myself for a few hours."

"O-kay." I don't like this tension between us.

A cold shower and a wardrobe change later, I meet Soph on the front steps of her building. As we walk, my boxy, pale gray linen dress allows me to stay cool in the early evening breezes, and I get a whiff of my own Dove deodorant that the wind carries into my nostrils. We sit inside De Witt Clinton Park on the turf, watching sweaty soccer players in neon-colored pinnies kicking around.

Sophia drums her fingers on her cheek as I explain the strange vibes I'm getting from my mom. "Weird. It's like Lily's freezing you out," Sophia says.

"Yeah, it's bizarre. I wonder if I should try talking to her again or something."

"Doesn't sound like she'd tell you even if you did."

"Yeah, guess not." I don't say much more because I want to change the topic. I turn to face Soph and squeeze her hand excitedly. "How did the audition go? Have you heard back?"

She shakes her head. "They're taking forever with the call-backs. It's usually so much faster."

"You're going to be Broadway's biggest star one day. I know it."

"Oh, you know it, huh? Okay, if one day I am, you can design the stage that I perform on."

"That's not really interior design, but I'd still be honored," I answer, bowing.

"When's your application due?"

"I'll mail in my portfolio in a week or so, probably. Maison & Saito Interiors said they won't announce the final candidates for the internship until mid-October, though."

Soph throws one arm around my shoulder. "Future famous interior designer, future famous Broadway performer. That's us."

"Done deal. Pizza?"

She grins. We peel stray blades of Astroturf off our clothes and walk toward Eighth Avenue, where the second-best pizza in NYC stands. 99 Cent Express Pizza will always be the taste of home to us and is easily our favorite pizza joint, no pun intended. It's not as iconic as Roberta's or Prince Street Pizza, but it's homier, and the guys who work there recognize us as regulars, which is always nice.

After we down our pizzas with root beer—the most under-rated of all beverages—I grudgingly start heading back toward our street.

We wave from our respective stoops across the street from each other, and I head into my building, panting by the time I reach the top of the three measly flights. When I unlock the door marked 3F, I can barely push it open and stick my head in halfway. There are boxes pushed up against the door and scattered all over our tiny living room.

"Mo-om?" I shout through the crack of the door.

She helps open the door, and I stare wordlessly around the apartment.

"Did you get a sudden itch to redo our apartment?"

She sits on the sofa and gestures for me to sit across from her on our small ottoman. She sighs and looks at me for a long time before speaking. "We're moving," she says, with the same direct tone she'd use to say "Here's dinner."

"Like . . . to a different unit? A different building? I didn't even know you were looking at apartments. I could've come with you."

"No." She shakes her head. "To Korea."

I can't read her expression clearly. She looks sad yet determined, like staying is not an option.

I look at the dining table on our left, the boxes strewn about, her bedroom floor where her clothes and books and laptop lie haphazardly in a pile.

"What?" Everything feels hazy to me suddenly.

"We're moving. To Seoul, to live with your dad."

I'm confused and starting to feel nauseous. I'm positive I'm mishearing my mom.

"What?" I repeat. "Like on a vacation?"

"Mel, we're moving to Korea."

I don't think I believe her, but I see the mess, the boxes, the clothes, and I know we are, but it isn't registering. I keep staring at the boxes and wondering if I'm actually here or not. Or if I'm imagining everything.

"How . . . why . . ." I barely manage to get any words out. "*When?*"

My mom sighs again. "Monday night. Our flight departs at 12:50 a.m." When I don't say anything, she continues. "I'm sorry it has to be such a surprise to you, Melody, but your dad has actually been talking to me about this for a while—"

"All those phone calls. These last few weeks."

My mom stutters for a moment. "Uh, y-yes. Mel, I know—"

I cut her off, my rising anger quickly replacing my confusion. "And you never thought to tell me?" I glare at her, knowing she can see the hurt in my eyes. "Is it because I tried weed? I promise I'll never do it again, you know I won't. You know I keep my promises." My voice is higher than normal and coming out squeaky, like I'm begging her for something. I stand up, feeling all too claustrophobic in this chaotic living room.

She shakes her head. "It's not about the weed, Mel. We've lived apart from your father since you were a baby and I really believed it was for the best, that you should be raised here in the States. But now you have less than two years before you'll go off to college, and after a lot of conversations, we both agree it'll be good for you to spend some time with him before you leave for God knows where."

"That's what summers are for, aren't they?" I don't understand why all of a sudden my mom has this new mantra. Why now? Why when I'm about to start junior year? We've been fine on our own this whole time, just the two of us.

My mom pats the sofa but I don't join her. "Please, honey? Sit. When you were younger, you used to cry all the time because we lived so far from your dad. Don't you want to try being close again?"

"He visits us plenty. Why doesn't *he* move here, if he's so keen on spending time with me again?"

"You know he can't do that with his job."

"No, I know that he doesn't *want* to with his job."

"I've always had a democracy in this house, you know that. I'm not overbearing because that's how my mom was, and it drove me crazy. It suffocated me, and I didn't want to suffocate you. I try to always let you make your own choices . . . but this time it's different. It'll be better in Korea, better for you to also be with your father, to get to know him better."

My voice grows louder, maybe to make up for how quiet she's being. "We're not really moving, right? You're just saying these things because you're angry." My eyes are watering now, and I tighten my lips to keep the tears from falling.

"The decision's already been made, Mel. You just need to trust me on this one. We made this choice a while ago, actually, but I just hadn't been able to tell you. I knew you wouldn't take it well. I should've told you sooner."

"I can't believe you've been hiding this decision from me. How long have you been planning this, huh?" My voice turns cruel. I can't help it; I feel betrayed. "And what happened to 'everything is a democracy in our household'? Did you decide to throw that out the window because Dad wants me to come to Korea all of a sudden? Do you not have an opinion about uprooting both our lives and moving to a foreign country? When are you planning to move us back? Do I even have a say? Our lives are here, Umma. Our friends are here. You don't know or have anyone in Korea except Dad, and you barely even talk to him. Oh, and your sister, someone that I don't even know because you *never* talk to her."

My mom looks at me, her face contorted with pain, probably at the mention of her sister. I know it was a low blow, bringing in my estranged aunt like that. "Go to your room and start packing," she says. "You'll complete junior year in Korea. I'm sorry it has to be this way, Mel, but it does."

She grabs a few unfolded boxes from her room and puts them into my hands. "The movers come Monday afternoon."

THE NEXT THIRTY-SIX HOURS GO BY IN A HAZE OF Chinese takeout food, Taco Bell, and endless boxes stacked against the wall. How do you pack up sixteen years of stuff in a day? I guess it's easier than you'd think if your home is seven hundred square feet.

We're leaving in a few hours and my eyes are swollen from crying. I'm in Sophia's room, downloading the KakaoTalk app for her on her phone.

"I can't believe you're leaving like this," Soph says as she looks at me from the floor with her legs propped up against the wall. "This came out of nowhere."

"Yeah." It's all I can manage. "I use this app to talk to my dad and my halmoni. She prefers it over text. It's basically WhatsApp but for Koreans." Soph and I send each other crying emojis in our new KakaoTalk (KaTok or Tok, for short) chat and giggle, but there's a bitterness underneath.

"How's your mom?"

I pick at the wall. "We've barely talked. And I'm not interested in how she's doing. Do you think I could emancipate myself from her? Then I could stay here," I say, only half joking.

Soph squeezes my hand. "You'd regret it."

"Maybe my mom's been tricking me this entire time. Acting like everything's fine, acting like we're so close and always telling each other everything, and bam—we're going to Korea." I pause. "I think I really hurt her." I recall her face when I mentioned Aunt Rebecca and accused her of barely speaking to either of them. It was true, wasn't it?

"I really hope this isn't because of the weed. I still feel so shitty. I'm sorry, Mel," Soph says. She scoots closer to me and leans her head on my knee.

"It's not. She said it's been a decision for a long time, apparently."

"Either way, I guess you're leaving."

"Yeah," I say again, feeling numb inside.

When I reach the steps of my building, I turn around to wave a final goodbye to Soph.

"LOVE YOU, SOPH!" I scream across the way.

"LOVE YOU MORE, MEL!" she shouts back.

After I finally force myself to turn away from my best friend and head inside, I go upstairs to my apartment and stare around my almost-empty bedroom. My limbs feel weak and lifeless as I muster whatever energy I have left to pack my bag for the plane and gently slide my portfolio into my tote. I won't let Korea stop me from sending in my internship application to Maison & Saito.

By the time we finish the final bits of packing and watching the movers haul our boxes away, we're a little behind schedule and rush into our Uber. The last forty-eight hours happened so quickly that even after the car ride to the airport and checking in our bags, this all still feels like a bad dream.

"Are you sad?" I ask my mom, giving in to the urge to talk

to her as we wait to board. The thought of having to entertain myself for fourteen hours feels dreadful and impossible.

"Of course I am, honey. This isn't easy for either of us." Then she rubs my back like when I was little, but it's not as comforting as it once was.

"Then why are we going? You can say no. We can still probably go back."

She pulls her hand away abruptly. Whatever momentary softness my mom had immediately disappears under a stiff exterior. "Please stop making this harder than it already is, Mel."

I ignore her and scroll through Instagram and see that I've been tagged in a post by Sophia. It's a 'gram of us from last summer, when we went to Coney Island. We're on the beach, lying on our beach towels in matching polka dot bikinis.

The Korean Air flight crew calls for all first-class passengers to begin boarding. I pay no attention until my mom tugs at my cardigan.

"Come on, Mel. That's us."

I look at her in confusion and bring my ticket closer to my face. Sure enough, there it is in all caps at the top: FIRST.

THREE

I whisper because it feels weird to say out loud. Like confirming that we're trying to take something that doesn't belong to us. "Mom, are you sure these are ours?"

She nods and tugs me toward her. "It's your dad's doing. Or your grandfather's doing, technically. Anyway, come on, Melody."

I'm still confused but I gather my things—making sure to be careful with my portfolio—and fumble after my mom. She looks about as uncomfortable as I do, but we smile and nod politely back at the flight attendants as they lead us to our seats. My mouth falls open at the sight of the private suites. I count. There are only fourteen seats, but not even half are filled. As my mom and I settle into our compartments, a flight attendant comes to take our cardigans and hang them up for us. I let her take mine while I remain shocked at just about everything. Even though my mom and I are sitting next to each other, the sliding partition doors might as well separate our seats by rows. It feels like a private jet, or I imagine this is what a private jet probably feels like. I look at my mom for a hint of shock in her face, but her face is void of emotion, or like she's deep in thought about something else, something faraway.

"Mom, Mom," I whisper-call to her.

She looks up at me after stowing away her purse.

"They give you *pajamas*."

"What?"

"Look," I say, pointing. "Pajamas. I'm going to change into mine." I walk over to the lavatory, and I'm satisfied to see that it's available. Two bathrooms for fourteen seats. It's a ratio unthinkable in economy.

It's past 1:00 a.m. so I go back to my suite and am stunned to see it has been turned into a bed. How'd they do that so fast? The lights are off and a flight attendant comes to close my door, and I awkwardly stand back up to thank her. I never would have guessed that sleep could come so easily and comfortably inside an airplane. The last thought in my head before I fall asleep is that these pajamas are softer than the ones I own at home.

When I wake up hours later, I roll around in my bed and then browse the mini storage compartments within my suite and find the menu card. It's extensive, like a restaurant menu. When I slide open my compartment door, I see my mom telling her order to a tall, poised flight attendant dressed, like all the others, in all turquoise. She comes to me after, and I point at the Western breakfast options and mumble a polite thank-you in my only half-fluent Korean. I haven't been on many flights that serve complimentary meals, but even in restaurants the food I'm used to ordering is never this decadent. I take photos of every dish as I make my way through each beautifully plated course and finish it off with omija tea—a first for me. It tastes like a fancy berry tea. After watching *Paddington* on a screen twice the size of a normal economy screen, I wander into my mom's compartment and sit across from her.

"Why did Grandpa fly us first class?" I stare at her sternly, waiting for a response.

"Because *he* only flies first class, Mel."

I look at her suspiciously. "Whenever Appa visited us in New York, did he also always fly first class?"

She distractedly pulls out a magazine. "No idea."

My frustration takes hold, and I snatch the magazine from her hands. "Mom. Stop avoiding me. *Why are we going to Korea?*"

"How many times do I need to tell you that your dad just wants you to be there with him? He's been asking me for a while, but I always said no until now. You can confirm it for yourself in seven hours when we land."

I close her compartment door. "Why didn't we just go with him when I was a baby and he moved back?" Why hadn't I ever asked her this before? I guess growing up far apart from my dad felt so normal that I never thought to. We were a business family, that was it.

My mom takes the magazine back and puts it into its rightful place. "He promised to come back."

I look at her intently, waiting impatiently for her to continue.

She looks back, as if debating whether to divulge more information. "When you were two, he moved back so he could make money faster. We were struggling in New York to make ends meet. But . . . well, he entered into your grandfather's world and was so determined to work his way up that he kept putting off his return to New York. Thirteen years later, he's still there and we're still here."

I nod slowly, memories of me crying every time I said good-bye to him as he left for the airport, back to the other side of the world, filling up my head. "But why couldn't we go with him?"

My mom looks at me with resignation, like she knows I'm not leaving until she gives me some answers. "I couldn't. Not after how hard my parents worked to move us to Flushing. It's hard to understand, Melody, but I couldn't do that. Go backward in their eyes and move back to the country they left. It would've discounted their immense sacrifice." Her lips are tight in a straight line, and I know that's all I'm going to get. There are so many more questions I want to ask all of a sudden, but I think she sees the curiosity in my eyes because she holds her hand up. "Things are different now, and it would be nice for you to be in Korea with your dad and get to know your culture, your country, and your father more. So just try to make the best of it, okay?"

I stand up to leave when I think of a question I can't help but blurt out. A small potential bright spot in this whole move. "Will we get to see Rebecca Eemo?" I haven't seen my aunt since I was in elementary school—the first and last time I visited Korea. But I remember I liked her. She had a fun energy.

My mom purses her lips. "We'll see."

If there's anyone that can hold a grudge, it's my mom. I vaguely remember a fight that she and my eemo got into years ago in Seoul, the night before we were heading back to New York. I heard yelling even though I was in the other room at the hotel we were staying at. Ever since then, we never spoke much with her. My mom said my aunt never became an adult and that she would be a bad influence on me. So that was that. And every time I tried to bring her up, my mom would get angry in a way she never did at any other time. Eventually, I stopped asking.

Multiple times, the flight attendant comes by with various wines and champagnes, and I politely decline them all. By the time we're almost in Korea, I'm super full from all the food they served throughout—including an eight-course meal for dinner—and admittedly, I feel a tiny bit sad to leave the plane, but I'll never share that piece of information with anyone else. At the end of the flight, the attendants come and thank my mom and me for flying with Korean Air, and I bow repeatedly and thank them back.

There must be some sort of airplane class system in the cargo hold, because our bags are among the first out while everyone else stands around waiting. I don't remember much about Seoul, and I don't expect to like it very much, but Incheon International Airport is sublime. Clean, massive, not crowded. I sigh as I realize that I am officially on the other side of the world from home. As we exit through the doors below signs informing us that we cannot return to this area once we've left, my heart beats faster in anticipation. Because of what, I'm not sure. My mom tells me "they" are waiting outside the arrivals entrance, but whatever thought I might have had circling my jet-lagged brain just then is wiped out when I am greeted by the intense humidity of a Seoul summer. It feels like a dirty mop slapping me in the face, the kind you find leaning against a questionable wall in a public gym.

Then I see the "they." My dad and a man in a black suit who I assume is his driver are standing by the open trunk of a Range Rover. When our eyes meet, there's no waiting gesture of embrace, which isn't particularly surprising since he's not the affectionate type. Nothing's been said yet, no greetings whatsoever, but I already feel awkward. I try to study his face as casually as I can, but his eyes give nothing away. He looks at me as if he's waiting for me to enter his conference room for a business meeting. I glance at my mom and she's giving him a small smile, but she looks as uncomfortable as my dad does. The man in the suit takes our suitcases and insas to my mom. She bows her head, too, and then nudges me to do the same.

"Anyoung haseyo," I say to him.

"Hi, Appa," I say to my dad.

He extends his hand and I shake it. "Solmi. How was the flight?" He sounds formal and I fidget. I think of those people I've seen in Union Square holding FREE HUGS signs and imagine my dad being offered a hug.

"It was okay," I lie. *Best flight of my life.*

He nods curtly. The man in the suit opens the door for us, and we slide into the back seat and start the drive to my dad's apartment.

"Did you always have a driver, Dad?"

He shakes his head. "Since about five years ago. And an upgraded car when I made partner this past year." I can hear the pride in his voice.

"Ahjusshi," I say, inching my body a little closer to the driver's seat, "what's your name?" I ask in Korean.

He just smiles awkwardly at me, but before he can respond, my dad jumps in.

"Solmi, we do not talk to the driver when he is working. Sit back against your seat."

I silently sulk back into my seat and look out the window. My parents make brief small talk about the flight, the move, the arrival of our boxes, and even though I don't fully understand every word they're saying, it feels tight and unnatural, the way they talk to each other. I also notice that the taxis in Korea are silver or black instead of yellow, and whether it's the winding car ride or the suffocating silence, I feel nauseous and homesick. A cab is not a cab if it's not yellow.

"Hell's Kitchen feels so far away," I say out loud to no one in particular, but for everyone to hear.

My appa frowns at me, and I can see the disapproval and wrinkles on his face and forehead. "Hannam-dong is one of the most coveted neighborhoods in Seoul. I'm sure you'll adjust just fine. It's a much nicer home than your previous apartment."

The way my dad says "previous apartment" makes me feel an irrational surge of anger, like he has a personal vendetta against it. I wish I could tell him that it's natural for me to miss my own home and to give me a break, but I turn back to face the window instead. I don't feel comfortable enough to say what's on my mind. Not with him.

Some of the buildings are ridiculously tall and have large Korean letters emblazoned on them. I imagine they're big companies, but the buildings are significantly taller than some I've seen in New York. I squint to try and read them, but the driver is going too fast for my slow Korean reading skills. After some time, we drive through an area that's a stark contrast from the neighborhood with the tall buildings. It looks a lot older, the buildings are much lower, and the signs on them are mostly big red or blue letters that look dusty and on the brink of collapse. At a stop sign, I roll down my window and look at the strange things the street vendors are selling. These street stores sell kitchen and bathroom supplies outside. There are toilet brushes, plastic chairs, even bags of chips that hang from plastic rods.

We must have driven almost an hour by the time we enter into an area where the driver seems to be slowing. I start squirming in my seat, trying to find a new comfortable position. I slouch low and prop up my knees against the driver's seat, but my dad swats at them and makes me sit up straight.

"We'll be home soon, Solmi, just sit up and sit still. This isn't your bedroom."

We drive slowly through the neighborhood, and here the buildings all look fancy. There are a lot of little stores that are selling jewelry and clothes, endless cute-looking cafés, and a lot of Italian restaurants. Everything looks modern and polished.

No Name Driver pulls up to a building and comes to a stop. There are midsized cream-colored buildings behind black iron gates, looming over me, looking more like they were built to keep people out than welcome people in. Once I get out of the car, I can see two or three buildings, but it looks like there are more hidden behind. After we thank the driver, I follow my parents past the intimidating iron gates. The complex beyond them is solely comprised of similar cream-colored buildings and a central courtyard with a seating area and a currently unoccupied playground. I notice the exterior of these buildings seems to be some sort of smooth stone, and I wonder if the interior is as lavish looking. The stone slab on our building reads:

4, HANNAM TOWERS

My dad scans his key card, and we get inside an elevator that greets us in Korean. Our apartment is located on floor eight, which appears to be the highest floor. When the elevator opens, I see a long hallway and only one door. This must be ours.

"Only one apartment per floor seems like a bad use of space," I comment.

"Or a way of maintaining privacy," my dad responds.

He punches a code into the keypad that unlocks the door, and I follow him in.

"This is our luxury villa. The master bedroom and your bedroom are upstairs. The guest room, study room, and my office are down the hall."

I consider asking why a study room and his office are two separate rooms, but shock numbs my mouth and I'm unable to say anything as I slowly slip off my shoes and take in my new home. The foyer is decorated with oversized canvas paintings and opens up into an enormous living room. Panoramic floor-to-ceiling windows line the entirety of the space that eventually connects to an open kitchen layout. Just the living room alone, though, is more than twice the size of our Hell's Kitchen apartment. I can't tell if the windows make the ceiling look taller, but it must be at least twenty feet high. Off to the side is a sort of second, slightly smaller (but still huge) living room. The furniture is pretty much what I would imagine a wealthy middle-aged man to have—minimal, dark and muted colors, with random sculptures and paintings that look too expensive to touch. I walk toward the window, feeling completely flabbergasted, and join my mom, who looks out the tall windows onto our view.

"It's the Han River," she explains.

My dad heads toward the kitchen, so I turn to my mom. "Did you know he lived in a mansion?" My voice comes out quiet enough that my dad can't hear us.

Her expression reveals nothing. "It's not a mansion," she answers, and walks toward the kitchen to join my father. I can't decide if she looks resentful or sad.

I follow her in and run my hands along the black marble kitchen island, surrounded by black cabinets. The walls in the living room and kitchen are plain white but two sides are painted in a dark shade of navy blue, serving as beautiful accents for the rest of the space. The kitchen floor is some sort of matte gray porcelain, while the living room looks like white desert oak flooring. I wonder how impressed my parents would be if I pointed out how much I knew about the materials and design of this home. Or if they'd just be angry that I'm wasting my energy and brain space on knowledge like this.

"What do you think? You haven't seen your own room yet." I don't think it's in my head that I sense a hint of excitement in my dad's voice, like I could be bought with a nice room. The stairs start from the living room and are covered on one side by frosted glass paneling. I hold back any expression of anticipation as I head up the stairs to find my room. When I open the large ivory door, my breath catches in my throat. "Oh my holy *moly*." I take a cautious step inside, as if rushing in is out of place with the luxury of this room. Or, like my dad would somehow sense that I ran in and would come upstairs just to yell at me, saying a young lady doesn't rush. With every additional step I take, I realize that this is what my dad probably always wanted for me. I see now why he always lectured me on how my bedroom was furnished in New York. I mean, I knew he always hated our plebeian lifestyle—I still remember his words—because he was always making comments about my "too colorful" room or my "disgraceful" eating habits. *Stop slouching, Solmi; Use a proper napkin, not a tissue or paper towel, Solmi; Photos aren't artwork to hang up, Solmi; blah blah blah.* But my room in New York wouldn't be able to fit even half of the furniture in my new room.

A mini living room is set up near my bed, with a three-seater suede sofa and an oval antique mirror table with two uncomfortable-looking chairs. My bed is very high up and the sheets are a pale gray shade of satin. Next to my bed is a nightstand with a crystal vase filled with peonies. Two large paintings of different shapes that look more like they belong in the Museum of Modern Art hang on the wall above the sofa. It's fine, not super attractive, but has an elevated air to it. Another painting hangs across my bed, which I immediately decide I'll replace unless I want to wake up to see an oil-painted rice paddy every morning. Past the sofa and the bed is a separate workspace with a long desk and an accent chair. An empty bookshelf is next to the desk, waiting to be filled. It's instantly my favorite piece of furniture in this oversized apartment. It's a shelf that will be completely and utterly me, irrelevant to my dad's more opulent tastes. I think of my small bedroom back home. I think of my IKEA furniture and HomeGoods linen baskets, and I miss everything so much my heart feels like someone is pushing down on it. But a small thought creeps up into my mind: Why couldn't we have lived like this in New York? How have my mom and dad been living so differently all my life? And why did I never know this? Before I head back downstairs, I see a piece of paper with a Wi-Fi name and password; when I connect, a stream of messages come through all at once on KakaoTalk. For the first time since leaving New York, a genuine smile spreads across my face.

SOPH

had the most boring day without you.

can't believe you'll be on a plane for another 8 hours 😭😭😭😭😭😭😭

what the hell why does it take so damn long to get to Korea?! 🇰🇷

text when you land. Must know you're alive!!!! 💀👍

hey fave designer, here's your reminder that you better submit your design application soon!!!

Sophia's last message makes me feel motivated. Everything here is closed still, but in a few hours, I need to find a way to mail in my portfolio after some finishing touches. I can't miss the deadline because of an address change debacle. Deep down, I know that even if I get selected, I'll need to somehow convince my mom, who doesn't think interior design is a legitimate career option, and my dad, who has no idea I even enjoy design and considers my choices too "colorful," to send me to

New York for the first weekend of November, which seems highly unlikely. But I'll deal with that if I even get selected for the final in-person round. For now, baby steps.

Taking a deep breath, I open my laptop and head to the homepage of Maison & Saito Interiors. I created a login for my profile a while ago, and even though it's completely blank, just seeing my name on the M&S website gives me butterflies. I wonder what it'd be like to work at a place like that, one of the best interior design firms in the world. Because the position is for rising seniors only, this is my one shot. I comb through the scanned files on my drive. It makes me miss New York so much. Almost all my sketches of the city are included, from Harlem to Prospect Park, Central Park and the West Village, the Bronx and Bushwick. Flushing to Hell's Kitchen, of course. It's everything I've known until now, everything I miss and everything I wish I could go back to. Most of my portfolio was created in secret, over lazy summer days and spring evenings when my mom was at work or running errands. I don't realize that tears are streaming down my cheeks and only notice because my laptop keys have fat droplets on them. I pull on the bottom of my T-shirt and wipe the keypad dry, then wipe my eyes.

i'm alive!! barely. jk.

miss you so much.

you still better tell me all the details
from your audition, my superstar
best friend.

so jetlagged.

this place is nutso.

Before going back downstairs, I lie down on my satin sheets for a moment, the exhaustion of a supremely long (albeit supremely fancy) flight washing over me. I can faintly hear my mom's voice calling me from downstairs, but sleep comes to me before I can will my body to get up and face my parents again.

FOUR

hen I wake up, it's past lunchtime. I can't believe I slept for almost six hours straight in the middle of the morning. It's still Wednesday, and even though it's the middle of the night in New York, my stomach growls. I tiptoe downstairs, not comfortable enough here to roam around freely. My mom is sitting in the den by herself, reading or watching something on her phone.

"Morning," I mumble.

My mom starts when she sees me.

I look at her suspiciously. "Why so surprised? Didn't see me?"

She gives me a half smile, and for a brief second, our relationship feels normal again. "Didn't hear you. Did you sleep well, Mel?"

I nod and sit down next to her on the sofa. "Mom," I say slowly, "is Halmoni or Rebecca Eemo sick?"

I feel a wave of relief as my mom's mouth opens slightly in confusion. "No, of course not, honey. Why would you think that?"

I shake my head. "Everything just seemed sudden. Us moving here, all of that."

My mom hands me an unopened yogurt and spoon and pats the seat next to her. "Mel, I really am sorry I sprung this on you. In my head, it had gone on for a while, and I was so conflicted I didn't want to bring you into it. But ultimately, I do think this is the right choice."

I pick at my yogurt for a few seconds. "Did Dad always live here?"

"No, not in this villa. It's recent. Since he became a partner at your grandfather's law firm."

"Wow. He got a lot of upgrades when he became a partner, huh? So he didn't *always* live this ridiculously lavish life?"

Mom raises her eyebrows at me. "What's going on inside that head of yours?"

I let out an exasperated sigh and stand up in frustration. "I don't know exactly, Mom. You uprooted our lives and moved us to Korea right before my school year was going to start, and it turns out my dad lives in a huge mansion apartment with five bedrooms and a driver, while we lived in a tiny walk-up apartment my whole life. I don't know what's going on inside my head, either, but I sure as hell can tell you I'm confused because no one's being honest with me."

My mom releases an equally loud, even more tired-sounding sigh and pinches her forehead. "Feeling a little dramatic, are we? This villa isn't paid for by your dad. It's your grandfather's money."

"Harabeoji is paying for this?"

"Paid. He already bought it for your dad. For us."

Before I can ask anything else, my dad walks in. "There you are."

"Hi, Appa."

"Here." My dad hands me a weighted black credit card. "This doesn't have a limit, and it's under your name and active, but don't go too crazy."

"Yeobo," my mom says, standing up and taking the credit card from me, "she's a student, she doesn't need a credit card."

My dad frowns but speaks calmly. "She's almost an adult— sixteen in the US but eighteen in Korea. A young woman of her age should have a credit card on hand, especially for emergencies."

"Melody is—"

But my dad cuts her off. "I already have it under her name, and she'll need it once school starts for eating out with her peers. And she might need it tomorrow when she meets Junghoon," he says gruffly.

At this unknown name, I jump in on the conversation. "Wait, wait, wait. Who's Junghoon?"

By the guilty look on my mom's face, I can tell she's in on this.

"A young, smart boy," my dad responds matter-of-factly, and extremely unhelpfully.

"Good for him, but that tells me nothing. Mom?"

My mom averts her gaze.

"Solmi," my dad cuts in. "Junghoon Kim is the son of one of Korea's most preeminent professors. Some people think their family is not that wealthy, but I think they secretly are. And I got you a meeting with him. It's important you associate with the right people now that you're in Korea. Junghoon's father was also very excited for this to happen. I will not have my daughter running around with just anyone." My dad tugs on the lapels of his jacket, straightening them out.

In that moment, I piece it together.

"You're setting me up on a blind date?" Though I don't intend it to, it comes out like I'm asking a question.

"It's not a blind date, Solmi," my dad says. "He goes to your school, so it's a good way for you to meet a classmate before you start on Monday."

"Then why can't I just meet him on Monday?" I keep my voice measured because he is sounding increasingly annoyed.

"Solmi, you accept help when your parents help you."

My eyes fall to the floor and I twist my fingers uncomfortably. I look to my mom for support, but she doesn't say anything. "I'm not interested, but thank you," I say, trying again to stand up for myself.

"This is not up for discussion." My dad doesn't even look at me; his eyes are focused on the paper in front of him.

If my mom had told me this, I'd fight her. My dad and I don't fight, though. We don't laugh together, either. It's always been surface level, which I never minded, but up until now, I was never in a situation where I was forced by him to do anything I didn't want to do. My dad takes my silence as obedience. And I guess I do, too.

"Try to sleep at a normal time tonight so you're not so jet-lagged tomorrow. The driver will be picking you up at eleven a.m. to take you to the meeting location. You both must be tired. I'll go warm up lunch," my dad says, ending the discussion and walking away. I can see him from the den at an angle, grabbing bowls and plates.

"The ahjumma came by while you were asleep. She made a lot of food," my mom says, as if changing the topic would make me feel any better.

"I didn't realize coming to Korea meant letting Dad control my life," I say to her quietly. My shoulders tighten and rise toward my ears. "And I don't *want* to use a driver. Tell Dad it's all his."

"Seoul International Academy starts Monday. Your dad is just trying to help so the transition is easier for you." She reaches over to pat down my hair, but I swat her hand away.

"I don't mind being friendless for a few days, okay?" I speak slowly, using all my strength to keep my voice calm. "I don't know why you're taking his side when he's the one that never came back to us. I'll go on this forced date just to get out of this apartment."

We make our way to the dining table, and halfway through lunch, when I sneak a glance at her, her eyes are focused on her food, wordlessly moving the soup around with her spoon. Neither of us talk for the entire meal. I spend the early afternoon unpacking my boxes with my door closed and wondering if Sophia has already gone to bed. A couple of hours into it, I hear the vibration of my phone on the bookshelf and immediately rush to it.

"You're awake! And you read my mind. Thank God you called," I say, my voice coming out high pitched in my excitement at seeing her face.

"Finally," she says, grinning. "Miss you so much. Tell me everything. Although, I guess there isn't much yet, huh?"

"That's what you'd think," I say, and then I give her the full rundown of the new apartment, the flight over, and of course, the forced date happening in less than twenty-four hours.

"That's wild. Aren't we too young to be going on blind dates? Isn't that what moms do if we're forty and single?"

"He said it like it was the most normal thing."

"So are you going?"

I look at the ceiling and think for a second before I answer her. "On the one hand, I want to get out of this apartment, away from my parents. And honestly, I feel uncomfortable about disagreeing with my dad so outright. I've never been super comfortable with him in general, you know?"

"Yeah. He's very . . . uh . . . formal."

"On the other hand, I want to take a stand. Like a You-Can't-Control-Me Stand."

Sophia laughs and then frowns. "I guess you can look at it as an introduction to Seoul? I'm sure a lot has changed since the one time you went when you were like six."

"Maybe. I'll think about it. I don't have to decide right now, anyway."

She gives me a knowing look, and it's so familiar that it aches not being in the same room as her. "Pretty sure your dad already decided for you. Plus, you're too obedient and uncomfortable with him to say no."

"Whatever. I don't care what he wants," I lie. Of course I care. She's right. Soph knows better than anyone how bad I am at resisting authority, especially when that authority is my dad. The fact that we've never really had a meaningful conversation before makes saying "no" feel like a declaration of war. I'd be starting a battle I'd end up losing because one, I'm "just a kid"; two, I'm in an unfamiliar country; and three, it's the first time our family is living under one roof together, and I'm not ready for an emotional blowup twenty-four hours in.

○ ○ ○

JET LAG MAKES YOU HUNGRY AND NOT HUNGRY AT weird hours, so that night, I end up skipping dinner. Surprisingly, I manage to keep myself awake until 11:00 p.m., and when I wake up the next morning, it's a little before seven. Melody one, jet lag zero. The morning passes quickly as I beat almost fifteen levels on *Candy Crush*, and then I finally get out of bed and look through my clothes. I have no interest in impressing my prospective classmate, but I won't leave the apartment looking like a slob, either. Eventually I find myself standing with cropped wide-legged jeans and a baggy beige plaid tee draped over me in front of my full-length mirror, which is perfectly propped up against the wall and showing me a complete head-to-toe reflection of myself. I could fit three of me side by side in this mirror, whereas my narrow white over-the-door IKEA mirror in New York was just barely big enough to check my outfits.

I head downstairs in my pajamas and find it completely empty. My dad is back at work, I assume, but he messages me to say that the driver will be waiting at the designated time outside our home. I guess he's sending him from the office. I open the fridge and find grapefruit juice and boil myself an egg.

"Knock-knock."

I turn my head in surprise. You really can't hear when someone is walking around this place.

"How's your jet lag?" my mom asks me.

"There's no door, why are you knocking?" I ignore her question.

She comes closer to me and sits down on a dining chair.

"Your dad is trying," she says, "in his own way."

"And if you were trying, you would have told him he's being unreasonable," I snap at her.

The bags under her eyes make me feel almost guilty. "Mel, we're all trying our best to make this work and keep the peace. You think you can do your part?" She doesn't sound mad as she says this. More sad, which makes me feel worse.

I turn my attention to peeling my soft-boiled egg. "Are you going to start working here, like you did back home?" I ask without looking up.

"Probably not. I'll have plenty to do helping you adjust to your new school and taking care of other things while we're living here. I do miss everyone at Two Points, though."

My mom's been the receptionist at a tech firm in Midtown Manhattan for as long as I can remember. It'll probably feel weird for her to suddenly stop working now, but I don't want to bring it up.

"I'm sixteen. I don't need help adjusting. But what other things?" I think of Aunt Rebecca, and I wonder if that's what my mom is thinking about, too.

"It's been so many years since I last lived here, just people to see, people to catch up with. Just stuff. Melody, I know you don't want to meet Junghoon, but you're just meeting a new friend. That's all it is, okay? Think of it like that and who knows, you might have a better time than you think. All I'm asking is for a little bit of openness."

Without a word, I take my egg and juice upstairs back to my room.

○ ○ ○

IN THE SHORT AMOUNT OF TIME I'M LYING ON MY bed after consuming my sad and lonely breakfast, I speed-read through *Coraline*—one of my comfort reads—and drift into a fantasy about "other parents." Eventually, I throw on the outfit I picked out earlier and grab my Strand tote and go outside to meet the driver. I'm morally opposed to taking this ride, but I don't know how to get around Seoul yet, so I accept it for now. I need to learn to find my own way around the city as soon as possible. In the car ride over, I send Soph an update and a barf emoji, though she's probably sleeping by now. The driver stops on a long street lined with cafés and boutique stores. Dad said I was meeting this guy at a place called Like Coffee. I search for the name, but there aren't many signs. All the storefronts look so hipster; the only signs that stick out are logos or random letters. One store's sign just says *W::*.

Eventually I see it: in a thin, cursive-type font, a sign that reads:

likecoffee

It kind of looks like it's trying too hard, but it also looks chic and minimalistic. I catch my reflection before I push open the door; my neon yellow flats match my neutral outfit nicely. My hair is up in a messy bun so that my gold hoops shine against the blazing sun outside. I go inside and scan the room, not entirely sure who I should be looking for. I've never seen the guy, and Appa didn't show me a picture. An overeager hand waves at me from across the room, attached to a boy who has a too-large grin on his face.

I dread this instantly. Uneasy, I make my way over to him

and stick out my hand like I'm here for a job interview.

"Solmi!" He leans in for a hug as I sit down across him, and it's a very cringy few seconds as he leans forward more and more to try to properly hug me.

"Awk-ward," I say, leaning my head farther back and lightly pushing him away. "And it's Melody."

"I knew it was you from the moment you walked in," he says, beaming. He's not ugly; he has smallish eyes, and his hair is parted mostly to one side but isn't waxed or styled much.

"How'd you know it was me?" I ask. "You're Junghoon?"

He nods. "My father showed me a picture of you that Abeonim sent. You look different, though. More beautiful." He uses the formal word for "father" when he references my dad and it makes me cringe.

He's staring at me all googly-eyed and grinning, and I'm suddenly seized with an impulse to poke him to see if he's real. He seems like he popped out of one of the cheesy K-dramas my mom watches. When I squint at him, his face shows a flicker of discomfort, but it's so fleeting that I can't be sure I really saw it.

"Let's go get coffee." He's acting all cute. Not that I find him cute, but *he* thinks he's being cute. "Something wrong?"

I could think of twenty things wrong, but I just look at him and shrug instead. "Okay."

"My treat. What can I get you?" he says, cocking his head to the side and gesturing to the seat to get me to sit down again, the smile never leaving his face.

I fight the urge to grimace outright and fail. "I'll pay for my own."

He shakes his head. "You're adorable. No, really, I'll pay."

Adorable? I don't deign to respond to this and instead pull out the credit card my dad gave me, which I didn't think I needed but turns out to be very useful right now. I twiddle it between my fingers tauntingly. "Unlimited." I flash him my fakest smile and head over to the register without looking back.

When I return with my iced Americano, I find Junghoon has moved to the same side of the table as me and is now sitting next to my tote bag. "What are you doing?"

"I wanted to sit a little closer to you. The table is so wide."

I really think this guy is pranking me. I exaggeratedly look around us for a secret video camera or a cast of TV crew members. "Are you going to get your coffee?"

He pats the seat next to him. "Yep, I was saving our seats. I'll go get mine now," he says cheerfully.

I sit down and watch him as he walks toward the register. The second he starts placing his order, I grab my things and rush out of the café as fast as I can. Three minutes with Junghoon is three more than I can handle. I barely make it out the door (damn the little silver bell!) when a hand grabs mine. A K-drama moment! One of those scenes in dramas I always wish guys would stop doing.

Instinctively, I pull away with all my strength. "What the hell are you doing?" I say a little too loudly, my annoyance unmistakable.

His smile finally falters. Around us, people start staring, and a few shuffle past me from the street into the coffee shop.

"Are you leaving?" He has a look of mixed confusion and annoyance on his face.

"Yes."

"Why?"

A small part of me feels guilty. It's mostly my dad I'm mad at. "Sorry. I just, this isn't what I imagined my first few days in Korea to look like, okay?" I speed walk down the main road. I must have caught him off guard, because he remains standing there for a few seconds before jogging to catch up with me.

"Wait, hold on!"

When I hear his footsteps, I turn around so suddenly that my now-loose bun whips his face and he nearly bangs into me.

"Clearly I made you mad, but I wasn't trying to," he says. "I'm sorry, okay?"

My expression must soften a little, because he continues.

"I was just trying to get to know you. Honest."

I chew my lips again. "Fine. But no more calling me adorable or anything resembling that." I continue walking a few steps before I turn around and look at him. "Are you coming? Might as well explore."

His grin comes back. "So we're continuing our date?"

Ha. So it *is* a date. We walk silently down the main road, and I notice that the street is lined with vendors selling beautiful jewelry. My eyes linger on a booth with dainty gold jewelry.

"What is this place?" I ask him.

"This area is called Garosugil. It's popular for its boutique stores and some designer brands nearby, I think. I don't really come here often."

I walk over to the gold jewelry booth and try on some bracelets. I pick up a thin gold bangle and ask how much it is. When the ahjumma working the booth tells me the price in Korean won, I shut my eyes to figure out the conversion into dollars. Then I slip the bracelet off and put it back on its display. Eighty dollars is a lot more than I'd ever pay for a flimsy bracelet, but before I realize what he's doing, Junghoon hands his card to the owner and adds a thicker gold bracelet to the purchase, which he slips onto his own arm. In one swift motion, he puts the thinner of the two around my wrist.

"No, I really—"

He cuts me off.

"Look," he says, shaking his wrist at me. "Couple bracelets!"

Dear Lord.

"Couple bracelets?" I repeat.

"Do you like them?"

I stare at him, not in the mood to argue again with a future-classmate-slash-current-stranger. "Umm, I mean, I don't want it though. And I don't need you to—"

"You never know what the future holds," he says with a nudge. I am in too much shock to immediately respond to this statement.

Finally I shake my head at him. "You really are straight out of a Korean drama," I say as I continue walking.

"So, what do you want to know about Korea?" he asks, while casually slinging his arm around my shoulders. I not-so-casually wiggle out from underneath it.

"Okay, listen. Can you please relax with the physical contact? This week already sucks and I don't need it getting any worse. We don't know each other like that, okay?"

He doesn't say anything back, which is a relief. I'm just trying to make it home in one piece without pissing off my dad too much if he gets wind of this horrible date. I look at my cell phone. The driver is picking me back up at 3:00 p.m. I need to last three more hours.

For a while, we walk past bougie-looking stores in silence,

and for the first time since meeting Junghoon, I'm not completely annoyed. The street we're on now is wider and cleaner, and the people-watching is entertainment enough.

We walk into a store that looks like it only sells clothes in neutral colors: white, beige, gray. It's a dream. This is my ideal wardrobe—plus of course, my essential single pop of color, like my neon yellow flats. Right on cue, Junghoon breaks the silence, and I am immediately back to screaming internally in annoyance. "Here," he says, extending his arm, "give me your bag."

"What?" I shake my head and instead turn to browse through a rack of soft beige and brown dresses and blouses.

"I'll take your bag."

"I'd ask why you're offering, but I'm not sure I want to know."

"I can hold it for you while you try on clothes."

I sigh. "I can hold my own bag, Junghoon. Been doing it all my life, believe it or not."

"Okay. I guess I find your self-reliance attractive," he says, walking around the store.

I stare at his back. I find it very odd that he doesn't *look* like the type of guy to say the things he's been saying. Or the type of guy to casually throw an arm around a girl he just met. But maybe I just don't know Korean guys. I switch over to a different section of the boutique displaying beautiful silk tops. I stop in front of a stylish white blouse and imagine it with my bright red skinny jeans. I look at the price tag and am instantly appalled. "Four hundred twenty dollars for a T-shirt?"

Junghoon walks over and sees the satin blouse I'm holding up.

"That anyone would pay four hundred twenty dollars for a shirt with fabric this thin and no real design or any sort of embroidery on it seems beyond unreasonable." I insa to the salespeople and head back into the humid August outdoors.

Junghoon frowns. "It's not that bad, in my opinion. If you really love it, I don't—"

I put my hand up close to his face. "Don't finish that sentence. *Please.*"

He makes his mouth small and doesn't say anything.

I rub my eyes, exhausted. I'm jet-lagged, Junghoon's still annoying, and I haven't eaten a proper lunch yet. "Is there anywhere we can grab a quick bite before I head back home? I'm starving."

His eyes light up. "I know a place," he says, pulling me by my arm until we get to a small restaurant with red signage against a white backdrop. Next to the restaurant name, white plastic rice cakes stick out in 3D.

"Okay, can you let go and talk now?"

"Oops," he says, dropping my arm. "This place has the best ddukbokki you'll ever eat."

I look above me at the laminated menu stuck to the walls. It's written in cute fonts and lists various combinations of spicy rice cakes and deep-fried foods, ranging from squid to vegetables to fried seaweed rolls. Luckily, underneath the many, many Korean words there are English translations. My mouth is watering, and even though I've never tried this place before— or any place in Korea, for that matter—I know it's going to be good. The spicy aroma of gochujang paste fills the small restaurant. One ahjumma working behind the steamy foods and stirring rice cakes asks us for our order. I let Junghoon place the order while I point to a few things that interest me. Within a few minutes, our food is ready, and Junghoon goes to grab a tray and brings everything back. I can see the steam rising from our late lunch, the mountain of rice cakes lathered in a deep red sauce.

"This looks amazing."

"Wait till you actually try it."

We plunge our chopsticks into the bowl and make sure the dduk is well coated in the sauce before stuffing our faces. It seems stupid of me to have not guessed how spicy this would be; Junghoon doesn't seem to experience this at all, but my mouth feels like an army of bees have just flown in and stung it. The heat of the rice cakes in my mouth combined with the thick red pepper sauce swirling around inside make my throat feel like it's burning. But through the suffering, I'm also marveling at the taste. I've had ddukbokki a lot in K-town back home, but it never tasted this good. Not even close. After I gulp down multiple cups of water and recover somewhat, I watch Junghoon in grudging admiration as he eats his ddukbokki unconcernedly, swallowing one rice cake after another without so much as taking a sip of water.

"Is this not spicy at all to you?" I ask.

"This restaurant is actually not known for their spiciness. If you think this is spicy, Solmi, you've been in America for way too long."

It feels weird to hear my Korean name spoken out loud by someone else. It's usually only in legal documents or spoken in disappointed tones by my dad. "Melody," I remind him, since I mentioned that the very first time he called me Solmi.

"Huh?"

"It's Melody. I don't like being called Solmi."

"Why not?"

"Because. I just prefer Melody. It feels more me than 'Solmi' does."

"Well, that seems a little discriminatory."

"You don't get to judge that."

"I'm not judging, I'm just sharing an opinion. It just seems a little arbitrary that you would have such a strong dislike for your Korean name, when it's your *actual* name. Legally, I'm guessing your birth certificate says 'Solmi' on it? Thereby, Solmi is your real name."

"Yeah, yeah, yeah. Using words like 'thereby' don't make you sound any smarter. We get it, your dad is a professor. Hurrah."

"Fine, Melody it is."

"Thank you. Do you have an English name?"

"No, just Junghoon."

"Right," I say, pointing my chopsticks at him, "so you wouldn't understand."

I turn my attention back toward my food and pick up a crispy seaweed roll. I dip it into the ddukbokki sauce and savor the combination of the crispy fried seaweed, the soft clear vermicelli noodles inside, and the rich, thick sauce melting together inside my mouth. Junghoon, perhaps sensing my earlier agitation, grins at my satisfied expression and proceeds to also dip the fried vegetables in the sauce. I feel like we've both learned that silence is golden with us, so we finish the rest of our food quietly and place the empty bowls and plates by the drop-off station and head out.

I have one more hour to kill, and I'm typing out a message to Sophia when Junghoon nudges me.

"So you want to meet up again tomorrow?"

I shouldn't even be shocked by his off-putting questions and comments after just a couple of hours in his company, but I am. "No, not really," I manage to say. "Not at all, actually. And I wouldn't believe you if you said you did!"

He walks over to a street vendor nearby with a bunch of hoodies and tees bearing the Supreme logo on them. "Once you get to know me, I'm *supreme*," he says, pointing at the tees and grinning.

I try to suppress my laughter and shake my head. "To someone in this world, I'm sure you are."

"To most people, believe it or not," he answers, walking back over from the vendor. "When's your driver coming anyway?"

"At three."

He looks at his phone. "Fifty-two minutes." And then sighs.

I study his expression. "I'm getting the sense you also don't want to be here."

Junghoon doesn't say anything. "Why don't we walk that way? We haven't gone down that street yet."

I trail behind him a few steps, and as we turn a corner, I see a store I am immediately drawn to. Through the glass window, I can see little trinkets, small wooden sculptures, and notebooks. It looks like a design store. "Hey," I call out to Junghoon. "Come back, let's go in here."

Without a word, he turns around and follows me in. This Junghoon I can get on board with.

Inside the store, I feel an overwhelming sense of calm. Large green plants dot the space, making it feel more like an oasis than a concept store. In the corner of the store is a small coffee bar with wooden stumps for sitting and small black circular tables. The store itself sells a variety of small vases, minimalist stationery, artistic-looking paper holders, and other small home decor items. The pleasure of wandering through this newly discovered sanctuary takes my mind off Junghoon, off my parents, off being in Korea. Right now, I'm just browsing a design shop and in love. When I wake from my trance, Junghoon is nowhere to be found. I finally leave the store and find him waiting outside.

"How long have you been out here?"

He shrugs. "It's almost three. Is your driver coming here?"

"I told him I'll meet him at the subway stop."

"Hope you enjoyed the ddukbokki."

"I did. I really did," I tell him honestly. A lingering awkward pause fills the air. "Well, see you Monday, I guess." I turn around and walk toward the subway stop.

"It's the other way," he calls from behind me, and I can tell by the way he's saying it that he's almost teasing me.

I silently turn around, raising my hand to cover the side of my face and avoid eye contact when I walk past him.

A surge of relief washes over me when I see the familiar car drive up. Overcome with jet lag, sleep hits me hard when I slouch into my seat, and however many minutes later, the driver is gently shaking me awake, informing me that I'm home. It takes a moment for me to adjust, and for a very brief second, I feel disoriented and confused about where I am.

Then I remember.

Oh, right. I'm still in Korea.

FIVE

*A*fter the worst blind date, the rest of the weekend goes by too quickly, most of it spent in intermittent naps or being just barely awake enough to eat and then go knock out again. On Friday, while my dad is at work, I carefully put my portfolio into a box and ask my mom to help me send a package to Sophia. She believes me when I tell her it's filled with snacks and a cute dress I bought while out with Junghoon. I did buy her a cute little trinket from the design store though, so hopefully she'll like that. By Sunday evening, I feel mildly better, but not at all ready to start at a new school. I'm still feeling groggy when I realize someone is calling me from my door.

"It's dinnertime, Solmi." I can hear my dad's voice from the threshold.

My head hurts from a weekend of too much sleeping, but the pleasant aroma of Korean food draws me downstairs.

"Finally awake?" my dad asks me once I join him at the dining table.

"Yeah, jet lag sucks." I pull up a chair and sit slouched in it while studying the fancy-looking plates in front of me. Thin, flat, charcoal-colored stoneware plates with heavy silverware are set on the table. The table is covered in galbijjim, at least seven different traditional side dishes, and doenjang jjigae. Steam rises from the stone pot in the center, which has a beautiful wooden ladle next to it, and my mom brings over little bowls filled with rice for each of us. In the hours I was awake on Saturday, I skillfully avoided my dad or pretended to be asleep when I heard him poking his head through the door, so the topic of my horrid date with Junghoon has not yet been discussed. I think of Mister Dumpling and its ten-dollar dinner combo of General Tso chicken and fried rice that my mom and I used to get at least twice a week. Mr. Wu—the owner of Mister Dumpling, which is right in the building next to ours—always gave us extra helpings of chicken and fortune cookies.

My dad eats a spoonful of rice and turns to me. "Good of you for trying with Junghoon. His father told me you two had a decent time. As friends. But keep him in your network."

I pretend to rub my eyes so my dad doesn't see them practically rolling over backward. *Network?* Really? I open my mouth to protest, but he hands me a thick stack of paper before I can say anything.

"Here is all the information you need to know about your classes. The administrator at Seoul International Academy—SIA—will give you details on your exact schedule tomorrow." Maybe that's what my dad was trying to give me on Saturday.

I take them from him and study them. The classes seem challenging, but nothing completely outside of what I'd expect for junior year. AP World History, AP English, Pre-Calculus . . . Honors Korean?

"Wait, what's this?" I pull out the sheet with "Honors Korean" on it.

"Your Korean class," he says.

"I'm nowhere good enough to take an honors class in Korean, Appa."

"You can catch up. You took Korean classes in Queens, didn't you?"

"In Flushing. But that was when I was in elementary school. It's been years."

"Exactly," he says. "You are Korean. You need to know how to speak your country's language."

"Yeobo, I think Honors Korean will be too tough for Melody right now," my mom chimes in as she brings over three glasses of water.

"Thank you. How am I supposed to be the top student if I'm forced into a class I *know* is beyond my level?"

"You'll catch up," he says sternly.

"She shouldn't need to catch up. She can start where she belongs and learn at an appropriate pace," my mom argues back.

"It's not up to her to decide that."

"It's *her* schedule." My mom's voice is rising to match my dad's.

I slouch lower in my seat, uncomfortable and guilty that they're fighting already because of me, though I'm grateful my mom is finally saying something back to him.

"She's Korean. She should be in Honors Korean." My dad's lips are tight as a line as he looks at my mom.

"Us coming to Korea doesn't mean you get to decide all of Melody's schedule." My mom stands up, fists clenched.

I grab her arm. "It's . . . it's okay, Umma. I will. I'll catch up." I wish I didn't have to, but for the peace of their relationship, I force myself to believe I can.

My mom squeezes my arm in a futile attempt to encourage me as she sits back down and regains her composure. After a few moments of silence, my mom breaks the ice. "So, tell us more about Junghoon? You've been in your room all weekend." She forces a smile, but I can tell she's stressed inside.

I poke at a grain of rice. "Very Korean." I shudder at the unwelcomed memory of him slinging his arm around me. "It was fine. He was fine. It was nice getting to meet a classmate, I guess," I add, trying to throw out whatever words might fully divert our topic from this almost-fight.

"Did you enjoy exploring Seoul?" she asks.

I nod. "Yeah, I guess so. I went to a cool design store, which I liked. And the ddukbokki here is so much better."

My dad shows a small smile when I praise the food.

I bring a spoonful of stew to my mouth and study it before slurping. "I still haven't met the ahjumma. Does she come every day?"

"Three times a week. She wasn't here during the weekend, but she made all this on Friday while you were asleep, again."

"Is she going to join us for some dinners?"

My dad scoffs in a way that makes me feel a little stupid. "She's just the help, Solmi."

"I'm sure she has a name, and I'm sure she eats," I mutter. I purse my lips together tightly, wishing I had the boldness to say this louder. Is there anyone more elitist than my father? I force a fake smile and excuse myself to go back to my room, where I eagerly open KakaoTalk to call Sophia.

"I haven't talked to you in days," she says, greeting me with the same level of excitement I feel to see her. Seeing Soph, even through a screen, washes away thoughts I have about my dad, about my whole situation, my life, really, and I feel comfortable again.

"That's because I've been basically sleeping on and off for the last two days."

"Bad jet lag?"

"Absolutely horrible."

"Is that your *room?*" Sophia asks me, squinting at her screen and trying to see past me.

I flip the camera around and give her a tour of my room.

"Your room is as big as your New York apartment!"

"It is *massive.* Did you get the package?"

"My fake for-Sophia-but-really-for-Maison-and-Saito package?"

"Exactly the one."

"Not yet. But didn't you only ship it out on Friday? I'm sure it takes longer than a few days to get here."

I bite my lip nervously. "Yeah, you're probably right. I just don't want to miss the deadline. That would be the saddest way to not be selected for the final round."

"You should have listened to me and sent it in while you were in New York."

"I couldn't. I had to properly look at it and add finishing touches to it. And I was too busy being consumed with anger about my mom ruining my life."

"Okay, okay, now for the important part of this call. Tell me everything about your blind date," Soph says expectantly.

I update her on every detail from my "date" with Junghoon, the T-shirt and bracelet shenanigans, the design concept store, the ddukbokki that burned my insides, and then the Honors Korean conversation at dinner. At the end of our phone chat—which is cut short because it's the first day of junior year for her—I make her promise to update me on her callbacks.

"Clinton Park High isn't going to be the same without you today."

"Seoul International Academy is going to suck since you won't be there."

After we hang up, I open my sketchbook to a new page and end up drawing Clinton Park High. The gray cement building, the heavy doors, the hallways with blue lockers and our mascot, a tiger. I draw the back of me and Soph, walking with our arms linked. I'm wearing high-waisted shorts with a men's medium tee tucked into them, and Soph is wearing a red cotton dress with faded dandelions printed all over. Before I sleep, I study the information on my new classes one last time and stare at the uniform that hangs ominously on my door. What I'd give to be back home, breezing through school instead of worrying about tomorrow. A tear unexpectedly falls down my cheek, and I wipe it away bitterly and force myself to sleep instead.

IT'S 5:04 A.M. AND I AM AS AWAKE AS NEW YORKERS on a summer evening. I wish I could sleep another two hours before I have to get ready for school. Propping myself up against my large decorative pillows, I hold the phone in front of my face and video-call Sophia, but she doesn't pick up this time. I reflect on how normal I felt only days ago as we talked about junior year. Never would I have imagined that it would start out this way. I open my KakaoTalk and see a message she sent while I was asleep.

SOPH

mr. reuben said he missed having you in class because you were the only one that seemed to understand symbolism (besides me)

lol 😖 wish me luck, day one at SIA starts in two hours.

I glare at my uniform, mocking me from the entryway. "You scream private school," I say to it. I bring it down from its hanger and hold it up against myself in front of my mirror. A pleated navy skirt with a beige checkered stripe running around an inch from the hem, a white blouse, and a navy tie. In a bag on the small sofa are the other uniform accessories my dad purchased: a thin checkered vest, a ribbonlike tie, a blazer, a cardigan, and knee-high socks. I don't bother taking anything out of the bag since I'll be wearing the bare minimum of this forced outfit. I throw the uniform over my chair and plop back onto my bed and read until it's time to get ready. I hear padded footsteps coming down the hallway, and a moment later, my mom pokes her head through the door.

"Morning, honey. Happy first day of school," she says, walking over and kissing the top of my head.

"Morning. Thanks," I mumble.

She sits on my bed with me and plays with my hair. "How do

you feel? I can't believe my little girl is a junior in high school."

"Old and sad."

At my answer, my mom bursts out laughing. I involuntarily smile at the sound of her laughter, which I haven't heard much of since coming to Seoul.

"You're so young, and in time, you'll feel better. I promise."

When my mom heads downstairs to make breakfast and coffee, I begin getting ready, which doesn't take long when you have a uniform. I apply my winged eyeliner, put on some hoops, and throw my hair up into my signature bun. When I look at myself in the full-length mirror, I have to admit I don't hate how I look. It's a somewhat okay schoolgirl-chic vibe. I make a wry face at myself for liking the attire even a little bit and head downstairs. My mom has changed into her around-the-house T-shirt, and I don't say anything but silently appreciate it. It's her oversized I AM RUFUS tee that I won at a carnival in Jersey, with a worn-out picture of the naked mole rat from *Kim Possible*. She grins when she catches me looking at her shirt and hands me a cup of coffee, and I join her to gulp down my yogurt.

"Your father left for work earlier, but he said you could take the driver to school."

"No thanks. I'll take the bus. I can't give Dad the satisfaction of puppeteering every aspect of my life."

"Melody, please. The driver already took your dad to work and is waiting outside for you. I can't have my only offspring getting lost and disappearing on her first day of school. Now go, before you're late," she says, rushing me out the door with my backpack and cardigan.

"Fine, but it's still summer. I don't want this," I say, tossing the cardigan inside the apartment and speed walking to the elevator.

In less than twenty minutes, the driver slows down at a large uphill. There are other cars in front of us, all similar, like this one. Black vehicles waiting single file to enter through the main campus gate. I look outside the window for a bus stop and see one at a distance, up a set of cement stairs. It feels pretty far from the school. At first glance, SIA doesn't look like a school: It looks more like an expensive hybrid between a college campus and a giant estate, with modern glass exteriors and marble pillars flanking the entrance. What I assume is the main building of the school is tall, wide, and very formidable in appearance. At a distance, I see a large grass field and a few smaller buildings. The main grounds of the school are packed with clusters of students of all ages, hugging each other and taking first-day-of-school selfies. I feel so out of place as I walk past the other kids and look for the administrator's office. My mom had offered to come with me, but I didn't let her. If I had known how big the school was, maybe I would have. I make my way toward the main gates, where a large sign spells out SEOUL INTERNATIONAL ACADEMY.

In the main lobby, I weave through crowds of students more or less dressed the same and find my way to the office, where I receive my new-student orientation packet. A few students glance my way and I pretend not to notice. I hope there are other new kids in my grade. After getting a brief overview of the basics from an expressionless administrative employee, I climb up three flights of stairs to find my homeroom. I notice the lockers here are all a dark grayish-navy color. When I open mine, I can't help but feel satisfied at how spacious they are, too. No more shoving all my books and quickly slamming the door shut so they don't fall out.

I approach a door with a sign that tells me I'm at the right spot.

ELEVENTH GRADE HOMEROOM 2—Miss Smith

Taking a deep breath, I walk in and slide into a seat in the back row. My mind goes back to Clinton High, where I always sat up front. Right now, I don't want to be seen by strangers. The class has less than thirty students, much smaller than what I'm used to back home. A thin, youngish-looking Korean woman walks in wearing a hip-hugging pencil skirt and a form-fitting blazer, with heels that look like they could puncture clumsy toes. She's the hot-teacher type, the type high school boys will talk about when she's not there. But she doesn't smile or have the warmth of an older, veteran teacher.

She drops her stack of books on the table, producing a bang and silencing the class. "I'm Miss Smith." She has a British accent. "Most of you know me, some of you don't. I am the junior class Homeroom 2 teacher, and the AP English and English Literature teacher. Whoever has AP English—expect it to be a challenge. We have one new student—"

The dark walnut door slides open so fast it hits the doorframe multiple times, making Miss Smith pinch the back of her neck, and a tall boy rushes into the empty seat next to me.

"Chae Wonjae!" she shouts in perfect Korean. "It's the first day of school. How can you possibly be late?"

The tall boy grins and shrugs. "The driver took a wrong turn, Miss Smith," he says coolly, as if having a geographically challenged driver is something beyond his control.

"As I was saying," she continues, throwing Wonjae a disapproving look, "we have a new student from New York. Melody Solmi Lee, would you like to give a brief introduction about yourself?"

I stand and smooth my skirt, giving the class an awkward wave. "I'm Melody . . . My parents forced me to come here, I'd rather be in New York, and nice to meet you. Um . . . anything else?"

Miss Smith shakes her head. "That's fine. Be seated." As I sit, I steal glances at Chae Wonjae, who seems to show no remorse for his loud interruption. I wish he wasn't, but *wow* he is hot.

The first half of the day goes by quickly, and I'm forced to do that stupid introduction for every single class. This gets repetitive, so by third period, I am introducing myself to my unsuspecting classmates as Luna. It seems random enough to be funny. The teachers don't seem to be that amused, though. My fourth period is Pre-Calc, and I'm about to sit down (back row again) when a boy and girl approach me, their arms linked.

"Hi," says the girl. She's Korean, too, as is the boy, and it's surprisingly nice to have so many faces that are similar to my own. She looks so much cuter in her uniform than I do, and her legs look long, even though she's wearing high-top sneakers.

My jaw aches a little after fake smiling at teachers all day, but I give her one anyway. "Hey."

"So, you don't want to be here, huh?"

I shake my head. "Nope."

"Who would? New York's so much more fun," the guy says.

My ears perk up. "You've been?"

"We've both been. My family usually goes once a year," he says.

I let out a gentle snort. "Not the same as living there." I feel like a jerk almost immediately after I say that, and I hope I didn't just ruin my chance at having a somewhat friend. "Sorry," I add, just in case.

This guy has thin eyebrows but a great big mess of hair. He has a smaller nose and average-sized eyes. And large lips. "Someone's a New York snob," he teases.

I smile sheepishly.

"Kimbeom," he says, extending his hand to me. His uniform pants have definitely been tailored. They're a lot tighter than the other students'.

I shake it, and I'm relieved he doesn't take offense.

"Yura," the girl says. Her hair is slightly wavy, like a perm that's coming undone, and she's not wearing any makeup. Her thick lashes make it look like she's wearing eyeliner, though. She looks like she'd be a very popular student, and I wonder why she seems to be going out of her way to be nice to me.

"Hello?" she says to me, smiling. She waves her hand in front of my face, and I glance at her perfectly manicured nails. She has a bright red half-French manicure.

"Oh, sorry. I blanked out for a second," I answer. "I'm Melody." I hope my expression conveys how thankful I feel in that moment that someone finally talked to me.

The teacher walks in, so they scramble into their seats. I don't pay attention to the other students and this time, the teacher either forgets that I'm a new student or doesn't care, but either way I don't have to give an introduction.

Pre-Calc ends up being hard. Really hard. Math was one of

the easier subjects for me at Clinton, so by the end of the class, I'm frazzled and frustrated. Thank God it's lunchtime.

"Want to head to lunch together?"

I turn around and realize Yura is talking to me, so I nod, hopefully not too aggressively. "Sure. Thanks." *Thank God.* I seriously contemplated going to the library for the entire lunch period to avoid sitting alone. She walks with me to my locker and waits as I put my stuff away. Our lockers turn out to be near each other, so after she's done stashing her things in hers, we head downstairs to the cafeteria. At first glance, the cafeteria doesn't seem all that special or private school-ish, but the food appears to be actually edible, not like American cafeteria food. I can appreciate that. We get our lunches and sit down at one of the many dark wooden tables (real wood!) and Kimbeom joins us shortly after.

I look at his tray, empty besides a can of Korean soda. "Why aren't you eating?"

"Going to ditch my next period and go to a restaurant with real food."

"This is a lot more real than my previous school's lunch," I say as I recall Clinton's mystery meats. I'm thinking about the uneven plastic tables from my old cafeteria when the loud clatter of a tray hitting the table jolts me out of my thoughts. I look up and see that we have been joined by another boy, the hot one I was staring at in homeroom.

"Who's this?" he asks.

I look at him with mild annoyance at the way he's talking as if I'm not right here.

"This is Melody," Kimbeom says, introducing me.

"She's in our homeroom, idiot," Yura says.

"Ah, the new girl. I'm Wonjae," Late Boy says to me with a goofy smirk.

I take another long look at him. He's wearing navy slacks and a white button-up shirt with a beige tie. But he's also wearing a navy vest and a cardigan with SIA's crest sewn on. He looks like a walking catalog for the school's uniform.

Before I comment, he leans in closer so we're face-to-face. "Why are you checking me out so intently?"

I don't avert my gaze, despite the unwelcome tingles I feel in my body with a guy I barely know five inches away from me. "I was trying to figure out if the school pays you to advertise their clothes." Sarcasm is the best way to cover up anything.

"Well, seeing as you have goose bumps on your arms, I'm guessing you're cold and wish you had your cardigan on you." He pauses. "Unless there's another reason for goose bumps." Then he laughs like he's the funniest guy in the world. "The school blasts the air conditioners every day. Rookie mistake, but you'll learn soon enough," he says, tsk-tsking and standing up. "I'm going to go eat with Junghoon. Bye, New Girl." Something in his tone, the way he talks, is very mocking, like he's laughing about something I'm not in on, and it bugs me instantly. *Of course* he's looking for Junghoon, I'm not even surprised that the two annoying guys I've met from this school are friends.

"Everyone seems to know everyone here," I say to Yura and Kimbeom.

Kimbeom nods. "It's a small school. There are only two home-room classes for juniors, so less than fifty of us total. I wish it was still summer vacation." He looks dreamily at his soda can.

"That's because you got to spend it with Rishaan in Singapore, cruising on yachts and sleeping in beautiful hotels and doing nothing but ordering room service," Yura says pointedly. "Rishaan is Beomee's boyfriend. He moved to Singapore earlier in the spring, though. But before he left, the two of them were basically the envy couple of the school," she explains to me.

Blush rises to his cheeks. "We've been together for almost a full year now. He is *dreamy.*"

"Very yummy," she says, giggling. "You two are lucky. Meanwhile, I spent the summer in board meetings and being forced to meet boring old people in suits every other day."

"Board meetings?"

Yura groans. "My mom wants to start having me see more of what she does at Dynasty before I take over her business one day. One day far, far into the future, when she's too old to do it herself, but that's years away."

"Dynasty is one of the biggest department stores in Seoul. Yura's mom owns it. She's a big fancy boss lady," Kimbeom adds.

"Oh, wow. That must be a lot of pressure for you," I say.

She waves like it's no big deal. "It's fine. My brother's a lost cause to them, so they're forcing me to take over one day. I get to shop there for free and already have lifetime job security." She grins and gets up. "Bell's gonna ring soon."

I pick up my own tray and follow after her, smiling slightly.

I know the rest of the day will be easier since my main classes (AP English, Chemistry, AP World History, and Pre-Calc) were all before lunch. Since it's the first day, study hall is designated as quiet time to read through all our course syllabi. I spot Junghoon, but we don't make eye contact. I see him again for seventh period Creative Writing and groan inwardly. He's sitting in the opposite corner of the classroom. I send him a silent thank-you with my mind that he told his dad that we mutually agreed we were better as friends. Saved me a forced second date with him.

One more class and the day is over, but it's the one I dread the most: Honors Korean. The teacher, Mrs. Lee, thankfully doesn't give us any major assignments on day one, but it already feels harder than any other class at SIA. She briefly runs through a midterm project we'll be paired up for and informs us of monthly Korean exams. Great, I have a month to become fluent in Korean.

"Can you even speak Korean?" a teasing voice whispers from behind me.

I throw a defensive look halfway in the direction of what I now recognize as Wonjae's voice. "Better than you can speak English," I lie.

"Want my cardigan, New Girl?"

"Nope, not cold," I lie, even though I'm freezing and, yes, would actually like his cardigan. Instead I bury my attention into my textbook. After class, I see Yura by the lockers and rush up to ask her a question before she leaves. "Hey," I say, forcing some pep into my voice. "Do you know how to get to Hannam-dong from here?"

"Fastest way is by car. Why?"

I shake my head. "No, like a subway or something. I live around there."

Her eyes light up. "Wait! Me too! Do you live in Hannam Towers?"

"How'd you know?"

"A few of us from Homeroom 2 live in that area, and we're all in HT," she says. "It's a pretty popular residential building in the neighborhood. Okay, if you're dead set on taking public transit, you can walk down the big hill and up the stairs past the CU convenience store and take bus 402. Get off at Hannam O-guri, the Hannam intersection. It's a pain, though. The stairs are annoying."

I give her a big smile. "Thanks."

"So why are you taking the bus?"

"To annoy my dad. And to be myself," I add, which she laughs at.

"See you tomorrow."

Before Yura heads down the hallway, I shout at her back, "Was Pre-Calc hard for you?"

She turns around and shakes her head. "No, you?"

I bite my lip. "Nope," I answer, in a lame attempt to save face.

Walking up the hill, I feel a stab of guilt about leaving the driver hanging. He's probably still waiting at the school parking lot, wondering why his boss's daughter hasn't shown up yet. But he wouldn't be fired for this, right? It's completely out of his control that I just didn't show up. I really hope my dad doesn't blame him.

When I reach the convenience store, I stop inside for a snack. It's a wonder how clean these convenience stores are compared to 7-Elevens in New York. The bell dings when I push open the door, and a guy who looks like he could be in college greets me politely. Food in convenience stores seems the most interesting, no matter where you are in the world, but this one in Korea ranks high among the convenience stores I've been to: varieties of flattened sausages on a stick, triangular kimbaps, instant noodles, and actual full-on meals that are prepackaged fill the aisles. I'm exhausted and still jet-lagged, so I quickly browse the section of small kimbaps and pick the least suspicious-looking one, with a picture of a chicken. I pay for it with the credit card my dad gave me (which is proving to be useful on many occasions now) and carry it delicately to the bus stop. It seems easily smushable.

At the bus stop, there's this wooden shelter where a few grandpas and grandmas are sitting, and it has a roof so it's giving shade to them. I kind of want to join them, but I don't. I just sit down on the plastic chairs by the bus stop, and I closely study the arrows to unwrap it the right way.

"That impressed by mass-manufactured junk food?"

I jerk my head up and see Wonjae with his window down from a car. A driver has his eyes fixed on the road.

"Want a ride?" he asks. His eyes are so laser focused on me that it makes me feel a little exposed.

I shake my head, averting my eyes. "Nope, waiting for the bus."

"I can see that. Where do you live?"

"Hannam-dong."

His expression tells me something, but I'm not sure what. "You sure you don't want a ride?" he asks again.

What would I say in a car with a guy I just met that I find annoyingly attractive?! I shrug. "I'm good, thanks," I say, hoping he can't see any red in my cheeks. Plus, if I was going to take a car, I would've gone with my dad's driver.

"Suit yourself. Bye, New Girl."

I focus my attention back on the samgak kimbap and carefully peel the arrows off the wrapper. It doesn't work; half my kimbap drops to the ground with an ugly *thud*, and the kim, which is supposed to stay in one piece, rips in three places.

Pride takes over and I throw the rest in the garbage can next to me. *Fine, Korea. You don't want me to eat your food? I don't want it anyway.*

When the bus comes, I'm relieved to discover my credit card also functions as a transportation card, and I tap it against the machine as instructed by the driver. It takes me a bit to figure out how to get to Hannam Towers after the bus drops me off, but eventually, I see the cream-colored buildings. I start walking through the courtyard toward our building when I see an unwelcome presence reading on a stone bench.

My mouth falls open in surprise. "You're *stalking* me now?"

Junghoon looks up from his book. "Don't flatter yourself."

"What other explanation is there, then?"

"The natural guess is that I could also live here."

Oh. "Well, I hope it's not my building."

Junghoon looks at me like he is already tired of this conversation, which, funnily enough, is how I feel as well. "I can't be stalking you because I'm not interested in you." At my confused expression, he continues. "My dad forced me to go on that date. Didn't yours force you?"

"Yeah, so?"

"So I don't know what your relationship with your family is like, or if you tell your parents everything, but I needed to convince you that I was 'into you' so you wouldn't rat me out. My dad wanted me to get on your dad's good side, so I was forced to try and make a good impression."

"I would never!" I protest, crossing my arms.

"I wouldn't know that. Anyway, let's clear the air. I'm not into you, Melody. And for the record, I didn't actually want to get matching bracelets with you and I wasn't dying to hold your bag, either. I just had to do all that to cover my back."

My words come out awkward and stilted. "Fine. Good. I'm glad." I think back to the date and how off I thought Junghoon was. How his actions didn't seem totally aligned with his facial expressions or the kind of person he came off as. It makes much more sense now. He faked it. "You're a horrible actor, do you know that?" I add.

He snorts and turns his attention back to his book. "If I'm such a bad actor, I'm not sure why you would have thought I followed you all the way to your home," he says without looking up at me.

Dang. Good comeback. Junghoon 1, Melody 0.

SIX

At home, I give my mom a brief overview, the usual first-day-of-school-was-fine speech to avoid any real questions like how truly difficult Pre-Calc and Honors Korean were, and head upstairs to my room to check my M&S application status. I feel hopeful until I open the online portal and log in. The status update bar next to my name remains blank. I send Soph a quick Kakao message.

> facetime when you're awake?
>
> did u get the package yet?

That night, I wait in the den until I finally hear the tune in the door passcode and my dad walks in. "I don't need your driver," I say to him, as confidently as I can, but my voice is shaking. I'm used to ignoring his remarks or blankly nodding along, not really standing up for myself. My eyes dart to the clock behind him; it's after midnight. He looks exhausted.

"The driver waited for you for almost an hour, Solmi, and instead of calling, you turned your phone off. Go to your room. I don't even want to look at you right now." I can hear the annoyance in his voice.

The benefit to not having a real relationship with your dad is that his insults don't cut as deep. The next morning, I'm content to discover that the driver is not waiting outside for me. Turns out Google Maps isn't the most efficient in its route suggestions with transportation in Seoul, though, and it takes almost an hour to get to SIA. The 402 bus may come to Hannam O-guri, but it doesn't go to SIA. Thankfully, I anticipated struggles and left earlier. It's fine. A small price to pay for my freedom and a semblance of normalcy. During Pre-Calc, Yura and Kimbeom invite me to join them after school to go hang out at a café. Yura's driver is going to pick us up, and I'm admittedly relieved I get a brief break from the bus system. It is deceivingly difficult to learn.

"Where are we going?" I ask once we're in Yura's car.

"Just a café near our apartment," she answers. During the drive there, the route looks and feels familiar, if anything can be familiar after just one week.

We pull up to a coffee shop I've seen near Hannam Towers. It's called CappOH!ccino and I haven't been inside yet, but it's one of the many well-designed cafés in the neighborhood. From the outside, this one seems like it has more flair than other coffee shops in the area.

"Do you hang out here often?"

"Kimbeom also lives here, so it's been our go-to place lately."

"What tower are you?" Kimbeom asks.

"Four. You?"

Yura squeezes me so tightly I choke. "Same! Kimbeom's in two, and two other people from our homeroom are in towers three and one. I love that we're in the same tower. What floor are you?"

I can't help but smile back at seeing how excited she is. "Floor eight."

"I'm six. Perfect."

Being in the same building reminds me of Sophia and how our buildings faced each other. Yura isn't Soph, but it is nice to have the only female friend I seem to have made live in the same building as me. We enter the café and I'm amazed; the café's interior takes my breath away. Two-seater suede sofas in different shades of pink, mint-colored leather chairs, and squiggly shaped tables are spaced throughout. There's a long island of baked goods and cute trinkets, which, upon further examination, appear to be unique to this particular café's brand. The walls are covered in plants and different-colored neon signs.

"Wow, this place is so cool." A café like this in New York would definitely be packed with people, but this one isn't. It's also a perfect day for an iced caramel macchiato, and I find it hard to believe that any place in the world could make coffee better than New York can, but when we get our drinks, I take a sip and am pleasantly surprised. Based on the name, I'll definitely have to get a cappuccino next time.

"I texted the others to come by if they were around," Yura says, checking her phone. "Junghoon's almost here."

Kimbeom looks askance at her. "Should we leave you two alone? Oops, too late." He waves at someone behind me.

Before I have a chance to gag, Junghoon and Wonjae sit

down at a small two-seater circular table right next to us.

"Wow, New Girl again." I don't think it's in my head, but his eyes definitely linger on me.

I smize at Wonjae before glaring at Junghoon. "Why are *you* here?"

He shoots daggers at me. "You have a lot of nerve talking to people like that on your second day. Do you even have friends?"

"Junghoon," Yura says with a tone of surprise. Then she looks between the two of us. "Wait, how do you two know each other?"

Neither of us say anything; I sit on my hands. Junghoon's right. They're *his* friends more than they are mine. I barely know them. "Actually, I have to get going."

"Why so fast?" Kimbeom asks, blissfully sipping his iced mocha.

"AP English assignment." I grab my things and look at everyone before I leave. "I'm also still a little jet-lagged," I add, hoping this solidifies my lie. We just have to read *Hamlet* by next week, but since none of them are in that class with me, they won't call me on my fake excuse. "See you tomorrow?"

They all wave, and no one seems suspicious, which is a huge relief. The truth is, I feel overwhelmed. Like I'm expected to just take all of this in stride as being normal. None of this is normal to me. I'm supposed to be in New York, breezing through my first week of school at Clinton High and eating pizza with Sophia after, not taking a car with rich new classmates to a fancy coffee shop, pretending like this has always been my life.

The next morning, my dad is downstairs reading the paper. I'm surprised to see him since he usually leaves before me, but when he looks up, he smiles and folds the newspaper.

"Were you waiting for me?" I ask him.

He nods. "Change of schedule today after school for you. The driver will be dropping you off and picking you up from SIA today."

"But I don't need—"

"There's someone I'd like you to meet. He's the son of a good friend. His father runs Joobang, the big home goods retailer. It's a giant company, but it's a family business. The son, Colin Joo, is about your age. One year older."

I sit there, not believing what I'm hearing. "But school already started, Appa. And you agreed that I—"

"He's not from your school. He's from ISS—International School of Seoul. I've met Colin a few times with his father, and he's shaping up to be a good man. You'll like him more than Junghoon, I hope."

"Appa—"

He cuts me off again.

"I know you threw a fit about taking a bus to school, but today, the driver will take you and pick you up. And in the future, when I schedule something for you, you will be using the driver. Do you understand? He'll pick you up at three p.m. sharp to take you to the restaurant where you'll meet Colin." His voice sends chills down my spine, and I don't have it in me to disobey him.

My fists clench but I follow my dad outside quietly, mentally kicking myself for not being able to stand my ground; the drive to the school is completely silent. I can't tell if my dad knows that I am fuming next to him in the back seat, but if he does, he doesn't show it, and his eyes never leave his phone. My blood boils and I feel heat emanating from my face. As soon as we get to school, I get out and slam the door, racing off before my dad rolls down his window to lecture me.

EIGHT HOURS OF SCHOOL PASS BY IN A DISTRACTED blur, and I dread each approaching hour more than the last. I think I end up listening to less than 50 percent of Mrs. Lee's lecture during Honors Korean. It's hard enough to pay attention and barely understand the multiple Korean idioms she keeps making us memorize, but my forced afternoon plans don't make it any easier to focus. With every day that passes in Seoul, the feeling of losing control over my life intensifies, and by three p.m., I consider skipping the date altogether, just to see what would happen. But my mom's voice begging me to try and keep the peace in the household echoes loudly in my head, so I slump reluctantly into the car and let the driver whisk me away to my second first date.

It's the middle of the afternoon, so I'm not sure why we're at a restaurant, but I'm not totally opposed to eating a second lunch. The driver tells me we're in a neighborhood called Cheongdam-dong. This restaurant is—like pretty much everywhere else I've been since I arrived in Seoul—absolutely beautiful. It has a gray exterior and black window frames, giving it a very modern but gothic look. A dainty sign with an ink drawing of a bowl of pasta hangs above the door. Inside, tall flowers adorn each table, and glass pendant lights hang at varying lengths from the high ceiling. Sheer curtains divide sections of the restaurant.

"Wow," I say quietly. A woman in a white blouse and black

dress pants greets me and gestures for me to follow her. I wonder how she knew who I was meeting. The farther we go into the restaurant, the more it feels like an airy indoor garden, with bright greenery lining the walls.

The hostess leads me over to a table near the window, where a guy dressed in a school uniform is sitting by himself. Colin Joo. He's studying the menu. I take a deep breath. "Just eat and go home," I tell myself.

"Colin?"

"That's me." He has dark eyes and severely waxed hair.

I sit across from him and watch him sip from a tall champagne glass.

"You're drinking at four in the afternoon?"

"If I could get away with it, I'd have started drinking much earlier," he says without glancing up. "Care to join me?" he asks, raising his speedily emptied glass.

I shake my head. "I'm good, thanks."

The edges of his lips curve up a millimeter as he meets my eye. "More for me," he says as the server refills his portion.

Where does my dad find people like this?

"I'm an actor. And I go to Hong Kong on weekends," he says, unprompted. "What about you?" He doesn't really sound like he wants to know what I do, more like he wants to test that what I do is interesting enough for him.

"How are you an actor when you're in school?"

"School is just a formality," he answers.

"And Hong Kong?"

He smirks. "The best night scene. You can come with me one weekend if you'd like."

"I'm still good."

"Fine by me." His voice is low and he talks slowly, and it makes me want to vomit. "So, Melody, what makes you think you'd be a good wife for me? Why did my dad want me to meet you? Your dad was very hopeful for this to work, by the way." He crosses his arms and leans back into his seat like a he's a big-shot executive interviewing an intern.

For the faintest moment, I think I must have misheard him. "Excuse me?"

"You heard me."

I lean forward and drop my voice to mimic his exaggerat-edly low tone. "Do you talk like this because being yourself doesn't ever work with girls?"

He smiles again, in that same way where only the edges curve. It makes me want to slap his haughty face. He leans in, too, so that our faces are very close, and talks just above a whis-per. "It works pretty easily when you have endless money."

And the way he says it—with his pompous air and his con-descending smile—causes something in me to snap. Maybe it's just all my anger from this morning, or the fact that my first date with Junghoon was already a forced part of my new life here that I didn't welcome, but the frustration that's been sim-mering in me all day finally erupts. I reach over swiftly to grab his glass and splash the newly poured champagne in his face. "You're a dick." I set the glass down, sling my backpack over my shoulder, and rush out without looking back. The driver was going to pick me up at six p.m., but I text him to let him know that I won't need him.

After asking multiple strangers, I finally find my way to the subway stop, and an employee helps me download the subway map on my phone in English. It's surprising in an almost-jarring way when I discover the station is sparkling clean. It almost feels wrong, like there *should* be rats. And like it should smell like nighttime, post-drunken urine. Fortunately, the subway system seems easily navigable, the way that all stops and directions are written in Korean, English, and Chinese. Unfortunately, my confidence leads me to take the wrong subway line two times, with two different lines, but finally, I make it to Hannam station and find my way home from there. Despite all the time I spent being outside and walking around getting lost, I'm still fuming by the time I get home. It's a lot earlier than my parents are probably expecting me, but when I press in the code that unlocks our apartment, I hear angry voices echoing through the living room, reaching me in the foyer. It's enough for me to momentarily forget about my horrible five minutes with Colin, and I wedge a shoe in the threshold so the tune doesn't sing when the door closes completely and tiptoe in the direction of their voices. I hide behind one of the walls connecting the living room to the kitchen and listen.

"Well, I didn't come for you," my mom says, clearly exasperated. "I don't want Melody to fall into your world. You're always falling for his false promises." Her voice is cold.

"If you're going to push back on everything I try to do for Solmi, for this family, why did you even agree to come, then?" My dad's words are just as biting, but there's a tinge of hurt to his voice.

"I came because Umma needed me to reconcile with Jieun, and I met her on Friday. But seeing you living like this is a daily reminder of what you clearly chose to prioritize over your family." Her voice is quieter, and I have to strain to really hear her. Jieun. That's Aunt Rebecca's Korean name. She came for my aunt? A moment later, when I hear loud footsteps approaching from the kitchen, I rush back to the front door and close it loudly.

"Oh, hi, honey," my mom says, coming into the foyer just in time for me to act like I am slipping my shoes off. "How was meeting Colin?" There's no sign on her face that she was just in the middle of a fight with my dad.

I look at her blankly. I can't believe how normal she pretends to be, and suddenly, after being so close to her my whole life, I realize something.

I don't think I trust her anymore.

SEVEN

my dad follows my mom out to the foyer and looks shocked to see me. "Why are you home so early?"

"Because your friend's precious son is a misogynistic asshole, Appa. I can't believe you made me meet him."

My dad furrows his brows at my word choice. "Colin Joo is from a very well-respected family, Solmi. You're not a little girl anymore. You need to think about your future, your family's future. The person you end up with is the family we're forever tied to. Your life is not only about your own happiness. Do you understand that? I'll call Colin's dad, maybe we can work something out for next week and—" He walks back toward the kitchen, presumably to grab his phone.

I take a deep breath, count to five in my head to calm my anger, and follow him. "I went on this date, for you, because you asked me to, and I went on the date with Junghoon, also for you, but I'm not a puppet, Appa. And this one ended when it started because Colin is an elitist, patronizing scumbag."

"Watch your language and do not disrespect me in my own house!" my dad thunders. "This was for your own good."

I feel small, but it's too late to back down now. "Appa, I *went* on the dates, out of obedience to you. Isn't that enough?" My voice comes out as a pitiful whimper.

He leans his hands on the dining table and looks at me while I instinctively back away. "You've been in America for too long. Look at you, talking to me like this. You think like such an American. You act like the only thing that matters is your own happiness," he says, lowering his voice and shaking his head. "Don't you ever disrespect me again."

"Yeobo," my mom says, leaning close to him so he straightens up, "that's enough." Her voice is patient, but there's a firmness to it that quiets him momentarily.

"Go to your room," my dad says without looking at me.

I bite my lower lip to hold back tears, so hard that I taste blood. I turn my back to him and stand still. "If all that mattered was my happiness, I'd still be in New York right now. Without you." I immediately run up the stairs.

My mom comes upstairs a few minutes later, but I'm not in the mood to speak with her, either. She went to see my aunt and didn't tell me about it. She was fighting with my dad right until I came home and acted like everything was fine when I walked through the door.

"Hey, you," she says softly to me.

Back home, I would have confronted her about something like this immediately, but things are different here. The change is palpable. Things are hushed, conflicts get swept under the rug, and my mom seems more distant than ever.

"I'll talk to your father," she says, rubbing my back.

I pull away from her. "I just want to be alone right now."

She nods and leaves my room. I spend the rest of the evening hungry and alone, with a daunting textbook of sajaseongeos, or four-character idioms derived from Chinese characters. I study one phrase particularly closely: *dong mun seo dab*, the literal translation being "East Question West Answer." It's when you ask something and someone responds with an answer that doesn't make any sense.

Otherwise known as my regular interactions with my dad.

I WAKE UP EARLIER THAN NORMAL, JUST IN TIME to see an incoming video call from Sophia.

"Hi," I say as her face fills up the screen. "I missed seeing your face."

"Me too. So, I have news."

"Tell me, tell me. Good? Bad?" But by the lack of her excitement, I'm guessing not so great.

"First the bad news. I didn't get the callback."

My face falls immediately. "I'm so sorry, Soph. I know you really wanted that one." Her face reflects my own sadness, and I wish I was there to give her a huge hug.

"It's okay. There'll be others, I'm sure. The other piece of news . . ."

I wait patiently for her to continue.

"My dad is *dating*."

I gasp. Soph's dad hasn't seriously dated anyone since her mom passed away, which was when Soph was less than a year old. "Like more-than-one-date dating?"

She nods, her eyes as big as mine. "Yep. They saw each other three times this past week, but turns out, he's been seeing her for two months. He didn't tell me until he felt like it was at least a little bit more serious."

"Holy moly. *Two* months! Wo-ow. Go, Mr. Taye. He must really like her. Have you met her yet?"

"No, not yet. It feels weird. Obviously I'm not unhappy about it, but I'm not super over the moon, either, which makes me feel bad. I don't know. I just kind of assumed my dad would live with just me forever, you know?"

I nod; I know exactly what she means. That's what I assumed my life with my mom was always going to be, too.

"Keep me posted the second you meet her. I want to hear all about it."

"I will. Also, I got your portfolio and did overnight shipping, so it should be there by the weekend."

"Oh, thanks so much, Soph!"

"And I *loved* the little decorative ceramic monkey. Perfect to display on my nightstand. It's like a piece of you."

"Yay! I'm glad you like it."

"Your portfolio will get there in time, Mel. Stop worrying," Soph says, reading my face.

I force an assured smile. "So, how's school been?"

"School feels the same, except not at all since you're in Korea. AP classes are a pain. I'm taking AP Physics and AP US History. Not a fan," she says, grimacing.

"I hear you. My dad signed me up for Honors Korean, which doesn't even make sense because the classes here are already so much harder. I don't even know *how* he got me into it. A classmate told me they were all full."

"You were one of the smartest students at Clinton. You'll be fine. But no more talking about classes, I'm getting a headache. What fun things have you done lately?"

Nothing has really felt that fun, but I think of something to tell her because she seems so excited to hear about Korea. "The cafés here are really nice. They're all beautiful and well designed. Not much besides that."

"Are there any non-Koreans at your school? Maybe you can meet people outside of school, since you don't seem to like any of the dudes you've met so far," she teases.

I think about this for a second. SIA is mostly Koreans, like a good 80 percent. "Not really? I mean, not in the few places I've visited so far." I make a mental note to ask Yura or Kimbeom about this at school. "Oh, guess what? I blew up on my dad."

"*What?*" Sophia knows I've never talked back to my dad. The fight is as big of a shock to her as it was to me, and I fill her in on as much as I can before I need to get ready for school. I promise to keep her posted if my dad sets me up on any more crazy dates, and I rush out the door.

For today, SIA isn't as bad because I'd rather be here than at home. I wait for Yura by our lockers so we can head to homeroom together. Having this little morning routine with her, even though it's only my first week, has been comforting. I wave at her from a distance as she approaches and then immediately proceed to share the details of my very crappy evening.

"Wait, Colin Joo? The guy who's going to take over Joobang, right?" she asks me as we settle into our seats.

"Yeah, you know him?"

"Unfortunately. He's the absolute worst."

"How do you know him?"

"The international school world is pretty small. But yeah, he's a gigantic asshole."

I nod vehemently. "*Such* an asshole."

Classes are getting increasingly harder, and the only one that still feels easy and natural to me is AP English. By the end of the day, my brain feels overloaded with information. I find Yura by the school entrance with Wonjae and wait at a distance for him to leave, but he doesn't. It almost feels like he knows I'm waiting for him to leave so he purposely doesn't. And he definitely sees me awkwardly lingering. Yura catches my eye and waves me over.

"Hey," she says in her usual cheerful tone.

"Hi, quick question. Do you know where non-Koreans hang out in Seoul? Is there like a particular place a lot of people go?"

She taps her chin while she thinks. "You mean where expats hang out? Hmm."

I wave it off. "It's okay if you—"

"Itaewon, mostly. Right?" she asks Wonjae.

"Yeah, probably."

I smile gratefully. "Thanks. Can you teach me how to get there from Hannam Towers? I'm going to go home and change and then go there. With this whole fight with my parents and my dad actually thinking a prick like Colin is a decent guy, I just want to be outside the apartment for a bit longer."

"Colin Joo?" Wonjae chimes in.

Oh, great. I lightly roll my eyes at the mention of Colin's name again. "Unfortunately."

"You met Colin! My man, Colin. How's he doing? Did you go on a setup with him and scare him away the way you scared Junghoon?" he teases.

Yura smacks him. "Shut up, Colin is horrible. Don't pay attention to him, Mel. He hates Colin's guts, too."

I ignore his comment and wave at her. "Itaewon. Got it." She promises to Kakao me information on the best bus app to download in Korea, and I head up the stairs toward the bus stop. Once I'm home, I change out of my uniform and Google "Itaewon, Seoul."

An area popular with expats and foreigners, Itaewon is also one of the primary hotspots for nightlife in Seoul.

I'm not too keen on going to what sounds like mostly a bar scene alone, especially given that I've never even had alcohol before, but if my parents aren't telling me the truth, I don't need to tell them the truth, either. I pick a bar at random to map directions to on my phone and close my laptop with determination.

Armed with Yura's helpful tips on public transportation in Seoul and my sketchbook and tote, I go into the living room where my mom is sitting, her phone in hand. "I'm meeting Yura and we're grabbing dinner," I say to her.

"Where?" she asks.

"Nearby." Technically, Itaewon is pretty close to Hannam-dong, so it's the partial truth.

"Don't be home too late."

I get to Itaewon, and in a weird way, I feel instantly better. It's not that it looks like New York at all, but there really are a lot of foreigners, more than I expected, and the diversity makes me feel at home. People in all directions are loudly speaking English, French, and some other languages I can't immediately decipher, and through a nearby window, I can see groups of non-Asians clinking their beer mugs and yelling at a TV screen, which is showing a baseball game. It is simultaneously sad and funny to me that the sight of white people yelling while watching sports makes me feel at home. The mid-September air has become slightly less humid, and now that it's evening, people are wearing thin cardigans over their summer outfits. The blacktop streets are lined with bars on both sides, with people standing around tables or sitting on high-top stools. I walk from one end of the street to the other, trying to decide which bar to enter. I finally see one I like. It seems a little quieter, and there's no TV inside, which means no loud sports-watching parties.

I see a booth that's empty, and when I settle in, a young waiter comes by with a menu. I worry that he might ask for my ID, in which case I'd be kicked out immediately, but he doesn't. Black lampshades hang over every table, giving the bar a very dim, hipster ambience, and people are talking quietly, which is exactly what I was looking for. I browse the menu of drinks and order the cheapest one, then pull out my sketchbook and appreciate the quiet. A bar like this in New York would be fully packed with a line out the door; it's nice to be able to just walk in and grab a seat. I begin drawing my surroundings, sketching out the decor and even the people sitting at the high tables drinking. When my summery cocktail arrives, I look at it nervously and ask for a cup of water. It doesn't seem prudent to have my first drink without anyone around me that I know. Instead, I focus on darkening the black lampshades and sketching out the actual bar, which has wineglasses hanging from the top. I go through three cups of water and watch as the condensation on my cocktail glass creates a thicker and thicker ring on the table.

"There you are," a familiar voice says, startling me.

It's the person I'd least expect and who just made this evening a lot more interesting. "What are you doing here?" I ask Wonjae, an obvious tone of surprise in my voice. I instinctively tuck my messy hair strands behind my ear.

"I got bored. Remembered you saying you wanted to drink at Itaewon."

"Whoa, okay, I did not say I wanted to drink. I just said I wanted to visit a place with expats. And anyway, I've never actually had alcohol before."

"What the hell are you doing at a bar by yourself, then?" Wonjae looks genuinely concerned. He slides into the opposite side of my booth. "You don't mind, right?" he asks, holding up my drink that I hadn't touched.

"Go nuts."

"So you didn't answer my question. You come to a bar by yourself on a school night, order a drink that you don't actually plan on consuming, draw in a sketchbook instead . . . What's going on there, New Girl?" Wonjae says. I can't tell if he's amused or impressed as he peers over the table to glance at my drawing.

I close my sketchbook and put it back in my bag, smirking at him. "I'm a woman of many mysteries. And my name is Melody," I say emphatically.

"A good name," he says, taking another sip of my drink. He has long fingers and hair parted to one side like every other guy in Korea. Even though he's not wearing his uniform, he still looks relatively more formal, in a light blue button-up shirt and gray jeans. He has big monolid eyes and a big nose, too. His lips, even when he's not smiling, seem like they curve a little upward in a very boyish, admittedly adorable way. "Wow, you picked a packed place."

I look around and notice he's right. I hadn't realized when I was deep into drawing the bar, but all the booths and smaller seating areas are mostly taken now.

We make polite small talk about school and classes we're taking this semester, and everything feels surprisingly easy.

"So do you like living here?" I ask him.

He cups the base of my cocktail with his fingers. "It's definitely the best. I've lived in Boston, Singapore, and Hong Kong, and I can testify that Seoul is superior," he says, grinning wide.

"Why's that?"

"Clean subways, Wi-Fi everywhere, amazing food, best nightlife, the list goes on."

I nod slowly, taking in his points. When I check my phone, I'm surprised to see it's after nine. "I should get home. It's pretty late."

"It's only nine fifteen. Do you want to at least try a beer before you go?" A second later, he adds, "I mean, no pressure though, obviously."

And for whatever reason that can't be explained by logic, I decide I do want to try a beer, so we order one each. Now I can check two things off that list of what other precocious teens have already done. When the beers come, we clink our mugs and I take a small sip. My first sip of freedom. It doesn't taste very good, but I force down a few more gulps. Each time I take sip, I feel like I have control over my life again, though deep down I know this isn't true. I stretch out my legs for a moment and accidentally graze Wonjae's knee. I pull them back sharply in embarrassment, but if he notices, he doesn't say anything.

For a second I think I feel him inching forward. We're still sitting across from each other and back to talking about Honors Korean, Pre-Calc, and other casual topics, but the only thing that I am paying attention to is the feeling of our knees touching lightly again. My focus goes to his lips, which are now going on about what else is fun in Seoul. He looks so happy, the way he's talking about this city and sharing it with me, and for the very first time, I don't hate being in Korea.

EIGHT

*I*t's finally Friday; I survived my first week at Seoul International Academy, and more than anything, I am eager to do absolutely nothing this weekend except talk to Sophia and read books in my living room and watch endless television. During study hall, I catch Yura rolling up the waistband of her skirt to make it shorter, and I grin at her mischievousness. She throws a note at me and I open it.

Did you know I was into Junghoon?

My eyes widen and I look at her with a half-apologetic, half-shocked expression. Makes sense, when I think of the joke Kimbeom made that time at CappOH!ccino. If I had known, I wouldn't have gone on the setup. But then again, school hadn't even started then and Yura and I hadn't even met, so how could I have known? She's my only girlfriend I've made so far, and I'm instantly worried that she may be upset with me if she finds out I went on a "date" with Junghoon. Why did she wait an entire week to tell me? The second the bell rings, I rush to her seat and make my voice quieter. "Yura, I have to tell you something," I say, trying not to sound too guilty.

"Hmm?"

"My dad—and Junghoon's dad—forced us to meet. It was on Thursday—not yesterday, last Thursday." I'm stuttering out of nervousness. I don't think I realized how concerned I was that she might be pissed. "But I have *zero* interest. And he practically hates me, so it didn't even go well. Really, you can ask—"

Yura holds my shoulders. "I know already! That's why I was telling you. I figured you'd freak out if you found out later. Junghoon mentioned it at the café after you left. I swear I'm not mad. That's how Wonjae knew, too, remember? When you asked about Itaewon."

Oh yeah. "Really?" I ask, biting my lip. "Not mad?"

"Really."

I let out a relieved sigh. "Does he know?"

Yura shakes her head. "But I'm going to make him fall in love with me this year. That's the plan."

Her confidence is so endearing I can't help but smile, even though I can't comprehend what she sees in the guy. "What's your plan of seduction?" I tease her.

"I'll tell you once I have one. For now, I'm just going to force my presence on him so he begins to realize what he's missing in his life. We didn't hang out enough last year, so it's time to fix that. And soon," Yura says suggestively, "I'll have him wrapped around my finger." She wiggles her pinky in the air to emphasize her point and I just laugh.

I haven't seen Wonjae all day, and I half expect him to not show up to Honors Korean. But he does. "Thought you ditched school today," I say when he slides into his desk behind me.

He gives me the same goofy smirk that I recall from earlier this week in the cafeteria and doesn't say anything.

"What?" I ask him.

"Just interesting that you thought I ditched school."

"Yeah, what about it?"

He leans in slightly closer and I pull back, hiding the stiffness that comes over me when he does. "So does that mean you were looking for me today?"

I try to think of a witty comeback and am graciously saved by Mrs. Lee's entrance.

I've given up hope of being the top student here, but I'm still determined to get decent grades, so I shush him when she reaches her desk, where she stands intimidatingly silent at the front of the class for a minute. Wonjae doesn't respond to my shushing, but I can see from turning my face ever so slightly sideways that he's grinning. Mrs. Lee gives us more assigned readings and informs the class of an upcoming exam in two weeks. The test will cover history, culture, and traditional sayings, followed by a reading comprehension and essay portion—both of which will be in Korean. My chest tightens in anxiety at the thought of having to learn as much Korean as I possibly can within the next two weeks.

At home, my mom is waiting for me in the kitchen and has peanut butter sandwiches cut up into little triangles. It's what she always prepared if I came home from school in a bad mood or if we had an argument. A sort of peacemaking snack in our household.

"Come eat, honey," she says. "Peanut butter triangle?" She hands me a small sandwich.

I take it and sit down next to her, dropping my heavy back-pack on the ground.

"How was your first week of school, overall?"

"I'd rather be at Clinton, but it was fine, considering."

"What's making you so angry, Mel?"

The fact that I know you're hiding something from me. "I don't want to talk about it, Mom. I just ended my first week at a new school, and I would really rather go to my room."

She sighs with a big heave of disappointment, but I can't be bothered to feel guilty. I don't know why I can't just ask her. Maybe it's because I know she's intentionally hiding it from me for whatever reason, and it hurts to think she'd keep stuff from her own daughter. I don't want to admit that she purposely didn't tell me something. I stand up when she doesn't say anything and grab my backpack again.

"Your dad wants us to visit your grandparents tomorrow," my mom says to my retreating back.

I turn around reluctantly, seeing my dream of doing nothing tomorrow flitter away. "Tomorrow? Do they even *want* to see me?"

"Of course they do. Why would you think they wouldn't?"

"I mean, it's not like they've ever called or sent me a single birthday card. Or shown even the slightest interest in getting to know their granddaughter. I've been around for sixteen years."

"They want to see you, Mel. Promise. We're having lunch at their home tomorrow."

In my room, I consider going back downstairs and telling my mom that I overheard their fight. But I can't erase the image of her acting so perfectly fine when she saw me, like they hadn't just had a screaming match. Do I even know who she really is?

LATE SATURDAY MORNING, WE PULL UP TO MY grandparents' home, and I learn that you don't need to live in suburbia to own a massive home. You just need to be filthy rich. A private black gate opens automatically when we buzz into the intercom. I'm mistaken if I thought our villa was grandiose; my grandparents' home is an actual, giant house—outdoor garden, terrace, patio, balcony, and all smack-dab in the middle of a bustling city.

"Is it just the two of them?" I ask.

My mom nods. I look at my dad, and I see sweat bleeding through his shirt. I don't think it's from the heat because the car was blasting the air conditioner, and we've only been standing outside for less than a minute.

"What are they like?" I whisper to my mom. She doesn't have a chance to answer, though, because the front door opens and a maid takes our coats as another hands us cold glasses of water.

The maids are wearing outfits that are fancier than the clothes I own, so I can only imagine what my halmoni and harabeoji are wearing. The floor is covered in beige travertine tile, and we step into house slippers and are led into the living room. A tall old man is seated on the armchair, and a very elegantly dressed older woman with huge pearl earrings and a matching ring is on a sofa next to him. My mom nudges me and I bow low to her, a ninety-degree insa the way my parents instructed me to do upon meeting them.

I sneak a quick glance around the living room; heavy-looking drapes hang from floor to ceiling behind the sofa, blocking some of the sun that's coming in brightly from the backyard.

Huge pillars stand in the middle that lead to the kitchen and neighboring area, and a very long table sits majestically in the dining room. A maid—different from the two who gave us water and took our coats—comes in with a platter of fruit and five cups of tea on a large wooden tray. I look at my dad, who is still standing; my grandfather looks him over sternly and finally tells him to have a seat. My dad bows again and sits on the sofa across from my grandmother.

"Solmi, we haven't seen you since you were a little girl," my grandfather says in Korean.

I give a small bow again and chuckle uncomfortably, in the way that you do when your super-intimidating grandparents say stuff you don't know how to respond to.

"We were cheated out of our time with you," my grandmother adds. In a not-so-subtle way, she *ahem*s in the direction of my mom, who looks at the ground.

"Will you be a lawyer when you get older? That seems to be the right path for you." my grandfather says.

"I don't really know," I respond in the best Korean I can summon. I focus on my enunciation and formal speaking. Informal Korean and formal Korean are so different, it takes mental energy to make sure I'm addressing my grandparents properly.

At my inability to confirm his wishes for me, my grandfather lets out a low grunt and picks at a piece of fruit. "You make sure of it," he says, turning to my dad.

"Being a lawyer is the proper path for the Lee family, Solmi," my grandfather says to me. "We will help you along the way. Don't worry."

I bow my head again and thank him, unsure of how else I

could possibly respond. Imagine the drama that would ensue if I casually mentioned to everyone in this room that I've actually applied for an interior design internship in New York and have zero interest in any nonartistic endeavor, especially law.

"You've grown well," my estranged grandmother says to me. "Tall, like your father."

"Gamsa hamnida." After thanking her, I reach over and bring my teacup to my lips, taking slow sips of my hot green tea.

Two maids prepare the dining table with more side dishes than I can count, along with a spicy-looking chicken dish and oxtail soup with rice. The table is covered in Korean food, and the medley of aromas wafts up my nose, making my stomach growl in hungry anticipation.

The adults exchange small talk, but I only understand snippets of it. My eyes continue to go to my parents and how different they seem here: my dad seems afraid and intimidated of his own father, which I find ironic but a little sad. If he doesn't enjoy that distant, obedience-centered relationship, why does he inflict that on me? His stoicism resembles my grandfather's so much I almost feel a little sorry for him. My grandmother makes a few more passive-aggressive jabs at my mom, and it's all I can do to hold my tongue so I don't turn this day into unwanted drama. My mom doesn't put up a fight, though. She just sits there, focused on the food in front of her and speaking only when asked a direct question.

"Is it good?" my grandmother asks me.

"Nae," I answer her, nodding.

"You probably don't get decent home-cooked meals in your apartment, so I'll have to feed you here. See, look how skinny you are." My grandmother turns her head sideways in my mom's direction. I'm about to say something when my mom reaches over and pats my hand.

"Good to see you eating all your food, Solmi," my mom says. She gives me a meaningful look and I know she wants me to keep my big mouth shut, but it's hard when you see your mom being basically verbally attacked.

I grumble silently. "It's delicious," I say, playing my assigned role of the obedient granddaughter.

Lunch drags on much longer than I desire, but finally we insa and follow my grandparents to the door.

"You'll come for Chuseok," my grandfather says matter-of-factly.

My parents bow and thank them for the food, and we get inside the car and head home.

"What's Chuseok?" I ask once the door is closed and I'm safely out of earshot from my grandparents.

"It's a traditional holiday, like Thanksgiving," my mom explains.

"It's a holiday celebrating the autumn harvest," my dad adds. "It's spent with family, so it makes sense that your grand-parents want us to join them."

"I wonder if I get days off from school, then."

"You do," my dad confirms. "Most of the week."

I grin to myself. Nice. Once we get home, my dad isolates himself in his home office, and my mom and I sit in the den. When I hear the door close behind him, I turn to my mom.

"So what are your thoughts on your in-laws?"

My mom squints at me, like she thinks I'm up to something. "Why?"

"Not a fan, right?"

My mom gives an accidental snort. "Not a fan."

I nod in agreement. "So Chuseok. It's about family?"

"Well, usually people will gather with all their extended relatives at Chuseok, yes, and eat a lot of food."

"So can Rebecca Eemo come?"

I can tell my mom is surprised by my question because she trips on her words as she answers.

"Oh, your aunt is out of town for a while, sweetie."

"Is that why I haven't seen her yet? She's been gone this entire time?"

My mom nods. "I gave her a call and she said she's traveling, but we'll see her when she comes back."

"She's really been gone since before we got to Korea?" I'm giving her a chance to come clean. *You told Dad you saw her on Friday.*

"Yeah, unfortunately," my mom lies.

"When is she back?" I look closely at my mom.

"I think she said late October." My mom pats my back and picks up a Korean book from the coffee table.

Liar.

NINE

I spend all of Sunday finishing homework assignments and starting my AP World History paper. I checked the status of my application on the M&S website yesterday and this afternoon, but there's still no update, and the worry that my portfolio never arrived in time gets bigger in my chest. The deadline is Wednesday, so I still have a few more days, thankfully.

That evening, our ahjumma calls in sick, so my mom prepares dinner. I've learned that the ahjumma comes in at ten a.m. and leaves at three p.m., so it's no wonder I've never met her. I haven't seen my mom cook anything since we came to Korea, but it smells like home: spaghetti and meatballs. When I was young, she'd make spaghetti and meatballs for me anytime I was really tired or stressed. She's not going to be on *Top Chef* anytime soon—or ever—and her marinara sauce is always too watery, but for some reason, whenever things felt tough, nothing tasted better than my mom's watery spaghetti. We sit around the table and my dad smiles.

"Your spaghetti and meatballs," he says.

"Mm-hmm," my mom says with no emotion.

I guess she made it for him, too, once upon a time. I try to imagine them as a young, newly married couple, but I can't see it. She plates his food and lays it down in front of him.

The tension between them is unmistakable, but like most parents who are in a fight with each other, they both direct their attention toward me.

"Mel? I thought you'd be more excited." She pretends to make a sad face, which I find mildly irritating.

It's hard to fake a smile when I think about her lying about my aunt being out of town, about my parents fighting in secret, about my grandparents deciding I'm going to become a lawyer, but I do it anyway. "I'm just tired from homework."

I stare at the one meal that reminds me of New York and our apartment, the one meal that always makes me feel better, hoping it'll help, but I feel farther from home and my mom than ever. I don't think my mom ever lied to me before. Or maybe she did and I never found out. Maybe we're not as close as I always thought we were. That hurts my heart in almost a literal way. We all eat silently. I focus all my attention on my watery noodles and escape to my room as soon as I'm done.

On Monday during lunch, Yura, Kimbeom, and I sit in the school lobby, which opens up into an enclosed courtyard with tall trees and stone tables. We're waiting for the lunch supervisor to leave the courtyard and hunt down a student in the cafeteria for making an intentional mess at multiple wooden tables in the lunch space, which Yura convinced him to do with her charming personality. That girl could get anyone to do anything for her with her celebrity-like face and her sweet charm. The second the tall, young (and kind of attractive) supervisor turns around, we dart through the main gates and out of school.

"We won't get in trouble for this?" I never skipped school back home, not that my teachers would have noticed.

"We do it all the time, don't worry. A ton of students leave for the lunch hour and come back," Yura says.

"I did that on the first day of school, remember?" Kimbeom says, winking.

These two transgressors somehow manage to convince me to skip *the rest of the day*. I shouldn't be skipping Honors Korean, but since it's the second half of the day and all my main subjects are over, I succumb to their plea and we go to Apgujeong for a late lunch. I'll study extra hard for Korean tonight.

"I think I've been near this area before," I say when I recognize a giant department store. It says GALLERIA on it, and the entire building is covered in shiny light-up scallop-shaped panels. My eyes went to it immediately when I first saw it. "This is near Garosugil, right?"

"Look who's starting to find her way around Seoul," Yura jokes.

"Ugh, it's near where I met Junghoon. The second-worst setup of my life."

Kimbeom and Yura start laughing at the distaste in my voice. "Come on, he's not so bad," Kimbeom says. The automatic glass doors slide open and we enter the department store. The bottom floor is a gourmet food hall and grocery store, so we walk around for a while, browsing our options. I can't get over how incredibly bougie this grocery store is. Employees in uniforms line every fruit and vegetable stand, offering to pick out the freshest produce for their customers. Who shops at places like this? There are more employees working individual stands than there are cashiers at a normal grocery store. I turn my attention back to the food hall and focus on what my stomach wants to eat.

"Yeah, you're *lucky*," Yura teases. "I'd *love* to go on a date with Junghoon," she adds, giggling.

"How many dates so far?" they ask me simultaneously.

"I wish I could forget," I groan. "Two in a week."

"Oh, I win. When I went to Hong Kong on a business trip with my mom, I met four guys in two evenings," Yura says nonchalantly while I gape at her in shock.

"That's wild."

"It is, but I got to eat two dinners on both days and was treated like royalty."

"Who was the second guy?" Kimbeom asks me.

My nose wrinkles at the mere thought of him. "Colin—"

"Joo," he finishes for me. "Okay, he is definitely the worst."

I nod, agreeing. "You just let your parents keep setting you up on these horrible dates?"

"I'm pretty sure if I put up a fight every time, my dad would just kick me out of the house," Kimbeom adds. "I don't know if he makes me go on so many dates because he knows about Rishaan or if he is so clueless that he thinks I've just not yet met a woman I'd be interested in."

My insides ache when he says this. It isn't right. "If your parents kick you out, you can come live with me." We settle on naengmyun because of the warm September day, and the first slurp of the ice-cold, tangy broth is immensely satisfying. The buckwheat noodles slide smoothly down my throat, and I immediately wash them down with more of the broth.

"I don't know. Sometimes I wonder if he really is just that clueless," he answers, pouring more vinegar into his bowl.

Yura leans her head on his shoulder sympathetically and twirls her noodles with her chopsticks. "Our parents are so great at the whole parenting thing."

I know it was meant as sarcasm, but this hits me harder than I think it was intended to.

"Are you both close with your parents?"

Yura shakes her head. "I used to be, when I was younger. My dad is pretty normal, but he's always busy and traveling. They started getting all controlling and manipulative about my life a few years ago."

I blink, taken aback. "Doesn't that make you mad?"

"It's fine," she says cheerily. "I shop for free and live in a fancy home. And all I have to do is attend board and shareholder meetings and pretend like I know what my mom is talking about." She takes another blissful bite of her naeng-myun and a chopstick full of banchan to go with it.

I don't want to make things uncomfortable, so I stop asking questions, but I can't help wondering if there's another layer under Yura's cheeriness. Maybe something not so positive. How could someone truly not care about being controlled?

"Why the sudden parental questions? Is everything okay?" Kimbeom asks.

"Everything's fine, I guess. It's just weird how secretive my parents are being these days. Well, my mom, I guess, I don't know if my dad was always like this or not. My mom doesn't want me to see my aunt even though I know she's here. She lied and said she was out of town. And I overheard my parents fighting but they acted completely fine the minute I walked through the door."

"Do you really think she's hiding something from you, though?" Kimbeom asks. He gathers the used napkins and chopsticks and puts them neatly inside his empty bowl.

"Yeah, can't it just be a typical fight and that your mom doesn't like your aunt for whatever reason?" Yura adds.

"But *why*? It's bugging me, not knowing."

Kimbeom looks at me. "Can I ask you something that might be a little presumptuous?"

I wait for him to continue.

"Why is this so important to you?"

"Why is what so important?"

"Why is it so important for you to find an answer? Clearly she doesn't want to tell you."

I stare at him. "Wait, are you seriously taking my mom's side right now?"

A cleaning woman comes by and takes our trays for us, and I insa to thank her.

"No, it's not that, just genuinely curious. I mean, if I tried to get to the bottom of every one of my parents' secrets or conversations, I wouldn't have time to graduate," he says.

Yura sticks out her bottom lip in thoughtful agreement. "True. My dad is gone at least two weekends a month. For all I know, he might have another family in a different city."

I can't tell if she's joking or not. "My mom and I don't have secrets. This is the first time," I tell them. "Our lives were never this complicated. Never full of secrets, being fake, lying to each other, barely talking."

"Yeah, I can't even imagine that," Kimbeom says.

"Well, why should there be secrets?" I challenge them. "Family isn't family if there are lies, secrets, and fights all the time. And at the very least, I feel like I deserve an honest answer about why my parents suddenly made me come to Korea. I know it's not simply for me to suddenly get to know my dad after all these years." I pick at a stain on the table with my nails. "It's just all so annoying. Being here, away from my home in New York, away from my best friend and my old school and not really knowing why."

Yura looks at me unsympathetically but not unkindly. "Oh, come on, Mel. Korea isn't that bad, honestly. I know you love New York and all that, but just give it time. And I'm not trying to get all nationalistic on you, but you *are* Korean," she says. "It wouldn't hurt for you to try a little bit to open your mind to being here." She gives me a loving pat and dabs her mouth with the corners of her napkin.

I want to tell her that she's wrong, because every additional day in Korea is one less in New York. I want to tell her she's being insensitive and just having a Korean face and a Korean name doesn't mean much to me. It never did. But I don't; I only just met Yura and Kimbeom. I can't be *that* girl. These are the two people who have kept me sane since SIA started, and I can't afford to lose them.

Yura insists on needing a new light coat to wear for fall, so we take the elevator and head to the women's wear floor. If I thought the little boutiques at Garosugil were expensive, this department store is on a whole new level.

"Are you sure you should be shopping here instead of, oh, you know, your mom's department store?" Kimbeom suggests.

Yura has a teasing twinkle in her eye. "This is my own form of rebellion." We browse Isabel Marant, Saint Laurent, and Chanel before Yura decides on a pale pink trench coat from Max Mara. I have never witnessed someone paying so much money so easily for a thin coat, but I keep my thoughts to myself.

"Uh-oh," Kimbeom says, looking at his phone. "Junghoon and Wonjae are bbijussuh for not telling them we were ditching for the day."

Yura giggles. "I had to keep Junghoon guessing. Wonjae's collateral damage since they're always together. Tell them to meet us at CappOH!ccino."

In just a week and one day, I feel like CappOH!ccino—or Cappo, as we call it—has quickly become our spot. Yura's driver picks us up and drives us to the coffee shop. It takes less than fifteen minutes to get there; I didn't realize it was so close. Slowly, I'm getting a handle on nearby neighborhoods. Inside Cappo, I wait for my drink, and only a few minutes later, Wonjae and Junghoon arrive and join us at a big round table by the glass door, shaking their heads at us.

"Hey," Yura says in a teasing voice, "no need to be rude."

"We have a right to be! I can't believe you three ditched without us," Wonjae says, sliding into a seat next to me. I try not to make it obvious that my body tenses in nervousness when he does.

I glance at Yura and see her holding back a smile. "Sorry, we didn't mean to," she says with a bit of taunt in her voice.

As an apology, I go to the counter and order pastries for everyone, even Junghoon. "Here, take it and forgive us," I say sweetly.

"Just this once," Wonjae says, picking a matcha croissant from the tray.

"Junghoon, which one?" I ask.

He takes a flaky pastry with a sausage inside, sprinkled with cheese. "Thanks."

"Who knew it was so easy to buy a guy's forgiveness?" I comment as I pluck a cream puff for myself.

An hour later, we all walk back to HT together, full and caffeinated. When I'm alone in my room, I log in to the M&S portal as habit, and don't expect to see any changes, but it reads:

Status: Received

A long, relieved sigh escapes my body, and I hug a pillow on my sofa. Maison & Saito finally received my portfolio! This means they'll be reviewing it soon. When Soph doesn't pick up, I text her the update and spend the rest of my day drawing whatever takes hold in my imagination.

Today was a good day.

TEN

School is a miserable blur the next day as we're given pop quizzes in both Pre-Calc and AP World History— my two hardest classes. When I come back home, I'm surprised to find my dad working in his home office. He's rarely home in time for dinner on most weekdays, so finding him here in the late afternoon is unusual.

"Solmi," he says, greeting me in the living room.

"Hi, Appa, you're home early."

He pats the spot next to him, and I let my backpack drop to the floor with a thud and hang up my cardigan on the brass coat rack nearby.

"How is school?"

"Fine," I lie. It's getting harder by the day. I start sweating. Does he know I skipped yesterday? The elective teachers aren't as strict, and Kimbeom told me their parents never find out. I discreetly wipe away the sweat from my forehead.

"Good. Education is very important. And Honors Korean?"

"It's hard," I answer honestly.

He nods like he understands. "You are Korean. It is right for you to be in the Honors class, and it will help you expedite your learning."

He pauses and I consider leaving for my room, but I sense he has more he wants to say.

"We can put the incident with you and Colin behind us. You are too different from each other to get along. I see that now."

My mouth opens in surprise. "Wow. Thank you, Appa, I—"

He raises one hand to show he isn't finished. "There's someone I want you to meet tomorrow. And I put a lot of thought and care into it, so I'd like you to respect that."

My shock at being set up on yet another blind date combined with my confusion at his noticeably softer tone leaves me wordless. He takes my silence as acquiescence.

"Tomorrow, the driver will be picking you up from your school. Are you socializing enough?"

I nod without emotion.

"Good. Very good. You're going to Café Dior in Cheongdamdong."

"Appa, can we talk—"

But he stands up and grabs his briefcase. "I came home to tell you this because I'll be busy this evening and the meeting is tomorrow after school."

He turns and walks to the front door, so I call out behind him the only thing I can to fight for the smallest ounce of freedom. "This is seriously the last time I'm using your driver."

"Suit yourself," he says as he leaves, not bothering to turn around.

That night, I'm still lying awake in my bed when I hear my dad come in. I look at the clock; it's 1:06 a.m. I consider going downstairs to at least ask for a name for the meeting tomorrow but decide against it. One, because I know he probably already sent the guy's dad my picture by now, and two, because a part of me thinks if I ask him any questions, he's going to take it as a sign of interest and continue with these horrendous setups.

IN THE MORNING, AS I APPLY MY EYELINER, I'M debating between taking a change of clothes with me to school to switch into for my date or just going in my uniform when my mom walks in. Even though she smiles at me, I feel like she, too, can sense the tension between us.

"So, Melody, I have to go out tomorrow evening and your dad won't be home till late. The ahjumma said she can stay late into the evening if you don't want to be alone. Or maybe you can go see Yura or one of your school friends?"

I don't turn around from the mirror and look at her in the reflection. "Where are you going?" I ask, though I already have a hunch. *You're going to go see Aunt Rebecca.*

"A friend of mine that I haven't connected with since I was young reached out to me. She lives in a different city but is in Seoul for a work thing." My mom doesn't look at me and lightly fluffs up my satin pillows.

"I'll be fine home alone," I tell her calmly.

I make the decision then and there. I'm going to follow my mom and put an end to this secrecy tomorrow evening. I'll implode if I don't get answers stat.

"Melody," my mom says, standing up and grabbing a brush next to me. "I know you've really hated these blind dates, but they mean a lot to your father." She gently brushes my hair while looking down. "I'll talk to him and make sure today's date is the last one, okay?"

I've already thought about not showing up to the meeting, fueled by an intense desire to prove him wrong and show him he doesn't have control over my life and that it's *my* life, not his, but this is ultimately overridden by a simultaneous, warring desire to make him proud of me.

"It's been exactly two weeks since we've come to Korea," I say out loud.

"I know, honey." There's sadness in her voice and I know she misses New York, too. I can hear it in the way she talks, even if she won't say it.

"THREE DATES IN TWO WEEKS. NOT BAD, NOT BAD," Kimbeom teases during study hall. By the time Creative Writing rolls around, my list of assignments has expanded from finishing *Hamlet* to include two more papers, a World War II essay from the perspective of the UK, the upcoming Korean exam, and an oil painting for my Fine Arts elective. The last one I'm more than happy to do, though.

In the week and a half of school, I've gotten accustomed to not sitting near Junghoon in class, but when I go to my usual seat, he's sitting in the desk next to mine.

I cock my head to one side. "Is your corner seat taken or something?"

He huffs. "Truce?"

It's hard to cover up my surprise. "Truce," I say, extending my hand. "For what it's worth, I'm sorry I kept saying you were a shitty date. It wasn't that bad."

He shakes it and gives me a wry smile. "Do you still want me to go sit in my corner?"

I think of Yura and how much she seems to like him. "No, stay. You introduced me to ddukbokki. That's worth a friendship for sure."

Creative Writing can be more fun now that I have a "friend" in the class. I grin to myself at the thought and pull out my notebook for class. Over the last few days, despite all my efforts, I find myself consistently getting nervous for my final period, Honors Korean. With Wonjae. He always sits behind me, and the thought of my not seeing him while he's doing God knows what behind me makes me unreasonably jumpy. Wonjae isn't in the classroom yet, so I quickly get out a small handheld mirror and let my hair fall out of its ponytail. I think it looks better from behind that way. We learn more about the Joseon dynasty today, and as I take notes, I look at the clock. Ten minutes, fifteen minutes, then thirty minutes go by, and Wonjae still hasn't shown up. I try not to let it distract me, though, because it shouldn't matter to me whether he's here or not. I wonder if he noticed my absence this keenly when I skipped two days ago. When Korean class ends, I don't have time to find Yura or Kimbeom because it's past three o'clock, and I know the driver has been waiting for me.

Inside the car, I look at the message my dad left me. The guy's name is Beom, which is a pretty unique name. All other Korean names are two syllables, excluding the last name. Like mine. Solmi. Sol-Mi. Lee-sol-mi. Three characters total. His name is, apparently, just Beom. Like Madonna or Lady Gaga.

"So," I say to the driver in Korean, "do you drive any other people around besides our family?"

"No," he says stoically. He keeps his eyes on the road.

"Does my dad go to a lot of places? I thought he would just stay in the office a lot," I continue.

"He has a lot of meetings all over Seoul," the driver says. Then he says something else, but my Korean isn't good enough to understand it, so I just smile politely and lean back into my seat.

The streets in Cheongdam-dong feel and look wider, and the roads look cleaner in this part of town. I guess I didn't notice this the first time I came to this part of the city because I had nothing to compare it to. Now, I can tell it's significantly cleaner and nicer than other areas of Seoul. It reminds me of a less crowded, more spacious Fifth Avenue in New York, where everyone who's anyone owns luxurious apartments overlooking Central Park. The driver comes to a slow stop and I step out of the car in front of a Christian Dior. The exterior is unlike any other designer-brand store I've seen, and I look up in awe. It almost looks like five oversized white sails connected together, piece by piece. I love it. I walk in and a woman in a chic suit with a name tag asks me where I would like to be escorted.

"The café?" I say in a hesitant voice, almost like a question.

She directs me to the elevator and I take it to the top floor, where the doors open up to an indoor and outdoor space flooded with natural light. What I like most about the space initially is the reflective, shapeless blob on the ceiling that functions as a mirror. I look around the room and do a double take when I spot someone I know.

"What are you doing here?" I say, walking over to Kimbeom. He's wearing red-and-orange-checkered pants with a light blue blazer.

"What am I doing here? Oh, please, you're the one that says you don't want to be affiliated with bougie places, and then I see you at Café Dior?" he teases.

"I am not here by choice, trust me."

He leans in conspiratorially. "Guess what?"

"What?" I whisper back.

"I'm your date."

"What!" I yell excitedly.

"Yeah," he says, grinning. "You like what you see?"

"*Love,*" I say, laughing. "Wait, so you're Beom? I didn't know it would be you."

He pretends to look concerned. "With those brains, good luck making it into college."

I shove him right as a server hands us each a glass of champagne. I bite my lip and bow a small apology when the champagne spills over the glass and gets on her uniform.

"Smooth," he comments as she escorts us to our table.

"Wait, so why didn't you tell me you were my date?" I ask.

"It was way more fun this way. You were being so dramatic about these setups from your dad, when I found out I was one of them, I couldn't resist," he says, grinning at me.

I shake my head. "And the reason you chose this extremely over-the-top café?"

"Because you, my friend, don't seem to enjoy the finer things in life, and I'm here to show you that they aren't half bad." The server hands us menus, but Kimbeom already knows what to order.

"Hey. It's not that I *don't* enjoy them, I'm just content with my plebeian lifestyle."

"You say that as if you don't have a personal driver," he teases.

"Not mine. My dad's, remember?"

"Mm-hmm," Kimbeom says, clearly not agreeing with the difference.

I flick his arm. "So you've been here a lot?"

"It's my go-to. Are you drinking that?"

I shake my head, and he takes my champagne.

I glance at the menu and then bring it closer to my face, thinking I've read it wrong. "It's eighteen dollars for a coffee?!"

"And they write 'Dior' on the pastries. And on the lattes. It's adorable."

"I just can't imagine spending eighteen dollars on a coffee."

"You know," Kimbeom says, pulling out his sunglasses from his man bag, "you say that like it's such an appalling thing, but eighteen dollars on coffee is only excessive to you."

"Um, I think eighteen dollars on coffee would be considered excessive for anybody," I say, but not rudely.

"I disagree. It's all relative."

"What do you mean?"

"You don't think spending one dollar on pizza is excessive, right?"

"No, of course not."

"Because you have more than enough to spend one dollar on pizza. People who come here and spend comfortably are not spending excessively; they're most likely spending within a budget that's reasonable for their means. It's not a lot to them. Get it?"

I suppose he has a point, but . . . "I'd argue that the average human would not think eighteen dollars for a coffee is normal, whereas one dollar on a slice of pizza is."

"You're a stubborn one," Kimbeom says as the pastries come out.

"I'm not stubborn, just rational."

"Stubborn people always say they're not stubborn," he teases.

He shifts his feet under the table, and his shoes immediately distract me from our bickering.

"Oh my God," I say.

"What?"

"You're wearing fur on your summer sandals. What is it with rich people and fur? Do you absolutely need to feel the skin of a dead animal on your body to make you feel good?"

He responds to this by putting a macaron in my gaping mouth. "Here, just eat already. And yes, I do, thank you. And it's not summer, it's almost the end of September, which means it's fall."

"Were your plaid pants not attention-grabbing enough for you?"

"Don't be jealous that you can't pull these pants off as well as I can."

He's not wrong about that.

"These pastries are so pretty I almost don't want to eat them. Almost," I say before swallowing my macaron. There's a rose-flavored dessert with edible petals on the pastry and perfect dots of strawberry coulis on the plate, which make the dessert look even fancier. When our eighteen-dollar coffees come, I lift up the teacup to look at it. The teacup is a delicate gold-and-beige thing of beauty, and the drink itself has *Dior* written on the latte foam in carefully stenciled espresso powder. I admit it looks pretty exquisite.

"You look like you're enjoying this," Kimbeom says. "Be honest."

"I am," I confess. "It's all so decadent."

"Then why are you so against nice things? Come on, talk to me."

I put the cup down and sigh. "I don't know, I just feel mad. And guilty. It's . . . a lot. Why do you think I'm so against nice things, though?"

"Forcing yourself to learn the bus system on your second day of school, your hatred for our overpriced uniforms, your disgust at eighteen-dollar coffees. Need I go on?"

He waits for me to continue.

I trace the pattern on my teacup. "I just didn't know my dad lived like this. I mean, I knew he must've been doing well for himself, since all he did was criticize our one-bedroom apartment in New York, but not like *this*. Not to this level, with a driver and a fancy villa, and sending his kid to a private school with ridiculous tuition. So that's the mad part. I feel like he kept things hidden from us, and while I know *you* weirdos think it's normal, it's not normal to me. Parents hiding things and stuff, to this extreme. And I'm also mad because I remember loving my aunt as a kid and I have no idea why my mom is so set on keeping her from me. I'll find out tomorrow, anyway."

"And the guilty part?"

I think of the guilt I feel. The guilt over the life my mom could have had in Korea, if she didn't think my being raised in America was the better option for me. The guilt over the fact that I'm so much closer to my mom than my dad. Aren't children supposed to love their parents equally? The guilt from thinking about how my mom raised me in a country foreign to her so it could be native to me. All the guilt I'd like to keep locked away inside and not talk about openly in a fancy rich-people café. "Stop bombarding me and eat." I take a leaf from his book and shut him up by forcing a forkful of strawberry cream cake into his mouth.

He puts his hands up defensively. "Okay, okay!" he says, barely able to talk with his mouth full.

"You're the best date I've had, though," I say, wanting to change the topic.

"I'm a great date. Though I wish my dad would stop with these setups. It's exhausting."

"Does Rishaan get upset about it?" I ask.

Kimbeom shakes his head and takes a sip of his coffee. "No, thankfully. But I'm sure he will eventually. We're still in our honeymoon phase, and it doesn't make it any easier that he's in Singapore now."

"Do you ever think of confronting your dad?"

Kimbeom shakes his head. "I shouldn't have to tell him who I am for him to notice me. It's not like I'm hiding it."

I lift up my teacup. "Cheers to that. I guess there's a lot of pressure on you when you're the only child, huh," I say.

"Oh." Kimbeom looks up from his plate. "I'm not the only child. I *am* the black sheep, though. I have an older brother."

The surprise on my face shows I had no idea. "Where is he?"

"College. He's at Harvard, he's the prized son of the household, heir to all Kim property, yada yada."

"Are you close with him?"

Kimbeom shakes his head. "He's five years older than me, and he never really got over having his 'only child' status taken away from him after I came along, so we never really got into a good rhythm."

"I'm sorry. That sucks."

He shrugs it off. "I have my mom. She's a real-life angel. If she ever wanted to leave my dad, I'd support it 100 percent and leave with her."

"Take her with you when we go off to college. She can go with you to Harvard and you can outshine him," I joke.

He smiles a little bitterly, and I know I've triggered something.

"Sorry, did I say something wrong?" I ask.

"I really do want to go to college in America. Maybe Stanford or Northwestern. But my dad wants me to take the suneung."

"The suneung?"

"It's basically the SAT for Korean universities. He's telling me it's good to 'keep my options open,'" he explains with air quotes, "but I think he just doesn't want to spend his precious money on sending me to America."

That makes no sense. "But your brother's already there . . ." My voice trails off.

"Yeah, which, to him, is enough to show that he's a good father. That's what favoritism looks like in Korea."

I shake my head in sympathy. "I officially support your mom's decision, too, if she ever wants to leave him." It makes a little more sense now how Kimbeom spends his finances the way he does. Maybe it's his own way of rebelling. In a twisted way, maybe it's the closest he feels to receiving even an ounce of love from his dad. The freedom to buy whatever, spend whatever, until one day he can't.

We continue stuffing our faces with tiny, expensive, bite-sized delights, and after an hour, we both lean back in our chairs. "I think I need to unbutton my pants," I say slowly, slouching in my velvet chair.

"Be a lady!"

"I will not!"

When the bill comes, I have to check to make sure my eyes did not, in fact, fall out of my head. "Did we seriously spend over two hundred dollars on dessert?"

"Two hundred thousand won. It's not exactly two hundred dollars. It's closer to one seventy."

"Close enough."

"Well, stop converting it all the time. You're in Korea now."

I know he doesn't mean to make me homesick by saying it, but I feel it. I don't say anything, though, because Kimbeom makes a fair point. I'm always automatically translating prices here into dollars. When I don't respond, I think he feels bad.

"Sorry," he mumbles. "I didn't mean—"

"I know."

"I'm sorry."

"It's fine. Really," I say, smiling so he knows I'm not mad. "I'm just . . . still not used to everything, you know? My mind still goes to US dollars over the Korean won."

"Yeah. I think we forget . . . because you're Korean. I just keep expecting you to be comfortable with everything, but I forget that you've only been here once before."

"Well, I have a good handle on Cheongdam-dong, Garosugil, and Hannam-dong. Anywhere we can go that isn't so high-rolling?"

He laughs loudly when I say this, and people look in our direction. "Let's explore Dior first," he says.

After Kimbeom purchases a belt and a pair of dress shoes, we go to the ladies' section. "Wow. These are gorgeous. Even I can appreciate a good bag," I say. "Why'd you get those shoes?"

"We have an extended family dinner next weekend so I need something nice to wear."

I nod like this is a completely normal and relatable situation to be in.

"These are our Lady Dior bags," the woman behind the counter says.

"Oh, these little ones are so cute." I pick up a glossy black one and try it on. "So impractical but so cute."

"We'll take one," Kimbeom says.

"Oh, no, wait, we won't, sorry."

"Come on, it'll be my welcome-to-Korea treat."

"Yeah, right. You already paid for dessert, which was also unnecessary. Don't even think about it."

"Totally necessary! If my dad found out I let you split the bill, he'd definitely make me go on more dates to redeem myself."

"As much as I appreciate the thought, this is beyond excessive."

"Yeah, but it's fun to be stupidly excessive every now and then," he says mischievously.

"True."

"So you'll let me?"

"Nope."

"You don't even know how much it is," he argues.

"Fine. How much is it?" I ask.

"3,800,000 won," the woman informs us. I'm trying to do the conversion but I'm failing.

Kimbeom looks at me. "A little under four grand," he says to help me out.

I pretend to faint. "And I thought this store couldn't get more ridiculous than their eighteen thousand won coffee," I say, thanking the woman and dragging Kimbeom out the door.

We spend another hour or so wandering the vicinity before my driver comes to pick me up.

"I think we're having a family dinner tonight."

"At home?" Kimbeom asks.

"Yeah."

"Lucky."

"More like uncomfortable." Before we part, we make a plan for what to tell our parents so that our stories align. We're both going to say that we're already getting to know each other at school, and while we had fun, we're better as friends. As long as both parents have that information, neither side can blame one of us for being rude. I get in the car, and as Kimbeom waves me off, I roll down the car window. "Thanks for being the best date!" I shout at him.

When I get home, I feed my dad the agreed-upon story, and to my surprise, he handles it fairly well.

"That's disappointing," he says but adds nothing more. We're gathered at the dining table, eating bulgogi and mukguk. The clear radish soup brings welcome relief for my stomach, which has essentially been pumped full of sugar and nothing else all afternoon.

I consider telling him that I'm done with the blind dates, but my current desire for a peaceful family dinner outweighs my hope for long-term freedom. Plus, my mom did say she'd talk to him.

"The café was a little excessive, wasn't it?" my mom says knowingly. Maybe she's been there before, but it definitely doesn't seem like anywhere she'd set foot in.

"Yeah."

"I read about it online," she explains before I can ask. "But it looked nice."

"I liked the interior of it a lot."

"Just the interior?" my dad chimes in.

"Well, it was pretty unusual, not what I expected of a big designer brand. There were a lot of funky shapes and really bold furniture pieces. Not boring and predictable." I can't help going on about the decor, because it's probably one of the more fun cafés I've seen, and I don't normally have a reason to discuss this with my parents. "And it wasn't tasteless or over the top, but well done."

My dad nods and it feels like approval. "You like interior design?"

"I love it," I say quietly, letting a small glimpse into my secret passion reveal itself.

"It's a hobby of hers," my mom adds quickly. "She just likes to look at fun decorations."

"Well, that's a little condescending." I shoot her an irritated glare. "It's more than just decorations."

"I just meant it's nothing serious, Melody."

"A hobby, huh?" my dad asks.

He seems interested in learning more, so for a moment, I consider telling him that I want to be a designer, that I applied for my dream internship in the field. But if my own mom, who knows me inside and out, doesn't support me, I can't imagine how my dad will take it.

"Yeah. A hobby."

"Mmm. Eat your dinner," he says, scraping rice out of his bowl.

Good thing I lied. I think of how Kimbeom doesn't feel accepted in his family, and for the first real moment, I understand him. But I know his pain is way worse.

ELEVEN

I get my pop quiz results back from Pre-Calc and quickly stow away the unforgivable C+ in my folder, too ashamed to look over the questions I got wrong. At lunch, I stew in my bitterness while Junghoon, Wonjae, Yura, and Kimbeom chat about weekend plans.

"What about you, Solmi?" Wonjae asks.

"Hm?" I am so deep in thought about the too-high academic standards at this school that I don't even have the mental energy to tell him to call me Melody.

"Plans?" Kimbeom repeats.

"Oh." I think of the fat red C+ on my paper. "Study. Homework. Study. Repeat."

"No breakfast, lunch, or dinner," Wonjae adds jokingly.

"Well, today I'm going to finally meet my aunt. I haven't seen her since I was in elementary school." The thought brings a smile to my face.

"Ooh, where?" Yura asks.

"No idea. Gonna follow my mom to find out."

Wonjae shakes his head and grins, like he's proud of my decision. "She has no idea you're following her?"

"Nope."

"And you don't plan on telling her."

"Correct."

He nods, impressed. "Text me an update."

I can't tell if he's casually showing interest in talking to me one-on-one during post-school hours or if he's genuinely curious about how my stalking plans will turn out. I guess I'll find out tonight either way. I clean up my table area and carry my tray to the drop-off section in our cafeteria and wish I'd mentioned that I don't have his phone number. My bowl shows no trace of miyukgook, which pleases the cooking staff when I hand over the empty dish that had been filled with seaweed soup. During eighth period, Mrs. Lee reminds us that we'll be getting our assignments for our partner project tomorrow. I'm relieved to learn that the project will be considered our midterm in lieu of a written exam, and that the presentation will be counted as part of the grade. *Thank God.* I just hope I get a decent partner.

"Good luck tonight," Wonjae says from behind me.

I turn my face a few degrees to my right so I can just see him in my periphery. "You didn't give me your number," I whisper so I don't get caught talking during Mrs. Lee's lecture. I turn my head back to face the front and try to take notes on the factional divides during the Joseon period, but my mind is elsewhere. Most of it is distracted thinking of tonight, thinking of meeting my aunt and what I know will end up being a fight with my mom. But there's one tiny portion of my brain that's also fixated on who's right behind me. As if he knows what I'm thinking about, Wonjae leans forward to whisper in my ear.

"Now you have no excuse." He slips me a piece of paper with his number scrawled on it.

I grip the paper tightly, the first time a boy has ever given me his number. I'm also relieved I'm sitting in front of him so he can't see my flushed cheeks. Trying to play coy, I give a slight smile and say nothing but nod my head just enough to acknowledge that I heard him. Meanwhile, my mind is a whirlwind.

A boy! Gave me! His number!

I should frame this.

When I get home, my mom is downstairs and shouts at me from the kitchen to let me know there are leftovers I can heat up.

"Thanks," I say loudly. I go up to change out of my uniform and check the M&S website. I'm really hoping for an update. I thought once I read "received," I'd be content, but I'm not. It's still September, though, and M&S won't be making their announcement about the final candidates for another month. I imagine the next few weeks will drive me crazy in anticipation.

Pulling open my dresser and wardrobe door, I study my options: a slim-fitting maroon-and-white-striped long-sleeve tee with white skinny jeans or a pale blue shift dress with puffy sleeves and yellow tassels on the hem. I take the dress off its hanger; it's more believable that I'd wear a dress at home than skinny jeans. When I go join my mom in the living room, she looks up from her afternoon coffee and book. Next to her book is her cell phone, and I'm so tempted to grab it to read her messages. I'm sure she's been exchanging texts with Aunt Rebecca.

"Well, don't you look nice," she says. "Coffee? Tea?"

I shake my head. "Just water. I'll get it." I open the refrigerator and grab the glass pitcher. "When are you leaving to meet your friend?"

"In a bit."

"Can I come?"

"Honey, you'd be bored. You wouldn't understand ahjumma talk." She smiles and walks away, and I hear her footsteps going up the stairs.

"Wait, so when exactly are you leaving?" I shout.

"Soon!" she shouts back. Her footsteps fade out of my hearing as she walks down the corridor into the master bedroom. Because my mom doesn't specify a time, I sit quietly in the den, reading *Hamlet* but not able to fully focus. Two hours later, I hear her coming downstairs, and she joins me in the den in a new outfit. She's wearing a long jacket that could easily be dressed up or down.

"I'm heading out now, Mel. You'll really be okay home alone?" she asks.

"Mom, I'm sixteen."

"Okay, okay," she says, walking toward the foyer. I can hear the smile in her voice. "Bye, honey."

To get out of our apartment complex and out onto the main road, it generally takes about five minutes at a normal pace. When I'm positive she's outside the building, I quickly put on my shoes and race out the door. Both elevators are at *L*, so I take the stairs, skipping two at a time. Once I'm outside and past the courtyard, beyond the iron gates, I see my mom up ahead.

I walk quickly, being cautious to make sure I'm far behind enough that she can't hear me but not too far that I lose her. When I see her walking past the taxi waiting area and the bus stop, I relax just a little. It would've been easy to lose her in a cab and easier to get caught in a bus. As I trail her to the subway, there are moments I feel like she senses me, but I think I'm being paranoid. I realize the benefit of being in Hannam-dong, which is centrally located: it doesn't take long to get anywhere.

The train ride is less than thirty minutes. I see her through the glass windows in the doors connecting our cars, and when she gets out, I scramble out just in time before the doors shut. The crowd makes it easy to keep close but out of sight. She wanders around a bit, looking for an exit. The subway stops here have numbers to accompany exits, which is genius. "Let's meet at exit 3" is so much easier than "Go to the exit near the back of the train, but the left one, not the right one," which would happen all the time in New York. She leaves through exit 4, weaving through a crowded street until she comes to a stop in front of a sign outside a club. I wait in a nearby convenience store until she enters. What on earth is my mom doing going to a club? I wait about five minutes then pull the door open slowly, nervous and unsure of what to expect. What if she's right there before I can catch her red-handed? A man standing by the door asks for my ID and thirteen thousand won for the entrance fee, roughly thirteen dollars. He puts a wristband on me to indicate that I can't purchase alcohol. It's a little dim inside, but I can already sense that everyone's focused on the woman singing on stage, the woman whose voice has captivated everyone's attention, including mine. I know that voice. I know it because it sounds remarkably similar to another I know so intimately.

But the singer's is slightly different. It's stronger, fuller, and has more heart and feeling to match the melody of the song. And even though it's been almost ten years since I've seen her, I know it immediately: that woman on stage is my aunt.

My mom is sitting a few tables away, not too far in front of me, but close enough that she would instantly be able to see me if she turns around. She's really focused on my aunt, and for the next hour, so am I. Or at least, I'm focused on watching my mom watch my aunt. My mom's eyes are glistening, almost like she's holding back tears. My heart feels like a balloon expanding in my chest as I listen to her sing. Aunt Rebecca has a petite frame but a large presence. She looks too trendy and cool to be only a few years younger than my mom. Baggy pants, a form-fitting top that exposes her shoulders, super-short hair, and side bangs that frame her face perfectly. She doesn't look like she's wearing much makeup, but her eyes feel catlike, and her dark eyebrows and thick mascara make her look intimidatingly unapproachable. Though I can't understand most of the lyrics, the tenderness in her voice makes me think she must be singing about souls or something else very fragile. It makes me feel sad but hopeful, like I've lost a treasure but I'm close to finding it again.

After the performance, I continue to watch my mom carefully. Aunt Rebecca and my mom make eye contact, and my mom nods her head toward the door. I swiftly move to a different table where I'm out of her line of vision and boldly follow them. They weave their way through the stairs and a few people and go out the door, through which I also exit once it feels safe enough to not get caught immediately. Out on the street, I hide behind a thick pole and neither of them see me.

"Stop showing up if you're just coming here to lecture me," my aunt says.

"Well, you wouldn't tell me last time and I need to tell Umma. Where are you living?" my mom asks, her voice demanding.

"Somewhere nice."

"I'm being serious, Jieun."

"Why does Umma need to know anyway?"

"She just wants to make sure you're doing okay. Roof over your head, making an income or a semblance of an income, etcetera."

"Semblance of an income? That's nice, sis. Tell Umma I'm doing great. And if that's all you're here for, then you can see yourself to the subway. Or your driver."

"Do you want me to help you find a job or something? Let me help."

I have to get closer when they move farther away, and I'm no longer fully hidden, but they're both so clearly annoyed with each other that they don't notice me. Well, my mom's back is to me, but my aunt doesn't recognize me at first, I guess.

She sighs and pinches her forehead, something my mom does a lot, too. "I *have* a job. You'll never see my side, Lil, so just drop it and go back—"

My aunt abruptly stops talking when her eyes lock onto mine. "Unni," she says in an almost whisper to my mom, which is what you call your older sister.

I'm not looking at my mom when she turns around. I'm looking back at my aunt, who I've missed for so many years. Her eyes continue to linger on me, and a moment later, she's right in front of me and wrapping me in a hug.

I hug her tightly back. "Hi, Eemo."

"Jieun-ah," my mom's voice sharply calls back to her sister; then she pierces me with a stern look. "Melody, what on earth are you doing here?"

"I followed you. Because I *knew* you were lying to me."

"Oh, Melody." My aunt is squeezing my shoulders, and my mom glares at her.

"Jieun, stay out of this."

"No, Mom, *you* stay out of this. I knew it," I say angrily, my voice slightly cracking. "You lied this entire time, saying Aunt Rebecca was out of the country."

Now it's my aunt's turn to be confused. "What? You told me Solmi was still in New York for the semester."

"Jieun," my mom snaps. "Worry about yourself. You have plenty to focus on without intruding into my daughter's life. Melody, let's go." She turns to leave, but my feet don't follow.

"No."

She turns around, already a few steps ahead. "What did you say?"

"You told Eemo I was still in New York? You were going to try to keep her away from me this entire time. You don't just get to force me to leave with you," I tell her loudly, the hurt in my voice obvious to anyone around.

"I do when you're a teenager. We're leaving. Right now. I'll explain things at home, Mel."

"I'm going to eat dinner with Eemo." I look at my aunt, who seems somewhere between amused and surprised at my proposition.

My mom walks rapidly toward me. "I said we can talk at home, Mel. For now, you need to listen to me."

I nudge my aunt, trying to signal her for some support, but then again, it's been ten-plus years, so maybe she feels awkward. Finally, she lets out a long, slow breath. She puts her arm around me lovingly. "Melody, we'll catch up. I promise. But maybe you should go home with your mom."

I look at the pavement, disappointed. Great. Now I have to go home after throwing a fit about not leaving. "Okay." Feeling awkward, I take off first and head into the subway station. I retrace my route home and rush into a subway car right as it pulls in so my mom is hopefully stuck getting the next one that comes. She calls me multiple times on my cell, but I send them all to voicemail. If I have to go back home, at least I'll go in peace by myself.

My mom must've taken a cab home because when I get in, she's already back, sitting on the entryway bench. I look at her and slip my shoes off, ignoring her as much as I can.

"Melody," my mom says, grabbing my hand as I try to walk past her. "Honey, let me explain. Sit down."

I yank my hand away. "Until you're ready to tell me the truth—the *full* truth—I don't want to listen. I knew you were lying, Mom. From the very beginning. Did you even think about how this would affect me? Do you know at all how hard this has been for me? I thought I'd be with Sophia, talking about colleges and walking to school together, but here I am, in a foreign country against my will, with absolutely no understanding as to why. I know you came because of something related to Eemo and Halmoni, and if you don't want to face your own reality, fine, but I'm done pretending to play along." She looks surprised, hurt. I know what she's thinking: we don't fight like this, not ever. I'm thinking the same thing, too.

I rush upstairs and slam my door shut, which is hard because it's so heavy, but I manage to produce a somewhat satisfying bang. I can hear footsteps heading up the stairs, and I twist the lock in my room just in time. When I first came to Korea and started at SIA, my dad bought me noise-canceling headphones so I could drown out noise and focus on my studies without being disturbed. At the time, I thought it was a ridiculous purchase, given how big the villa is, but right now, the headphones are a welcome gift. Her voice, her incessant knocking—gone. Or maybe she stopped. Either way, I let the headphones drown out everything and lie on my bed, looking up at the eggshell-colored ceiling. Her lies weigh on me in a way that leaves me immobilized. I feel trapped in a small space where the only way out is to know the truth.

Why did we really move to Korea? She said we came here so I can live with my dad, but to be honest, he doesn't seem *that* intent on spending a ton of time with me anyway. But there's more to the story she's not telling me. What were Halmoni and Umma talking about just a few days before we left? Why does my mom hate Aunt Rebecca so much that she never let me see her after that one day in elementary school? Why won't my mom let her sister and her daughter have a relationship?

I never thought much about these questions, and even when I did, my mom's short answers satisfied any budding curiosity, but now those same questions are creeping back into my mind, and her once simple answers are no longer satisfying. Umma always said we were just a normal business family, and Dad had to live in Korea. That's the way it was. I accepted it. My aunt and my mom drifted apart when my aunt moved back to Seoul. That's natural. I hadn't gone back to Korea since elementary school because my mom couldn't take off work weeks at a time. Simple. Now I know all these answers were provided so easily because there's more to this story, more to my *mom's* story that she never told me. The cracks are forming, piece by piece. I am spiraling in my thoughts and my head feels like it's splitting with confusion. I let tears fall down the sides of my face and wet the pillowcases and turn my body sideways, staring as dark circles form on the rich silk.

I don't know how much time has gone by, but eventually, I take off the headphones because they're hurting my ears the way headbands hurt the sides of your head when you wear them for too long. I reach for my phone and see a missed call from Soph and a Kakao message from Wonjae. I look out my window and see the Han River glistening against the reflection of the city lights.

> soph! sorry 😞 i'll call you back soon, in
> the middle of an intense project. Boo.

I don't mean to lie, but it's easier than typing out the jumble of thoughts inside my head. Who would understand me? No one's family is this confusing.

> **WONJAE**
> how did it go?

I can see what the message says without having to open the text, so I leave it unread. A part of me wants to respond, to pour out everything to Wonjae. Sometimes, it's easier to lay my soul bare to those who don't fully know me. Like a clean slate of stories. And he seems easy to talk to. I think about how close he was to me when he slipped me his phone number. Before I left school, I slipped mine into his locker. I was too shy in the moment to give mine to him.

Instead, I turn to my bookshelf in search of a distraction. My shelf is now about one-third full. This one is way bigger than the makeshift shelf on my dresser in New York where I had stacked all my books between two bookends, so there's still a ton of space to fill. I pull out *Jane Eyre* and let the oversized accent chair hug my body as I prop my legs up and slouch down. *Jane Eyre* is one of what I call my At Least I'm Not books. At least I'm not Jane, discovering that my lover has been keeping his secret insane wife locked up on the third floor of his mansion home. At least I'm not Bertha, locked away by my husband.

Except that that's fiction and this isn't.

I try to find comfort in Jane's miserable situation, but instead, I end up quietly crying again into the imported Italian fabric of the chair, eventually falling asleep from the dizziness you get when you feel too much.

TWELVE

At some point during the night, my neck starts to throb with the pain of having slept at a wrong angle for too many hours, and I stumble my way back onto my bed. My stomach growls with the desire for food, and I realize how hungry I am since skipping dinner last night. The Roman numeral clock that hangs on my wall tells me it's 6:43 a.m. I throw my uniform on and sneak downstairs, but there's nothing I really want to eat at home. I leave a Post-it on the fridge telling my parents I've left early for school.

The sun is slow to rise and the sky is still a light gray when I leave the courtyard and walk toward the bus stop, where the street is lined with cafés getting ready to open, boutique stores still dark, and a pyeonuijeom store with a sleepy-looking cashier; the one in our neighborhood is called GS25, and it looks similar to the convenience store near school. I push open the glass door at GS25 and the bell startles the cashier, who mumbles a greeting. The ready-to-eat aisle options are overwhelming: There are endless types of jook, but I don't really like porridge so I skip those; there are full-on meals that just need to be heated up, like ddukbokki, chicken drumsticks, something squid related, and a few things I've never tried, like chicken feet. Hanging above on racks are rows and rows of sausages on sticks, which I almost immediately decide is what I want.

As I'm about to pay the sleepy cashier, who doesn't look much older than me, my eyes go to a cylindrical glass container with a bright red lid and red base. The glass is foggy from the steam inside, and three-tiered steel plates hold individual white buns, which I recognize from my mom's Korean dramas: jjin bbang. I can't choose between the sausage-on-a-stick and this, so I go with both. The cashier tells me that the red bean jjin bbang is the most popular; it's only nine hundred won, which means it might be the cheapest thing I've eaten since coming here. Less than a dollar! The sleepy boy points to the microwave in the back if I want to heat up the sausage. *Yes, please.* One minute later, my mouth is watering at the smell. The counter where the microwave is also has stools, a coffee and hot water dispenser, and trash bins for food waste and regular waste. I pull out a stool, unwrap the sausage from its sealed packaging, and stuff it in my mouth. The juicy taste satisfies the grumbling in my stomach that's been loudly begging for food. Once that's gone, I turn my attention to the jjin bbang. There's a papery thin wrapper stuck to the bread, and I gently peel it off before I take my first bite. The red bean paste overflows out of the bun, and I quickly put it to my mouth to keep it from falling; the sweetness of the red bean and chewiness of the steamed bread make for a pleasing combination in my mouth. This might be— no, is most definitely—the best thing I've eaten in Seoul so far. Better even than spicy rice cakes. I have to open my mouth while chewing to let the steam escape so it doesn't burn my throat, but no one sees me through the glass windows since it's still early.

Eventually, as the time on my phone and the slow increase of people outside tell me, it's almost time for first period, and I know I need to get to school. The bus stop at Hannam O-guri has a lot of blue buses that come and go. Two different buses take me to the same stop near school, but when the first one comes, my feet refuse to move. After twenty minutes and three buses pass, I finally get on the fourth one and sit down by a window. The bus is filled with students in the same uniform, probably all headed toward the same public school. Their uniform is markedly different from mine; the white blouses have Korean name tags sewn onto them, the skirt is black, and a lot of the girls wear thin ribbons instead of ties like us. Their jackets have the name of their Korean high school on it; I wonder how far it is from SIA if we're all on the same bus.

Instead of walking my usual route to the SIA campus, I sit down at the bottom of the stairs and stretch out my legs. School seems meaningless today, and I realize how much I don't want to see anyone right now. Eventually, I walk around aimlessly, but not toward school. I'm not sure where in Yongsan I am, and I'm far enough away from SIA that I feel less stressed about my impulsive choice to ditch school. For the second time in my life, for the second time in a month. My classmates at Clinton would be shocked to hear it. There are a lot of PC bangs around me, which I've learned are just large rooms with rows and rows of computers mostly for customers who have some particular need for fast internet or gamers who seek in-person camaraderie and high computer power. Amid the sea of PC bang signs, I see a sign that looks different; it's not for a PC bang, but a multi-bang. It's written in bright colors and looks more attractive than the PC bang signs. *Bang* is "room," so the concept of a multi-room piques my interest enough that I go up a narrow staircase and open the entrance to the multi-bang. When I enter, I notice other students that look my age, also in uniforms. It's surprising and reassuring to know how many other students skipped school today, even if I don't know them. The man behind the counter says he charges fifteen thousand won per hour, and after I pay him, he points to a snack station where I can help myself. I pour a handful of popcorn and Korean snacks into a bowl and grab a soda and follow the ahjusshi into the room he assigns me. There's a button for me to press if I have any questions on how things work. I look around at the small room; it feels more like a large closet. For such a small space, there's a lot going on here: a giant TV, a Nintendo Switch, a Wii, a selection of movies, a USB port apparently for if you want to bring your own films, comic books, and microphones for karaoke. I smile and make myself comfortable against the cushions, flipping through movie selections. I don't check my phone for a few hours; instead I stuff myself with ice cream, snacks, and soda for lunch while enjoying *Pirates of the Caribbean.*

YURA

you're late! mr. sullivan gave a pop quiz
today for AP World.

where are you???

text me when you see this

hi, yeah i didn't go today . . .

YURA
where are you??????

some multibang . . . lol
near SIA

YURA
omg. Meet me after school at the
bottom of the hill?

okay but don't tell the others.
not in the mood to see anyone today
☹

YURA

At 3:10 on the dot, Yura is at the bottom of the hill, slightly out of breath. I'm sitting on a bench with my hands in my jacket pockets when she slides next to me.

"Hey," she says, looping her arm through mine. "Want to come over?"

I give her a grateful look. "Your parents won't force me to invite my parents over or anything like that, right?"

She gives me a squeeze. "Nope." We head for her car, where her driver is waiting and opens the door for us.

In the car, I remember I promised to call Soph back and try her, but she doesn't pick up. It's only after that I realize it's 5:30 a.m. in New York. She messaged me last night saying she wanted to talk about her dad's girlfriend situation, but the time difference is making spontaneous phone calls increasingly difficult. For now, I put my phone away, resolving to text her later.

It's a weird feeling to go to my building but get off on a different floor. I guess I assumed our villas would look or feel similar because we lived in the same building, so I am shocked when Yura pulls open the door. And also immediately ashamed, as a future designer, for thinking any two homes could look the same.

The entryway hall is much longer in Yura's home, and it expands into a significantly larger living room, with an even higher ceiling. The walls aren't solid colors but rather painted in abstract patterns; textured furniture and accessories, from a wool rug to (faux?) fur throws and pillows, adorn the living room. Floor-to-ceiling mirrors face the floor-to-ceiling windows, giving the living room an even larger feel.

"Holy moly. Your house is huge," I say, sounding out of breath. "How is it *this* big?"

"Oh, my parents also bought the unit upstairs, and they combined them into one huge apartment."

"Wow. This apartment feels like a totally different building."

"Come on, I'll show you to my room." She has to drag me through the hallways because I'm taking in all the artwork and furniture as I walk. It's no wonder her mom owns a department store; this entire home feels like one—although not like your average modern department store. It feels much more personal and thoughtfully designed, likely by someone with expensive and inimitably eclectic taste.

Yura's room is even more glamorous than I thought it'd be, but in a way that doesn't feel exactly *her*. Yura is more classy, elegant in an effortless way. She's the kind of girl you wish you could be but never are. But you can't hate her, either, because she's not stuck up, even with all her charm and looks, and she's just so incredibly kind. This room doesn't give off that vibe; it's not subtle, it's the textbook definition of glamour and luxury. Gold-framed mirrors, a huge chandelier, a marble desk that looks too glossy to be productive at.

"Wow," I exclaim again. "What a room."

"Welcome to my extremely un-humble abode," she says jokingly, opening her arms wide.

"Un-humble . . . is about right." I laugh.

"I mean, come on, does this look like me?" she says, holding up a furry tiger-striped pillow. She throws it at me and laughs, too. We put our bags down and I plop onto an ivory leather ottoman. Right next to it is a silver coffee table, and just as we get comfortable, a maid comes in with water, a charcuterie board, fruit, and a small bowl of snacks.

"Gamsa hamnida," we say in unison to the maid. I pull a grape from its stem and pop one in my mouth.

"So," Yura says, poking the ottoman. "Your new friends are a bad influence on you, huh?"

I look up, confused.

"We made you skip school, what, less than two weeks ago? You were so paranoid then, and here you are now, skipping all eight hours and missing a pop quiz." She doesn't say this accusingly; I can tell she's worried but trying to make light of the fact that I didn't show up today.

I sigh very loudly. "So, your bedroom isn't really decorated to your taste?" I ask, diverting the topic.

She looks at me pointedly. "Okay, changing the subject, got it. Well, it was all done by mom's interior design team. They didn't ask for my input or my preferences, even though it's *my* room, so here we are."

"So if you could change it however you want, would you?"

She shakes her head. "I could have if I wanted to, I guess, but I don't really have much of an eye for design, just fashion."

An idea pops into my head. An idea that makes me feel more like myself than anything else has in a long time. "What if you had a friend who loves interior design and offered to help?"

"I would absolutely take my interior-design-loving friend up on that."

"I need a distraction," I say honestly.

"Perfect, I need a designer."

I could hug her so tight she'd cry. "Okay, so first, I need to ask you a series of questions."

"When's the shopping portion?"

"After I get a better understanding of what you're looking for." I realize I don't actually know any furniture stores in this area or in Seoul. "But you're going to have to take us to the actual stores . . ."

Yura waves away my hesitation. "I'll take us around."

We sit on her navy velvet carpet, crisscross style, and I pull out a pen and paper. "It's against my values to spend a million dollars redesigning your room. I propose, since you have all the nice stuff anyway, let's set a budget and find things within a set range that we can buy to create a more personal touch."

She looks at me skeptically. "You won't even be the one paying for it!"

"Come on," I insist. "It'll make it more rewarding than swiping your credit card for whatever you want, trust me."

She opens her mouth to keep arguing but then shakes her head, giving in. "Fi-ne. What's the proposed budget?"

I give her a thumbs-up and grin. "I'm thinking around two hundred thousand won?"

"Wait, are you bad at conversion or do you really mean under two hundred dollars?" she asks. "No way. That's not even the price of one paperweight."

"Okay, I'm sorry, are you a fifty-year-old man designing his home office? Why on earth would you even need a paperweight?"

"Fine, it's not even the price of a set of bookends."

"It's the price of ten. We can do this."

"I know we *can*, Mel, I just don't *want* to. 1,500,000 won. Deal?"

"Five hundred thousand won." I flash her a provoking smile. The same dare-you-to-ditch-with-us smile she and Kimbeom gave me my first time skipping school.

"Fine, now ask your questions." She heaves a loud sigh, but I can tell she's excited. It's contagious; I can already imagine how her room will look once she's let me have at it. More authentic, more Yura.

I squeal. "Okay, question one. What is your source of inspiration?"

"Junghoon." She answers so seriously we both burst out giggling.

"Rule number one: teenage boys cannot be an inspiration."

"Okay, just kidding. I don't know, I don't have any." She shrugs. "Next question!"

"Everyone has an inspiration. What's your dream in life?"

For the slightest—almost unnoticeable—moment, Yura's eyes seem to dim. But before I can say anything, she bounces back. "To take over my mom's company," she answers.

"You sound bored saying that. Besides that, if you weren't forced to, what would be your life dream?"

She gets to her feet and looks around the room. "I want fun pictures. None of this abstract crap," she says, pointing to the walls.

I let the abrupt change of topic slide, picking up on her unwillingness to answer my question head-on. "O-kay. Moving on. What's the kind of imagery you like, then? What pictures bring you joy?"

"Casual ones."

"What do you mean, casual ones? Nature, oil abstracts, illustrations?"

"I just want my room to be a place I can feel carefree."

I nod, taking in what my first client is telling me and trying to visualize how to make her feel carefree in this space. "Are you open to rearranging?"

"Yep. Down for any changes. My bookshelf is a mess, but I don't know what to do about that."

I ask a few more questions and jot down her answers. "Okay. I think we're ready. Where can we go to get small home decor items?"

"Hmmm. Kyobo has cute little trinkets and random things you can buy. And books, obviously; it's a massive bookstore.

There's one in Gangnam, not far from here. I can have my driver take us—"

"I want to travel sans driver today," I say, cutting her off.

She makes a motion with her hands as if strangling the air. "You're killing me, Mel. But fine. Only because you're so sad. Do you want to talk about it?"

I shake my head. "Do you want to talk about what you were thinking about twenty seconds ago when you avoided my question?"

I say it playfully, but Yura looks at me, visibly annoyed for the first time since I've met her. "Mel, drop it."

I bite my lips awkwardly. "Sorry. I didn't mean to bring up something personal."

Yura shakes her head, back to her old self. I've never seen anyone so capable of literally shaking things off so easily. "It's all good. Kyobo time."

We walk to the Hannam-dong bus stop and hop on one of the many buses that go to Gangnam. It drops us off right in front of Kyobo, a wide red-brick building with a huge lobby and a coffee shop and restaurant on the ground floor. I make for the information desk, but Yura guides me to the elevator, off to the side. The familiar hush of a bookstore makes me feel at ease and excited at the same time.

"Do you have any preference on genre for books?" I whisper.

"Nope, unless you recommend any."

"Where's the English books section?"

When we get there, I pull *The Picture of Dorian Gray*, *The Importance of Being Earnest*, and *Lady Windermere's Fan* from the *W* shelf.

Yura watches me with amusement as I pull out my choices.

"Have you read any of these or do you own them already?" I ask.

She shakes her head. "No, but I take it you really like books by dead Irish men, huh?"

"Just this one dead Irish man, and they're good at distracting me. Okay, perfect. Now we need to get some special edition books."

"Why?"

"They look good on a shelf, facing out so people can see the cover. Trust me." I'm running on adrenaline now, and when I don't think too much, I'm in my element. I close my eyes for a moment, mentally rearranging Yura's furniture and reorganizing her bookshelf. I pull out the paper with my notes and draw a makeshift blueprint of her room from memory. She watches me in awe as I sketch out her room and furniture.

"You have a photographic memory!" Yura squeaks.

"Do I? I think I just remember people's bookshelves easily."

After buying copies of *Alice's Adventures in Wonderland* and *Anne of Green Gables* with illustrated covers, we head downstairs on the escalator, where, as Yura says, the "trinkets" are.

She grabs an item on display when we get down. "Ooh, Polaroid cameras! I need one of those. This can't be part of the budget, because I actually need this. And we can take cute photos today."

I submit to this, and we both continue walking around the floor. I'm amazed by how wide the space is and the variety of items for sale. There are records, music players, toys and books for children, stationery, professional art materials, frames, and a ton of little household and lifestyle items: clocks, wallets, and surprisingly enough, paperweights.

"Other places in Seoul seem much more crowded compared to this place. I mean in terms of shopping," I comment.

"Yeah, a lot of outdoor touristy shopping areas like Myeong-dong will be crowded, but places like this, or cafés in certain neighborhoods and department stores, aren't too bad. Except on weekends."

"I see," I say, picking up a paperweight shaped like a teacup and imagining it on Yura's bookshelf. The joke is on me, I guess, because this paperweight would look great. I could set up half the books horizontally and stack them, with the teacup paperweight on the top, and display the more artistic-looking ones facing out with a picture frame or a candle next to them. I add it to our basket.

In the stationery section, we pick out wooden clips and rolls of twine of varying colors and thicknesses for a gallery wall. I see a corner with all types of paintings, drawings, and posters and pull Yura in that direction. I find some beautiful drawings of dancers—ballerinas in dainty costumes—and a snowy painting that makes you feel refreshed just looking at it, just like Yura wanted. I pull the two posters out and show them to her. "Perfect, right?" I ask eagerly.

"I don't like those. Nothing winter, no dancing, okay?" The way Yura says this makes me think I offended her somehow.

But once again, she's immediately back to her sunny self. "What about this one?" She pulls out a drawing of a little child holding up a balloon in a grassy field near a stream. It's very peaceful. I nod my approval.

After we finish checking out, we head outside, satisfied with our haul.

"Okay, on to the next," I say. "Do you know a furniture store around here? A place with pillows, throws, maybe some lounge cushions or something."

"Mm-hmm. And it's not far from here. We can walk." We tighten our jackets against the brisk wind and link our arms closely together as we walk down the wide Gangnam streets.

"Does it snow a lot here?" I ask as we walk past a Baskin-Robbins with a snowman drawn on the windowpane.

"Yeah. Most winters it'll snow at least a few times. It gets really cold, too."

"Colder than New York?"

"I think so. I've only been to New York twice during the winter, so I'm not sure. Less windy here, though."

I turn so fast to look at her that I crick my neck. "When was the last time you went? Where did you stay? How long were you there for?"

She giggles at my questions. "You really miss it still, huh? We usually stay at the Four Seasons in FiDi, and I'm not really ever there for long. And my parents always have a packed agenda, so I never get to do anything fun. Next time I go, you can show me around."

"It'd be so much fun. I'd take to you all the places rich people don't know exist," I say.

Soon, we arrive at a street lined with furniture stores. "What is this place?"

"It's a street known for furniture shopping. It's part of Gangnam, called Nonhyun-dong."

"Amazing." Because we've decided on a budget, we stick to this one store I like the look of. Yura tells me that it's well known in Korea for its good design and affordability, sort of like a Korean IKEA.

"Perfect. No wonder I felt it calling to me."

Almost two hours later, we're sitting on beanbags that face each other, reviewing our final choices for purchase: a yellow pillow threaded with a delicate navy pattern, a baby pink pillow with thick faux fur, a navy linen pillow, and two small beanbags.

"I'm not sure these beanbags will go with your room, to be honest," I say to her.

"Yeah, but ugh, they're so comfy," she says, leaning farther back into her beanbag, now almost flat on the floor.

"Well, we can get rid of the two chairs you have with the gold metal legs, and put these beanbags there instead," I suggest. "But not these colors. If they're surrounding the silver coffee table, we need something more muted, like a neutral color."

"What about that beige one?" Yura points at a lonely beanbag sitting a few feet away.

"Well, little grasshopper, my job here is done," I say in my wisest voice. "That's perfect. We'll get two of those."

She bows and I stick an imaginary gold star sticker on her forehead, and we carry everything down to the cash register.

"Where will you put all the stuff you're not going to use anymore?" I ask her as we wait in line.

"We have an empty-ish study and lounge room, so I can just put it there."

I let Yura convince me to take a cab home with our now very heavy haul, and we drag it all upstairs to her room with the help of her ahjumma.

It's almost dinnertime when I finish rearranging her furniture and decorating her bookshelf. When I take a step back to appreciate my work, I'm glad to see Yura smiling like she's got a hanger in her mouth. "I *love* it, Mel," she says, hugging me.

"Can't breathe," I choke. I release a sigh of happiness. I wonder if this is what it feels like to have a happy client. It's wonderful.

"It's so nice that I have someone to do this with."

"Do what with?"

Yura gestures at the air. "High school. You know, before you came along, it was just me and Kimbeom, sometimes Junghoon and Wonjae. Oh, by the way, we all know you two are flirting not so secretly."

"We are not!" I say, hoping she'll believe me. Even if I feel a little tense and nervous around Wonjae sometimes, I am definitely not ready to admit that to anyone, not even myself.

"Oh sure, sure," she says, her eyes twinkling.

"How's your seduction plan going?" I ask, trying to divert the topic.

Yura flips her hair. "I play coy and I'll rope him in one of these days."

"One day soon, I'm sure of it."

"You know," she says, with a mysterious air, "we *have* been texting a lot. Sometimes, he KaToks me in the evenings, asking what I'm up to."

"Yura, he's definitely interested!"

We sprawl out on her floor, exhausted from what feels like a week's worth of work, and snap a few photos on her new Polaroid together and some on my phone of her room as well, to commemorate my success with my happy first client.

"Guess I should head home," I say reluctantly.

"You can sleep over if you want," Yura says, but I shake my

head no. I appreciate her offer, but I know I need to get back home.

"I have so much catching up to do anyway. I'll probably have to lock myself in my room all weekend and study."

Yura waves goodbye and promises to send me all her notes from the lectures I missed and says she'll get Junghoon's notes as well from Creative Writing. I take the stairs up to my apartment and—out of habit by now—open my phone web browser to Maison & Saito's website to check on the status of my application. I almost trip on the next stair when I notice there's been a change in my status.

Status: Under Review

My application is being reviewed. Mine! A warmth spreads through my chest as I open my apartment door. This entire day was the medicine I needed, and I'm ready to rest when I hear loud—very loud—footsteps rapidly coming in my direction.

"Lee Solmi!" my dad's voice booms through the foyer, and my entire body turns to stone.

THIRTEEN

I race through a list of all the possible reasons my dad could be mad: Did he find out I ditched school today? Did he somehow learn I lied about my date with Kimbeom? Did he find out about the champagne-in-the-face incident with Colin Joo? Although he technically already yelled at me about that. I stand up straight, wondering if he can hear my heart palpitating.

"Yes, Appa?" My voice comes out clear and innocent and masks my fear. He's right in front of me, and I haven't even taken my left shoe off.

In his hand is a crumpled-up sheet of paper. He unfolds it ominously in front of me, and before he's done, I know what it is. He holds up my Pre-Calc pop quiz, the one I threw away. The large C+ mocks me from the top of the page.

I suddenly find that I have forgotten how to breathe. "You were in my room?" I'm paralyzed with fear that he saw my portfolio stashed in the bookshelf.

He walks toward the den, and I know I'm expected to follow. My dad slams the quiz down on the coffee table between us and sits himself on the sofa. "This is unacceptable," he says, the sound of the slam still reverberating in my ears. I stand stock-still, staring at the floor.

"What do you do all day if not study?" he asks. I stand there silently, not taking my eyes off a light yellow stain on the ivory rug.

"Answer me, Solmi," he says. His quietness is scarier than his yelling.

"I do study, Appa. But SIA is harder than my public school back home." I'm not lying, and my cheeks are red from embarrassment. It's not like it makes me happy to see a C+ when I study hard. "Pre-Calc isn't easy, and I really have been—"

"If you bring home another C+, I will personally make sure you are escorted to every class."

In an attempt to salvage what little pride I have left, I peel my eyes away from the floor and look straight at him. "It's not my fault that it's taking more time to get used to, okay? You think transitioning to a new school in a foreign country is easy? I hate getting C's in my classes, too."

My voice is shaking, but I try my best to sound calm.

"It's been a month. This isn't a foreign country. It's your homeland. The sooner you accept that, the sooner you'll perform the way you should at SIA. Don't let me see this again."

I wait until my dad's footsteps are out of range before I go to my room.

I'm only in my room for an hour when my dad knocks on my door. "Dinner."

"No, thank you."

"Eating dinner is not an option. You eat so you can study. Now come down."

Faced with the risk of him fully entering and seeing my

interior design sketches now scattered all over my desk and getting angrier that I'm "wasting" my time, I capitulate, trudging down the stairs and into the dining room.

My mom's become a pro at heating up dishes that the ahjumma makes. Today we're eating soondubu and bulgogi. I watch her place the dishes in front of us, wondering if she's going to try to make any amends or small talk with me in front of my dad.

"Solmi, do you need a tutor?" my dad asks.

I shake my head vigorously. "I'll bring my grades up."

"If you can't bring them up soon, I'm going to get you one," he says.

I eat my dinner silently, just relieved that my parents didn't find out that I skipped school today. I watch them interact. Their conversation feels strained, uncomfortable. I wonder if my dad knows my mom went to go see Aunt Rebecca the other day.

"Did you go meet someone today?" my dad asks my mom as he brings a spoonful of soondubu to his mouth. She's wearing outdoor clothes instead of her usual loungewear.

"A few hours ago. Are you still going to Singapore?"

He shakes his head. "Got canceled, so I'll be here. I may have to go to Taiwan after Chuseok, but we'll see."

My mom isn't asking me questions, but maybe my dad doesn't know about our fight and she's trying to keep it that way. That'd be my best guess. I wonder who she went to meet. Was it my aunt again? We go the entire dinner not speaking, and it doesn't seem to concern my dad; does he not realize she and I rarely go this long without talking?

I excuse myself after dinner and lock my door again. Yura

and Kimbeom send me all the materials I missed from school today, and I sit on my sofa and try calling Sophia, but she doesn't pick up. She's probably in the middle of class right now. Sighing, I put my phone away and go to bed feeling a lot of things I can't put a name to.

I successfully avoid my mom for most of the weekend until Sunday afternoon rolls around, when I'm sitting on my floor, surrounded by watercolor pencils and old fabrics cut out of dresses I'm not wearing anymore, and creating a collage. I'm so focused that I don't hear my mom setting down a tray of peanut butter sandwiches next to me.

I jump, leaving a streak of light green paint across the corner of an old white T-shirt. "Thanks a lot," I grumble.

"Mel, you can't avoid me forever."

"Try me, I bet I can."

"Do you want one?" she says, handing me a cut-out sandwich.

I look up at her. "No. What I want is for you to tell me what you and Halmoni talked about, why you lied to me about going to see Aunt Rebecca. And why you're always fighting with her. And she's who you saw today, right? When will I get to spend any time with her?"

She sighs. "Listen, kid. There are things you can't possibly ever fully understand. Know why? Because you're sixteen, Melody. You need to accept at some point that I have my reasons for the choices I make for this family and go with it, okay? And if part of that means sometimes you feel left in the dark, well, you'll understand when you have children of your own."

I don't respond and focus on blotting out the green streak and cutting up a piece of yellow fabric to glue onto my blossoming collage. I can feel her eyes watching me, waiting for me to look up. I don't.

Eventually, she gets up to leave, closing the door on her way out.

When I run out of glue and tape, I wander around the house wondering where I could find some. My first guess is my dad's office, but he's out at a work dinner so I can't ask him. I know he'd be angry if I went into his home office without permission, but what he doesn't know won't hurt him. I sneak in, closing the door behind me slowly. I spot a roll of tape and grab it, but then I think: I've never been in here before and I don't plan on coming back, so what's the harm in looking around a bit? I pull open some drawers and rifle through some papers, but everything is in Korean and nothing looks even remotely interesting. I'm about to leave when on the walnut bookshelf, I see a leather notebook that looks very worn out. Old leather-bound books always have a great story behind them. I pull it out gently, immediately realizing what it is. It's not a book. It's a journal, written in Korean. I sit on the floor and slowly begin translating bits and pieces of it.

> June 1999
> I can't wait for New York. My dream.
> Wall Street.

"Wall Street" is written in English, but I don't know what he's saying about it. But my dad was once excited about going to New York, years ago. 1999 . . . five years before I was born. He must've met my mom pretty soon after. Already knowing I need to read more of this precious journal, I replace the spot on the shelf where it was originally with another book that's a similar color. I carry the diary carefully and rush upstairs to my room, where I spend the rest of the evening slowly trying to decipher the unfamiliar Korean words and my dad's messy handwriting. I can't believe I found this. I wonder how much time I have before he notices it's gone. Or maybe he'll never notice. I flip to another page with neater penmanship.

2002
Jieun leaving is bad for the child. Lily is sad every day.

I guess my mom was really sad about Aunt Rebecca leaving New York to go back to Seoul. If I had a sister and we had to live apart, I guess I'd be sad, too. I try to read other entries, but it's hard to read messy Korean writing and even harder to understand what he's talking about. I find one from May 2000.

Wall Street . . . not New York. Tired.
Best thing to meet Lily. My sweet flower.

I only understand parts of it, but I can tell he was enamored with my mom. It's weird to read that, seeing them now. They're not hostile toward each other, but they're not loving, either. I wonder how they both really feel. I wonder what job my dad did on Wall Street. It's strange to think of my parents as young adults, not much older than I am now. Well, not *that* much older, anyway. That night, I go to bed vowing to learn more Korean so I can read through these pages and figure out their story for myself.

At school the next day, I have an exceptionally hard time focusing and catching up on material. Teachers don't ask why I didn't show up yesterday, which confuses me, but I also don't press since it means I'm not in trouble. During AP World History, I get my WWII paper back, and I am relieved when I see a B at the top of my paper. It's a little disheartening that I'm relieved about a B, but it is what it is. It's good enough for now. At lunch, I don't tell the others why I skipped school or how my weekend was, but no one pries, and it feels like a normal Monday.

"Oh, but one piece of good news," I say to them in the cafeteria, trying to keep a handle on my excitement. "My application for the M&S internship is now 'under review.'"

"What's that mean, then? When do you find out?" Kimbeom asks me.

Junghoon and Wonjae are nowhere to be found, and Yura guesses they ditched lunch to go eat "real food."

"Soon. I think definitely in the next two weeks."

When it's time for Korean class, I realize how three days of not seeing Wonjae feels a lot longer. But when I see him seated at his usual desk, right behind mine, I wave as casually as I can. Before I can say anything, Mrs. Lee walks in, looking like she's just returned from an extremely important person's funeral. She's wearing black heels, wide black pants, and a black blouse that looks sheer but doesn't actually show anything.

"Like I mentioned, instead of midterms, you'll be given a project. You'll have three and a half weeks, including the holiday week. Presentations will be the Thursday before finals. Consider yourselves lucky."

The class groans in unison at the thought of having to work

on a project during the upcoming holiday week, but I remain quiet. A project for Korean class is the best-case scenario for me because it means no exam.

"You'll each be assigned a district, or a gu, in Seoul. Study it, research it, make that location your personal area of expertise. You'll be doing a presentation on it in whatever creative format you wish: this could be an architectural structure you've created, a PowerPoint deck, a written paper—this is the least interesting presentation format, but it has been done before—the list goes on. I will also be the ultimate judge of how well you know the history of your assigned district. Any questions?"

Wonjae raises his hand. "Are there any creative formats that are off-limits?" I turn to look at him; he's grinning a goofy grin, and the rest of the class snickers encouragingly.

Mrs. Lee holds up her hand as if to stop him right there. "No improv." Before he has a second to respond, she continues. "Here are the pairings."

I listen for my name, and I make a silent wish to be paired with someone smart.

Then I hear it: "Wonjae Chae, Melody Lee. Your district: Jongno-gu."

I shut my eyes tightly. I'm nervous and excited and awkward all at once. I never responded to his text on Friday, mostly because I didn't want to deal with the reality of the big fight with my mom, and he didn't message me to follow up. Not that I expected him to, but it did make me wonder if he was annoyed. It was his first text to me, and I know it's too late now, but I wish I didn't ignore it. My embarrassment has my hand unexpectedly shooting into the air like an overeager teacher's pet.

Then my mouth follows, stupidly saying something I already know I don't mean.

"Can we request new partners?"

Why did I just say that? I inwardly curse my uncooperative vocal cords. It's like they know my heart can't handle an overload of one-on-one time with Wonjae.

Mrs. Lee peers at me over her glasses. "No, you may not. Anything else?"

I slump back into my seat, mortified. I turn my head to sneak a glance at Wonjae, and he's stifling a laugh.

"Why do you not want to work with me?" he whispers.

"I didn't mean it," I say truthfully. "Really. It just came out." I hope I sound believable, because it's true. I actually couldn't think of a better partner for me. Forced alone time with Wonjae sounds . . . well, pretty good.

Before class ends, Mrs. Lee reminds us of our monthly Korean quiz this Friday. Wonjae taps my shoulder. "So, when are we meeting to discuss the project?"

"How soon should we start?" I ask.

"Well, I mean, if we want to make sure we get A's . . ." He trickles off with a crooked smile.

"Makes sense." I smile back, hoping I come off at least a little flirty. "I'm free tonight," I add.

"Cool, Cappo at six?"

I nod. "I'll be the one with the coffee."

WHEN I GET HOME, THERE ARE CHEESE, CRACKERS, dried fruit, and sliced fruit on the kitchen table. My mom puts her book down and greets me in the foyer before gesturing me over toward the snacks. "How was school?" she asks.

"Fine." There's a slight awkward pause between us. I think about the days when we would talk for hours, homework took no time, and exams were easy. I can't believe it was only a month ago.

"I made a snack for you. Like old times." Maybe we're both thinking the same thing. That we miss New York. And our apartment.

I stare at the snacks. "I don't remember you giving me dried fruit and bougie-looking cheese before."

"Well, the Taco Bell here doesn't taste the same," she says, smiling.

I don't say anything, instead focusing on putting a piece of cheese on top of a cracker and then putting both in my mouth.

"You ready to talk yet?" my mom asks. "Or are you going to keep ignoring me and leaving for school before I get a chance to wake up and see you?"

I put a dried prune back down onto the marble board. "You've been lying to me my entire life. Would *you* be ready to talk?"

My mom purses her lips. "Honey, not telling you the reason for every little thing in our lives is not the same as lying."

"Yes, it is. It's a lie of omission, which is still a lie. And besides, if I said I'm ready to talk, then what? Are you going to give me answers? And you *did* lie to me, FYI."

"What are your questions?"

"Same ones as yesterday, Mom. Why do you not like Rebecca Eemo? Why did you never let me build a relationship with her? She's my aunt."

"Rebecca hasn't matured yet, Mel. She's off singing and doing God knows what else, not at all being responsible with her life. She isn't exactly a role model, and she certainly isn't a good influence on you. That was never a secret."

I shake my head. "There's more. There's more to why you don't want us to be close."

"Your grandma wanted me to come to Korea and patch things up with her. She's getting older, you know. She wanted to make sure her daughters would have each other after she's gone."

"O-kay," I say, glad for some sort of information, "but what was there to patch up in the first place?"

My mom just sits there in silence.

I look at her, disappointed. If she won't even open up about her own sister, there's no way she's telling me anything I want to know about my dad. "Well, I have to do my homework until I meet up with my Korean class project partner tonight." I stand up to leave, but I turn around before going up the stairs. "You think I'm so unaware, Mom, but I'm not."

I leave a little earlier than necessary so I can avoid dinner and tell my mom that I'm eating with Wonjae, even though I'm not. I'm planning to read my book until he gets here, but when I open the glass doors, I see him already seated at a table.

"You're early," I say to him, shrugging off my jacket.

He waves as I sit down across him. "Want some coffee?"

"I'll go get my own." I browse the pastries and buy two madeleines and a latte. I hand a madeleine to him, and he smiles charmingly and opens his mouth.

I laugh and shake my head. "You are fully capable of feeding yourself," I say awkwardly, and push the madeleine on a plate toward him. Because I kind of do want to feed it to him. But I can't; I'm not smooth enough.

"All right. Let's get to work. Do you know anything about Jongno-gu?" Wonjae asks.

I shake my head.

"Okay. Where to start? It's pretty much the cultural center of Seoul, so in that sense, I think we got an easy assignment. The main palaces and cultural sights are basically all in Jongno-gu, but I think it would be too predictable to do a presentation on those." He taps his pen against his chin as he thinks.

"Hmm, okay, what else is around there? I did read about the palace and other historical areas, but I agree, it feels a little bland."

"Cafés . . . stores . . ."

"All Seoul has are cafés and shops, right? And bars."

"Um, yeah, like most cities everywhere. And it has a lot more than that. New York isn't that different," he says, sounding defensive.

I gape at this profound display of ignorance. "Are you kidding me? New York has so much more to do than Seoul in terms of activities, culture, food, and everything else."

"Okay, okay. Focus."

I take a satisfied sip of my matcha latte. "So, is there anything different about these coffee shops or stores in Jongno versus other places, like Garosugil or Gangnam?"

Then he slaps the table in an *aha!* manner. "Actually, there is."

"I've never seen you so excited before."

"Maybe I need to hang out with more exciting people," he says, sticking his tongue out at me. I roll my eyes but let myself laugh.

He opens his phone map to show me. "There's this up-and-coming area. It's pretty popular now with locals, but tourists don't really know about it yet, so it feels like a neighborhood secret. It's called Ikseon-dong."

I listen intently until he stops talking and looks up suddenly from his phone, like he's just thought of something.

"Let's go," he says, standing up and picking up his coffee.

"What? Go where?"

"Ikseon-dong."

I'm tempted to say "no," to tell him his idea is all play and no work, but a voice inside my head admits that I'd much rather be with Wonjae than my mom. I place my coffee cup in the return bin and give him a thumbs-up. He exits first as I wipe my hands on a napkin, and I see him outside hailing a cab.

"Let's just take the bus or subway," I say, wrapping my jacket tighter around myself as I join him.

"You don't even know how far it is," he says. "What if it's over an hour away?"

"It's not. It's within Seoul, and I've seen Jongno on the subway map a million times. I know it's not more than thirty minutes away." I feel proud that I know more about Korea than he expected.

He relents. "Okay, fine, but only because traffic is heavy."

When we get off the train at Jongno 3-ga subway station—it turns out there's a million different Jongo-something stops, so I'm glad I'm with Wonjae—we walk toward exit 4. I'd never admit it to Wonjae, but I'm getting more and more excited for this because I have a feeling it's going to be different from everything else I've seen of Seoul so far. I can just sense it in the air.

"I'm still surprised every time I ride a clean escalator in the subway. And they're so long. I think the only escalators this long in New York are at the major transfer stops," I say as we step onto the escalators.

Disappointment washes over me as we emerge onto the street. I stare at low-rise buildings that look dilapidated or like dust has made its home on the facades permanently. "What is this place?" There are a few cleaner-looking convenience stores, but nothing remotely impressive. Plastic blue trash cans line the street, and full black trash bags line the sidewalk.

"You've been here less than one second, Judge Judy."

"Hey, it's not my fault you hyped this place up."

"Just be patient." He walks ahead of me, so I follow him as he makes turns into small alleyways. We pass by a restaurant that has red plastic stools and steel tabletops and no formal entrance. It's completely empty, but there are a few older ahjummas working in the kitchen. When I stop to observe, Wonjae notices and walks back to me.

"They're preparing for the dinner rush. This place gets popping by eight p.m."

I don't believe him. It's almost seven o'clock. Shouldn't people be here by now?

"Welcome to Ikseon-dong," he says. He's spreading his arms out like he owns these alleyways.

"Doesn't look like there's much around here. The streets are so narrow. Is there more inside these alleys?"

"Follow me. Have you tried hodduk?"

"Nope."

"There's a bit of a line, but it's worth it."

I can see in my periphery that Wonjae is inching closer to

me as I stand there shivering in the crisp fall air. It's slightly colder than normal today. When it's finally our turn, we get our hodduk—which turns out to be some sort of filled pancake folded into a paper cup—and I bite into it slowly, heeding Wonjae's warning that it's hot. Honey oozes out of the pancake and fills my mouth, along with some other tastes I can't quite identify: Rice? Walnuts?

"Holy moly," I say. "Okay, I'll give you this. I have yet to eat food here that isn't freaking amazing."

Wonjae fans the steam coming out of his open mouth. "Korea has the best food in the world, in my completely unbiased opinion."

"Unbiased, huh? Have you tried a lot of other foods?" We start walking deeper into the alleyways, and the farther we go, the more people there are. It almost feels like a festival here, with many outdoor vendors and a lot of outdoor seating, despite the chilly air. We squeeze past other students taking pictures and couples holding hands and taking selfies. "Are you sure this place is up and coming? It's packed," I tease him.

"Seriously. My bad. It's been a while since I've been here, but the last time I came, it wasn't this crowded. And yeah, I have, when I wasn't living in Korea, anyway."

I turn to face him, curious. "You didn't always live in Korea?"

"Singapore, Hong Kong, Massachusetts."

"I had no idea."

"Funny, I mentioned it in Itaewon," he says, smirking.

"Massachusetts," I say wistfully. "America."

Wonjae laughs, and I secretly feel pleased about it.

"Where in Massachusetts?"

"A boarding school."

"Mm-hmm," I say, my fail-safe response for getting the other person to talk more.

"My grandfather forced me to go to all these other boarding schools there, and I hated every single one of them. Singapore wasn't bad because I loved the food there, but none of those places felt like home to me. I've only been in Korea consistently since the seventh grade."

"Then how are you so good at Korean?"

"I came back every break and spent bits and pieces of my elementary school years here. Or did study-exchange programs here whenever I could."

"Ah, worked the system, I see."

"Exactly."

As we walk around, I think about how Wonjae felt most at home in Korea, even when he hadn't lived here. Maybe one day Korea can feel like home to me, too.

The stores are really cute, and there's a wide variety of them: lots of cafés, some non-Korean restaurants, street vendors with jewelry, and clothing stores. I want to go into all of them, but the most noticeable thing about them is the architecture. I couldn't really tell at first, but as we get deeper into the alley-ways and emerge from the throngs of people taking selfies, I see now all the exteriors are made of wood. The interiors are more modern, with glass displays or tables and mannequins set up near the doors. When we walk close enough to a building, I can hardly resist.

"How old is this place?" I ask, running my hands over the walls. "I can't believe these roofs. Look at this!" I touch the edges of a door. Most of them are a dusty black color but very traditional-looking. All the roofs are the same style; the shingles look like they've been individually stacked on top of each other, resembling small parallel cylinders forming a pyramid.

"Cool, huh? These are called hanoks," Wonjae explains.

"These stores?"

"Yeah, technically. They've been converted from old homes. Some people actually still live in these hanoks, but a lot of them have been turned into what you see now. Jewelry and clothing stores, restaurants, bars."

"Wow." The alleyways are lively with decorations. One café crowded with girls taking pictures of each other has greenery climbing over their doors and cute chalkboard signs; another alleyway is bursting with plants and has colorful upside-down umbrellas hanging overhead, making for a very Insta-worthy spot.

"You want a photo?"

I look up at the umbrellas and all the little succulents but shake my head. "It feels *too* Korean for me. And like I'm buying into their marketing scheme of taking pictures under these umbrellas."

"You're right. It's a ploy. How dare people try to make a place aesthetically pleasing so that people stop to document it. Monsters."

He has a point. "Okay, one picture."

I end up loving how the picture turns out. I consider asking if he wants to take a selfie with me, but I chicken out. We keep walking and he points to a café. "This is my favorite café. It's not as popular because it's not one of those made-for-Instagram type of places, but I think it has the best Korean desserts."

There are two massive wooden doors that sit on oversized hinges, and when we open one, it emits that perfect old creaking sound. Flat round stones pave a walkway from the doors toward the café, with an abundance of plants and flowers on both sides. Inside, the tables are low, and we have to take our shoes off and sit on the raised floor. Wonjae orders desserts from the menu that he seems to know are good, and when they come out, I admire the presentation and all the colors on the plate. I follow what Wonjae does: using a mini wooden fork, we stab the green rice cake and dip it in the honey. The rich sweetness of the honey and the chewiness of the rice cake together are heaven. The rice cake is slightly toasted, too, adding a delightful crunch to every bite.

I've never eaten sweet dduk like this before. Only the plain kind that's in ddukbokki, with the spicy sauce. He sips his cinnamon tea, and I drink some of my yuzu tea. It's sweet and tangy at the same time and somehow refreshing, even though it's hot.

"Wow, this dduk," I say, going in for my third piece.

"Save room for the other desserts."

"This place is like a time portal. I feel like I'm in a period drama."

"Yeah, it's like a traditional tearoom." Wonjae picks up a different dessert that has the same cylindrical shape as the green dduk but looks puffier and hands it to me. "Try this one. I think you'll like it."

I take it from him, but again, I wished I'd opened my mouth and let him feed it to me, an homage to our missed moment from the café.

I bite into it, not knowing what to expect. It's crispy at first bite, but then chewy, and it tastes like sweet rice. I close my eyes and soak it in. "Mmm."

"Good, right? This is called yugwa. It's made from glutinous rice."

"Koreans really love our rice and honey, don't we?"

Wonjae raises his eyebrows meaningfully.

"What?" I ask him.

"Nothing. Just that you said 'we.' And 'our.'"

I shake my head at him. "So? I mean, look at my face. I'm obviously Korean."

He *hmms* nonchalantly. "So . . . what do you think of Ikseon-dong?"

I put my fork down and take another sip of my tea. "I love it. I think it's the best place I've visited so far in Seoul. These hanoks are so beautiful. I've never seen anything like them. I'm just so impressed with how they turned them all into stores, but, like, not in an overly commercial way, you know? I love that they all look like they're small businesses and not a bunch of franchises. It's thoughtful."

"Wow, you actually like something about Korea, huh?"

I take another bite of the chewy yugwa and let it melt inside my mouth and manage to stick my tongue out at him.

For the next half hour, I try a few new desserts that Wonjae orders, and all of them taste equally delicious. The table is wide, but something about sitting shoeless in a small café makes the vibe between us feel more intimate. Something I've come to notice is how much I laugh around Wonjae and, despite the butterflies that never disappear, the comfort I feel when I'm with him. Tonight, it's no different.

As we head out and we weave our way through crowds again, I'm incessantly hitting refresh on the M&S portal page on my phone.

"You've been checking your phone a lot today," he comments.

I look up at him, startled, not realizing he had noticed that, not even realizing how obsessively I have been refreshing it.

"Habit," I say. I end up telling him more about Maison & Saito's interior design competition.

"It's under review now, so I'm just waiting to see if I was selected for the final round."

"Hope you get it."

"Me too."

"But it's not the end of the world if you don't. I mean, it's just an internship for one summer."

A sudden urge to flick his forehead comes over me. "It is the end of the world. To me, anyway. Being accepted into the final round is my ticket out of here."

Wonjae looks surprised. "You're leaving us so soon?"

I'm about to respond when I spot a cute store with double doors that are wide open and step inside.

The store feels warm and cozy, with tables lined with autumn hats and scarves, racks draped with elegant fall coats, and shoes and bags displayed in the corner. The interior is also all wood, and the exposed entryway is paved with rocks you have to walk across to get to the inside.

"I can almost imagine what the house used to look like when it was someone's home," I tell Wonjae. "And maybe. I need to get accepted first. Then I need to convince my parents, who have no idea I want to seriously pursue interior design, to let me fly to New York for the weekend to attend the competition."

Wonjae whistles. "Good luck with that," he says, not insincerely.

I try on a headband with a giant bow on our way out and clap my hand over my mouth when I catch my reflection. "I look ridiculous."

"You said it, not me," he says, grinning. He shrugs after. "Kind of cute, though."

An involuntary grin washes over me, and I try to keep it cool. I know I just said I look ridiculous, but his comment is enough to convince me to buy the headband. A memento of today. "I'll be right back," I say, trying to sneakily make my purchase without him noticing. We retrace our steps the way we came in, just to check in at the previously empty restaurant. He was right: it's now absolutely packed.

"You win," I say, looking at the tables covered with grilled meats, bottles of soju, and a ton of rice and side dishes. "Where'd all these people come from?"

"It's the post-work dinner rush. A lot of stressed-out employees trying to blow off steam."

As we walk toward the station, I spot something I didn't notice before. Or maybe it wasn't set up before. "What's all that?" I only see it from an angle, but it's a line of reddish umbrellas, orange tents, and steel carts emitting steam.

"Oh. It's the Ikseon-dong street food."

"I only see one or two at a time in other places. Is this area famous for street food?"

"Yeah, I mean there used to be a lot more pochas in Korea, but over the years they've sort of been disappearing. You won't find as many of these large hubs, but this is one of the few. It's a lot of seafood, anju—which are random snacks—and drinks. Super fun."

"Looks like it," I say kind of wistfully. It's in that moment of staring at orange tents and seeing the sky get darker that I realize I don't want this night with Wonjae to end.

"We can come again next time if you want," he offers.

"Well," I say as casually as I could, "what are you doing tonight? I guess you eat with your parents?"

"Parent, singular." When I don't know what to say, he just smiles kindly. "Don't worry about it."

I smile back. "Sorry. I didn't know . . ." My voice trails off.

"Didn't expect you to. Anyway, no, my mom is actually gone for a few days to my grandparents' place. Why?"

"Want to just, um, get anju and seafood here tonight, then?" I gesture to the tents. If he's surprised, he doesn't show it.

"After you," he says, lightly bringing his hand to my lower back and guiding me in front of him, sending tingles straight down my spine. We walk down the long street lined with bright orange tents on both sides. Some tents are packed with people while others are emptier; I point to one that has only one table occupied, by a young-looking couple.

"What about there?" I ask.

"It's pretty empty, which means it's probably not that good."

"But if it's empty, the owner would be that much happier if we go in. As opposed to an owner in a crowded tent, who's probably already happy with their crowded tent and who could potentially be stingy with us since they have so many other customers." I tap him lightly with my elbow. "Get what I'm saying?"

"All right, fine, but if the food at this pocha tastes bad, don't go around Seoul bad-mouthing all pochas."

Because of the wind outside, the tent flaps are all down, and we pull open the heavy clear plastic flap before we go in.

We insa to the elderly woman, and she points with a spatula to a table where we can seat ourselves. We pull blue plastic stools out from underneath and get situated.

"Any preference?" Wonjae asks. The offerings are extensive; almost half the counter space is used to display raw seafood. There's a large grill in the back and bottles and bottles of liquor and soda.

"Wow. I wouldn't even know where to begin."

"So you're good leaving it up to me?"

I nod tentatively. "Nothing too out there, okay?"

"Got it." He calls the ahjumma "Eemo" and orders a few dishes for us.

"Why did you call her your aunt?" I ask.

"It's just an affectionate term. A lot of people, when you order food from intimate places like this, you refer to the owner of the establishment as Eemo or Unni or Noona."

"Speaking of aunts, I'm sorry I never texted back . . ."

Wonjae shrugs it off. "It didn't go well, I'm guessing?"

I shake my head. "Not exactly."

"I figured. Well, uhm, I'm here, you know, if you, you know—" He shifts uncomfortably, but it's very sweet.

I nod without looking up. "I know. Thanks."

Before things get any more awkward, we're saved by the eemo, who covers our table with food and a bottle of something white and two gold bowls.

"This is makgeolli, which is Korean rice wine, and this is raw squid, soondae, and rabbokki. Here," he says, handing me a pair of disposable wooden chopsticks.

I survey the dishes before me with some trepidation. "Isn't soondae blood sausage? Also, *raw* squid? And what's rabbokki?"

The rabbokki looks the most appetizing to me because it looks like ddukbokki, which I love.

"It's basically ddukbokki but with ramen noodles added. Ramen plus ddukbokki: rabokki. And spicy, like any other ddukbokki sauce, slightly sweeter. And soondae is not bad at all. You eat sausages, don't you? And the inside of the soondae pieces isn't even sausage. It's just vermicelli noodles. Just try one." He dips a piece of soondae in a pinkish salt and puts it on my plate.

I pick it up, close my eyes, and warily put the piece into my mouth.

"Good, right? Admit it."

I chew slowly, soaking it in. The soondae is a little salty, warm and chewy, easy to eat, and who doesn't love noodles?

"That is . . . *bloody* delicious." I say it so seriously Wonjae just looks at me before he bursts out laughing. I join him.

"I knew you'd like it. So, since you liked it, you need to try the ojingeo."

I shake my head aggressively. "Never. It's *moving*. I can literally *see* it moving in front of me."

"Dip it in the gochujang. Come on, trust me."

I slowly reach for a tentacle, and when I poke it gingerly, it squirms and I freak out and drop my chopsticks. "Nope, not happening."

"Come on." He picks a small one that isn't so squirmy and coats it in the sauce. I guess he thinks I won't pick it up again if he puts it on my plate, so he leans forward and holds out the piece in his chopsticks toward my mouth. My brain sends happy tingles throughout my body, and I bite my lip nervously. A welcome, exciting K-drama moment, and it's happening to me right now. I lean over the table toward him, closing my eyes, wondering if Wonjae can see how nervous I am to be this close to him, and trying to focus on the taste and not the moving invertebrate inside my mouth, and—

I fail and ungracefully spit it out. The K-drama moment is gone. "Congratulations, Wonjae. You've introduced me to the first inedible dish I've had in Korea."

"That's a you-problem. Most people love this. And all you really taste is the red pepper sauce anyway. Mmm. So fresh." He opens the makgeolli and pours the rice wine into the bowls. "Here. This will get rid of the aftertaste since you hate it so much." We clink to cheers, and I take my first sip of rice wine.

"Holy moly, yum."

"Better than that beer in Itaewon?"

"Way better. I could drink this every day."

"You probably shouldn't."

"Probably not," I say, grinning wide.

The rest of our time in the tent is spent mourning how hard Pre-Calc is and brainstorming more ideas for our Korean project. I can see the appeal of these pojangmachas; inside the tent, with drinks and heat lamps and no one else around us, my eyes are so focused on Wonjae that I notice every detail of his face, every line that crinkles around the edges of his eyes when he laughs, the subtle movements of his arm on the table inching closer to mine until they casually touch.

And it's not just that I'm getting closer to Wonjae that makes me feel this bubbly, warm, almost fuzzy feeling . . . it's that, for the first time, I feel closer to Korea, too.

FOURTEEN

My first thought when I wake is: *Will Wonjae be my first kiss?* My second thought is: *I'm going to be late for school!* I rush out and just barely make it to Miss Smith's homeroom class right before the bell rings.

Yura is showing pictures of her new room to Kimbeom, Junghoon, and Wonjae when I join them. "Hi," I say, slightly flushed. Whether it's from running up the stairs or because I was thinking of Wonjae's lips, I'm not sure.

"Ooh, it's much more you. Good job, Mel," Kimbeom compliments.

"Thanks. I'm pretty proud of it," I say, stealing a glance at Wonjae, who's looking intently at the photos Yura is scrolling through. As the day goes on, Wonjae and I don't talk much, and I gradually come to think we were just caught up in the heat of the fall evening air by ourselves, without our usual friends to keep things fun and light. Maybe we were bored. Whatever flirty vibes I was feeling yesterday, none of it is here today, which makes me believe he likely dismissed it, too. Which is fine since I need to focus anyway. The monthly Korean quiz is this Friday, so I have to pay attention. I can't afford to get distracted.

The rest of the week moves quicker than most, with my determination to ace the quiz overpowering any other thoughts. I mostly only see my friends during lunch period and in Honors Korean, so it's hard to scrutinize Wonjae's possible romantic interest toward me, especially when Mrs. Lee speeds so fast through her lectures that I can't waste a minute trying to flirt.

At home, I spend most of my afternoons this week studying. If my dad flipped out about my C in Pre-Calc, he definitely won't be any more gracious with a C in Korean. In the middle of studying one evening, my mind wanders to his diary, and when I'm confident that no one will be entering my room unannounced, I open it to try and translate more of the pages. It's Thursday night, but I tell myself that reading his pages is technically studying Korean.

> April 2003
> Cleaned another house. Really big.
> Very tiring.
> Solmi is so little. Lily is happy. Love.

My eyes grow a little dim over this page. This is the year I was born, the year before my dad moved to Korea and my mom and I didn't. It makes me feel closer to him, reading this page. I'm sure his writing is more eloquent than my rough translations, but I'm able to grasp these basics. I study the first line closer. He went from Wall Street to cleaning houses? Why? And how did he become a partner living in a five-bedroom villa? I flip to the end of the journal, but it's blank. I realize, despite the thickness of the notebook itself, only half of it is filled. Starting from the end of the journal, I work my way back to find the exact last page of his entry. It's an entry from 2004; I guess my dad wasn't exempt from the universal truth that people never finish their journals. It's a longer entry, filling about three-fourths of the page, all in Korean I can't read legibly. I sigh, frustrated, wishing I could ask someone to translate this for me. I even try using a translation app on my phone, but it can't detect the my dad's scrawls, unfortunately.

I close the journal and stash it inside one of the satin pillowcases behind two large decorative pillows. I go to bed that night thinking about my dad's life in New York.

Every period, I try to study my Honors Korean notes, which I place surreptitiously under the textbooks I'm supposed to be focusing on. The panic about the quiz and the pressure from my dad feels heavy as I enter Mrs. Lee's class, but by 3:05 p.m., I'm out the door and feeling slightly better than I expected about the exam. What a relief it's over. I'm at my locker packing up my books for the weekend when Yura comes running toward me excitedly.

"Gue-ess wha-at," she says, all sing-songy.

"Something exciting."

"So, during AP World, I wrote a note to Junghoon saying that I didn't do well on the essay and needed some tutoring. And since we take Physics together for second period, I mentioned that I'm struggling in that class, too."

My brows knit in confusion. "I didn't know you were struggling in those classes."

"Not really, per se, but it's still a good excuse to casually create dates."

"Does Junghoon do that well in his classes?" I try to hide the twinge of jealousy I feel.

"You didn't know?" Yura asks. "He's jungyo ildung."

"First place in what now?"

"In school. He has the highest grades in our whole school."

"Wow," I say, truly impressed.

"Anyway, my plan worked, and he's going to tutor me tomorrow." Her cheeks are rosy with giddiness. "Project Palm of My Hand is in motion."

"You know that makes it sound like he's going to become your little servant."

Yura sticks out her lower lip in thought. "Project Wrapped Around My Finger?"

"Sounds a little naughty."

"Good, it will be," Yura says, giving me an exaggerated wink.

I tell Yura to keep me posted on the ambush date she has planned, and I head home. My mind wanders back to my appa's journal, and I'm a little relieved to learn he won't be joining us for dinner this evening when I get home. It's not rational, but I feel like unless I stop thinking about it, he'll be able to sniff out my thoughts over kimchi jjigae or something and realize I stole his diary from sixteen plus years ago and that will be the end of my life. The exhaustion from the past several days of sneaky diary reading and prepping for my Korean quiz takes over finally, and I read on my bed until I fall asleep.

I wake up when a pillow is thrown at my face, leaving me feeling disoriented. I reach for my phone. It's barely 6:40 a.m., and as I squint toward the culprit, I see my dad. We are not at all pillow-throwing level of close, so I look at him, baffled, my hair a mess, my eyes bleary. There's a faint trace of a smile on his face. I flip over to turn my back to him, hoping he'll leave me alone and let me sleep until a godly hour on this Saturday morning. And not throw another pillow at me.

"Good morning, Solmi, wake up," he says, more cheer in his voice than I'm used to hearing.

I ignore him again. The door is wide open, but he knocks on it loudly, incessantly.

I groan just as loudly, hoping he will take the hint. When he doesn't, I surrender inwardly and turn back over. "Yes, Appa?"

"We're going hiking today."

"*We* as in . . ."

"We, our family. We're leaving in twenty minutes, so start getting ready," he says as he walks out. I sit up groggily, confused by the visible cheerfulness he is exuding.

I throw on sweats and a T-shirt and meet my parents downstairs in time for a quick breakfast. During the car ride, there's old-school American music playing, and both my parents are humming along. I feel like I woke up in an alternate universe. This is a side of them I've never seen before, and I don't understand where it came from.

"So where did this sudden need to go on a family hike come from?" I ask.

"It's the best time to go. The leaves are changing this week," my mom answers, rolling down the window just a crack. My mom is singing "Jolene," and when I look at my dad, I can tell he is looking at her out of the corner of his eye and enjoying her singing. I wonder if she used to sing a lot when they lived together, too. At every stop light, he glances over at her. It's my first time hearing her sing since we came to Korea, and it makes me think of my aunt. I think they sound kind of similar, like they'd have very compatible voices.

A quick nap, some *Candy Crush*, a bottle of hojicha, and a bag of Korean corn chips later, we finally arrive at the base of the mountain. We stretch our limbs and take in the crisp morning air. My dad told me the name of the mountain in the car, but I wasn't paying attention, and I nod while he rambles on about the mountain and our hike. "Your mom and I used to go hiking a lot, Solmi," he informs me.

"How come there are so many people already here at this hour?" I ask as we start heading toward the base. On my left is a group of ahjummas all wearing bright red visors, colorful pants, and moisture-wicking polo shirts. I try my best to suppress a grin at this intense-looking, middle-aged hiking group.

My dad brings us some sad-looking beanies. "They'll keep our heads warm," he says, handing each of us one. Mine's orange and my mom's is red and his is brown. We look like colorful croissants. My mom lets out a genuine laugh when she puts hers on, and she helps my dad with his.

The hike is not all that bad. It's a consistent, gradual incline, and my mom was right: The leaves are changing color and there's a beautiful gradation already on the ground, making each crunch under my feet very satisfying. The leaves look different than the ones in New York. My favorite ones are the yellow ginkgo leaves that resemble clovers. I trail a few steps behind my parents, cherishing this alone time in nature. A little while later, I'm walking with my eyes fixed on the ground, trying to step in all the crunchiest-looking leaf piles, and when I look up, I see my parents doing something I've never seen them do before in my entire life: they are holding hands. It's almost like they don't even notice I'm there, and it's even more jarring than when my dad threw a pillow at my face three hours ago. It's a glimpse into their past, before me, before the separation in New York and Korea, before whatever happened over the years that drove them apart. I thought seeing my parents like this would produce a warm, fuzzy feeling in my heart, but it only makes me feel suspicious and confused. Did my mom force me to come to Korea for her own sake? Because she wanted to? So she could patch things up with my dad and Aunt Rebecca?

When I catch up to them, their hands pull apart and I pretend not to notice. "How much longer till we reach the top?"

"Still a bit, but let's stop for a break," my dad says, pointing at a little store. There's nowhere to sit; it's just a station with hot foods where you stand and eat before you keep going. Like a mini pocha.

"Is that odeng?" I point to a steel compartment with steam issuing from the top and a bunch of wooden skewers sticking out. I rush over there first and breathe deeply. "Mmm, it is." We all hover over the narrow counter as we bite into our fish cakes and warm our stomachs with the hot broth the halmoni hands us. I smile at her. "Gamsa hamnida," I say, thanking her as I take the cup.

She compliments me to my parents in words I don't fully understand, but I get the gist of it. In this chilly early morning air, I close my eyes and can smell so many things: the fish cake, the soup, the leaves, the cold, and even a hint of my mom's perfume. It's so light and barely there, but I can smell it. There's a spray bottle filled with soy sauce, which looks super unappetizing, but which I've learned from my outings is completely necessary with odeng, so I grab it and spray it on both sides of what fish cake still remains on my stick.

"Hey, look at you," my dad says, patting me on the back. "You've been learning the locals' way."

I smile sheepishly. "I went to Ikseon-dong." I don't know why, of all facts, I choose to tell him that, but I do.

"Did you like it?"

I nod. "It was really pretty. A lot of people, though."

"Good, good. Maybe we'll go together sometime."

He sounds as awkward saying it as I do hearing it, but I think this family hike is bringing out some sort of fatherly gene in him he was previously lacking. I don't have the heart to tell him I'd rather not go to Ikseon-dong with him, mostly because I want to let it remain a place that I went to with Wonjae. I can't have my dad of all people come and ruin that perfect memory for me. But I give him a thumbs-up anyway.

Another thirty minutes later, my mom tells me we're almost near the top. The higher we go, the more that the tension I've built up toward my mom and dad releases. The wind, the colder air up top, the leaves blowing around all the hikers— all of it makes me feel like everything that felt hard or serious at the base of the mountain is somehow not worth worrying about anymore. Pretty soon we reach the peak, and the views are breathtaking. People all around us are spreading their arms wide and taking lots of selfies. Some are shouting at the horizon, and no one seems to mind too much. At the top, I feel a sense of accomplishment and a rush of adrenaline. I wonder what it'd feel like to have your first kiss at the top of a mountain after a long hike, looking out onto this view. I bet it'd be intense.

I force myself to stop thinking about this in case my cheeks start turning red. My mom calls my name, and from how easily startled I am, she's lucky I wasn't on the edge of the mountain. My parents are a few yards away from me, waving me over to a spot where more people are gathered.

While the view is breathtaking, I soon discover an even more impressive fact: Despite it being the peak of the mountain, this area is still flat. There are two restaurants, a souvenir shop, bathrooms, even a coffee shop that boasts a "Fantastic View!" There is something Koreans do supremely well that I've noticed in my one month here, and it is that they turn everything into an experience, and apparently summiting this mountain is no exception. There are seating areas with flat wooden blocks where you have to sit crisscross style, or small plastic stools. The restaurants are actual restaurants where you get seated with menus and such, not just pojangmachas. We pick a restaurant that serves kalguksu after agreeing that piping-hot knife-cut noodles will be just the thing for a post-hike reward.

Once we're seated, the ahjumma serves us with hot tea, and my parents decide to order some makgeolli.

My mom nudges me. "Isn't it impressive how they can set up a full restaurant up here?"

My dad grins and eats a spoonful of his noodles. "Food always tastes better in the mountains." He lifts the gold kettle and pours the makgeolli into bowls.

"Kunbae," he says, lifting up his gold bowl and clinking it against my mom's. My dad hands me an extra bowl. "Solmi, you want to try some?"

"Yeobo!" my mom chides.

"It's good that she tries her first alcoholic drink with her parents."

I pretend to be interested in my noodles to hide my face.

My mom just shakes her head and says "Fine, fine" and lets my dad pour a little bit of makgeolli into my bowl. "Just a sip, okay?"

I bring it to my lips and pretend to hesitate. *I already know how this tastes, you goons! And I love it.* "Not bad," I say to them.

After the kalguksu, my dad picks up a roll of kimbap from a different vendor, and we walk to the edge of the mountain peak where people are seated and find an empty spot. My mom puts coins into a vending machine and gets three cups of hot coffee.

"Appa?" I try not to betray any signs that I've begun to dig into his past. "Did you have a dream for your life when you were my age?"

He's hunched over with his hands on his knees, looking out onto the view. He doesn't seem to be taken aback by the question. "My dream . . . my dream was to be successful."

I try to imagine what Young Dad's version of success would have been. "But success is subjective."

He dusts off a light brown mark on his pants, likely carried there by the wind, and stands up. "That's not what successful people say." His tone puts an end to this discussion; I already know whatever other deep question I might try to probe him with won't be answered.

Maybe this is what Kimbeom and Yura were talking about. Something about Korean families and all their secrets. Maybe secrets are what maintain the peace in the family, like responsibilities and burdens that parents feel they need to keep from their children, and that they thus hide away for years and years and years. A can of worms that piles up dust from never being opened. As I think about how peaceful this hike has been, how pleasant and comfortable my parents seemed with each other, a small voice suggests I should stop trying to stir up family drama and accept that this is the new normal, that my dad has his secrets and my mom has hers. That they're doing it for my sake, for our sake, for the sake of peace.

But the more I know, the harder that is to do, and the louder voice inside me reminds me that I'm family, too, and I deserve to know their story, each of their full stories. After all, I'm a product of it.

Saturday continues to turn out to be as unexpected as the hike itself. I feel like my parents are off in some distant past that for some reason has come back today. I'm upstairs in my room, but I hear comfortable laughter at least three different times. It's mostly Umma's voice laughing, but I can hear happy-sounding low grunts here and there. I close my door and turn to my phone. Finally, a familiar face pops up on my screen.

"Mel!" Soph yells into the camera.

"It feels like forever since we caught up!"

"I know, seriously." There's a short pause. "So, what's new?"

I pucker my lips as I think of something interesting. "Oh, you know. Nothing too crazy. Oh wait, yeah, my application status changed to under review."

"One step closer, Mel. Have you talked to your parents?"

I shake my head. "I'll talk to them if there's anything to talk about. I think I'm supposed to hear this week," I say nervously. My potential ticket out of here.

"I'm sure they'll be super supportive."

I smile at Soph's assurance, but that doesn't sound like my parents.

"How's your dad's girlfriend?"

"I don't know. She wants to meet up with me alone, without my dad. A girls-only date, as she calls it."

I grimace. "Do you want that?"

Soph glances off to the side. "I mean, I don't know. Not really."

"You should tell your dad you don't want to, then, Soph. Just be honest with him."

Soph looks at me pointedly. "Oh, come on, Mel, you're queen of keeping secrets from your parents. I'll be honest with my dad if you tell yours that you love interior design and plan on forgoing whatever career trajectory he's mapped out for you," she says teasingly.

"So not the same, Soph." I keep my tone light, but I am mildly annoyed. What does Soph know about having to pursue a dream in secret? Her dad supports her in everything she wants to do. Her dad doesn't dictate her life for her and set her up on awkward dates. For as long as I can, I plan to keep M&S and my hopes for this internship private, away from the judgment and disapproval of my parents. And it's not just because of the disapproval factor. It's one of those things you keep to yourself because the dream is too all-consuming, and showing someone too much of it makes it seem that much more unattainable.

"How has Korea been?" Soph asks me.

"School is hard. Really hard, Soph. But Yura lives only two floors below me, and our other friends also live in HT, which is pretty convenient and kinda fun."

"HT?"

"Oh. Hannam Towers. It's the apartment complex we all live in. Yura's home is massive. I went over the other week and we redecorated her room, but Soph, this home looks straight up like a department store. Her mom actually owns a huge one in Seoul." I start talking faster as I go into the details of Yura's room and the changes we implemented until I notice Soph's expression gradually changing. She looks . . . bored. And it stings. "Anyway, other than that, it's just been fine."

"My dad's calling me for breakfast, Mel."

"Yeah, I should go study, too."

We hang up and I feel uneasy about our phone call, but I brush it off and try not to read into it. A message pops up in Kakao to distract me from spiraling too far into insecurity about it at this moment. My body tenses in giddiness when I see the message. Or rather, who the message is from.

WONJAE
any fun weekend plans?

> lol the weekend's almost over

WONJAE
well, tuesday we don't have school
remember? so i guess it's kind of like
a long weekend.

Oh, right. I completely forgot about that. Tuesday is the annual Teachers' Work Day or something at SIA. It's a day that all the teachers come together and have a bunch of meetings and exchange ideas and prepare for the second half of the semester.

> ooh yeah. well . . . we sadly still have
> school on monday lol

WONJAE

I wonder what I can say to keep the conversation going. I type, delete, type, delete. I need to text something fast in case he saw that I've read his message. It'd be weird to respond five minutes later if he knows I've already seen his emoji that whole time. Maintaining good texting etiquette is so draining.

> i told my dad about Ikseon-dong
> and he wanted to come with me
> next time 😂

> never! lol

WONJAE
did you tell him you went with me?

I type in "no haha, he would've read into it" but backspace the second part.

> no haha

I don't know what to say next, and I guess neither does Wonjae, so it's a pretty short-lived conversation. I hear footsteps padding down the hallway on the upstairs floor, across from my room. It's my mom. I take a deep breath. She's in a good mood with my dad, it's a weekend, and we're all full from a good meal. I miss the ease of our conversations and the comfort of having my mom as my friend and confidante.

I gather my courage and go to the master bedroom, softly knocking on the door before opening it. She's reading on the long sofa and has a cup of tea on the small oak coffee table in front of her. The evening light from the window and the dim nightstand light beside her combine to cast a shadow across her face.

"Hey, you," she says warmly. My body relaxes just a little.

"Hi, Mom. Can I come in?"

"Always."

I stare at the beige-and-ivory pattern on the sofa where we're seated. "Did you have fun today?"

"I did," she says, looking relaxed. It's refreshing to see her look so at peace. "Did you?"

"Mmm. I guess so, but it was a little weird, you know? Kind of."

"What do you mean?"

"I mean, it's not like you and Dad ever showed much affection to each other. And in the month we've been here, you two didn't seem especially fond of each other." I fidget in my seat when my mom looks at me, confused.

"When did we seem unfond of each other?"

I sit on my hands and cross my toes over each other, a nervous habit. "I overheard you two fighting. About how he's not the reason you came back."

My mom looks like she's been caught doing something and

is guilty of it. "Oh, Mel, I just said that in anger. Of course he's a big reason we came back. Your dad's been wanting us to move to Korea for a long time."

"Yeah, okay, but it wasn't all for him, right?" I try not to seem too probing in case she decides to withhold information again.

"The timing just made sense. Before you're any older. SIA is a good school. It'll help you get into a better college."

I resist the urge to shake her and force the full truth out. I recognize it again: a lie of omission. My jaws are clenched in frustration. "But what about your forever fight with Eemo?"

"We're not fighting, Mel. We just grew apart, okay?"

"But why? You grew apart because of something, right?"

My mom averts her eyes for only a half moment, but it's moment enough to confirm my suspicion. Something happened between them, something big enough to create this rift. I sit silently, not letting my gaze leave her while I wait for her to answer.

"Look, I'm seeing Jieun sometime next week. You want to come?"

My eyes get round when she says this very unexpected thing. "Wait, seriously?"

My mom pats my knee and stands up. "Yes, seriously. I'll let you know when. Then enough with these questions, got it?"

I nod without a word. A real chance to hang out with the both of them.

I leave the room and sit on my bed, opening to a different page in my dad's diary. The only words I can make out, though, are "abeonim" and "Korea." That night, I fall asleep clutching my dad's diary, as if holding on to it will help me understand it more. Or him.

FIFTEEN

My friends are squished at a smaller table today because our usual area was occupied, and they're talking about plans for tonight. My mind feels hazy, though, and I'm too distracted to participate. Since our kind-of-awkward video call, Soph and I haven't texted once, and, granted, our call was only twenty-four hours ago, but it feels weird to message her for some reason. And even though I know my mom isn't telling me the full story yet, I feel hopeful, like she's maybe coming around. The whole day, my mind oscillates between Soph, my mom, and the internship. Any day now, Maison & Saito Interiors will be releasing their final-round candidates. I nervously tap on the "Application Status" button, but nothing's changed.

"Hello?" Yura's waving her hand in my face.

"Huh?" I look up from my phone. "Sorry. What'd you say?"

"That we're going out tonight. And you have to join."

I shake my head. "I'm good."

"Melody, come *on*. I think you'll love it," Yura pleads.

"Yeah, plus, you've been here for a month now and you have yet to experience the Seoul nightlife," Kimbeom adds.

I promise my friends I'll think about it and skip study hall to go for a walk. The autonomy we get in these classes is surreal but very satisfying. The teachers here treat you like you're in college. If you don't show up, that's your fault, but you'd better figure out how to get back on track if you fall behind. I see a playground in an apartment complex nearby, so I walk over there and sit on the bench, pulling out my sketchbook. I start drawing my surroundings, a way for my mind to relax and not think about anything besides the swings and the monkey bars. I come back before seventh-period art, and soon, I'm sitting in Korean class while Mrs. Lee talks about the Goryeo dynasty.

"I'm handing back the exams from last week," she says, and immediately every muscle in my body tenses. A chance to prove to my dad that I can catch up and do well in a class that's objectively way beyond my knowledge. "Some of you really need to ace this upcoming project if you don't want to retake this class," she says as she walks around, dropping papers on students' desks. When she hands me mine, she slows just for a second. We make eye contact, and she says in a low voice, "You need to catch up, Solmi, or you shouldn't have been in the honors class." She says it quietly enough so only I hear, I think, but it's still mortifying. At the top of the page, in her usual red ink: D. As if her comment to me wasn't shameful enough, there's something written at the top: *Please see me after class.*

I flip over my quiz and stuff it into my backpack, refusing to let my eyes water. *Breathe in, breathe out.* I've never gotten a D in my entire life. At Clinton, I don't think I could get a D even if I didn't study at all. The worst part is that I actually studied hard for this quiz.

When class ends, Wonjae lingers, but I tell him I need to talk to Mrs. Lee really quickly about something.

"Oh. I have to take the bus home, so I thought we could go together," he says.

I consider his offer, and I know it's a complete lie because if his driver couldn't come get him, he'd at least just take a taxi. I force a smile and nod. "Sure. I'll be out in a few minutes."

I go to Mrs. Lee's desk, where she's sitting frowning at a stack of papers and marking a lot of reds through them. "You wanted to see me?" My voice comes out high pitched.

She doesn't look up. "You're aware that this quiz was worth fifteen percent of your grade this semester?"

"Yes, ma'am," I answer quietly.

"The midterm project is worth twenty-five percent. You're aware of that, too?"

Her voice is not kind. She grades the stack of papers with swift agility, like she's done this a thousand times over, which she probably has.

"I told the class the grade breakdown at the beginning of the term. Three monthly quizzes, fifteen percent each; midterm project, twenty-five percent; finals, thirty percent."

"Yes, I remember."

"Fifteen percent of your grade is a D. I rarely call in students because you are treated like responsible young adults at SIA. I am not here to hold your hand as you learn a language you should already know."

My face feels hot and red, and it's getting harder for me to hold back my tears now.

"I highly recommend you find yourself a tutor, Miss Lee, otherwise you may as well take another language course next year with students a grade below you. That is all."

I leave without saying a word and race out of school, wiping the tears away quickly with the sleeve of my cardigan as I walk down the hill. I completely forget that Wonjae just told me he'd meet me, and there he is, waiting by the bus stop. I dry my face as much as I can, but I'm sure it looks blotchy and stupid.

"Whoa," Wonjae says when he sees me.

I look at him through red eyes. "Thanks." I tighten my hold on my backpack straps and sit on the wooden square, letting my legs dangle.

"Hey, you okay?"

"No," I manage to say.

"Hey, hey, hey." Wonjae stands up and faces me, holding my shoulders lightly. "What's wrong?" His voice is gentle, like he's talking to someone who just got badly bruised up.

"I got a D on my Korean quiz." I feel pathetic for saying that, then even worse when he looks at me pitifully. It's one of those things that, when you say it out loud, instantly makes you feel worse instead of better.

"I know you were studying hard for that . . ." His voice trails off.

"Which makes it worse." I shake my head. "I don't want to talk about this anymore." I release a loud breath and wipe the edges of my eyes again and stand up. "The bus is coming."

We're walking slowly from the bus stop to HT when Wonjae breaks the silence.

"Clubbing might not be the worst idea," he says.

I look at him sideways. "I don't think I deserve to have fun right now."

"It's more like blowing off steam, you know? Recharging, upping your energy so you have motivation to study again."

"What a way to spin it," I say back, but I'm also bitterly laughing. "Is everyone going?"

Wonjae nods. "Kimbeom said his dad is driving him crazy lately, so he's definitely going. With or without us. So, what do you say?"

I shake my head. "I don't think so."

When I get home, the apartment feels larger than usual, and I wander into the living room to see if my mom is anywhere to be found. She's not. "Mom?" I call out as I head toward the master bedroom. She's not home, but there's a note stuck on the fridge.

Mel, had to step out for a few hours. Errands, etc.
I'll see you for dinner tonight.

She could have texted me this, but I know she wrote it on the fridge because otherwise I'd simply text back: *What errands? Are you on your way to see Eemo?* I know she's with her.

I pull out a snack and sit at the kitchen table alone. I write a note back and stick it under hers. It's a spontaneous decision, one that's feeling better by the second.

I'm going out with my friends tonight.
Will be home late. Don't wait up.

I stare at my reflection before leaving. It feels club appropriate.

A lot of texts between me and Yura have led to this final out-fit: black leather shorts with sheer black tights underneath and an oversized, one-shoulder, neon yellow long-sleeve top. It's just sheer enough that you can see the outline of my black bralette.

"Ooh la la, who are you trying to impress?" Yura says the second she sees me. Then she leans in closer so only I can hear her. "I know who you're trying to impress," she whispers, affecting a suggestive air.

I shove her playfully, and we meet the boys out in the courtyard.

My eyes go to Wonjae, who's waving us over. He's dressed in black jeans that fit well, not tight enough where I'd think he's trying too hard, but not baggy like they're going to fall off his body. His sky-blue V-neck outlines his toned arms, and I peel my eyes away when I feel a jab in my side. "Ow!"

"Okay, little Miss Googly Eyes, you're being a little obvious," Yura jokes.

I scrunch up my face and pretend to look guilty. "Oopsie."

We opt for easy-to-eat sandwiches for a light dinner so we don't have the delicious but unsexy smell of Korean food on our clothes when we go clubbing. At a nearby speakeasy, we grab a booth and order some light bites and cocktails. I'm so excited, I blurt out, "My first cocktail!" Okay, *too* excited. I'm pretty sure my mom would be furious if she found out, but the drinking age in Korea is younger, I learned, than in the US, and bars aren't that strict here anyway. I study the menu and order something Yura tells me will likely be sweeter and less deadly.

"No, usually the sweetest ones are the deadliest," Junghoon

says. There's a flirtiness in his voice, and he glances at Yura when he says this. A softness to his words that I've never, ever heard from him. She's doing it; I can see it. He's into her, whether he realizes it or not. Yura and I exchange a knowing glance, and we high-five, gleefully ignoring the confused looks on the boys' faces.

When my cocktail comes, I take my first small sip. It's citrusy but sweet. "What is this again?"

"It's a yuzu cocktail," she explains. "With some lychee."

It tastes like a sweet mixture of honey and lemon. I can hardly taste any alcohol in it. I'm acutely aware that Wonjae and I are next to each other because my left hand and Wonjae's right hand are almost touching. I want to peek under the table to see if Yura and Junghoon are doing the same thing. It's close to 11:00 p.m. when we make our way toward the club.

The club is called Octagon, and there's a long line out the door; I see a lot of tight outfits and high heels. And, as I would have expected, there's a giant octagon shape above the club, gleaming in silver light. Despite the long line, Wonjae goes up to the guy at the front—the bouncer, Yura says—who greets Wonjae like his best friend and unlatches a velvet rope, allowing us to go in through a different entrance.

I don't want to be impressed by this, but it beats waiting in a long line.

The club is huge and dark, and a ton of people are already dancing, strobed in bright light. It's a lot bigger than I imagined. I thought it'd be one large floor, but there are levels above and below and private rooms and rows of tables. A guy Wonjae calls "Hyung" directs us to our table, and Kimbeom and Yura start opening the bottles that are already waiting for us. There's champagne, vodka, and some juices to mix in with the hard liquor.

Yura cheerfully pours copious amounts of champagne into all of our glasses, and we kunbae together, letting the loud clinking of the glasses mark the beginning of our night in Octagon. I sip mine slowly, careful to remember that I already had a cocktail before coming here. Yura and Junghoon are talking to each other, and I notice her giggling. Kimbeom ditches us when a few people he seems to recognize wave at him to join them. Less than five seconds later, he's on the dance floor with his other friends and releasing the stress his father is probably causing him. I watch from a distance and start to take off my jacket, hiding my purse and valuables underneath it on the sofa, just in case.

"Cute top," Wonjae says to me. In the loud club, his voice appears in my ear from a lot closer than I thought he was, and I turn around so fast I feel my neck crack.

"Thanks!" I shout over the music. "It's pretty cool in here!"

The four of us talk about school, about plans for Chuseok—which is only a week away now—and winter break plans, even though that's still two months away. Kimbeom comes back from the dance floor already sweaty, gleefully panting.

"The music is so good right now." He picks up a bottle of vodka and pours it into shot glasses for all of us.

"To no more stress," Kimbeom shouts, and we all cheers together and throw back a shot.

I then take a few more generous sips of my champagne, adding a little bit of orange juice to make it sweeter. Yura pulls me to the dance floor with her, and I'm dancing away my stress about school, my fear of being stuck in Korea forever, the distance between me and my parents, the weird unspoken rift between me and Soph. To be able to release my guilt like this, even temporarily, feels amazing. Eventually, Wonjae, Kimbeom, and Junghoon join us, and the five of us are cheering, drinking, and dancing together. This is unlike any night I've ever experienced . . . and it's so much fun. When I finally wear myself out dancing, I wobble back to the sofa, where I plop down and pour my third or fourth glass of champagne.

Wonjae is back at the table already, alone and on his phone, sitting not too far from me. The alcohol makes me bold; I've seen this happen in movies and now I know it's real.

"Hi," I say, scooting closer to him.

He gives me a funny look. "Hey," he says. "You okay?"

I nod and bring my hands to my cheeks. They feel warm. "Yeah. Just needed to take a break from the dance floor. Ikseondong was so fun!"

He puts his phone away and looks at me, laughing. "Yeah, you mentioned already. You don't need to shout, you're already close," he teases.

"Oh," I say a little too loudly.

"Feeling better from earlier today?" he asks.

"Mm-hmm. Dancing really is a stress reliever. I think I'll come to Octagon every weekend." My words come out a little slower than usual. I inch in a tiny bit closer, close enough that I can talk at a normal volume and he can hear me perfectly fine. If I lower my head just a bit, I can smell his clean, fresh laundry scent.

"I'm glad you came," he says. A warm, kind smile spreads

across his face. It's a smile that makes me feel like he sees only me right now, and there's a glittering sensation in my chest as my heart rate goes up.

But that glittering has a side effect of apparently making me wild, because a moment later, my body is moving on autopilot and I'm leaning forward and pressing my lips to his. I pull back in shock, and he does, too. My eyes are big, my cheeks are burning, but the next second he leans in and our lips meet again. He wraps his arms around my waist, and our long kiss becomes several kisses, growing in intensity. He moves a hand up to my cheek and draws me even closer to him. My hands are on his shoulders and sliding down his back and I lean deeper into him, tugging at the bottom of his shirt.

My head is spinning now and I'm smiling a lot, and in between kisses, we drink more champagne. His lips taste sweet, and I can't tell if my dizzy buzz is from this champagne or from kissing or both. My eyes flutter open for a brief second just in time to spot the others leaving the dance floor, though they don't see us through the crowds. I pull away and scooch to a more friend-zone safe spot and pour myself another drink.

For the rest of the night, Wonjae and I sneak little glances at each other, but nothing more. I attach myself to Yura's hip, and we weave through crowds and dance in different locations throughout the night. The club gets even more packed as the night goes on, and whether it's the dizzying strobe lights flashing all over or that there's barely any space to actually move or that I had three drinks too many, my mind keeps going back to the kiss, and I want to find Wonjae for more.

We find the boys sitting around our table playing drinking

games. After we join in for a few rounds, we all decide it's time to get something to eat. I open my phone to see four missed calls and a bunch of texts from my mom.

UMMA
where are you?

it's almost two in the morning and you haven't called.

melody, call me when you read this message.

When we step outside, I tell my friends I'll be right back and walk a few steps to the side to call my mom.

"Hello? Melody?" Her voice is urgent.

"Mom, I'm fine. I told you I'd be home late."

"Where are you?"

"Gangnam. With my friends. I left a note on the fridge, just like you left a note on the fridge."

"Are you drunk?" The rising anger in her voice sobers me up a little.

"No," I lie. "But I told you I was going out. I left it there, in plain sight."

"You're drunk. You just repeated yourself."

"I'm *not* drunk, Mom. I'm with the others who all live in HT, so I'll get home safely, okay?" I hang up the phone before she has a chance to respond.

"Okay, where are we going?" I say, so eagerly that even I'm surprised.

"To the nearest pyeonuijeom!" Yura says, matching my enthusiasm.

"We're going to a convenience store?"

Kimbeom throws his arm around my shoulder. "Where the cup ramen is, we go."

We make our way to the nearest store that has enough stools outside and get our ramen. As we sit and wait for the boiling water to cook our noodles, I bring my hand down to my side, and as if he understands, Wonjae gently links his pinky with mine.

My heart is beating fast from excitement, or maybe the fear that our friends will see us, but we manage to stay that way and eat with our free hands. I think everyone's had a little too much to drink at this point to really pay attention because I don't even know how discreet I'm actually being. Kimbeom ends up buying two bottles of makgeolli, and we drink from small paper cups. It's soothing after the hard liquor and champagne, and the taste of the rice wine makes for a sweet finale of my first night out in Korea.

Kimbeom pours everyone seconds and raises his cup. "To us! May we all live next to each other until college and someday move back and live in one giant house together," he says. We raise our paper cups and kunbae to his sappy toast.

"So how is this for a night out in Korea, Melody?" Junghoon asks.

I quickly unlink my pinky from Wonjae's and pretend to think. "It was fun because of all of you," I say.

"Do you still prefer New York?" Kimbeom asks with a fake pout.

"It's still home for me, you know? And I want to go back for my design competition, but I don't even think I got in."

"You'll live," Junghoon says, characteristically curt.

"Aw, you sound like you actually care," I retort.

"Hey, no bickering on Mel's first night out," Yura warns us.

I inhale another mouthful of noodles, following this by lifting the large cup to my lips and slurping the soup. The heat spreads throughout my body. It's the perfect end to a perfect night after a not-perfect day. By the time we finish eating, we're all feeling even happier and more satisfied with hot food in our stomachs and the chill air on our faces. I check my phone: it's 3:43 a.m.

When we get to our apartment complex, Yura and I head in together since we're in the same building, so there's no need to worry about an awkward goodbye between me and Wonjae.

The lights are all off inside, meaning my parents must be asleep. I'm relieved; I'm pretty sure my breath smells like alcohol. Or alcohol mixed with Shin Ramen. I have no energy to even wash up, and I pass out the second my face hits my pillow.

SIXTEEN

When I wake up, the ceiling is moving and my head is pounding. I close my eyes again to stop the spinning ceiling and turn slowly onto my side. As I reach for my phone to see what time it is, I notice two Advils and a large glass of water sitting on my nightstand. I guzzle down the entire cup, not realizing how dehydrated I was, and let out a groan in my head. If my mom suspects I was inebriated, she's going to kick me out of this house. I stuff my face into my pillow, and in the darkness, I remember something besides the late-night noodles, drinks, and dancing. Wonjae and the kiss.

My first kiss!

I finally gather enough energy and willpower to get out of bed and shower. I wash away the smell of the nightclub and try to let the lukewarm water wake me up. It's Tuesday morning, and I head downstairs. As I'm waiting for the Advil to kick in, I pour myself a cup of coffee. I thought I was alone, but I can hear the rustle of a page turning. And then footsteps.

"Hi," I say sheepishly to my mom as she walks into the kitchen. I'm standing behind our kitchen island, and she pulls out a dining chair.

"Sit," she orders. "Coming home in the middle of the night after doing God knows what, getting drunk, being hungover. Are you out of your mind?"

I play with the handle of my coffee mug in front of me, trying to hide the fact that my head is throbbing.

"Well? Do you have anything to say?" she asks me.

I shake my head. Footsteps sound from the hallway, so I spin my head around. I would have thought my dad had left for work already, but I guess not.

"You're up early. Did you have a good time yesterday?" he asks. There's a hint of a proud glimmer in his eye, and he's definitely more lax than my mom is about my staying out late. I don't know how other kids deal with the whole two-parent thing. It's double the stress, double the emotions to read, and double the potential discipline.

This feels like a trick question. "Umm . . . yes?"

My dad turns to my mom. "Yeobo, don't be so upset at Solmi. She was safe with her friends and was having a fun night out." She looks thunderous at this, but I'm grateful. I relax just a little bit. *My dad just took my side.*

He nods. "Good," he says.

"What do you mean, 'good'?" my mom says.

"A girl her age needs some proper socializing. She was smart, safe, and had a good time with good friends. And you told me she messaged you that she was coming home with the other kids in Hannam Towers. Don't be so overprotective, Eunji."

My mom glares at him. "Proper socializing? Don't talk like

Melody doesn't know already how to make decent friends," my mom says, standing up and taking my mug from me and tossing it into the sink, even though I was still mid-drink. I look at the empty spot on the dining table where my coffee was two seconds ago and then look up at my parents. I'm cringing and slouching lower in my seat, but I can't look away.

"You call getting high with public school kids on the street in broad daylight proper socializing? Melody is meant for more, she's able to do more and be more, and you don't recognize that. Her being with better friends will help her get on the proper path."

"I wasn't high. It—" Neither of them pays any attention to me, and my mom cuts me off.

"So because I want her to live a life that isn't dictated for her, that means I don't recognize her potential? Did you ever think that she doesn't want to live the life you want for her? Is that so hard for your pride to accept that? That she doesn't plan to be a slave to her father's empty promises and unmet expectations? She's not you." She says those last three words slowly enough to emphasize something about my dad that hurts him deep. Rubbing salt into past wounds is always painful.

I muster up some courage to speak again. After all, it's not like my mom is exactly letting me live my life freely, either. "You never asked me what—"

My dad snaps at me with a frustrated look on his face. "This doesn't concern you."

"How does this not concern me, it's *about* me!" I bring my hand to by forehead and squeeze the sides to try and get rid of the throbbing.

"Melody!" my mom shouts at me. "Enough. Go to your room."

I shut my mouth but don't leave, and they don't seem to notice.

"She needs to make sure she's on the right track. I don't want her to end up like . . ." He pauses.

"Like my sister?" my mom finishes. Her voice is quiet and angry and disappointed, all in one.

"That's not what I was going to say," my dad says, but he doesn't sound convincing at all.

"Melody isn't that impractical. She'll be smart and she won't pursue something frivolous, but it's not for you or your father."

My dad scoffs at my mom, and I want to shake him, shouting, *Are you stupid! You can't scoff at an angry woman!* but I just keep sitting there as if I've lost all words and the ability to speak in sentences. "You act like you're so above me, as if choosing her career for her is any better than my wanting her to be in the right part of society?"

"Helping her choose a career that will put her on a stable path and guarantee a good life is not about me wanting her to be in a particular place in society. It's for her own good, not mine or the family's reputation." My mom pauses. "Melody, I told you to go to your room. Now."

I scurry away because I know things will get worse if I don't listen now. Korean parents will never stop treating you like you are their child, no matter how old you get. Not that a junior in high school is an adult, but Mr. Taye is always saying how once Soph goes to college, she'll make her own choices and become an adult. I don't think my mom or dad has ever said those things or felt that way. I'm pretty sure they're still going to be fighting this fight when I'm thirty.

When I get to my room, I look at my phone, but there aren't

any messages from Soph. I consider messaging her first, but instead my fingers find their way to the M&S portal and log in. I hesitate but click refresh on my application status. My thumb hovers over the screen, twitching slightly as I wait for the screen to load.

Status: Selected

I blink a few times because I can't believe what I'm seeing. Selected? What does this mean? Am I in the final round? There's a sentence underneath it.

Congratulations, Melody Lee! You've been accepted into the final round of Maison & Saito Interiors' Young Designers Summer Internship Competition. Please check your email for further details.

I log in to my Gmail, and there I see it: the email from M&S detailing all the next steps for selected final-round candidates. My palms are sweating with anticipation, my heart is still thumping, now from excitement and a disbelief that I was accepted. To have this chance, from the thousands of others that also applied, is a miracle of its own to me. The email outlines details that were already shared earlier during the application process. The competition will be in person in NYC during the first week of November. The prompt will be released on the Saturday, followed three days later by an in-person presentation on Monday morning at the M&S headquarters in SoHo.

"SoHo," I say softly. It's been less than two months since I moved to Korea, but SoHo sounds so far away, like a dream that

I can't imagine coming true. I take a deep breath. I have no idea how I'm going to convince my parents to let me go, and now I find myself regretting never having mentioned applying for this internship. Maybe a part of me never thought I'd even get in. How could I, though, when my dad just wants me to "social-ize" and my mom is so dead set on my choosing a career path that "isn't impractical?" They are literally downstairs fighting about my future. Sure, it might be a bit harder to find stability through it than becoming an engineer, but I know if I try hard enough, eventually, I'll have a shot at that.

I think of my aunt. I don't know her story, but I know she's a singer, the only other creative person in this family, and I know she'd understand me better than my own parents do. I open my door a crack and listen quietly. There are no more raised voices, so the fight must have subsided, but I hear too many footsteps to just be one person. That means my dad is still home.

Here we go.

I tiptoe into the den so quietly they don't notice me at first. They're sitting around the coffee table with a few papers in their hands, and I know I need to tell them now.

"Can we talk?" My voice comes out squeakier than I expected.

"Not unless you're groveling or coming to me with a list of chores you plan on doing around the house to make up for the damage you caused," my mom says. "I aged at least five years in one night because of you, Mel."

I chew on the insides of my mouth nervously and sit on the sofa facing them. "I promise to come back to you with a list of things I'll do. But this is a different talk." At their silence, I continue. "So . . . as you know, I love design." I clear my throat to calm myself down a bit, but instead I end up speaking too quickly and not stopping to take any breaths in between my words. "There's a huge firm, one of the best in the world, called Maison & Saito Interiors, and I applied for their Young Designers internship competition. I got accepted into the final round even though I thought I didn't have a shot. I have to be in New York for it, though. It's during a weekend, the first weekend of November, and it's really, *really* hard to make it to the final round. I was one of the very few who did out of thousands who applied, and I didn't know I'd be in Korea, and please, will you let me go to New York for this? Please?" I finally release the breath I was holding.

My dad hands me the papers he has in his hand. I take them and my face falls. "Where did you find these?" He went through my stuff *again*?

"That's not important. I told you to fix this."

Hideous C's and not-good-enough B's stand out in harsh relief on my various essays, quizzes, and assignments. Thank God I threw away the D quiz at school.

"Melody, why didn't you tell us you've been struggling this much in school?" my mom asks.

"I'm not struggling that much," I say quietly, already knowing they don't believe me. "SIA is harder." I feel two feet tall.

My dad speaks up. "SIA will get you farther in life."

"You don't know that. Public schools are just as good, Appa." I consider launching into my argument that public schools can be more advantageous than private schools, but I think about my greater goal here and close my mouth, looking humbly at the ground to show my penitence. "Could I please, please go to New York for the competition? I'll do anything."

I look up to see my mom shaking her head. "Melody—"

"Please," I beg them. "I know it sounds ridiculous to you, but being a designer is what I want. Please let me go. Just this once. And I swear, Mom, a place like M&S can eventually lead me to the stable life you want so badly for me. I promise I'm not thinking about living on some street corner, drawing for money outside." She doesn't need to know that I actually think that sounds a little fun.

"Melody, your passion for decorating is just a hobby, I promise you. I know you love it, and that's fine, but it's not enough for—"

My dad interrupts her. "I will be open to having this discussion about sending you to New York for this competition on a few conditions." My mom shoots him another deadly glare, and my ears perk up. "While you were upstairs, I made a call to the dean's office. Your grade point average is basically a B-, borderline C+, as of now, which we all agree does not reflect your true potential. And your mother is right. You can't be out getting drunk every weekend, especially when your grades are this low."

"It wasn't every weekend . . . I would never get drunk every—"

My dad raises his hand to indicate he isn't finished talking. "Regardless, that is unacceptable."

My dad's favorite word.

"You're basically flunking your classes," he adds. I want to interrupt him to say a B is actually above average, but again, I lock my mouth. "Your midterms are in two and a half weeks. Get straight A's on *all* of them, and I will consider sending you to New York."

My eyes widen in shock. "That's it?" Well, not *it*, exactly, since that's going to be extremely hard, next to impossible, honestly, but it's still something. "Okay, great, I can do that."

My mom shakes her head again. "This is a waste of your time, Mel. Trust me. You enjoy decorating, but you'll want a different career. I'm your mother. Don't you trust me?"

I look at her for a long time with a frown, and she looks a little hurt that I don't respond immediately, but the truth is, I don't. Not anymore. "It's more than a hobby to me," I say with confidence.

"My answer is no."

"*Dad* already said yes."

"Melody, this is not up for discussion." My mom sounds annoyed with me.

"Just like how none of my questions are up for discussion? You only talk about what *you* want to share, and I never realized that until we moved to Korea. I've asked you so many times about Aunt Rebecca, about coming here, and you never give me an honest answer. If you want to live your life hating her, then fine by me, but you don't need to keep *me* from her. Your anger toward her dictates *my* relationship with her, which is unfair to me and to Eemo. You only want me to see certain parts of your life, and it's so ridiculous that while you hide parts of the truth, you raised me to think you were always honest with me, always saying I could tell you anything, and that families don't keep secrets. So, no, I don't trust you."

My dad looks very confused by this outburst. "Solmi, do not talk to your mother that way. It's disrespectful."

I scowl at him. "It's not my fault I'm perpetually confused. It makes zero sense to me that you two go on pretending like everything is fine, like it's completely normal that we didn't live together for fourteen years and now suddenly here we are, hiking like a real family on weekends, when the truth is nobody knows how to act when we're together under one roof."

My parents just look at me with astounded expressions. My mind feels foggy and clouded with suppressed information and frustration. I'm not sure where this outburst came from, and I instantly regret saying all of it. If this is the reason they decide to ban me from this competition . . .

My mom sighs loudly and stands up, hovering over me in a intimidating motherly way. "You know what, Mel? Fine. But I'm adding another condition for going to New York: fix your attitude," she says, giving me her ultimate Stern Mom Look.

I open my mouth then close it again.

"I'm serious, Melody Solmi Lee. Starting right this second."

I nod without another word. I can suppress all of this for another two weeks.

She looks skeptically at me once more. "I will," I say sincerely. "Wait, can I still go with you when you go see Rebecca Eemo this time? *Please?*"

She looks at me for a long time. "If you fix your attitude starting *now*, then yes."

My dad looks at me with a solemn face. "Solmi, this doesn't mean you're automatically going. When exams end, we can have a follow-up conversation about it."

I nod multiple times, and the corners of my mouth turn up. The hope of being one step closer to going is enough for now.

My dad rubs his face with his hands. "I have a lunch meeting and need to get going now," he says, standing up.

"I'm going to go study," I tell them as I head for the stairs.

Time to get those A's.

SEVENTEEN

I wake up feeling exhausted. After getting the best news in the world yesterday, I spent the rest of the afternoon holed up in my room studying, but I'm not sure how much studying I actually got done. Instead, I sat on my Italian-fabric accent chair and replayed the kiss for so many hours that it seeped into my dream last night. We haven't texted since the kiss, so I'm not sure what to expect when I see him in homeroom in less than one hour.

When I get to school, I wait in the bathroom by the lobby, where I can watch students trickling in. Finally, Yura arrives and I pull her into the girls' locker room area.

"Ow, Mel, and hi," she says, hugging me. I've learned by now how affectionate Yura is.

I look around and make sure no one's in here. "Don't say a word about this to anyone yet."

Yura looks at me confused. "About—?"

"Wonjae and I kissed."

She grabs the edge of the sink with dramatic flair. "When? Tell me everything. Also, I *knew* it. I called it."

"Actually, you were there. It was at Octagon, when everyone was dancing. I don't know, it just kind of happened."

"*How* did I miss this? Was it good? Was it steamy?"

"I have no frame of reference—it was my first kiss! But I'm pretty sure it was steamy." I giggle at the memory of his hand around my waist.

"Holy moly!" she screams. "By the way, it's your fault I say 'holy moly' now. I used to be cool," she teases me. "Wow, first kiss. Does he know?"

I shake my head. "No. I mean, I'm sixteen. I don't want to go around parading the fact that I haven't kissed anyone before now."

Yura nods, understanding me instantly. I'm not ashamed, but a lot of girls my age have already kissed boys by now. "So, did you two meet up yesterday?"

"Nope."

"Oh. Did you at least talk?"

I shake my head. "Neither of us texted each other."

"What, why? You could've messaged him first. Why didn't you?"

"I just . . . I don't know, it felt awkward and I freaked out! He's usually the one to text, so I guess I just kind of waited."

"Maybe that's why he wanted you to text him. Do you regret the kiss?"

"No . . ." I say slowly, trying to find the right words. "Definitely not. I just don't know what we are, you know? It happened so suddenly and it's not like we're dating and I don't know how he feels about me."

"Well, I'm guessing you would have found out how he feels if you bothered to send him a message!"

We rush to homeroom as the bell rings, so Wonjae and I

don't have a chance to interact, which comes as a relief to me in my current awkward state.

At lunch, Yura is my fairy godmother and keeps the conversations easy and group inclusive so Wonjae and I don't have much room to say anything between just the two of us, which is exactly what I need. When I do have an uninterrupted second to daydream, I see myself as a senior designer at Maison & Saito Interiors, who kisses boys and isn't awkward about it.

"Hey." My shoulders rise up to my ears when I hear the very familiar voice. I can feel Wonjae's breath on the back of my neck. I lasted almost an entire day managing to avoid him, but there's no one to save me in Korean class when it's just the two of us. I don't know why I'm avoiding him, really. It's just that navigating new territory isn't my thing, and I was drunk when this happened, so it feels all the weirder now, fully sober and in school.

I turn to the side and force a smile. "Hey," I whisper back.

"Some kiss, huh?"

My cheeks burn and I don't know what to say. I wrack my brain for things I've heard in movies. "I had a great time last night," I finally answer, trying my best to sound casual.

Wonjae leans in closer. "Me too. Sorry I didn't have a chance to KaTok you. My grandfather kept me occupied with work meetings all weekend."

"No worries. I was busy, too." I think about my portfolio acceptance, and I have to exercise restraint so a grin doesn't automatically spread over my face. The news is still fresh, and I want to keep it to myself for a little while longer. "Anyway, I was pretty drunk, I think. I hardly remember it," I lie, hoping I sound like a pro-kisser. Then I feel stupid for saying that. Why did I lie? I remember every little detail, drunk or not. *I can't get enough. I wish we could replay that night over and over again* is what I wish I could say.

He frowns a little but doesn't say anything. "Guess I was the only one that enjoyed it, then," he says, and before I have a chance to respond, Mrs. Lee gathers everyone's attention by loudly clapping her hands together like we're in kindergarten.

"Since everyone recently took their monthly quiz, we're going to use today's class to brainstorm for your partner projects. Get into your pairs. Quickly."

I hang my head and flip my desk around as slowly as possible. I need to know what Wonjae's thinking about. Does he like me? He's looking furtively at his phone under his desk, so I take a moment to really look at him. One month ago, I would not have considered this guy even close to the type of person I'd dream of kissing. I'm Melody Lee from New York, where I prided myself in dollar pizzas and Taco Bell. That's who I am. I've never been into boys who are heirs to their family's multimillion-dollar companies or have drivers to take them everywhere. I shake my head. I can't stop thinking about our kiss, but I will force myself to, somehow. But then I look at him and wish he'd kiss me again.

"Hey," I say, and Wonjae looks up. My heart does that fluttery thing again, but I continue. "Okay, so how do we want to do the presentation?" I ask him.

"PowerPoint?"

I make a face. "That's so unoriginal."

"It's the easiest," he says matter-of-factly.

"Is it going to get us an A?"

"Do I look like Mrs. Lee to you?"

"We need to do a presentation that will guarantee us an A."

"All right, then you think of something brilliant," Wonjae says. "I'm fine with whatever."

"Maybe a sculpture of some sort?"

"That could work. So why the obsession about getting an A on this?"

"I have to get an A on this project so I can focus the rest of my energy on getting A's on all the other midterms," I say. "I've been getting C's and B's on almost all our assignments." I think of a brilliant idea and fidget in my seat before I gather my courage and ask him my favor. "Will you help me? Be my Korean tutor?"

He puckers his lips, appearing to be deep in thought. He rubs his chin with his hands and scrutinizes me. I make myself look as pitiful as possible.

"Okay," he says, still looking at me.

"Wait, really?" I half expected him to say no. Okay, maybe he *does* like me? It's obvious we're flirting, but he just said yes to basically one-on-one time with me. That must mean something. Right?

"What?"

"You'll help me?"

"Yep."

"It's just, well, you didn't hesitate much." I'm babbling at this point, and I wish I could tape my own mouth shut.

"Did you want me to hesitate?"

"No, that's not what I meant. Thank you. I need help making sure my assignment this week is perfect, and then prepping for next month's quiz. And I need that A on this project." I feel better and more hopeful already.

"Whoa, whoa, that's a lot of pressure on a tutor." He's sort of teasing, I can tell. "Are you paying me?"

I stick my tongue out at him. "Your Korean is fluent. And you don't need me to pay you; you're heir to millions of dollars."

"True, but that doesn't mean you can take advantage of me." He winks, and I wonder if there's a different meaning behind what he just said.

"Well, I don't have any money to pay you, but I'll buy your coffee every time you tutor me. Deal?"

He grins. "Deal."

"There's no catch?" I ask, still suspicious.

"You have to actually try and take my suggestions when I'm trying to help you."

"Well, obviously," I say.

Wonjae shakes his head. "Obvious to who? You're the most tunnel-visioned, stubborn person I've ever met. If you want me to be your tutor, you need to promise to not always think you're right. Because you're not, Melody." He says it gently enough that I know he's not criticizing me, but there's truth in what he says.

It stings a little, and I wonder if this is something about me that bothers him. I hope not. For now, I need to focus on getting to New York. "Deal."

"Meet me at the bottom of the hill after school."

At 3:00 p.m., I rush to my locker to grab all my books for tonight before meeting Wonjae.

Yura's already there, waiting for me. "Want to come over tonight?"

"Ugh, I wish. Maybe. It depends how much I get done."

"Okay. What's the rush?" she asks, watching me stuff as much schoolwork as I can into my backpack.

"Um. Wonjae's tutoring me in Korean and we have to discuss our project." I pull out a few textbooks from my locker.

She gives me a knowing grin.

"What?" I squeak.

"What? I didn't say a word," she says, poking my side playfully. "I need to go meet my mom for some fabric show, something, something. Have fun and text me tonight!"

I wave at her happily and meet Wonjae at the bottom of the hill. We start walking down the sidewalk, the opposite of my usual route up the stairs to the bus stop. "Where are we going?"

"To my designated study spot," he says. "I'm letting you in on a secret of mine."

About ten minutes later, we're standing at the gates in front of what looks like a public school. It's a massive red-brick building with a dirt field that feels too large for any school.

"A school?" I ask.

"Follow me."

We weave through some trees behind the building until we come to a small playground. It's completely empty, which seems out of place given how big this school is.

"Whoa," I say. "It's like a secret garden."

"Okay, it is not a secret garden. You're ruining my macho reputation," he says, flexing his nonexistent bicep. Well, it's not *totally* nonexistent. It's kind of there and kind of nice.

We drop our bags to the ground and fall onto the swings, swaying back and forth.

"So you come here to study?"

"A lot of the time. Actually, when the school lets out, it's good background noise. No one ever comes back here. I think it's the old playground or something."

"Thanks for bringing me to your cool study spot."

"Anytime."

We talk more about the project and how to incorporate the traditional hanoks into our presentation and what we liked and didn't like about Ikseon-dong. I only have a list of things I liked. Nothing is bad about those magical alleyways. After brainstorming some ideas, we decide to take a break, and Wonjae jogs over to the vending machine near the entrance of the school, returning with two cans of hot coffee.

"At times like this, Korea seems pretty cool," I say, sipping the coffee.

"When you're with me?" he teases.

I roll my eyes. "No. When you can get a good coffee from a vending machine. That kind of stuff." My mind goes back to the hanoks we saw that day. "Did you know hanoks were used for the aristocrats way back when in Korea?"

He looks at me with raised eyebrows. "No! You don't say."

"Oh. Well, did you also know that the walls aren't normal walls? They're made from hanji, which is super eco-friendly and has a lot of benefits besides letting the sunlight in naturally without opening windows. The traditional handmade paper is lubricated and made waterproof, which is how they can use paper for windows and stuff. And all hanoks have courtyards. That's part of the aesthetic in its traditional sense."

"Impressive. I didn't know you were that interested in traditional housing."

"I just think it's pretty incredible," I say, trying not to sound too much like a nerd obsessed with old homes.

We set up goals and days we'll meet for tutoring. The study plan makes me more excited about Korean class, and I'm determined to apply the same level of ambition to all my other classes. I *will* go to New York.

This ends up being a short study session since we just list out goals and talk about random things, and not more than an hour later we start heading back to Hannam Towers together, making a pit stop for some bungeoppang. It's a new street snack for me, and I marvel as the ahjusshi flips the fish-shaped irons over and fills them with batter poured from a giant gold kettle and scoops red bean filling into the center. We bite into the crispy bread with the mochi-like texture and red bean oozing out. The pleasure of the sweet taste and doughy texture whirling around in our mouths in a cozy tent like this makes me feel some type of way. Maybe it's because it reminds me of the orange tents we ate at in Ikseon-dong. By the time I get home, my stomach is warm and my mind is ready. I go straight to my room and study for the rest of the evening, occasionally checking my phone for messages.

I don't realize how much time has passed when I hear my mom's voice telling me to come downstairs for dinner. My dad's already at the table.

"Oh, when'd you get home?" I ask him.

"Solmi, that's no way to greet your father," he scolds. "I got home over an hour ago."

"But it's a weekday."

"I can't come to my own home on a weekday?"

"No, sorry, I mean, I just meant that on weekdays you usually come home late."

"Well, I don't know what to tell you. Things are slow before Chuseok. I can go into my study if you'd like to think I'm still at work."

I scowl. "Not what I meant."

"Attitude," my mom says in a warning tone.

I smile politely at my dad. "What I meant is that I'm glad you're here for dinner. It's usually just me and Umma." I smile at my mom with my crescent moon eyes. My dad gives a small, almost happy grunt at my new acknowledgment of him.

After dinner, I help my mom put the plates away. I can tell from her furrowed brows that she's thinking about something hard. "Yes?" I pry.

"Can't get anything past you, can I?" she jokes. "Okay. I'm meeting Rebecca in half an hour at a café nearby. Are you coming? You should also consider studying."

I almost drop a plate in excitement. "YES, I AM COMING! I'll stay up late to study if I have to. Let me go get changed."

Thirty minutes later, my mom, Aunt Rebecca, and I are seated in a café I haven't been to. It's smaller and feels more like a bakery. I'm waiting for one of them to break the ice, but neither of them is. So I do.

"Are you busy lately with performances?" I ask her.

She smiles at me. "Very, actually. Been getting busier by the day."

I raise my hand up for a semi-awkward high five. "That's good, right?"

"It's great."

"What do you do when you're not performing?" my mom asks.

"Usually practicing, but when I'm prepared, I try to reach

out to secure more gigs, but it's getting harder and harder to do that on my own. I'm actually planning on hiring a manager."

I make an O with my mouth. "That's so cool! A real manager. To book your gigs?"

Aunt Rebecca nods. "To help keep me going, basically. An assistant, a manager, hopefully a jack-of-all-trades."

My mom shakes her head immediately, and my body tenses from the feeling of an impending lecture. "Rebecca, you should be saving money. Just because it's going well now doesn't guarantee anything. You have to prepare for the worst."

My aunt closes her eyes, probably to calm herself down. *Hey, I do that too, Eemo.* "Unni, I'm managing just fine, and actually very well, which is why I made a decision to hire an assistant. When are you going to stop lecturing me about my choices and give me the respect I deserve as an adult? Maybe one day you'll even actually support me."

I bite my lips, praying against a fight.

"I can't support you being irresponsible, Jieun."

Eemo purses her lips. "Let's change the topic. Mel, how's school and friends?"

I exhale slowly and quietly, determined to help deter this fight. I talk about my friends, the difficulties of SIA, and all the street food I've consumed. Thanks to my jabbering, Mom and Aunt Rebecca manage to slide past their contentious topic and make pleasantries about life in Seoul and what my dad's been doing at work, boring adult stuff like that.

Two hours later, we say goodbye and we're back home. "That wasn't too bad, right?" I say to my mom, forcing myself to be more cheerful so she'll see that it isn't bad for me to come along when she meets her.

She pats my head like I'm a little kid and smiles. "Don't you have midterms to ace, Mel?"

Once I'm back in my room, I grab my phone to video call Soph to update her on my amazing news about M&S. I wait in anticipation for her to pick up, and finally, her face fills my screen.

"Soph," I practically scream into the phone. "I have to tell you the biggest news."

"Hi! I want to hear all about it, but I'm going to brunch with my dad's girlfriend right now. I love her now, by the way. We're going to Blue Dog. I'm actually late, but text it to me, okay?"

The screen goes black as fast as it lit up. I sigh, trying not to get too irritated. Blue Dog. I haven't been there in ages. But this is too big of a deal for me to text, so I decide I'll just tell her the next time we video chat. And just like that, a wave of homesickness takes over. I pull my sketchbook from the bookshelf and let myself draw, deciding to take a break from schoolwork for just one evening. Hours in, I'm looking at my finished sketch, surprised to discover how quickly my hands were moving, like they were longing to draw this. I look at my dad's smiling face, where I've given him wrinkles around the edges of his eyes, more than he has in real life because he doesn't smile that much. He's turned to the side, watching my mom, who's laughing a big open-mouthed laugh and looking at me. My face isn't in the sketch; it's just the back of my head. The biggest difference between this sketch and our reality is the setting. Our dining table and plates are not fancy ones inside a villa. In the background, I've drawn our narrow sink in Hell's Kitchen, the floral contact-paper countertop and a candle I bought from the Chelsea flea market years ago. It's faded, and only I can tell exactly what those items are, but it's home, as I imagine it. A home that never happened: me, my mom, my dad living together—happily—on 50th and Ninth.

EIGHTEEN

At school, I'm so much happier than usual that everyone seems to notice. Even Junghoon, whom I barely talk to unless we're in a group.

I'm walking down the hill from SIA, excited for the day to be done, when Junghoon jogs a few steps to catch up to me. "You've been very cheery these last two days," he observes.

I look at him, momentarily surprised. "Life's been sweeter to me these past two days." I shrug my shoulders cheerfully and keep walking. Yura was pulled out of school in the middle of the day for a work trip her mom forced her to accompany her on, so the day felt slower than usual.

I break the awkward silence when he doesn't ask a follow-up question about my sweeter life. "So, any other dates lately?" I pry.

"Not since the worst first date I've ever been on."

I ignore him and keep walking.

"Oh, that was you, by the way."

I stick my tongue out at him.

"Only half joking," he says.

I pretend-glare at him. "Why are you following me anyway?"

Junghoon shakes his head like he's not surprised by my question. "Once again, Melody Lee, not everyone who walks in your same direction is following you." Unlike a month ago, he doesn't say all of this in a tone of pure contempt.

I scoff and try to hide my embarrassment. "Why are you going this way?"

"The bus stop," Junghoon says plainly. "It's this way."

"*You* take the bus?"

"Why are you so surprised?"

"No driver today?"

"Or ever."

"Wait, what?" I don't mask my surprise.

"I never had a driver." He doesn't seem to care much about my surprise as we reach the bus stop.

"I thought you did."

"Nope. You just think you're the only one who's different from all of our rich classmates when you're not."

"No, I don't. What do you mean?" I ask defensively.

"Just that you think you're not a part of a certain lifestyle when you actually are."

"That's not true. I'm not."

"Suit yourself. Just sharing my thoughts," he says dismissively.

"Well, they're not welcome," I snap at him.

He shrugs, and that's the extent of our conversation.

When we get on the bus, we both tap our bus passes against the scanner and immediately head for seats on opposite sides of the aisle.

I pull out my phone to text Yura.

ran into Junghoon at the bus stop.

I look outside the window the entire ride home, thinking how strange it is we never ran into each other on our way home before.

"Do you know when Yura's coming back home?" I ask him as we step off the bus.

"Um. Later, before dinner."

"Nice."

"Why?"

"I was going to go over tonight because I couldn't yesterday."

"Pretty sure she's busy tonight, though."

I eye him suspiciously. "How do you know?"

He shrugs. "I just have a feeling."

I message Yura once I'm home again to see if she's free later at night. For the rest of the day, I focus on finishing my homework and readings for AP English. I pull out my big poster board that I've been brainstorming our Korean project on. Wonjae and I discussed more ideas for our project, and we're thinking of doing a collage to complement our structure of old and new Korea in Ikseon-dong. Our project will show the history of how these hanoks were turned into cafés and bookstores and such, as well as what could be even further into the future. Following a pattern, analyzing a present-day neighborhood, and creating an imagined future. I'm getting more and more excited about this project and begin drawing my ideas out on paper. About an hour later, my dad materializes next to me, making me jump out of my skin.

"Jeez, you scared me!" I yelp.

He laughs awkwardly. "What is all this?" he asks, gesturing at my poster and the initial drawings of my new hanok city. I explain our project to him and what Wonjae and I are thinking about.

"You like hanoks?"

"I love them. It's so cool to see a country preserve old architecture and adapt it for modern living as opposed to demolishing and building something else over it. America shouldn't be a young country, but a lot of people think it is because there weren't people who cared enough to preserve what Native Americans first created, before they were ruthlessly wiped out by colonizers. And now, as soon as a place starts gentrifying, we tear things down and build tall modern buildings in their place."

"I see. That's horrible." He *hmms* slowly. "You know, Solmi, there's a place called Gangneung. It's full of hanoks that you can rent and sleep in. You grill meat outside and walk in rice fields. Your mom and I went a long time ago. Maybe your friends would want to go with you."

"Is it far? Are you giving me permission to go on an overnight trip?"

"It's a few hours by car and worth a weekend trip. Keep studying. I've bothered you enough," he says as he walks out.

He definitely just gave me permission to go away for a weekend. I open KakaoTalk and decide to start a group chat. A small part of me hesitates for a moment as my thumb hovers over the "start new chat" option. I know it shouldn't be a big deal, but starting a group chat is like solidifying a friendship. Creating a group chat feels permanent, like I'm acknowledging that I'm here to stay. But I'm overthinking things again.

I tap the button and name the chat room: HT Chingoos. Hannam Tower Friends. It sounds pleasant enough.

hiiii friends

YURA
heart this! Hi.

KIMBEOM
WHOAAA

JUNGHOON

WONJAE
well, I'm honored.

YURA
😵 haha. HT Chingoos. that's cute.

friends, i have a crazy proposition.

YURA
???

I tell them about going to Gangneung, about the hanoks and my newly established need to go and experience them.

WONJAE
i actually know a place there. i'm down.

KIMBEOM
next week is chuseok though.
when would we go?

JUNGHOON
i can't during chuseok.
have a million relatives to visit.

WONJAE
tomorrow?

I think about this for a second. Since we're all preparing for exams and it's about to be Korea's biggest holiday, schoolwork is lighter than usual . . . Tomorrow could actually work.

YURA
leave tomorrow after school
come back Sun night?

JUNGHOON

KIMBEOM
ALL THE YES.

WONJAE
mel?

definitely down.

Also, in a roundabout way, this trip is for schoolwork, so I don't even have to feel bad for taking time away from my studies.

ON FRIDAY, CLASSES PASS IN A JOYFUL BLUR, ALL of us talking about our first group road trip together. Junghoon is insistent that we leave before rush hour, so when we get home, we only have one hour to pack and meet in the courtyard.

I'm packing my duffel, aggressively stuffing as many cute-and-comfortable clothes into it as I can, when my mom comes into the room and sits on the bed. I'm torn between wanting to ignore her and being polite so I can score some brownie points on the attitude front. "Hi," I say to her.

"Your dad told me you're going on a trip? Why didn't you tell me?" She sounds somewhere between trying to be gentle but clearly agitated.

I shove a pair of baggy but stylish corduroy pants into my bag even though the seams look like they might burst. "I thought Appa would tell you, and I already got his permission," I say, trying to avoid sounding defensive.

"He just did. I'm glad you're getting to know different parts of Korea. Gangneung is one of the most beautiful places in the country."

I nod in acknowledgment but don't make eye contact. I wish I could share with her how excited I feel about this trip, how I may or may not have a small crush on Wonjae, how I've come to love Yura, how off things feel with Sophia. Every time

I come close to wanting to share what I've been feeling this last month—the good and the cringey—I think of Aunt Rebecca; I think of my mom's lies and the fact that she closed off a huge part of herself from me while raising me to be fully and unabashedly honest with family. I zip up my duffel, praying the zipper doesn't break midway from the overstuffed clothes. "Yeah, he mentioned that," I say quietly.

Mom looks at me like she's waiting for me to say something. Like she knows there's a bunch of things I wish I could tell her.

"I'll be back Sunday." Avoiding her gaze, I leave my room and head downstairs quickly.

I meet everyone in the courtyard, and we walk together toward Kimbeom's car. Well, *one* of his dad's cars. We pile into the Benz, and I yank a bag of snacks out of my duffel to share. As we hit the road, I open the car window a little to let the breeze hit my face. The air is just cold enough to feel chilly, but something in the wind makes me feel hopeful.

"There's a hyugaeso coming up. Should we drop by?" Junghoon asks the group.

It's been about an hour and a half, and we all decide that we need some classic rest-stop food, so we step out and stretch our legs. I get out of the car, not expecting much, but am greeted with the sight of an entire plaza of restaurants, clean bathrooms, street food, and a massive indoor food court. "*Wow*, look at this place!" I exclaim.

Yura laughs. "It's just a normal hyugaeso. So easy to impress," she teases.

We go to the street cart with the most customers and stuff our faces with ddukbokki, soondae, and fried kimbap. After washing it all down with odeng broth, we head inside to warm ourselves up and pick up more snacks for the road. There's a ton of people sitting at long tables eating all different types of Korean stews; the aroma is too much for my self-restraint. "Wanna split a ramen with me?" I ask Yura.

"Always," she says.

I'm so full, but I can't help it. Everything smells so good. We slurp down the soup in a second, but not before the boys find us and steal a bite, too. Happy and stuffed, we all finally head back to the car and continue the drive to Gangneung. I don't mean to fall asleep, but I do, and when I'm gently shaken awake, I realize I was leaning my head on Wonjae the entire time.

"We're here, sleepyhead," he says.

I spit out the cracker that was inserted into my half-open mouth.

"Very funny," I say as they laugh.

When we pull up to the small parking area, the sky outside is dark.

"Your obsession with hanoks can continue this weekend," Wonjae says as we walk down the pavement leading to the rental home.

"I welcome all hanok lessons."

"This is my favorite place to stay in Gangneung."

"It better be, since you're the one who refused to stay anywhere else," I tell him. "What do you love so much about this place, anyway?"

"The people who run it. They're this amazing grandma and grandpa couple. They've been running this hanok rental for over thirty years, before staying in hanoks was even a trend. And plus, they love me," he says, grinning.

It turns out he is right about this. Before we even reach the main entrance, the owners run out to greet Wonjae with a hug and pat him on the back, showering him in all the usual old folk comments, like "When did you get so tall?" and "Do you have a girlfriend yet?" and—my personal favorite because it's crazy—"You get more handsome each time we see you; you missed your calling as an actor."

I shake my head at him in disbelief. "Told ya," he says, and goes over to coo at their dog. It's a common breed I've seen a few times in Seoul: a Korean jindo. Its soft white fur and intense, sharp eyes make it look like dog royalty.

The elderly couple leads us to the hanok, and we slide open the traditional wooden door covered in hanji and take a peek inside. The whole space is seven different rooms that have individual bathrooms and kitchens. Each one is a modest studio space layout, with a small kitchen in one half and a TV and living room space set up in the other. No sofa or bed, just lots of stacked mats, a low coffee table, and pillows filled with some sort of heavy beans. Apparently it's a Korean-style pillow that helps the elderly sleep better. The mats and heavy blankets are brightly colored and give a pop to the otherwise neutral, wooden rooms. The hanok complex feels a lot more traditional than the modernized versions I've seen on Instagram, in a good way. An authentic vibe. The entire space feels cozy and perfect for a wintry night in. The floors are heated by ondol, or underfloor heating, and I drop my bag and sprawl out on it, letting the heat warm every inch of me. For privacy's sake, we rented out the whole property so we'd have the place and grills to ourselves. It's an unnecessary extravagance, but Wonjae insisted, and the hosts adore him, so I don't think they charged a ton extra. Plus, the privacy definitely adds a cozier vibe to everything.

I'm forced to get up when the grandpa insists on giving "Wonjae's best friends" a tour of the backyard beyond the hanok. The seven rooms are all under one structure, which look onto the central courtyard. We follow him out back to a huge field behind the home, which has a garden full of different vegetables and giant stalks of wheat. To the left of the rental is a chicken coop, something I've never seen in real life before. The whole hanok is built atop a wooden platform so that you have to step up a bit before reaching your door. I go back into the room after exploring with the grandpa and put my hands back on the floor, taking off my socks to let the ondol thaw my toes.

"Should we go down to the river now or tomorrow?" Yura asks the group.

"Tomorrow. It's probably too dark and cold for the river right now," Wonjae says. "Tonight, let's grab groceries for dinner and rest. I'll drive to the store. I just need one person to come with me to help me carry everything back."

The boys' backs are turned to us, and Yura winks at me. "I'm going to rinse the dishes and set up the mats and stuff with Junghoon. Mel, you go since you're not doing anything."

I shoot her a thumbs-up and pull my socks back on, trying not to be too nervous about our grocery-run "date."

We get to the grocery store and head for the meat/gogi aisle. "Well, we definitely want some samgyupsal—pork belly is so good on the grill. And we should get some makgeolli after. It's the best drink to have outdoors, especially with gogi," he suggests.

I feel like we're a young married couple, grocery shopping

together in the evening before dinner. I try to sound casual, subtly resting one hand on the side of the cart. "Sounds good to me. Can we get the flavored one? Like we had from that night after Octagon? I remember it being yummier than the regular makgeolli." I shut my eyes, cursing myself. Did I have to mention the one night we kissed? He's definitely going to think I'm thinking about that now.

He nudges me playfully. "The peach one is pretty good, and the banana flavor grows on you."

I squash the tingling sensation and focus on finding the flavored makgeolli. I look over the options carefully before deciding to choose two peach, one chestnut, and one banana.

"Are you excited to sleep on the floor tonight?" he asks.

"Actually, I am. It's hard to believe how traditional homes like this still exist with how modern everything in Korea is now."

The grocery trip is quick, and we make small talk, but it's nothing super awkward or uncomfortable. Actually, everything feels relatively natural with Wonjae. Almost like he's a close friend. A close friend who I kissed one time and who gives me constant butterflies. When we get back, Kimbeom is starting up the grill and setting up all the utensils and plates. From a distance, I see Yura inside the sliding door with lettuce in her hands.

"Bring on the meat," Yura shouts from the kitchen, waving at us. "Kimbeom, do you want to start grilling? We're washing the sangchu now."

We join Kimbeom and unload the groceries while Junghoon and Yura bring everything outside. The elderly hosts come to join us, as is tradition, says Wonjae, and we pass out bowls and plates for the rice and side dishes. The grandma prepared an entire big pot of rice for us and brings out her homemade kimchi. If ever people said store-bought tastes the same as homemade, they are so wrong. Homemade kimchi—when made right—is vastly superior, and that is a hill I am willing to die on. I grab three layers of kimchi with my disposable chopsticks and savor its freshness. Kimbeom uses tongs to put some of it on the grill, and the smell of slightly burnt kimchi coupled with the pork belly makes my mouth water. The crispness of the almost-winter air, the jindo dog scrounging for food on the ground, and the chestnut makgeolli make for an amazing night outdoors. The grandpa gives a small toast and welcomes "all of Wonjae's friends" and raises his glass, which, as culture dictates when serving an elder, Wonjae poured for him with two hands.

"Kunbae!" he says as we cheers using both hands to hold our glasses, to show our respect to the oldest person in the group. Yura, Junghoon, Kimbeom, and Wonjae all grab a bit of rice and put it on the lettuce, then place a piece of samgyupsal on top after dipping it in salted sesame oil, and finish by adding in a dash of a spicy Korean condiment called ssamjang. I copy them and stuff the giant lettuce-wrapped first bite into my mouth. The mixture of flavors, from the buttery sesame oil to the sweetness of the rice and the tang of ssamjang, makes my mouth melt. And, if possible, the homemade kimchi tastes even better grilled.

As the evening progresses, our cheeks get rosy with the alcohol and the heat of the grill, and we all pull out chairs and sit around the newly made fire as the grandpa tells us stories of Wonjae and his family when he was little. He speaks in Korean, but I understand small portions of it. "Wonjae and his parents were some of our very first guests at our hanok rental home. Wonjae still manages to visit every so often, and he's really starting to look just like his dad." The grandpa pats Wonjae's back like he's proud, and the way he looks at him is full of love and gentleness, and maybe a little sadness. He disappears into the rooms to bring us some soju, which warms my stomach and washes away the greasy aftertaste from eating too much meat. Everyone else drinks it straight, but Yura squeezes fresh lemon juice into ours, which makes it taste 200 percent better.

After we help our hosts put away the leftover kimchi and tidy up the grill area, we head back inside the hanok rooms. My hands are red from the cold, and I blow into them for a few minutes before Wonjae and I begin to do the dishes together while everyone else disappears to shower.

"So you've been here a lot alone?" I ask Wonjae.

"I came by myself twice. Just to get away and spend time with them. My family used to come at least twice a year. My mom says this was my dad's favorite place." He smiles down at the spoons before putting them inside the drawer.

I don't want to pry, so I focus on drying the last few dishes with a towel.

"He passed away when I was still young, so I don't remember much. I was five at the time. We still came back for a few years after that, until the end of elementary school, but I think it got too hard for my mom to come back here without him so often."

I lightly touch his arm. "I'm so sorry. It must be painful to not have a lot of memories of him."

"It's okay. I just get sad for my mom sometimes, raising me

alone and living under a lot of pressure from my grandpa."

I nod slowly, even though I don't fully understand. But you don't need to understand to be there for someone. "Why do you come back here?"

Wonjae sighs. "I have this memory of my dad walking through the back garden here with me. And another one of my parents in the outdoor wooden lounge area. It's not much, but they're some of the only memories I have of him from when I was old enough to remember. Coming here helps me remember him. I feel like I forget him as I get older, and it . . ." His voice slows down. "It makes me feel guilty."

I look at him, unable to say anything remotely comforting, and I hope in my face he can see how much I hurt for him. I consider saying something or giving him a hug or just something to show him I care, but as I dry the final dish, the others pile into the room. I smile helplessly at Wonjae, and he shrugs and walks over to them, motioning for me to join in.

After we've all changed into comfortable clothes, we sit around in one of the more spacious rooms with a television on in the background and a deck of cards, drinks, and anju. I don't have another moment with Wonjae alone, so I etch this conversation into my mind so I can bring it up again hopefully when the time is right. I grab a fistful of peanuts. The small snacks really help balance out the drinking. I don't plan on reliving my post-Octagon hangover.

"Okay, so what should we cheers to for our first drink?" Kimbeom asks.

"Whatever happened to the good ol' days of drinking soda?" I say. "I'm still red from the soju."

"Well, high school is about upping your tolerance to prepare you for college life," Kimbeom says, reaching over to pour beer in my glass.

I laugh and let him fill it to the brim. "Fine, well, I have something to share." The others look at me in anticipation, and I know I'm ready to finally get my good news out there. I've enjoyed holding it so close to me and only me the last few days, besides my parents.

"I got into Maison & Saito's final round in New York."

Yura shrieks so loudly I think my eardrums burst. "I KNEW IT!"

"You did not!" I say, but it's nice to have the ego boost when you don't have it for yourself.

"Everyone hold up your glasses right now," she demands.

"To Melody," Junghoon says first, and I gasp—half in genuine surprise, half in jest—at his charitableness.

"Wow, I'm floored," I joke.

"To Melody!" Kimbeom echoes, and we all clink our glasses together.

We're sitting on the floor with our legs partially covered by the table, and I feel a firm hand squeeze my knee. I know without looking that it's Wonjae, and I feel myself blush. Luckily, the Asian Glow I get when I drink is a curse on my face that works out to be a blessing just this one time.

"So your parents are letting you go?" Wonjae asks.

"Only if I get A's in all my classes. That's why I absolutely need to do well on all my exams and assignments."

"Ahh," Wonjae says, "you mean, that's why you need a genius tutor."

I nudge him and raise my glass to toast myself. "I will toast to my parents letting me go to New York so I can achieve my dream career, against their wishes of me becoming a doctor or lawyer."

"To dreams! Kunbae!" we sing in unison.

Hours of games later, we sprawl out on the floor, happily exhausted.

"I'm too tired to move," Yura whispers to me.

"Me too."

"Goodnight, everyone," Junghoon says.

I look to my right. Wonjae is lying next to me. Not like right next to me, but close enough that I can see his satisfied expression staring up at the ceiling. He turns his head toward me and I feel a warm hand gently taking hold of mine. "Night, everyone," he says out loud, but he's looking only at me. I smile back at him and turn my head toward the window, where I can see an endless array of stars painted in the dark black sky. They look like little specks of hope scattered everywhere, flicked across the sky from an artist's paintbrush.

WE MUST'VE SLEPT REALLY LATE BECAUSE WHEN we wake up, it's past lunchtime. We get dressed and gather our things and stretch out in the courtyard. There's a small tree in the center, with a stone border circling it. I'm looking at it closely when Kimbeom shouts at me to come in and finish getting ready so we can get to the stream.

An hour later, we're at the stream, and despite the cold weather, we take off our shoes and on a group dare, dip our toes into the water. It is freezing and we last about twelve seconds. The air out here is so crisp and clean, unlike Seoul or

Manhattan. I inhale the air deeply as I let the cold water numb my toes before we all climb back into the car to warm our frozen feet.

"Why did we do that?" Junghoon asks.

"Because we're dumb," Wonjae says.

"Daring, you mean," Yura adds.

"What's for lunch?" Kimbeom asks.

"I thought we're going to get coffee." My stomach growls at the same time Wonjae's does.

We get to a large café—three floors total—and I take in the winter aesthetic. "Wow, Korea really starts on the holiday decor early," I say, looking at a plastic snowman in the corner and fake green table wreaths that decorate a seating area. We find a table that faces a window looking out onto the beach. The view outside is stunning, and I'm surprised that the place is empty on a Saturday afternoon.

Junghoon takes a cup of hot coffee off the tray and places it on top of a napkin in front of Yura. I take another cup and sip on a hot Americano.

Inspired by the view, Kimbeom forces all of us to go to the beach after, and we decide to walk the beachfront and see what restaurant we'll end up at. The group kind of naturally breaks up, and Yura and I end up trailing behind the boys as they walk a few steps in front of us. It helps that we're directly behind them and not getting hit by the wind as much.

"I have news, too," Yura says, cozying up to me tighter so we can keep each other warm.

I wait for her to continue and try not to focus on the cold.

"Junghoon and I are officially together," she says in an excited whisper that is somehow almost a shout.

"Oh my gosh!" I whisper as loudly as I think I can get away with without the boys hearing. "Why didn't you tell me, and since when?"

"Since Thursday. He's been my boyfriend for forty-eight hours. I am so happy."

We keep walking. "That's major. You did it. Not that I doubted you. He's had heart eyes for you since the moment he met you, I'm sure."

She smirks charmingly. "So now that we're actually official, you two need to be nicer to each other."

"Okay, okay. So, can I ask what you like most about him? I support you, Yura, but I'm genuinely curious. He's so . . . I don't know. Straight-edged, annoying, opinionated. Always has to have the last word. Typical rich kid vibes, you know?"

Yura frowns and pulls her arm away from me. "Or you can say he's disciplined, driven, goal oriented, and has strong principles. And he's not rich, Mel. It's a little unfair for you to just assume he's a stereotypical rich kid when you hardly know him."

Oh yeah, the bus stop conversation. I forgot about that. I kick awkwardly at the hard sand beneath my shoes. "Sorry, I didn't mean to upset you so much . . ."

"Look, I don't like calling people out. I rarely do, but some-times you can be very judgmental, and you don't even know him very well. You just assumed he was rich, example one."

"Well, he goes to SIA," I say defensively.

Yura jams her hands into her jacket pockets in frustration. "So?" We're not walking anymore, just facing each other and not moving. "His dad is a renowned professor at SNU, so he's here on scholarship and financial aid because their family is within a certain income bracket that qualifies them for that.

And SNU helps with housing. Obviously he's not going around sharing that information, so that's why you had no idea. But case in point, Mel."

"*Okay,*" I snap, a little angrier than I intended. "I didn't realize," I add, softer this time. "I feel shitty, okay? I'm sorry."

For someone who has had her bluntness pointed out to her by others time and again, I'm just Jell-O inside.

Yura sighs and turns to keep walking. "I think it's funny that you don't like him."

"It's not that I don't like him—"

"Whatever. That you don't have any type of chemistry, as friends or otherwise."

"Okay. Why is that funny?"

Yura looks like she's biting back a smile. "I think you don't like him because he's basically a male version of you," she says.

I make a disgusted face.

"That's right! I'm going deep right now. Do you not like yourself?"

"We are nothing alike."

"Sure you are. I already told this to him, too. You also love having the last word, Mel. You are also very opinionated. Or, as I like to say: driven, smart, with strong principles and ideas to contribute."

I shake my head but can't help smiling. That's the effect Yura has on people. Yura isn't the first person who's told me I can be too judgmental, and being in Korea, it's made me realize that they've all been right. "Sorry," I say sincerely, attempting to link my arm back into hers. "I'll be nicer. Promise."

She squeezes me with her elbow and grins. "Don't be sorry to me. Say sorry to yourself because clearly there's an issue there," she jokes. "The only difference between you two is that he doesn't say much and you never shut up."

The boys turn around and register confusion when they see how far behind we are. They wave us over, so we speed walk—as much as you can speed walk in sand—and catch up to them to scout out a lunch spot.

Before we leave the beach, we get into a group hug position to keep each other warm and take a few selfies together, under the coercion of Kimbeom. We all pretend to grumble but love it, and it ends up being a cute photo, with the waves as a backdrop and the wind in our faces and hair blowing everywhere. I feel like the picture captures the best part of my life in Korea so far. All of us, hugging, smiling for the camera and teasing Kimbeom for being so cheesy. I sneak a glance at Yura, and she's nuzzling up to Junghoon and probably using this group photo as an excuse to cuddle with him publicly. It's pretty adorable.

Then, as I smile big for the camera for another selfie, in the most unexpected moment, I feel a hand grab mine and squeeze it tightly. My heart stops beating, a result of the kaleidoscope of butterflies that has just exploded inside me. I return his squeeze. A million questions run through my head, how I feel, if I want something more, if I don't, if I'm ready to even have a boyfriend, if I'll ever go back to New York. I hold his hand long enough to remember that it feels warm and strong, and it's a hand I want to hold again.

NINETEEN

*T*he rest of the day goes by too quickly, and Sunday morning rolls around sooner than I wished. We insa to the elderly hosts and hug the jindo goodbye. By the time I'm home, I'm wondering if the hand I held was from a dream, but the tingling sensation that still lingers in my own assures me that it wasn't. Monday whizzes by as the only full school day of the week, and when I get home, my mom tells me my dad will be coming home for dinner. He worked late on Sunday, so I haven't had a chance yet to see him since I got back. Before he gets home, I use this free time to pull out his journal from the pillowcase and look for an entry that looks more legible.

Korea
Solmi bigger now.
Lily is far away. I miss her. I miss Solmi.

I run my hands through this page, finding it hard to believe my dad missed us at one point. I wonder if he ever told my mom.

I hear my mom's voice calling me downstairs, so I shove it deep into the bookcase to change up the hiding space. Downstairs, my dad asks me about the trip.

"It was a lot of fun," I answer.

"Did your friends like it, too?"

I nod and dip my spoon into the bowl of doenjang jjigae the ahjumma made for us over the weekend while I was gone. I've gotten accustomed to eating Korean food every day, even on weekend mornings. And soybean paste stew is definitely not something I'd thought I'd end up eating frequently, but it's hard to imagine life without its rich warmth now. It's like something in me always had a longing for certain foods that I never even thought about.

"You liked the hanoks?"

"Yep. It was a true hanok experience. We even barbecued gogi outside." I swallow another bite of food. "Thanks for telling me about Gangneung, Appa."

"I'm glad you had a good time, Solmi. So listen, we've actually decided to do a rather spontaneous gathering tomorrow evening, to celebrate the start of the Chuseok holiday," he says to both me and my mom. "Your friends and their parents in Hannam Towers."

My mom has a surprised expression on her face—not the pleased kind—and I'm guessing he didn't tell her about this, either. "What type of gathering?"

"At Plaza Hall for an intimate dinner. It's a restaurant in Cheongdam-dong," he says. "We've reserved a private room, and the chef is esteemed in the industry, so it'll be exquisite food, guaranteed. A younger friend of Wonjae's grandfather. The dress code is strictly formal, so be sure to spend some time buying a new outfit for tomorrow." He hands me a different credit card. A heavier, thicker one than the one he gave me when I first came to Korea.

"I can just wear what I have . . ." I say slowly, but my hand is already reaching for the card, and I'm a little excited, already thinking about what outfit to buy.

"I've seen the things you wear, and they're not appropriate for this restaurant," he says.

"Is it really necessary to buy an entire outfit for a small neighborhood dinner?" My mom waits for an answer from my dad.

"It's not just a neighborhood dinner, Yeobo, it's a kickoff to Chuseok, and I'm sure the kids will like it," my dad says. "You should buy a nice outfit, too. You can finally meet all the mothers. We haven't done a proper dinner together since Melody's come anyway."

My mom doesn't seem like she's into this idea. "I'll wear what I have," she says sharply. "And we came over a month ago, an introductory dinner is an unnecessary formality by now."

I pretend to be interested in consuming my jjigae and start daydreaming outfits in my head for tomorrow's dinner as my parents keep talking. Wonjae will be there; I need to look perfect.

Tuesday is a half day since it's the start of Chuseok, and the energy is contagious. Everyone is ready to leave and get on with their long, long weekend. Yura and I have a date planned right after school to go shopping for our outfits together. Her driver is waiting for us outside, and we slide into the BMW when he opens the car door.

"Although I'm not sure why you'd need a new dress; don't you go to a million of these types of dinners but fancier, for your mom's work and stuff?" I ask once we're inside the car.

"You can never have too many. Besides, you've never been to Dynasty. I can't wait to show you!"

Besides Galleria, I haven't been to any department stores in Seoul, so I'm eager to see what it's like. I've also only been to the ones in New York—Bergdorf's, Bloomingdales, Saks—a few times, usually during the holidays to enjoy the holiday festivities, but never to buy. The thought of trying on fancy dresses in a fancy department store sounds like an unrealized childhood dream, and I secretly can't wait. I just hope it isn't too expensive.

We pull up to a massive building that looks like it's made entirely of shiny reflective glass. Over the revolving doors, DYNASTY is engraved in thick gold letters.

"Whoa," I say. "This is a fancy department store."

When we walk in, there are tiers and tiers that you can see; escalators create an atrium throughout the levels so that shoppers can see into other floors from wherever they are. The escalators are covered on the sides with beautiful white marble, and multiple giant chandeliers hang from the ceiling, all at different levels, giving the space a sort of ethereal look. I'm dazzled by the beauty of the design, and Yura practically has to drag me toward the elevators.

"Come on," she says, laughing, "you're not finding a dress just standing there."

I follow her to the elevators, and we head to the top floor of the building, which she's only able to access with a key card. We reach a door that has her name on the wall.

"You have your own room?" I ask, amazed.

When she opens it, my feet are glued to the floor and I'm

unable to go inside. The room is basically a closet that's larger than two New York apartments. There are rows and rows of bags on shelves and dresses on racks.

"Is all of this yours?"

Yura nods modestly. "Yeah, it's all from my mom's store, though. Anything I buy from a different department store is at home."

"Your whole life is my dream wardrobe. Wow."

She laughs. "It's really not, but thanks. I like the collection up here. We can drop our stuff off and go to the dress section and try them up here."

We spend half an hour on the contemporary women's apparel floor and grab too many dresses and chic jumpsuits off racks, and staff members help us bring them back to Yura's closet.

As I change into a black midi dress, I raise my voice so it can be heard past the thick cloth curtain.

"Have you and the others done these dinners often?"

"Mm, when there were occasions, I guess so. Like a big promotion or a new job or whatever."

I come out and stand in front of the tall mirror and make a face. "Not the one, right?"

Yura shakes her head. "Here, try this one." It's navy blue and form fitting at the top but falls elegantly to the floor. I love the mix of edgy and classy in the dress—it only has a long sleeve on one side, which I don't know if I could pull off, but I try it on anyway.

I see my phone light up and buzz from the ottoman in the corner. It's Soph.

I pick up but answer without the video and bring it to my

ear. "Hey, Soph," I say, trying to zip up the side of my dress at the same time.

"Hi, where's your face?"

"I'm out right now with Yura at her mom's department store. Her dressing room or closet thing is the size of at least three of our New York City apartments. Wait, isn't it the middle of the night there?"

"Yeah, three a.m. I couldn't fall asleep. What was your big news?"

I hesitate before telling her. Her voice sounds distant, like she's not really interested in my news. "I made it to the final round of Maison & Saito."

"Oh, wow, congrats. That's huge." She sounds sincere, but not as excited for me as I had hoped.

"Thanks," I say awkwardly, because Soph doesn't seem especially thrilled. Not in the way she usually would've been anyway.

"So does this mean you're coming to New York?"

"I'm not sure. It depends if I get all A's on my midterms, which is in a week and a half."

"Wow, that's really major. I hope you come."

"Me too, Soph. I really hope I go, too. I'll keep you posted, okay? But I'm with Yura and I have to go now. Let's video chat this weekend?"

After I hang up, I slip my right arm into the sleeve, careful to not snag any of the delicate fabric. I hold the fabric by the zipper and finish pulling it up.

"How's Sophia doing?" Yura asks.

"I'm not sure. I think she's fine; things have just been feeling off between us lately, but I don't know why."

"Is she upset at you, or is it something else?"

I feel anxious at the thought. I hate it when someone gets upset at me. It's hard for me to continue my day without thinking about it every few minutes.

"I don't think so . . . It's just hard, being so far from each other." I face the gold-rimmed mirror and straighten out the bunched-up parts of the dress. This is the fourth dress I've tried on so far—not including three jumpsuits—and I think it's the best one by far.

"Okay, hopefully seventh time's the charm? How does this one look?" I ask, throwing my head back and placing a hand on my hip.

Yura claps her hands ecstatically. "This is the one."

"Really?" I look at myself again in the mirror. It's floor length, but not dramatic. There's just a slight shimmer to the dress, and it fits perfectly and outlines my form while giving enough room to eat freely. Parent appropriate enough. I love the way the one sleeve accents my left collarbone and long neck. I'm weirdly proud of my long neck. I look at the price tag: 900,000 won. Stunned, I quickly change out of it and hang it nicely back up. I can't be spending over eight hundred dollars on a dress for one evening. I should've known everything here would be super expensive.

Yura's choice is a boxy gold dress, beaded around the sleeves and neckline, which wraps around her thighs and makes her long, slim figure look even longer and slimmer. She pairs the dress with navy stilettos and a big leather bag from Chanel. An assistant comes back with beige heels and a long ivory cardigan for me to couple with the navy dress.

"I *do* love it," I say while I look at myself. "And I love your entire ensemble. You look like you need to be going to some fancy, exclusive party."

"Am I sensing hesitation?" she asks.

I don't want to offend Yura and her mom's department store by saying it's all overpriced, so I just give her a wry smile. "Just not sure it looks *that* amazing on me."

"Don't be ridiculous!" Yura says, dragging me to the dress I hung up. "It looked absolutely perfect on you. Especially with the heels and cardigan."

An employee at Dynasty takes the card my dad gave me and wraps up my new purchases in a beautiful sturdy box with a laced ribbon. As Yura and I happily head back to Hannam Towers together, my heart feels simultaneously over the moon to own such beautiful clothing and severely stressed at how much money I blew in one afternoon. But by the time the evening arrives, I'm even more excited than when I was shopping. I've never done a super-fancy dinner out, and definitely not with a group of parents and my friends. Despite the guilt, I feel classy at the thought of slipping into my new dress and accessories, and I wonder what Wonjae will be wearing. And if he'll notice how I look. And if he'll say anything if he does.

I'm drying my hair when my mom comes into the upstairs bathroom.

"Already washing up?" she shouts over the blow-dryer.

I turn it off. "Just want to start early."

"Wow, you're excited about tonight, hm?"

"Yeah, I guess. I mean, I get to see my friends. What's not to be excited about? Plus, I'm taking that whole new-leaf, good-attitude thing seriously."

"Are you going to return the credit card to your dad? I can

give it to him if you want to. Just give it to me now so you don't forget."

I hesitate before I respond. "He didn't ask for it back, so I feel like I could just hold on to it until he does, right?"

She frowns. "Mel, it's not your credit card. You're too young to have a card of your own."

"What? He gave me one the day we got to Korea." I'm not trying to argue, but it just doesn't seem really fair that *he* gave it to me, but *she's* taking it away.

"I made him put a limit on that one. How much did you spend?" she asks.

I feel uncomfortable saying the numbers out loud. "I don't know the exact amount."

"Ballpark."

I do the math in my head. The cardigan was around 600,000 won, the shoes were over 400,000 won, the dress was 900,000 won. Now I'm even more uncomfortable about answering.

"Less than two million won." My shoulders tense up, bracing for my mom to yell.

"You spent almost seventeen hundred dollars in two hours." Her voice is quiet, heavy with disappointment.

"Well, didn't you buy anything?" I feel defensive and attacked. It's not like I went out seeking things to spend money on.

"A woman my age spending seventeen hundred dollars on an outfit versus a sixteen-year-old girl spending seventeen hundred dollars is different, Melody."

"I was just listening to what Appa told me to do."

"Because you always listened so well before?"

My eyes meet hers, and I glare at her, hurt. "Contrary to what you might think, I actually do try to listen to him. And to you, even when you're being shady and secretive. Do you want me to return the dress, then? I'm sure that'd make Dad real happy. I could wear my usual T-shirt and jeans instead."

My mom rubs her neck with her hand and closes her eyes before opening them again and staring at me. "What has gotten into you?" Now she's annoyed. "Don't treat money like it grows overnight. You can't admit that the amount you spent was excessive?"

I wrap the blow-dryer cord around it and place it under the sink. "Fine! I'll return it, then. Happy?"

"That's not what I'm saying, Melody. Wear the dress, it's fine. But there's no need for you to keep holding on to a credit card. Go get it right now and bring it to me. This is not up for discussion anymore." She does that Mom Voice thing where you know you need to listen. It's like an octave higher than what a normal voice should sound like. I am tempted to roll my eyes but look straight instead and grab the credit card from my bag.

"Thank you," she says when I hand it over without a word.

I stalk back to my room and close the door so I won't be interrupted anymore.

My dad comes home with the driver to pick us up to go to Plaza Hall. He looks at my mom and smiles, and she gives a very, *very* small smile back. She's wearing a black dress that's cinched at the waist, with puffy sleeves, and a pearl necklace with diamond earrings. She looks like a Korean celebrity.

"Solmi, you look really nice," my dad says very formally.

"Thank you," I say. He doesn't look it, but I can tell by the tone of his voice that he's satisfied.

When we arrive at Plaza Hall, my dad lifts up one arm so my mom can link hers, and they walk in together like that. We ascend a set of stairs with attendants waiting by the door to open the private dining room for us. Inside is a long table, and most of the other families are already seated around it. I think only Kimbeom's family hasn't yet arrived. Everyone looks so elegant, and it looks and feels like the type of fancy dinner party I've only seen in movies. I feel more sophisticated than I've ever felt in my life, especially in my new dress, regardless of the price tag and drama it came with.

There's classical music playing and waiters showing us to our seats and taking our coats. The ceilings are high, and the chairs are gold with white linen cushions. The table setting looks almost like one for a wedding. A big floral centerpiece with blush pink peonies and vines overflowing from its gold vase graces the navy tablecloth. I don't even think it's peony season, so I know it must have been imported. Gold and ivory plate settings are elegantly displayed at each seat, along with gold-rimmed champagne glasses.

Wonjae walks up to me. "Nice hair."

I frown. "I didn't do anything to my hair."

He grins. "I know. Looks good."

I smile to myself and mindlessly touch my hair, held in place with just a clip in the back, and sit down where the server has shown me. We do a whole exchange of insas to all the parents while the servers pour champagne and we toast to a fun night ahead. Kimbeom is still not here, though. I message the chat but there's no response, except from the rest of us who are here, sending funny Kakao emojis saying we miss him. Never mind that we just saw him a few hours ago at school.

Halfway through the third appetizer, the door opens and Kimbeom and his parents walk in. The parents are smiling and looking polite and normal, but I can already tell that something's off. He's faking a smile and insas to the adults before sitting down.

are you okay, beomee??

I wish I could whisper to him, but the way everyone is seated, there's absolutely no way any of us can speak privately without at least one set of parents overhearing. Kimbeom doesn't respond for the rest of dinner, but after the adults have eaten most of the meal and desserts are being prepared, they start mingling around the room and we all get together at the end of the table where he's sitting, looking miserable.

"What's wrong, Beom-ah?" Yura asks.

"My dad officially knows," he says. "He knows I'm gay and he told me to fix myself." He wipes away the tears in his eyes before the adults can see. We sit there silently because what he shares is too horrible. How do we respond to that?

"I'm sorry, man," Wonjae says first. "That's fucked up."

I've never heard him swear, but if ever a time called for profanity, this does. "It really is," I add quietly.

"He wants to send me to a boarding school in Boston," he says, even quieter than me.

"What? Why?" Yura asks.

"Because he's ashamed. He doesn't want people to find out." His dad's words sound so cold, even as I hear them through Kimbeom. How could a parent be this way? Anger bubbles up inside me.

"You can't go," Junghoon says. "That's ridiculous."

"My mom doesn't want to send me. She's fighting my dad,

but of course, at dinner, they'll act like the picture-perfect family we aren't," he says with some hardness. "It makes me almost want to shout it to everyone, especially tonight. You know what's worse? I actually wanted to go to America for college, but he's just sending me there since it's far away and plans to bring me back for university here."

Yura gives him a hug. "I'm sorry, Beomee. This is not okay." Her eyes are welling up, too, and he leans against her and closes his eyes.

"Thanks," he says, his voice barely audible. When he makes eye contact with his dad, he sits up straight. "Okay, no more about this. I don't want to deal with my dad when we get home if he sees me sulking all night. I'd rather just be able to avoid him for now."

I slowly glance around the room. Everyone looks so happy, but how do they all really feel? Why does image matter so much to these families, who already have personal drivers, money, and education? I would never have guessed that my family subscribed to this kind of ridiculous and controlling lifestyle, but from my seat I see my mom smiling and laughing and drinking champagne and talking to the other moms as if they've been lifelong friends. All these parents who are puppeteering our futures. For what reason? Because they so firmly believe that they know what's best for us? Or because they care so much about their own reputations that they're willing to prioritize them over their children's happiness? These are thoughts I never would have had in America, not in New York with just me and my mom. And yet, from where I am sitting, I can hardly recognize her in her beautiful puffy-sleeved dress and pearls. My eyes focus back on Kimbeom and how sad he looks, sitting there slumped over his food, holding a spoon but not bothering to eat. I grip his arm.

"This isn't right." I stand up to say—what, I don't know, something, anything. Yura shushes me and tries to pull me back down.

"Mel," she says gently, "I know you're angry. I know this isn't normal to you. But they are still our parents, and this is not the place to cause a scene."

Kimbeom smiles sadly and shakes his head. "Thanks, Mel. But I just want to forget it all, okay? I'll figure it out."

I guess it works out that the table is so damn long since none of the adults actually notice our entire interaction and my near-blowup. I clench my teeth and sit back down. "I hate this, Kimbeom. I'm sorry," I say, but my words feel empty and unhelpful.

Toward the end of the night, as we're forced to talk about other things besides how horrible Kimbeom's dad is, I excuse myself and walk toward the bathroom to have a moment alone, but Wonjae is right behind me. "Can I help you?" I try to make my voice playful and light.

"Oh, I thought you were leaving and signaling for me to follow you."

"Oh yeah? What signal?"

He taps his head. "Telepathy," he says, grinning.

I bite my lips to hold back my laugh. "Who raised you to be so confident?" I tease.

"It's a defense mechanism," he answers. "So, where are you going?"

"The ladies' room."

"So I guess I can't follow you in there, huh?"

"It'd probably be frowned upon."

I want to flirt more with him, but the more I see of these families and their ridiculous ideologies, the more I don't want to be a part of it all. And falling for an heir of a huge corporation feels like the fast track to accepting something that feels unnatural and wrong. Besides, I just need to focus on getting home. Wonjae has to remain a friend, at least for now.

When I get back to the dining room, the vibes are definitely off. I scan the room and immediately feel the attention centering on Kimbeom, who's standing—and swaying slightly—in the middle of the room. Yura's tugging on his arm in a manner that seems like she's trying to tell him to stop whatever he's doing.

"My boy's had too much to drink," Kimbeom's dad says casually with a forced laugh. He snaps his fingers at the servers. "Desserts." They obediently filter out of the room to bring the next course of pastries.

"Abeonim, what is your goal for me in life?" Kimbeom is slurring his words. His cheeks are bright red, and he blinks slowly. His mom is seated in her chair, not saying a word or looking at her husband.

Wonjae is standing nearby, so I walk up to him and whisper, "What the hell happened while I was in the bathroom?"

He leans in without looking at me. "Beom made a toast and said 'Cheers, to us, who love our secrets and pride more than each other,' and it got real awkward. I think everyone was just looking at his dad for an explanation, and that's when you walked in."

"Appa? I'm waiting," Beom says, in a singsong voice.

His dad's face grows red, and he walks over to Beom,

grabbing his shoulder firmly and pushing him into his chair. "Drink water." Then he turns around to look at the rest of us, grabbing another refilled champagne glass (where is all this endless champagne coming from?) and raising it. "A real toast. To our children, who have a lot to learn about moderating their alcohol limit, but we're proud of them anyway!"

All the parents echo his toast while we kids eye his dad with disappointment. Kimbeom sits there, his eyes red from trying not to let the tears fall down his face. Everything inside me hurts, and I set my glass down, refusing to toast to his dad's fakeness.

Eventually, the mood levels out again, which only means that the adults have glossed over whatever happened and moved on, and the desserts continue to arrive. The meal ends up being eight different courses, and the night goes on longer than I anticipated. I'm more than ready to go home when it all ends. Fine dining is not for everyone. How do people sit through a three-hour meal? The driver drops us off, and we insa before heading inside. My mom follows me into my room as I take out my small, thick gold hoops and put them away in my jewelry box.

"So, you're interested in Wonjae, huh?" she says.

"What? No," I answer, trying to not let my tone give anything away.

She smiles in that knowing way. "Whatever you say. Listen, sweetie, I didn't mean to snap at you. I just . . . I don't want you living life as if everything is handed to you. Because that's not true, and it's not how it should be."

I remove the clip from my hair, and the silence feels a little more relaxed between us. It's the most fully honest thing she's said to me since we moved here. I can tell by the way she talks, the way she sounds, that this was why she was so upset at my spending. I think about this evening, about how fake everything felt, about how sad it was to watch Kimbeom be so diminished by his own father.

"I've never spent money like that before. And I won't in the future."

She nods. "Did you have fun tonight?"

"Did *you*? Or were you faking it when you smiled for three hours straight at women you had only just met?" I know she knows I'm lightly teasing, and for the first time in a long time, our conversation feels natural.

"Hey, just because I'd prefer to be at home relaxing in my Rufus tee doesn't mean I was being fake and acting all night."

"Did you enjoy it, then?" I ask.

She laughs. "No. Absolutely not. It was pretentious and the food portions were way too small and it dragged out. Ridiculous. But *you* did."

"Maybe. But if I enjoyed it, I'd never tell you."

She rubs my back and looks at me with a sad smile. "Oh, Melody. It's not bad to enjoy it. I'm just saying it's not for me. Maybe it is for you."

My mom doesn't know how much I hate that. Because I did enjoy tonight, or at least, the dressing up and being fancy and all that, everything minus the part with Kimbeom's dad. I hate admitting that I enjoyed it. Embracing this means I'm letting go of my home, my real home in New York, the one that's waiting for me.

I clear my throat. "Yeah, well, tonight wasn't really for me, either. Kimbeom's dad is awful."

"What was all that about, anyway? No one seemed to notice, but I saw that whole exchange. Good job holding your tongue on whatever you were about to blurt out, by the way," she says, raising her eyebrows so high that wrinkles form on her forehead.

"His dad is threatening to send him to boarding school." I pause. "Because he's gay." Life isn't fair, and I feel stupid for being so upset about my grief over missing New York. It feels small compared to being punished for simply being.

My mom shakes her head. "What an asshole. Maybe you shouldn't have held your tongue."

It's a brief moment of solidarity between us, and I silently thank God that she understands.

TWENTY

*T*he next morning, I wish I could roll around in bed and do nothing but read, but it's Chuseok, which means it's the fateful day my grandparents said we'd be dining together. After a lot of nagging from my dad, I wear a pencil skirt and a frilly banana yellow top, making me look like I'm going to a Model UN conference. A lot of our friends are spending this morning and the rest of the week with different parts of their families, but since we only have my dad's parents in Seoul, our family plans stop after today, thankfully. Although I overheard my mom saying she'd take leftovers to my aunt.

We pull up to the familiar gates, the very green front yard with trees and plants even in the late fall season, and enter the house. My feet feel cold on the floor, and as if reading my mind, the maid who opened the door places three pairs of house slippers in front of us. I feel guilty, watching her serve my grandparents and us when this is a big family holiday. Shouldn't she be with her family, too? I bow my head and thank her before slipping my feet into a light green pair. We're led to the same living room we were in two weeks ago, and I insa to my grandparents.

"Happy Chuseok," I say loudly, trying to up the energy of the room. My grandma smiles and gestures to the empty armchair next to her. When lunch is ready, I discover a newfound appreciation for this holiday. If I thought the table was covered in food for our last meal here, it doesn't compare to the spread that's in front of us now. I learn some of the foods on the table are songpyeon rice cakes, hangwa—which also includes yugwa, the delicious rice puff snack I had with Wonjae—chaldduk, and a bunch of other variations of dduk. The smell of galbi jjim lingers in the air, and the waft coming from the freshly cooked stovetop rice makes my stomach growl immediately. We get seated, and I pick up my chopsticks to take some of the stir-fried japchae when my dad gives me a death glare and swats at my hand.

"Ow!"

"The elder takes the first bite, Solmi."

I duck my head and furtively look up at my grandpa. I apologize in formal Korean and put my heavy gold chopsticks back down and wait for my grandpa to slowly dip his spoon into his bowl of muguk before the rest of us dive into our foods. I look to both sides and across from me, making sure all the adults take at least one bite of something before I reach over for a deep-fried perilla leaf. The table is relatively devoid of conversation besides business talk between my grandpa and dad, which I can't understand. The meat on the braised short ribs falls off the bone with little effort, and I savor each bite of the savory galbi jjim. My mouth is half stuffed with crisp kimchi jeon, or pancake, when my grandma turns to my mom and addresses her in Korean.

"Is Solmi taking proper instrument lessons?"

"Aniyo," my mom answers politely, shaking her head.

"Why not? Sign her up for a private tutor for the flute or piano."

My grandma turns to me, looking a little bit scary in her overdone white powdered makeup. "A young woman needs to know how to play an instrument. Learn the flute; it's easy to carry around."

"Halmoni—" I begin to say.

"Don't worry. It isn't your fault you haven't had lessons yet."

I look at my mom, my lips pressed together in annoyance, but she gives me the Don't Say a Word eye. I look at my dad, waiting for him to say something, but his attention is focused on slurping the rest of his radish beef soup.

"Solmi should come to the office. I can give her an internship so she gets into a good law school later," my grandpa adds.

My dad finally looks up, and he looks a little scared, almost.

"Solmi doesn't need an internship right now, Abeoji," my dad says, calling his father by the formal name for dad.

"Of course she does. You started too late, and I was only able to help you because you're my son. The world won't be so kind to Solmi if she does nothing until she's an adult. She can come to my firm, and I'll have my director's team train her." My grandpa's voice is low, husky, and firm.

I'm biting down on my lip so hard I'm afraid it'll bleed, and I force myself to let go. "No, thank you," I say politely.

Everyone stares.

"Melody—" my mom says cautiously.

"I'm not interested in becoming a lawyer. Or a doctor. I'm

going to be an interior designer." I wish I knew the Korean word for an engineer. I would've added that into the mix.

"Solmi," my dad says, warning me. He turns his attention to my grandpa, who's seated at the head of the table. "I'll talk to her at home, Abeoji."

My grandma, who's seated at the other end of the massive dining table, looks sternly at my mom. "Keeping your child and her father so far apart, this is why Solmi doesn't know how to talk to her elders properly."

I stand up from the table, my anger taking hold. How dare they accuse my mom when their son is the one who left us! He chose a job over his family. He chose status and wealth under my grandfather over us. It wasn't my mom keeping the family apart. It was him. "My dad's the one who left us to come to Korea, to come and work for—"

Before I can finish, my dad slams his hand against the table. "Lee Solmi." His voice echoes throughout the large space and is heavy with anger. "Sit down and apologize this instant."

My mind feels foggy with frustration, and my body feels limp. "Jwesong hamnida," I say to him, bowing my head and slouching back onto my seat. My grandfather ignores me completely, glaring only at my dad.

I sit quietly for the rest of lunch and don't utter another word. During the car ride back home, the atmosphere is dead silent, and I'm slumped over in my seat, dreading going home.

When the front door closes behind our apartment, my dad immediately turns to lecture me. "Why don't you know how to control yourself? You're sixteen, not a child."

"What did I have to control? I barely know my grandpa, but he's trying to create an entire career path for me? I don't want to be a lawyer, you know that, Mom knows that. Why shouldn't he?" My anger boils over, and I don't break my dad's gaze.

"How dare you disrespect him in his own home?"

"Why is telling him what I'm passionate about disrespect-ful?" My voice comes out like a desperate plea, a plea for my dad to understand me. "I don't understand, Appa," I say quietly.

"Go to your room. I can't even look at you right now." My dad's voice is cold and unemotional, and without another word, he stalks into his study and slams the door behind him.

My mom guides me gently to the den and sits down next to me. "Honey, let's talk. What happened?"

Fat droplets create dark circles on the hem of my banana yellow blouse.

"I almost snapped."

"I'd say you did snap," she says, and chuckles in a comforting way.

"No, Appa cut me off and practically pushed me into my chair."

She nods slowly, sympathizing with me in silence.

"This is a lot for me, you know. No one told me about this part of the family. My strict, conservative grandparents, the secrets, the stories."

My mom frowns and cocks her head to the side. "What stories?"

"I've been asking you about Aunt Rebecca, why you two have such a sour relationship, why you never told me. You just said you grew apart, but now that we're here, it's clear something happened. And it isn't fair that you don't tell me these things. She's family, you know."

"I'm sorry, Melody, but you know, parents don't always tell their kids everything."

"Yeah, but you made me believe like what I knew *was* the full story. And . . ." My voice trails off, and I pause to consider if maybe I shouldn't say anything.

"And?"

I suck on the insides of my mouth for a moment longer. "And I found Appa's diary, from a long time ago. Before I was born. And he clearly used to be so in love with you. How could he just give you up, give *us* up like that? For what?"

I can tell from my mom's expression that she was not expecting that. "Oh boy. You better put it back, Mel. Your dad is not going to like that."

"How can you live with him after knowing he purposely stayed away from us for his own happiness? He hated cleaning houses more than he loved being with us."

Her eyes are wide with surprise. "You really studied that old thing, didn't you?"

I smile bitterly. "Honors Korean. It took so long. But I still don't understand most of it, and there aren't even a lot of entries. But I know he cleaned houses. I got that far."

She takes my hand in hers and pats it. "Sometimes, people make choices that others can't understand. Even their own family members. The things that go on in a human heart run so deep that oftentimes, only that one person knows how he truly feels. And even then, it's tricky."

"Can you please tell me what really happened between you and Eemo?" My anger has died down, but the frustration of not knowing hasn't.

"Just like your dad coming to Korea was his decision, your

aunt coming to Korea was also her decision. Rebecca's reasons for the choices she made are not mine to share, Mel. And you need to accept that. I shared your dad's side because he's your father. This is different, though."

My mom is so earnestly holding my hand, and I can tell she's made up her mind. Next to us, my phone starts buzzing on the coffee table. I open my messages, and it's Kimbeom saying he wants to get out of the house, away from his dad. As I'm about to flip over my phone, it lights up with a phone call: Wonjae Chae.

My mom playfully rubs my shoulders. "Hey, it's your crush," she says.

"He isn't my crush!"

"Sure, sweetie. I'll give you some privacy," she says, teasing. "Oh, and Melody, the diary?"

I scowl. "In my bookshelf, the third shelf on the way right, behind *Permanent Record.*"

She ruffles my hair, then picks up the empty cups on the table and walks out of the den. When I can no longer hear her footsteps, I finally answer.

"Hello?" I say, trying to sound casual, like boys are always calling me left and right.

"Hey, Mel. It's Wonjae."

"Yeah, I know." I hope he can tell that I'm smiling as I say this.

"So I actually can't meet tomorrow for our study session."

My face falls, and I try not to sound disappointed. "Oh, yeah, that's fine."

There's a pause on the other line. "I was wondering if you were free today instead?"

"Today?" I look at the clock. It's already 2:00 p.m.

"Yeah. I know it's a bit rushed and all, but—"

"Yeah, I'm free."

"Courtyard in half an hour?"

I nod even though he can't see me. "See you then."

"Oh, by the way, dress warmly. We're going to a different spot."

"Where?" I ask.

"Gyeongbokgung Palace."

"Where is that?"

"We're going to wear hanboks and take pictures and be true Korean and non-Korean tourists inside the palace grounds. It'll be relevant research for our project. It's in Jongro."

The thought of wearing hanboks actually sounds a little appalling, but also, maybe . . . fun? "I'm down to go and visit. But I don't know about wearing a hanbok."

"Why not?"

"Because."

"Because?"

"It just feels a little weird. It almost feels like cultural appropriation. I never grew up wearing hanboks, but now I'm going to wear one as a tourist because I'm wandering a palace? Feels shady."

"First of all, you're Korean. Second of all, it helps local businesses. Third of all, it's fun and it's not cultural appropriation. It's cultural exploration. Of your own culture. You've never worn a hanbok before, so aren't you at all curious?"

I am curious, but I stay quiet on the line.

"There's a famous hanok village right by the palace."

That's all he needs to say, and I'm sold. One second later,

I'm on the phone with Yura and explaining. "He just asked if I could meet him in thirty minutes."

"Oh my gosh, he's basically asking you out on a date, Mel. It's a Korean holiday—the biggest one of the year. It means something to couples, you know."

"Stop, I'm not thinking of it like that at all. Nothing's been confirmed, so we're still friends. For now."

"Say whatever you want. I'm not an idiot, either," she says.

"Anyway, you have to come with me, okay?"

"No way. I'm pretty sure he wants to be alone with you, Mel. Take the hint."

"Yura, please. We're not there yet, and honestly, I think it's going to be a little awkward. We've only studied in cafés or like, in brief moments at playgrounds or around the neighborhood. Never like this. If you don't come, I'm not going." I think of the night in Itaewon, our kiss at Octagon. Those times were different, though. We were under the influence, as they say.

"Oh my God, fine. But invite the others, too. I'm not third-wheeling."

"Just bring your boyfriend," I say, emphasizing the last word.

"So it can be a double date?" she asks with equal emphasis.

"I'm dragging Kimbeom along, too, since he wanted a distraction, anyway."

My plan works, and an hour later, we're crammed in a hanbok rental place and getting directed toward the many, many options. It feels endless. Racks and racks of colors, patterns, hair designs, and traditional purses surround me and Yura.

I slowly walk through the room, studying all the different hanbok options: I could match a black skirt with white floral print to a hot pink top, or a pale pink skirt to a navy top with a yellow print. There are so many color and pattern combinations—mostly all very vibrant—it feels overwhelming, in a magical way.

Finally, after much discussion with Yura, I settle on a navy skirt with a white print paired with a deep red top. Yura lands on a pale yellow skirt with a bright pink top. Hers looks more like the traditional colors, like the ones I see in posters around the area. In the dressing room, I have to wear a white undergarment first, and the woman who works there helps me into it and ties it tightly around my waist like a corset. The skirt is fitted around my waist and balloons out to the bottom, and the top is loose with long sleeves, and it ties together in the front with a bow. The ahjumma working there has to help me tie it, though, and I feel slightly less like a tourist when Yura also needs assistance tying hers, too. The fabric is slightly sheer, which is probably why we have to wear undergarments, but it feels very breathable and surprisingly comfortable. Just a little itchy.

The woman flatters us, saying how cute we look and how when we're young everything looks so beautiful on us. It feels like a backhanded compliment, but I take it and thank her politely. We get directed to the hair area, and a different ahjumma does our hair and we each choose an accessory for her to clip in. By the end of it, I feel like Korean royalty in a K-drama.

"Ta-da!" Yura says as we exit the dressing room and meet the boys. "You guys can be our manservants today."

The guys' hanboks look different; they're all long sleeve as well, but they're wearing puffy pants that look like Aladdin's. When we start walking, I see the palace, even from afar.

"Wow," I say as we get closer. "How does a big-ass palace like this just exist in the middle of the city?"

"Korea's big on cultural preservation," Wonjae explains. "This was the main palace during the Joseon dynasty, and it was built in—"

"The fourteenth century, I know," I say. "I'm in the Korean Honors class *with* you, you know," I tease.

"Guess you don't need a tutor, then, if you know everything," he says in a tight voice.

I brush off his comment and poke him playfully. "What I need is someone to take photos of me and Yura." I feel ridiculous walking around the palace grounds in our colorful outfits. The five of us must look so funny, but the deeper we go into the palace, the more we see others dressed in hanboks as well. The normalcy of it makes it funnier, and I allow myself to enjoy it. You just need to own these moments.

As we walk through the grounds, Kimbeom, in typical fashion, whips out his phone and snaps selfies with all of us. He seems to be in a much better mood than yesterday, and I want to ask him if he's okay, but sometimes, bringing up difficult topics isn't always the right answer. And today—or at least right now—what Kimbeom needs is a distraction. A fun day with his friends.

The palace is different from how I'd ordinarily imagine a place where royals once lived; it looks more like individual homes all built next to each other, with separate entrances for all. It's not a huge castle-like structure, where there's one grand entrance and then all the millions of rooms are connected. It's just as beautiful, though, and everything looks like it's mostly made from wood. The roofs look similar to those of the hanoks I saw in Ikseon-dong and Gangneung. Until coming here, I never knew I cared so much about roofs. Most of the rooms are furnished sparingly—there are some Buddha statues, mats for the temple and prayer rooms, old paintings hung on the walls, and some low tables. That's about it. My favorite part of the palace grounds is a square pond surrounded by trees. I imagine it would look beautiful during the early fall or spring months when surrounded by changing leaves or new flowers.

"Go pose there!" Yura demands.

There's a loose vine hanging from a tree, so I tug at it and pretend to be a fairy in the forest.

"Finger hearts!" she instructs.

Finger heart poses are everywhere in Korea, from TV shows and celebrities to students taking selfies. I cross my thumb with the side of my index finger at the first knuckle, with my other fingers closed into a fist, so that the outline of my thumb and finger form a tiny heart. It doesn't *really*, but it's close enough. I've also seen it in America, too. I never really cared about seeing random celebrities do this pose or paid much attention to pop culture in general.

I stick out my finger-heart pose toward the camera. Junghoon, Wonjae, and Kimbeom all jump in and pose with me as Yura snaps photos of all of us being silly. When we're finished taking pictures with different combinations of people and a few (okay, *many*) selfies later, we go visit the palace café, an obvious tourist addition and definitely not built in the fourteenth century. Kimbeom, Junghoon, and Yura scope out seats while Wonjae and I stand in line to grab drinks and snacks for everyone.

"Are you learning a lot about Korea so far?" he asks.

"Nothing I didn't already know from our Korean class, but it's still cool to see it in person."

"I never said anything about bringing the others, by the way," he says lightly.

"Oh. I—" I open my mouth to finish saying something but close it instead because nothing comes to mind.

He shrugs. "It's fine. Not a big deal." He sounded like he meant it, but if it really was fine, why would he mention it? Maybe Yura was right.

"Sorry," I mumble.

"Don't be. What are you ordering? We're up next."

I distract myself from reading too much into this by focusing on the menu instead. After ordering, we wander the café until we find the others. For the rest of the day, Wonjae doesn't say much to me. I can't figure out if I'm overanalyzing or if he really is kind of cold-shouldering me. I wish I could tell him I didn't mean to offend him, that I actually would love to hang out with just him, but I chicken out.

Yura breaks my train of thought when she clears her throat. "So, we were going to keep this a secret, but I already told Mel, so we'll share with you two as well. Junghoon and I are official!" She says this with so much delight, but the others just laugh. "Okay, see, *this* is why I needed a girlfriend like Melody. Does no one care?" She pouts.

"We don't not care, Yura. We're just not surprised," Kimbeom says. "It's about time you two made it official. You think no one saw you and Junghoon dancing at Octagon or your 'secret' texting whenever we're all together? You send a message and then suddenly Junghoon's on his phone." Kimbeom laughs and puts his arms around the both of them. "But we *are* happy for you, and we love you. Better?"

Yura turns up her nose. "It was *not* that obvious," she says.

"But whatever, I'm happy. And Junghoon is obviously happy."
We look at him, and he just takes her hand. It must be really
nice to have a boyfriend who's so different when he's just with
you. To be the only one who sees that side of him. Eventually,
we all return our hanboks and find a bench to sit on. We're a
domino effect of leaning heads: I lean on Kimbeom, he leans
on Yura, she leans on Junghoon, and Junghoon leans his head
on Wonjae. I wish someone would take a picture of us right
now.

"What now?" I ask.

"Sorry, chingoos, Hoonee and I are going on a date tonight,"
Yura says.

"Ugh, you have a nickname for him already?" I say, but it's
endearing. I've never seen friends become boyfriend and girlfriend before. I think about what it would be like if the same
thing happened with Wonjae and me. I wonder if we'd have fun
wandering Garosugil or Ikseon-dong again, or maybe an amusement park. I wonder if he'd put his arm around my waist or if
we'd hold hands or link arms.

Kimbeom is quiet before he speaks. "I have dinner with my
mom, actually. I think she wants to talk to me in person without
the pressure of my dad coming home, or the maids listening."

"Good luck, man. If it helps, I always thought your mom
was really chill. I'm sure she's on your side," Wonjae says
encouragingly.

"Thanks," he replies. "What are you doing?"

Wonjae shakes his head. "Nothing now, I guess. My grandfather had some work trip and the driver couldn't come from
the airport to get me in time, so I'm just going to take the long
way home tonight and enjoy the view."

I try to be as casual as I can. "I'll take the long way home with you. I'm headed home, too."

"Oh. We might as well split a cab, then."

I try not to show my disappointment.

"Or we can do it Melody-style and take the bus," he suggests, seemingly reading my face.

I'd be happier about this little win, but his suggestion doesn't come with much enthusiasm. I try to make up for my earlier misstep with extra pep in my voice. "Yay! Let's do it."

Everyone says goodbye, and Wonjae and I wait for the bus that takes us to Hannam O-guri. We don't say much; he spends half the time on his phone, and I'm not really used to being the first to initiate conversation with him, so I also just look at my phone and play *Candy Crush*. When two passengers get off, we slide into their long seat. His hands drop to his sides, so very close to my own fingers.

"So what are your plans this week?" I ask.

"Just study. Tutor you, work on the Korean project, and prep for midterms. My mom wants us to have dinner together tonight, so that," he says, not peeling his eyes from his phone.

I gather a single ounce of boldness and slide my fingers so that they touch his. Definitely not even close to holding hands, but I feel it—the spark. I want to hold his hand, but before I even have time to contemplate if I have that kind of audacity, he pulls his hands up and crosses his arms. "What about you?" he asks.

I blush, embarrassed. Did he do that on purpose? "Same. Being tutored by you and also preparing for all the exams and working on the Korean project. Should we meet up and start building things out? Sometime this week?"

He smiles faintly. "Yeah, maybe this week."

On the walk home, Wonjae keeps the conversation light and polite, so I can't even say he's being cold or off. But I feel it. It's different, and I don't know what changed. But by the end of the walk, I know I definitely care. I pull out my phone to text Soph. Boy talk might help ease whatever tension is happening with Soph, too. And I miss her.

> soph. big news. i think i'm kind of into someone.

> wanna talk soon?

> miss you

When we reach the courtyard where the buildings split off, he gives me a casual wave. "We can pick a day this weekend to study more, since today was more research for our Korean project."

I nod. "Text me when?"

Wonjae's hands are in his pockets, and he jerks his head by way of a nod. "See ya."

As happy as we look in all the photos we took today, I feel uneasy when I'm back home. I wish he was more excited at the prospect of tutoring me.

TWENTY-ONE

On Thursday morning, I lie in bed, cherishing the lazy day I didn't get to have yesterday. Despite the airy light flowing into my room from the long window and the degree of reconciliation I felt with my mom yesterday, I still wake up feeling frustrated and uncomfortable. My dad's blaringly loud voice yelling at me after my grandparents' lunch echoes throughout my mind, and I throw a pillow over my face to try and drown it out. But when I do, I think of Wonjae; I think of his subtle but noticeable irritation that I invited the others. Yura was definitely right on this one. My mom, who enjoys lounging at home as much as I do, messages me from her bedroom saying she needs to go buy groceries and will be home by the afternoon. And that there's food for me to heat up courtesy of the ahjumma.

is appa home?

UMMA
he has a lunch meeting but will be

home for dinner.

does he hate me now

UMMA
it'll be okay. he's not angry.

i'll talk to him when he's home okay?

I check my phone for new messages since I still haven't heard from Soph. I open our chatroom, and there's still a little red *1* next to my message, indicating that she hasn't seen it yet. I sigh and pull out *Hamilton* from my shelf and prop up my pillows to create an ideal reading nook. It's a thick book with images and stories detailing the making of the musical, and I think of Sophia as I peruse the pages. I wonder how auditions have been for her.

I get out of bed eventually and hear the shower running in the master bedroom. When I put my book back, I notice that my dad's journal is not on my shelf anymore. Guess my mom took it like she said she would. When I get to my parents' bedroom, I'm sitting on the white linen ottoman at the foot of their bed when a phone vibration on the console catches my eye. My mom's phone lights up with a message. It's Rebecca Eemo. I look through the crack of the closed sliding doors that lead into the master bathroom. I wait for a few seconds, and when the water continues to run, I grab her phone and slide it open. It's unlocked. It's impulsive and I'll probably get caught eventually, but for now, this is what I have to do. I'm careful to not click the Kakao message from her so it doesn't show up as read and instead go into my mom's contacts list to get her phone number. The water stops running, and panic floods through me as I quietly rush to the desk where the pens are. I scribble down the number, press the back arrow a million times, turn off the screen, and put it exactly back where it was. My heart is pounding, but my mom doesn't seem to hear anything outside the bathroom. If she comes out now, she'll definitely be able to tell I'm hiding something, so I quickly rush back into my room and stay inside until my mom shouts at me that she's leaving. I shout back a "bye" and get my phone, dialing the number on the back of my hand.

A handful of pleas, a lot of convincing arguments, and one hour later, I'm waiting inside Plants Flowers Coffee—a small garden-like café near our apartment—one I know my parents don't frequent. My hands are folded together, pressing on each other in nervous anticipation. As the bell tinkles at the top, I see my aunt walking in through the glass door. I wave to her from my seat and she smiles, making her way over. Hers is a face I don't know very well, yet feel strangely familiar with. I think that's what family must be; the assurance that even though you go a long time not ever really having known someone deeply, when you do meet them, there's an unspoken bond that draws you together.

"Hey, you," my eemo says, plopping her bag down on the seat next to hers. She's wearing a dark brown teddy coat and black leggings with black boots that have thin heels and pointed toes. "I'll get us coffee. What do you want?"

I suddenly feel a little shy, meeting her alone like this. "Um, can I have a hot caramel latte, please?"

She nods and five minutes later is back with our drinks. As she gets settled into her chair, she looks at me the way an adult eyes a mischievous child. "I can't believe I let you talk me into this. Your mom is not going to be happy that we met behind her back, you know."

"I know. But she's not going to tell me your story. Is that just a thing here?"

My eemo looks at me, confused. "Is what a thing?"

"Secrets in Korean families."

I'm being serious, but she just laughs. "I don't think secrets are unique to Korean families, Mel."

"Not Korean families, families *in* Korea. There's a difference. I was part of a Korean-American family in New York, and my life was nothing like this."

Again, my eemo laughs, so I silently pick up my mug and sip on my latte.

"Okay, what secrets?" she asks.

"Why do you and Mom hate each other so much?"

My aunt looks at her phone and mindlessly flips it over so the screen is facedown on the white oak table. "Look, Solmi—"

I cut her off before I hear another excuse to add to the pile of family secrets. "Please. Eemo, my own mom won't tell me anything. And I have a right to know. I've asked her a thousand times."

"What'd your mom say?"

I stick my lips out like a fish, thinking about what she said to me yesterday after the debacle at the grandparents'.

"Something about it not being her choice to explain because she's not the one that made that decision." The melted caramel balances out the otherwise slightly bitter latte, and I lick the coat of caramel on my lips.

Aunt Rebeca sighs and I sit up a little straighter; I can tell she's going to say something more helpful than anything my parents have shared with me so far, which isn't much to begin with. "For the record, we don't hate each other, kiddo. Okay. So you know how your mom wanted to be a singer when she was younger?"

My eyes go round. "She *what*?"

"Oh, damn it. Don't tell your mom. I had no idea she never told you that." My aunt looks flustered and hesitant to continue.

All the times I used to sit in front of the bathroom door and listen to her sing, the times I'd be getting ready to meet my friends and she'd be humming in the kitchen. The moments I'd try to sing and she'd harmonize with me, always making me sound much better than I actually was. My mind is doing a flipbook montage of these singing moments. What I always believed to be a simple hobby suddenly has so much more meaning, a series of blurred images brought sharply into focus.

I gather my thoughts and look straight at my aunt. "It's fine," I lie. It's not fine at all. How could she have never told me? I try to bury the hurt I feel so I can listen to the rest of Aunt Rebecca's story.

"We used to do it together. We'd perform at church or sometimes in coffee shops, if we got lucky enough. My mom—your grandmother—was really against it. We were a typical immigrant family, so she wanted us to pursue a more stable path."

"Just like my mom wants for me," I say, half joking, half bitter.

"Well, you are a daughter of an immigrant family," she says pointedly.

"But how could my own mother not understand me when she's the one who *was* me, however many years ago?"

"It's *because* she was you. She just doesn't want you to have to live a difficult life," my aunt says, but the way she says it makes me think she's talking more about herself.

I know the immigrant family story. Your parents or grandparents brought the entire family to America, started over with nothing, gave up their dreams so that you could have it all. Therefore, you are indebted to them for eternity. I've heard it many times. I put my coffee back down on the table and fold a napkin in half. "The whole point of the American Dream is to bring your children into a country that celebrates individual pursuits and encourages dream-chasing so they can have everything you couldn't. But even though they supposedly want to give you everything, parents limit their children and carve out a narrow path to force them on instead. Didn't they immigrate so their children could have choices they didn't have? A choice to pursue a path that genuinely makes us happy? Why bother coming—I mean"—I stop as I remember once again where I am—"going—in the first place, then?"

Aunt Rebecca shakes her head. "You aren't forced to walk the path they made for you. But pursuing your own dreams comes at a certain cost, and you have to decide if you're willing to pay it. It's hard for them to understand, because it's a luxury they never had. And if you knew what your parents went through so you can have all this, you wouldn't be saying everything you just said with that attitude."

I chew my lips and think before I speak. She has that same adult look that I always dread receiving from my parents. "O-okay . . ." I say, choosing my next words carefully, "so were you willing to pay the price of pursuing singing?"

My aunt lets out another loud sigh, as if she knows she's

going to regret what she's about to tell me. I come to the edge of my seat, back straight, ready to hear. "Lily wasn't telling you why we stopped talking because I'm the one that wronged her. We were both attending the City University of New York when she got pregnant with you. Your mom enjoyed school so much more than I did," my aunt says, smiling fondly, "and she convinced me to go to CUNY with her so we could perform together. Well, that's what she said, but I knew it was because she wanted me to get a degree." My aunt hesitates before she continues, and I gently place my hand on hers.

"And then?" I press politely.

"Then, when she had you, she decided to stop singing so she could get a normal salaried job and raise you responsibly." Her eyes get misty, and she chokes a little as she opens her mouth. I wait for her as she patiently gets a tissue out of her purse and dabs at her eyes. "Melody, I care about you so deeply."

"I know you do," I answer naturally. Sure, we've met less than five times in my life, but I feel it. That's the family bond thing.

"Okay. When Lily told me she was giving up on singing, I was so angry with her. I was only twenty-one at the time, so my maturity wasn't at an all-time high there. I dropped out of CUNY and moved to Seoul to pursue my singing career. I felt abandoned by my family at the time—my mom was against us so much she said she'd stop talking to us until we gave up on our foolish dreams, and now I'd lost my sister and singing partner."

I'm at a loss for words so I sit there, trying to find the right thing to say. I see a tear droplet form a circle on the napkin in front of my aunt.

"I didn't realize I was the one abandoning them. By the time I saw what a huge mistake I had made, years had gone by, and I just didn't have it in me to reach out."

My aunt was the one who left when my mom needed her the most. It wasn't just a casual "we drifted apart"; it was abandonment and betrayal.

My voice is quiet. "Is that why my mom—"

"Didn't tell you? Yeah, knowing Lily. She didn't want to make me look bad." She smiles bitterly. "It was an irreparable hurt that I inflicted on your mom, leaving her like that at age twenty-three with her first child. I should have been there. Should have helped her raise you. We had only lived in the States for a few years by then, and it still hadn't felt like home to either of us. And after all these years, you know, I just got uncomfortable even seeing her."

I think of how lonely my mom must have felt. I look my aunt straight in the eye, careful to see if she tries to hide something else. "Do you know why we came now? Why now, why not years ago?"

She averts her gaze for a half second.

"You *do*!"

My aunt nearly jumps out of her seat, and I see several heads turning in my direction in disapproval. "Oh gosh, that was loud."

"Sorry. But you *tried* just now to pretend like you didn't know, right? Please, can you tell me? No one else will."

I know I'm pushing my luck with everything she's already told me, but hey, if I convinced her to tell me all of that, what's one more thing?

"It was Mom's wish. Well, my mom."

"Halmoni?" I think of my mom and grandma's last conversation before we came to Korea, in that room with the doors closed. So I guess that part *was* my mom telling me the full truth about Grandma.

"She's been asking your mom every year, actually, to consider coming to Korea to mend things, but I think only this year your mom saw how much us being distant had taken a toll on your halmoni's health. But for us, I guess it's been so long since we saw and talked to each other that it felt easier to keep living this way." My aunt doesn't make eye contact with me, and I get a sense that she feels ashamed.

I try to sound as encouraging as possible. "I don't think it's ever too late."

Her eyes soften and she shakes her head. "I think I shared too much with you. Listen, I'm going to talk to your mom first, okay? You think you can keep this conversation between us until then?"

Disappointment passes through me as I nod my head. I was hoping I could run home and apologize to my mom and tell her everything I now knew. If only she had told me, I wouldn't have been so cold to her, blaming her for moving us to Korea, for trying to hide her sister's selfish decision, for listening to her mom even when she was the one who had been wronged. "Of course," I say brightly. I can almost see the tension easing from my aunt's shoulders.

My aunt takes my hand and squeezes it. "Thanks, Sol. It won't be for that long, okay?"

"No one's called me Sol before," I tell her.

"Oh. Do you prefer Melody instead?"

I shake my head, grinning up at her. "No, I like it."

"Good. A new nickname just between us."

"What can I call you?"

"Some of my close friends call me Reba."

I grin at her. "So what about Reba Eemo?"

She nods. "Works for me. Reba and Sol. Got a good ring to it."

I love my mom, but Reba Eemo is definitely cooler. With every passing minute, she feels guiltier that we're meeting without my mom's knowledge, so after we finish our drinks, we share one matcha croissant and head our separate ways. I'm less sad and anxious than I was the last, more dramatic time we parted, because it's different now. She has my number and I have hers. As I walk back to our villa, I remind myself not to say a word of this to my mom until she mentions it first.

My mom is still out, but my dad is in the den with a thick law book—his idea of leisure reading. I don't think we've ever been in the apartment together without my mom, and we haven't talked since yesterday's debacle at my grandparents' place, so I don't know what's going on in his Strict Korean Dad mind. I walk into the den tentatively. "Hi, Appa."

He looks startled to see me, then equally uncomfortable, which is actually relieving. "Oh, you were out? Did you have a good time?"

I freeze, hoping he won't ask any more questions. "Yep," I say. It's the safest answer. I guess he thought I was in my room. I stand awkwardly in the den, somewhat waiting for him to bring up yesterday's incident. Instead, he's perusing the book in front of him. Finally, he looks up at me as if wondering what I'm doing hovering over him.

"You may join me if you'd like," he says, gesturing to the round grande swivel chair next to him.

I consider bringing it up first, but I don't see the point. "Sure." I plop down and get my phone out, letting the silence between us gradually feel normal.

I look through photos of the HT Chingoos in our hanboks from Gyeongbokgung. I'm giggling to myself over a particularly bad photo when, most unexpectedly, my dad appears behind the swivel chair and sees a picture of me and Kimbeom, posing back to back with our arms crossed. We don't look as tough as we tried to look, and the next photo is just us laughing.

"That's a good picture," he says. I turn around. "Did I scare you again?" he asks. He's holding two cups of water, and places mine on the coffee table.

I nod and flip my phone over so the screen isn't showing.

"Did you go to the palace?"

"Yesterday." There's a very pregnant pause as we both register what this means. *Yes, Dad, right after you yelled at me because I told Grandpa about my dreams for my life.*

When he doesn't respond, I stand up to go to my room.

"Solmi." He looks nervous, which is completely unfamiliar territory for me.

"Yeah?" I ask.

"Did you like wearing the hanbok?"

I blink, unsure how I feel about his unexpected question. "It was a little itchy, but I liked the colors a lot. And the floral designs."

"Can you send me that picture of you wearing it?" Another question I wasn't expecting.

In the past month and a half of living in one household, there are certain habits I've gotten accustomed to with my dad. He reads a lot. In the mornings, he's always off to work, and if he makes it home for dinner, he's always reading the Korean paper before my mom serves him food. He's stoic, and the few times I've seen a less stoic side to him is when he's talking to my mom. But moments like him asking for a picture of me are the times I realize how awkward and estranged our relationship feels at the core of it all. We care, but we don't know how to show it. Maybe my mom never sent a lot of our New York photos to him. Maybe he never asked.

"Sure," I answer.

TWENTY-TWO

On Friday morning, I check my phone. Finally, a message from Sophia.

SOPH
hey, sorry. free to talk tonight
(ny time) if you are.

I video-call her, determined to ease whatever tension there's been between us lately. I think it's just not having enough time to chat face-to-face. Her face fills my screen, and I flail my free hand excitedly.

"HI, SOPH!"

"Hi!"

"I feel like I haven't seen your face in years."

"Yeah, definitely."

We quickly exhaust all the usual subjects and things still feel a little off, but not enough to say anything. It's the worst kind of discomfort, when you can't mention it because you come off like you're being overly sensitive, which I might be. But this is Sophia Taye—my best friend and diaper buddy.

"Soph?" I ask, partly just to fill the painful silence.

"Hmm?"

"Is everything okay?" I try to say it with a mix of genuine concern and lightness.

"Of course, why wouldn't they be?"

I force a smile. "I dunno. Do you feel like we just haven't talked as much lately?"

"I think it's been fine." Sophia is a master at sounding casual but never really showing how she might be feeling. Not right away, at least.

I suppress a frustrated sigh. "How have auditions been?" My voice is more chipper than I feel.

"It's just been. I haven't booked anything, and I got another rejection. But I auditioned for a side character role in a bigger production, so that'd be really cool." My shoulders relax as Soph talks about her auditions. Whenever she talks about plays and performing, there's a wonderful sparkle in her eye. I imagine that's how others see me and my passion for design. Or at least I hope.

"I hope you get it. What's the play about?"

"It's about transcultural experiences. A Latina family that adopts a Japanese girl, and the Japanese girl's closest friend, who she treats like a little sister, is Black, which is the role I auditioned for. I think it'd be really amazing to be a part of it."

"That *would* be amazing. When do you find out?"

"I think they'll do callbacks sometime next week, so we'll see. Do you think you'll be in New York soon?"

I bite my lip, thinking about the actual possibility. "I hope so.

I mean, the next two weeks basically determines it. I hope I do."

"Me too," Soph says, and for a moment, everything feels normal. "You can say bye to your life in Seoul and come back to New York for good. It's better here anyway," she adds, and I know she's teasing, but I'm surprised to find that I feel defensive.

"Yeah," I say, forcing a laugh.

"Things with your parents are good?"

"I guess . . . ? I never really know." How do I explain everything I have bottled up in me through a phone conversation? "Soph, do you ever feel like you don't really know anything about your dad from when he was younger? Like how he and your mom met, how he felt through years of raising you alone . . . all of that?"

She looks off to the side. "No, not really. My dad pretty much told me everything, and we don't really have secrets. Like you and your mom."

Right. Me and my mom.

I vaguely update Soph on Wonjae but don't mention the kissing portion. She doesn't sound super interested, so it's more of an awkward "I think I might be into this guy and I'll keep you posted" than it is me gushing about all the things I've been thinking lately. It's late in New York anyway, so we hang up shortly after and I pull out my sketchbook to draw away my anxious thoughts. I create a living room—a spacious one that opens into a gorgeous backyard—and finish it off by drawing a white picket fence and beautiful windowsills. It's what I imagine the American Dream would have looked like through the eyes of my New York grandma.

An email notification jolts me out of my drawing, and when I move my mouse around to light up my screen, I see an email from our AP World History teacher regarding our recent essay assignment. It's an update that our online portal for SIA has our grades in them, and I eagerly open mine: an A-. I smile widely, hardly able to contain my excitement. I finally got an A-! Even though it's not the midterm, my goal for New York feels a little more attainable.

I open Kakao and type a message to Wonjae letting him know about my small win. He congratulates me and says he got a B+, and I gloat teasingly. I want to keep talking but I don't know what to talk about; I don't think Wonjae is still annoyed that I invited others on an outing he had only intended for us, but maybe if I recreate an opportunity for it to be just us two, it'll make everything better. There must be a place the two of us can go together. I rush to my desk and pull out a crumpled piece of paper from my study hall notebook. When I was bored last week, I wrote out a list of places I'd like to eventually explore in Seoul. Some of them are museums and art galleries, but my eyes go down to number six: Lotte World. An amusement park would be the perfect place to go during school break and seems like a safe in-between of "going as friends" to maybe a little bit more.

wanna go to lotte world?

WONJAE
today?

i've never been and you can teach me
more korean

WONJAE

not sure an amusement park qualifies
as a proper study session . . .

well neither did dressing up
and going to a palace

WONJAE

arguably more than lotte world . . .

😢 come on, it'll be fun

WONJAE

lol ok. I'm game. Meet everyone
out front in an hour?

Everyone? I'm trying to subtly type out "No, just us two," when a message from Wonjae appears in the group chat and my shoulders slump in disappointment. He's already told the others in the HT Chingoos chat that we're going to Lotte World and everyone better come. For a brief moment today, I had considered: Maybe, if the vibe is just right, I would tell him today, in line or while we eat snacks or after the adrenaline rush of a fun roller coaster, that I might like him. That I do like him. But any hope of that has now been shunted aside. Everyone agrees to meet in the courtyard, and Yura tells us her driver can take us.

YURA

don't forget to wear your uniforms! 🔥

wait, what? why??

YURA

it's a thing here, you New Yorker. 😜 just wear it!

I grumble loudly to myself but throw on my uniform. I consider telling Yura that she was right all along and that today I was considering finally talking to Wonjae, but I can't bring myself to. Especially when he's being weird and distant with me. Imagine telling him and having him respond with zero interest while Yura eagerly waits for updates from her crushed friend. Mortifying.

Lotte World ends up being much farther than a lot of the other places I've gone to in Seoul. When we arrive, at first glance, it just looks like a huge department store. It already feels so different than any other theme park I've been to. To get to the few restaurants in front of the amusement park entrance, we pass by shoe stores, clothing stores, stationery stores, and a lot of toy shops. The building is also connected to Jamsil Station, so there's a lot of foot traffic, and the others expertly weave their way through the bustling crowds shopping on a long holiday weekend.

"Not everyone here is going to Lotte World, right?" I ask.

"Nope," Junghoon answers. "There's more here than just the amusement park." He reaches down and casually grabs Yura's hand, and I'm hit with a pang of jealousy.

Yura smiles coyly at him and turns her head sideways toward me. "Yeah, there are a ton of stores and restaurants. And the outside area is called Magic Island and also has movie theaters and more stores outside the amusement park itself."

It's a very strange concept; to me, amusement parks were always the ultimate destination, not just a part of one bigger attraction. It'd be like going to Six Flags and not actually going to Six Flags. I follow our group, and after we pay for our admissions tickets, we enter through the indoor portion of the amusement park through a short escalator. It doesn't feel like we're indoors, though, because the ceiling is so high. There's even a monorail that takes you to the outdoor part, which Kimbeom explains to me.

"Whoa," I say, looking up at the faraway ceiling, "a hot air balloon ride in an indoor amusement park. It's like an oxymoron."

"First things first. I need to find buttered squid," Yura says.

"What?"

"It's so good, Mel. It's a little nutty, and really buttery, and I'm pretty sure it's not real squid. But it's addicting." We find a cart that sells it, and she forces a piece into my mouth without ceremony. Wonjae buys a bag, too, claiming one is never enough.

"Holy moly," I say, savoring the buttery goodness. I end up eating more than half the bag of possibly fake squid with Yura as we scope out the shortest lines for rides. Wonjae laughs as I eat bite after bite and steal some of his, too. My heart flutters and I walk a little closer to him.

We choose the Viking ride since a ton of people fit on the giant swinging ship at once, and are about to get in line for it when I see a shop full of headbands. It looks like the Disneyland headbands that people wear, with the mouse ears, but ten times cuter. "Wait, I need to look at those." I drag the others with me and try on the ears that come as hairclips. Some of the headbands are even little balloons that are like antennae on your head. We each pick one out and put them on. It's only a few thousand won, so I convince the others to buy them. "Let me have the full experience!" I plead.

"True. What's a day at Lotte World without Lotty and Lorry ears?" Junghoon adds.

"Lotty and Lorry?"

"The mascots. You'll see them eventually. They're the animals that are all over the carts and stuff. It's all very cheesy."

I grin at Junghoon. "Look at this rapport we've established," I say, and he rolls his eyes. "Okay, Lotty and Lorry ears it is," I say, grabbing a different headband and putting my new Lorry ones on my head. Yura and Kimbeom settle on matching hair clips with a sunflower poking out the top and then force Junghoon to buy a headband with sparkling red hearts that balance on springs.

"You have to choose one, too," I say to Wonjae.

Yura chimes in. "Pick one for him!"

I blush. "Maybe this one?" I grab a matching Lotty headband and put it on him. He lets me, and I'm acutely aware of how close our bodies are.

"Works for me," he says, and pays for it before I have a chance to offer to buy it for him. But I'm happy enough. Secret couple headbands.

While we stand in line, I notice the swarms of couples everywhere. They look like my age, some older, some even younger. A lot of the couples that look my age are wearing matching sneakers, matching sweaters, and even matching backpacks. My mind flips back to when I first met Junghoon and the couple bracelets incident. I look at Wonjae. He was himself from the moment he met me. I can't believe I'm thinking this, but I kind of wish I had a matching sweater to wear with him. I see some cute ones, although most of them are super cheesy. Some are just normal clothes, no couple-y signs on the sweaters or backpacks.

Coming to an amusement park during a national Korean holiday was probably not my smartest idea, and the lines drag on for over an hour.

"Hey, why'd you tell us to wear our uniforms?" I ask Yura while we wait, only now realizing how many other students are all in uniforms. "No one's at school this week, right?"

She nods. "Yeah, because of Chuseok. A lot of people wear uniforms to Lotte World. It's just a thing here. That's what we do."

"Curiouser and curiouser."

"Okay, Lewis Carroll. There are a ton of rental places here, kind of like when we wore hanboks at the palace. People who don't go to public schools or private schools with uniforms actually come and rent school uniforms to wear."

"Like even adults?"

Kimbeom tilts his head to one side as if he's just realizing how strange that seems and nods. "Even adults. Maybe they miss the days of their youth."

"Maybe their boyfriends are into the uniform look," Wonjae adds, wiggling his eyebrows suggestively.

"Don't be gross," I say to him as the line lurches forward.

After a few adrenaline-filled rides, we go to one of the many cafés for a break. The one we pick serves bubble tea, and we all settle into stools shaped like fun, patterned mushrooms. Considering it's inside an amusement park, the decor is impressive. Parts of the walls are bookshelves, sparsely filled with books sorted by color, Lotte World sculptures, and framed pictures of celebrities with the amusement park mascots. Besides the mushroom stools, some chairs are more like swings, suspended by thick ropes around ivory tables.

We're sipping on our drinks peacefully when Kimbeom breaks the comfortable silence. "My mom threatened to leave my dad."

We all turn to look at him, shocked.

"What?" I ask, almost choking on a tapioca ball.

"Your mom would do that?" Yura asks.

He shrugs. "It might be just to scare him a little. Her family was more powerful than his when they got married, and I think they still are. It'd objectively be more of a loss to him if they divorced, so she told him that he needs to apologize to me and take back his boarding school threat or else my mom will leave him."

"Jeez, it's like a soap opera," I say. "Well, you deserve that apology."

Kimbeom doesn't want to spend a lot of time talking about this, so we take the tram to Magic Island. There are fewer rides outside, which I find ironic since there's technically more space out here, at least vertically. While we're in line for something called Comet Express, Yura shares her sudden need for dakkochi.

"More street food?" I ask.

She nods. "Junghoon-ah, let's go get some for everyone together." He puts his arm around her waist and they walk off. The familiar ache of envy fills me up, and I sneak a glance at Wonjae, but he's busy on his phone. I stand up taller and look at his screen discreetly.

WONJAE

lol. yeah, i could go over tonight,
but not until later.

SAEHA

😧 can't you come now?

WONJAE

no, i'm busy right now.
let's meet for coffee another day
if that works better?

SAEHA

no, i want you to come over tonight. 🍑

I quickly avert my eyes, realizing too late that I shouldn't have been prying. My face feels hot, but it's not because I'm embarrassed. My jealousy goes from zero to one hundred in a second, and my heart feels like it just hit a rock. It's too late. I know I shouldn't have read his romantic evening plans with whoever this Saeha girl is, but I did, and now any willpower I had in me to flirt with him, my hopes of finding a moment to tell him how I might feel, all seem useless and stupid. I've never heard of this girl before in any of our conversations, and nobody mentioned Wonjae was seeing someone. Yura would've definitely said something to me if he was. And come on, a peach emoji? My heart feels a mix of annoyance at this stranger I've never met and disappointment that I missed my chance. I should have been honest with him at the palace or the bus ride home. I try to peer at his screen again, but Kimbeom catches me looking at Wonjae's phone, and I bite my lip in embarrassment when Kimbeom cracks up laughing.

Wonjae puts it away in his back pocket. "What's so funny?"

Kimbeom shakes his head. "Nothing. I'm just laughing thinking about how fun Comet Express is going to be."

I don't get a chance to read what he said back, but I pray it's not a matched enthusiasm to go see her. The line barely moves, and the only happy couple in our group comes back with too much food, so while the others eat, I grab my phone out of my bag and message Sophia.

> hi bestie, here's an update on the guy i
> said i like.

> i still like him, but he's likely hooking up
> with another girl today

> wish i could talk to you

> i shouldn't have pried but i saw his
> phone at this place we're at and
> ughasdjklewfjnsd

We're almost at the front of the line when my phone buzzes multiple times.

SOPH
where are you?

sorry girl if it helps men come and go . . .

Lotte World. it's an amusement park.

yura and junghoon are the only happy
couple here now

they're so cute and i'm sad and jealous

I stare at my phone to see if Soph responds, but after two minutes, I put it away as we approach the front of the line. Each car allows two people, so I try to strategically place myself in the line so that I'll be in the same car as Wonjae. It doesn't work, and I end up with Kimbeom, and he nudges me the entire ride, teasing me about secretly reading Wonjae's phone.

"Jealous, are we?" he jokes.

"I just think it's tasteless that a girl would send a peach emoji to a guy, okay? I mean, have some dignity."

"Mm-hmm."

The ride is fun, if a little dizzying, which is a good distraction for me. After a handful more rides with extremely long lines, the sun has set and the sky is a beautiful shade of blue-gray. We don't feel the need to eat a real sit-down dinner since we've been snacking all day, and when we think to check the time, it's already 9:00 p.m. The day has flown by, and I try to sit next to Wonjae in all the rides whenever I can. I wish I could tell him how I feel, but what if he's over me? He's already talking to another girl, and it's because I never told him how I felt. Even when I'm happy to be next to him, one thought of Saeha and I feel like my stomach is being squeezed by a hanbok corset.

We walk at a slower pace toward the indoor entrance,

exhausted by the activities of the day. "Do we want to get drinks?" Yura asks.

Wonjae shrugs. "I might turn in early," he says.

I blurt out something I never thought I'd say. "Let's get matching shirts." My friends stare at me, waiting for an explanation.

"Memories and all that," I say, feeling cheesy. It'll be my way of holding on to tonight and all the hopes of what could have been.

Yura giggles. "I'm in. And always down for couple clothes," she says, grinning wide.

The other boys protest loudly but eventually capitulate. The words replay in my head. *Let's get matching shirts.* There's a sentence New York Melody would never have said.

The air is getting colder now, but before we head in, we stay outside a little longer to see all the twinkling lights. There's something magical about outdoor parks at night when all the lights come on. There's a bridge on Magic Island where you can see the lake, and we walk there to take in the full view of the evening lights. Ten minutes later, the nighttime wind makes our faces feel like they're about to fall off, and we huddle together for warmth.

After weaving in and out through crowds of students in high school uniforms or imposters in rented uniforms, we finally make it to the exit and the beginning of the other shops within the Lotte World building. I take a deep breath and lead the HT Chingoos with determination to find us the perfect matching shirts.

At the fifth store, I see Wonjae take out his phone. I check mine. It's 10:32 p.m., and I wish I was nearer so I could see his screen again. He types something, and the smallest glimmer of hope rises in me. Maybe he decided to not go. Maybe he feels the butterflies I've felt all day long. He saunters over to me and looks up from his phone.

"Hey," he says, "did you find something?"

"A few options." I show him the three I'm holding and take turns holding them up one by one against me. "What do you think?"

He stands back and studies me, pretending to think long and hard. I know he's just joking around, but his gaze makes me feel vulnerable, in a good way. Like he sees me, like there's only the two of us.

"First option," he finally says. It's a neutral boxy T-shirt, and where there might usually be a shirt pocket, two black stick figures are sewn on, holding stick-figure hands.

I grin at him. "That's the one I liked the best, too." *It can be us, holding hands in an imaginary world.*

He motions the rest of our friends over. "She finally chose one," he says.

Kimbeom turns his eyes upward. "Finally," he says. "After rejecting all the ones we suggested, this better be good."

I stick my tongue out at him and show him the shirt. "I'm sorry! I just wanted to find the perfect one to commemorate today. Hey, it's also on sale for seventy-five thousand won." I contemplate this: Did I really just suggest buying a shirt that costs more than seventy dollars at a sale price? I don't have time to dwell on it now, though, because we're already headed to the cashier.

"It's pretty cute," Yura admits.

After we pay, we discuss whose driver can come to pick us up. Not mine, I tell them. Before we can decide, Wonjae's car comes pulling up. When did he call his driver?

"Oh, are we all getting into your car?" I ask.

"Hmm?" He looks up from his phone after checking the time. "Oh, uh, is anyone heading home? I'm not going that way."

"Yeah, I am," Junghoon says. "We can call a cab." Yura and Kimbeom are the late-night partiers, so they've decided to go out to get a drink on their own.

Wonjae looks at me. "Sorry, I have to be somewhere." He doesn't say it coldly, but I stand there awkwardly and walk back to Junghoon.

I wave. "See ya," I say as casually as I can.

"Don't worry, he's probably still in love with you," Kimbeom says, throwing his arm around me.

I pull away and look at him with a frown. "I don't know what you're talking about."

"She's in denial," Yura adds.

Junghoon snorts. "Pretty obvious."

"All right, all right, everyone mind their own business. Junghoon, when's the call-taxi coming? He's taking forever," I complain.

"So impatient for someone who refused to take a car two months ago."

I throw my hands up in exasperation and wait by the curb until the taxi driver pulls up, and my mind fills with scenarios I hope never happen between Wonjae and Saeha. I don't even know what she looks like, but that doesn't stop my imagination from filling in her blank face with that of the last K-drama star I saw on TV.

In the car, Junghoon stares intently at me until I cave.

"Can I help you?" I ask.

"I don't know who she is," he says to me.

"Who who is?"

"The girl he's talking to."

I shrug. "Me neither."

Junghoon laughs a little, and I shoot him another dirty look.

"Sorry," he says. "I'm saying that to make you feel better."

"How's that?"

"Wonjae's one of my best friends. If I don't know the girl he's talking to, it's because she doesn't mean anything. It's probably some misunderstanding that you've blown up in your head by sneak-reading a few messages. This is why they say you should never look at other people's phones."

I sigh, feeling only slightly better, but more comfortable. "I was hoping it'd just be the two of us today, you know."

"Oops," Junghoon says, realizing what I mean. "Wonjae didn't run it by you before he texted all of us, huh?"

I shake my head. "I was going to tell him I'm kind of into him."

"Kind of?"

"I mean, I don't know exactly how I feel, but I know I'm into him." I pause for a moment, thinking about what Junghoon just said about secretly sneaking looks at people's phones. "Wait a minute. How did you know I saw his phone?" I say accusingly.

"Beomee told us. Melody, you can't half-ass your interest in someone and then expect them to be excited. That's probably why he invited us. He knew. You need to be all in."

"I'm not half-assing anything, Junghoon. It's just . . . confusing. He isn't who I thought I'd fall for and it feels conflicting with who I am and all that. You wouldn't get it." My voice is quieter.

"Conflicting because he's rich and a big heir to a big company and you're not? I wouldn't get it? I'm probably the poorest person at SIA dating the richest girl possible in our school. If anyone gets it, it's me. Yura's the last person I thought I'd end up with, but she's the best thing that's ever happened to me."

I smile at his affectionate words for Yura and shake my head. "That's only a part of it." I turn to the window so he knows I don't want to talk about this anymore. As much as I love my HT Chingoos, they don't understand. And as much as I love Sophia, she wouldn't understand. I wonder if anyone understands my specific feeling: living in a foreign city that's supposed to be your home, missing your actual home, having your dream feel so unattainable and faraway, falling for the type of boy that you would've laughed about only a few months ago, and the biggest thing of all: discovering past stories and flaws in your family that weigh on you in ways you can't express. How can I make anyone understand all that when our lives are so different? I can't, so I just continue staring out and wait for the magical feeling the city skyline usually gives me, but it doesn't come tonight.

TWENTY-THREE

All of us spend the weekend separately due to familial obligations, and on our last free morning, I wake up with the Sunday scaries. I have one week left to prepare for midterms; it seems cruel for exams to come so soon after Korea's biggest holiday. I don't know what time it is, but the fall morning is bright out, and the natural light in my room, usually a luxury, makes me grumpy. I'm still moping over Saeha and Wonjae and am tossing and turning in my bed. I have a pillow over my face when my mom opens my door without knocking.

"Stop being dramatic and get up, sweetie," she says, drawing my curtains apart and further brightening my room.

It's been two days since Lotte World, which means an ugly two days of me trying to focus on studying and not even coming close to succeeding.

"Don't act like you know everything in my life, Mom," I say, putting a second pillow over my face to darken my vision. "Leave me alone," I say despairingly.

"Let me take a wild guess. Wonjae or Sophia?" she says as she rips the pillows from my face. She smiles with that annoying Mom Knows All smile and draws out a scowl from me.

I grumble. "You stalked me, didn't you?"

"Come on, my dramatic daughter, we need to talk. Downstairs for breakfast." With swift sweep, she pulls the blanket off me so I'm forced to get up.

I sit up quickly, trying to get a glimpse of her face as she roams my room, straightening pillows, searching for signs that she and Auntie Reba talked. "About what?" I ask.

"Your dad went to play golf with some clients, but he'll be back in the afternoon and for dinner. You have ten minutes to wash up and look like a human being." With that, she walks out, leaving my door wide open. I swing my legs out of bed and throw on an oversized peach T-shirt dress.

When I reach the table, it's covered with various fruits, a DIY yogurt parfait station, avocados, sourdough bread, orange juice, and the most initially out of place, but still welcome, dish of all: maeuntang. Whether it's because I still have lingering greasy street foods from Lotte World in my body or consumed too many snacks in yesterday's study session while holed up in my room, the spicy seafood stew this morning is just what I need. "Mmm, smells amazing," I say to my mom. I get the ladle and scoop up a generous portion of the steaming soup and boiled fish from the stone pot. I dig in first, and my mom walks to join me at the table with water glasses and a juice cup, bearing an amused expression.

"Sorry. Too hungry," I say, my mouth full of rice. She doesn't take her eyes off of me and continues to smile.

"What?" I wipe my chin where I've dribbled some broth.

"You know, Mel, less than two months ago, I never would've thought you'd be eating maeuntang for breakfast," she says.

"Less than two months ago, you would not have forced me downstairs for a feast of a breakfast, including homemade stew and yogurt parfait," I argue back.

"Oh, come on, that's not fair. We made plenty of parfaits for breakfast. And how'd you know this was homemade and not from Ahjumma?"

"Umma, flip-cup Chobani topped with whipped cream is not a parfait. It's a fast track to diabetes. And I knew because it tastes different. Ahjumma's cooking tastes better."

"And yet here you are, unable to stop stuffing your face with my homemade Korean food. Must be somewhat edible."

I point my fork at her in agreement. "So," I say, "what'd you want to talk to me about?" I spread avocado on a slice of sourdough bread and cringe at the bad combination. Korean food and avocado toast do not pair well, but the crunch I get from the toasted bread is worth it.

She sighs and scooches her chair closer to mine. "I spoke with Rebecca."

I breathe out my relief; it was only a "secret" for three days, but it was three days too many. I look at my mom, hoping she's not angry. "I'm sorry I met with her without telling you."

My mom nods. "Yeah, you shouldn't have. But I probably should have shared all of this with you when you were younger."

"But why did you agree to come to Korea? If you hate Eemo so much?"

My mom stacks empty plates in front of her mindlessly. "Oh, I don't hate her. I just . . . am not quite sure if I've forgiven her yet. And I came because your grandma sacrificed everything to start over in America, for me and Jieun. When I was younger, I felt like I owed it to her to stay in the States, because of her sacrifice, but as she got older, what she really wanted was for her daughters to mend their relationship. I saw how this stress had been hanging over her head for so many years. She needs to know her daughters have each other, that we won't turn our backs on each other anymore. And I didn't know how to tell you because it's just a part of me I've been wanting to forget . . . There was no way for me to tell you the full story without telling you the part of me I was hiding, a part of me you've never known."

I fidget in my seat. "I wish I had, though." A question lingers in my mind, and I watch as a slippery piece of avocado slowly slides off my bread. "Do you miss it? The singing?"

She stops scooping fruit into her yogurt and pauses, as if to really ponder my question. "When I got pregnant with you, it was like . . . well, sort of like all these fuzzy images came into focus. It wasn't realistic to make a living and support you through gigs we got a few times a month. I needed a real job. One of those jobs my mom had been nagging me about. I think I felt closer to my mom that year than any other, and I had so much regret about not taking her advice earlier. I realized why she emphasized the need for a reality check and to be smarter about our paths. Rebecca didn't, though. She didn't understand. I wanted her to quit, too, to make it faster than I did, not have to wait for a child to help her realize she needed to be smarter. She was devastated, and that's when she left me for Korea. Your grandma was heartbroken; I think she was sick for almost two months when Jieun took off like that."

"*Two months?*" The thought of my lovely, frail grandmother being sick for two months makes me ache with sadness.

"She'd always yell at us, so angry that we'd dare to pursue an artistic endeavor when she had worked so hard to immigrate to the other side of the world. Why couldn't we be like the Chung kids, who were trying to become lawyers, or the Park kids, who were on their way to becoming a doctor and a teacher? But we were naive and stubborn."

My heart shatters into what feels like a hundred fractured pieces. She is fully convinced that giving up her dream to be a stable office employee was the best move. It was her most sacrificial decision, but on the journey, she forgot what it was to dream.

"Let's go to the living room." She stands up with a plate of freshly cut Korean pears and I follow. We seat ourselves on a large sectional sofa, and she hands me a small silver fruit fork. I'm about to ask her about my dad when she beats me to it, like she knew all along that I'd ask eventually.

"When your dad and I met, he was working on Wall Street. Your grandfather was furious that his only son didn't want to follow in his footsteps and go to law school. Your dad dreamed of being in finance, a self-made man in New York."

I tuck both my legs under me and take a bite of the crunchy white pear, leaning in and devouring every word. I've been waiting so long for this.

"But after just one year, in the aftermath of 9/11, he was let go from his job. Honestly, he was miserable there, always getting berated by his manager and being called names. By then, though, your grandfather had cut him off, so he was forced to work odd jobs so we could make ends meet."

Understanding slowly dawns on me, and I think of Appa's entry about cleaning houses.

"Your dad didn't mind at first," she says, smiling like she's in love again. "We were married, I was pregnant with you, and we were happy. But after a while, without any job offers and no prospects, he lost a lot of his energy. It was like he just became a shell of himself." She puts her fork down on the tray. "Your grandfather gave him a one-time offer, which I think your grandmother was behind: He had the option to come back to Korea, attend law school, and join his firm. Everything would be paid for, and all your dad had to do was agree to work for his dad's firm."

I stop eating my pear. "That's why he left. When I was young. He had to go back for business," I say slowly, repeating the words that were so often spoken to me.

"He said he'd come back after saving up enough. I didn't believe him. I knew he'd fall into your grandfather's world, but he insisted. He'd go to law school, work for a few years under his dad, and save up enough to come back and get a job here, and in the meantime, he'd send money. We both agreed we'd keep raising you here, and I got a stable job that paid me a good enough salary."

"But he didn't come back." My dad and my aunt—my mom's two closest companions—both left her for Korea.

She shakes her head. "When you were six, he finally had enough, but he wanted more. He had this gripping insecurity that ate away at him, this need to prove to his dad that he was capable of more. He desperately wanted us to come back to Korea to be with him."

"But you said no."

"I said no. And once I made enough to support you fully on my own, I stopped taking his money. I was devastated and furious with him, breaking his promise to us. He was so tired of living the way we had been before that he said he couldn't go back to it, and that every year, he was closer to winning his dad's approval." A tear unexpectedly trickles down her cheek, barely visible as she quickly wipes it away, erasing its existence.

I think about how my mom forgot what it was like to dream while all these things happened around her. How could she when she had no leisure, no support? "Do you think Appa regrets not coming back to live with us?" I ask quietly.

"I think, after so many years, you sometimes forget why you do what you do—or don't do. You just are. And somehow, in the blink of an eye, sixteen years go by." She smiles at me and pats my hair a few times. "But I have no regrets about the six-teen years you and I got to spend together," she says, kissing my cheek. "I do think, deep down, he might regret it. For what it's worth, I think he did really miss us."

"Well," I say, trying to lighten the mood, "we are very miss-able."

She chuckles at this.

"Are you . . . still furious with him?"

Without hesitation, she shakes her head. "I'm still adjust-ing to life here, that's for sure, but no, I'm not. I forgot what it's like to be with him, to do life together. We're like longtime friends who lost touch, trying to get to know each other again. We've both changed a lot over the years." She pauses. "I've been remembering why we fell in love, and I think I really needed that. I think your dad and I *both* really needed that."

I nod slowly, remembering when they held hands, how it

looked a little out of place, of them singing in the car, of their smiles at each other, sharing those marriage moments I hope to one day have, too. "Mom? I'm really sorry," I tell her quietly, "about the way I—"

"I know," she says, cutting me off.

"If I had known—"

"Don't worry," she assures me, squeezing my shoulder.

I lean my head on her, hoping she understands how I feel; how sorry I am that she had to raise me mostly alone, how guilty I feel for being so angry at her, how grateful I am for the way she raised me. My eyes well up and wander to the clock and I realize that it's well past lunchtime. I quickly wipe my eyes before my tears drop. "Mom . . . not to kill the mood, but I have to study. Midterms start in one week, and I need that plane ticket to New York."

She laughs and puts a piece of tissue in the trash bin next to the credenza. "Okay, okay."

I turn around to look at her before I head up the stairs. "I'm trying, too, you know. With Dad."

She nods, understanding. "I know you are."

TWENTY-FOUR

For the next few days, my days blur into each other, all spent in exactly the same way. Wake up, school, study at a café or at home, dinner, study, sleep, repeat. It's Wednesday evening, which means tomorrow is the day of our Honors Korean presentation. Wonjae and I agree to meet at 8:00 p.m. to put the finishing touches on it.

> hey, where should we meet?

> **WONJAE**
> wanna come over?

Since that one exchange during Lotte World, I've heard no news about Saeha and haven't seen anything out of the ordinary at school, so I take that as a good sign and play it cool.

> mmkay. where?

WONJAE
tower 3, floor 6

I quickly change out of the same pair of sweats I've worn for three days at home in the evenings and into white skinny jeans and a baggy black V-neck with a giant smiley face in the center. Alone with Wonjae.

I ring the doorbell, too nervous for my own good. I'm sixteen, but this is my first time going over to a guy's house where it's just me and him, and I am so jittery my armpits are sweating.

The built-in keypad hums a tune as he presses the unlock button from the inside. "Hey," he says, holding the door open while I walk in past him, carefully carrying our large project.

"Hi."

His layout is like the mirror version of our villa, but they've combined the office and guest room into one huge room—Wonjae's room. His ahjumma brings in warm tea and fruit and smiles at me like I'm her long-lost child and spends five minutes complimenting me. I blush, and Wonjae tries to wave her away.

He grins, looking a little embarrassed. "Sorry, she's been with our family since I was three."

"Hey, I have no complaints about anyone wanting to compliment me."

For a few minutes, we both admire the work we've done.

"Looks pretty good, right?" I ask.

He nods. "Belongs in a museum."

We look at the model we built with toothpicks, bright

fabrics, and small cardboard pieces. Our presentation will be on how traditional hanok villages in our designated region have been preserved yet modernized over time. The influence of the palaces surrounding the villages have been a cry to preserve, preserve, preserve, and yet to keep them relevant and interesting to locals and tourists alike, the region needs to keep up with the city's evolving trends and interests. It's eye-opening to see a country as old as Korea work to preserve its culture and somehow have one of the fastest growing economies in the world. It's made me respect the country more than I expected I would. I smile again at our project, confident that we'll get an A, but more because of everything that it's brought me: palace days with my closest friends, tutoring sessions with Wonjae, a weekend getaway in a hanok, and most importantly, a deeper understanding of this culture. I should thank Mrs. Lee even though she made me cry.

He pokes my side, and I jump in surprise. "Are you thinking something sentimental right now?" he asks me, jerking me away from my—yes—sentimental thoughts.

"It wasn't that sentimental."

"Here I am, cleaning up the fallen toothpicks and peeling off dried glue, and here you are lovingly gazing at it like it's completed. We still have to finish it, you know," he jokes. "And then you can smile some more when you get that A and take that flight to New York."

"That A and five others," I remind him. "Although I guess Creative Writing isn't really a midterm. I already handed in my short story for the class, which is considered the midterm."

"And?"

I lift my chin with pride. "A."

Wonjae whoops and high-fives me. "So four left to go."

I sigh. "I really hope I get to go. I miss New York so much."

"What happens if you get the internship?" he asks.

"I'm not sure. If I get it, I'd be there the summer before senior year."

"Would you come back for senior year?"

"I don't know. I guess it depends on my family."

I feel the silent tension again—the same tension I always feel with Wonjae. The tension that gives me confidence that I mean something to him.

"So, are you seeing anyone?"

Wonjae looks up from delicately putting a misplaced toothpick back in its place. "What? Nope." He pauses. "You?"

I think of Saeha and consider dropping her name, but mentioning another girl's name is a vibe killer. Maybe it really was nothing, like Junghoon was saying. I shake my head. "Nuh-uh."

"Cool. A little random."

"I was just curious."

"Oh yeah?" He looks at me for too long. "Why's that?"

"Huh?"

"Why were you curious?"

"Just because." I turn my attention back to our project as I feel my face heating up. "Let's finish the structure and then we can rehearse our presentation."

A few hours of intense concentration later, we stretch our bodies, which have been hunched over for too long. I want to stay longer, just to spend time together, to flirt a little more, but my mind is in exam mode, and Wonjae's clock indicates it's almost time for dinner, which means an entire day has passed. "I should get going."

"Want to go for a walk first?" he asks.

I pick at my lips, trying to decide. Then I shake my head, and it feels almost impossible to say no, but I have ninety-six hours until my first exam—actually less than that, considering the sixteen hours that will be spent in school. "I have to go study for Monday's exams. But can we raincheck?" I'm crying a river inside, but my goal is New York. Taking a romantic stroll with my crush will just have to wait.

When I get home, I'm barely inside long enough to scarf down dinner before I gather all my study materials and go to CappOH!ccino to do more cramming before exam week, otherwise known as The Week That Determines My Future.

THE SUN HASN'T RISEN YET; IT'S 5:45 A.M. ON Monday morning—the first day of exams. I open my phone out of habit and see a message from Sophia asking about Lotte World and Saeha. I hit the video-call button and I give her a brief update on my non-success.

"But whoever she is, she doesn't exist anymore in his life, I don't think."

"I thought you'd send me an update but you didn't, so I was just wondering," Soph says to me. I hear the passive-aggressive tone in her voice.

"Sorry, yeah, things got a bit busy. But you didn't respond to my Yura and Junghoon comment, either."

"I mean, I've never met them, so I didn't really know what to say. Good for them?"

I look at the screen, not saying anything. We've been talking less and less in recent days and I don't want to make things any weirder between us, so I keep my mouth shut.

"Anyway, it was fine. I am definitely interested in Wonjae, Soph. But for now, I'm just trying to get through exams. I went to his place yesterday."

"Didn't you say he's the heir to a huge company or something?"

I nod. "His grandfather's."

"Honestly doesn't sound like your type of guy."

I blink. "Yeah. I guess he wasn't really."

She shrugs. "Well, people change."

"What's that supposed to mean?" I ask, irritated. It's like she wants to start a fight.

"Nothing, just saying."

"Saying what, Soph?"

"That you've changed."

"No, I haven't," I say defensively.

"Is your driver here yet?" I know she's saying this in a condescending way, the way we used to make fun of people who we thought were shallow and cared too much about the world.

I clench my teeth. "I take the bus. You don't even know half the things that have been happening here, Soph. You have no right to judge me like this."

"It's not my fault I don't know what your life has become, Mel. You're the one that doesn't tell me anything anymore."

"Oh, like you do?" Our voices are getting louder over the phone.

"My life isn't the one that changed," she says. "Yours has, clearly, and you're leaving me out of it. That's fine. Just go run along to your new best friend Yuna and your millionaire boyfriend."

"*Yura*," I emphasize.

"Same thing."

"You know what? If you hadn't been so judgmental lately, I would have shared more. I've been dealing with my parents, my aunt, and crazy grandparents. And you don't know a thing about how hard it's been for me."

Sophia pouts mockingly. "Oh, you poor little rich girl with your rich friends and your private driver and your elitist school."

My eyes feel hot and threatened by tears. "That's not fair, Soph," I say quietly. It's the day of my midterms—the most important day for me thus far. I'm not letting anyone get into my head, not even Sophia. I glare at her before I hang up the phone.

I leave my house extra early and sit inside a pyeonuijeom with a carton of banana milk to clear my head before the big day. The midterms schedule is different from normal school hours. Most of us have half days with two midterms per day. Technically, I have my last midterm for PE on Wednesday, but I don't count that since it's a physical test. I walk into my AP English classroom, where Miss Smith is sitting with her back straight behind her massive desk. On the door, a sign hangs:

AP ENGLISH—MIDTERM IN SESSION

8:30–9:45

I take a deep breath and slide into my seat, tapping the top of my pencil against my desk. Five minutes until my first exam, one and a half hours until my next (Chemistry).

Three hours later, it's as if a giant block (or two giant blocks) has been lifted off my shoulders. I straighten up, feeling free. "Two down, two to go," I say to Yura, Kimbeom, Junghoon, and Wonjae as we exit the glass building of SIA. "And I'm pretty sure we aced our Korean presentation."

"You're smiling because AP English was easy for you," Wonjae complains. "English Lit was deceivingly difficult. Miss Smith is way too obsessed with analyzing dead German authors. I think I bombed that one."

"AP World and Pre-Calc will be hard for me and easy for you. So it's all fair," I say.

"Let's go celebrate the ending of our first day of finals," Yura says.

"You're always looking for a reason to celebrate," Junghoon remarks.

"It makes everything less miserable. Now who's down?"

I shake my head. "I can't. Every hour of cramming counts. Oh yeah, how was the PE exam?" I ask Yura and Kimbeom. Junghoon took fencing by himself, but they had their PE physical test today, while Wonjae and I have ours tomorrow.

"It was fine. Timed sit-ups and push-ups, running around the track, and whatever typical things you can think of," Kimbeom shares.

"At least that's one exam I have a guaranteed A on." I wave to my friends and get into the car, where the driver is waiting for me, and think of what Sophia said this morning. I'm only using the driver today and tomorrow to save time commuting and maximize studying. I slam my AP World History book shut in the car in frustration. I haven't changed. She doesn't understand. I vow to push the fight out of my mind and empty my headspace to only fit two things: AP World and Pre-Calc. The only two things that matter right now.

In the evening, my mom knocks and brings two slices of pizza to my room. "Brain food," she says, putting them next to me. I give her a thumbs-up without looking up from my books. I'm trying to memorize and review sine and cosine formulas when my stomach growls. I inhale both slices and finish reviewing all my materials. When I'm done, I stretch my neck and look at the clock. 2:32 a.m. I don't bother changing out of my lounge clothes and fall asleep instantly.

"HOLY FREAKIN' MOLY, I CAN'T BELIEVE IT. WE'RE done!" I'm gleefully sipping on my bubble tea at a café near school. It's called Bbo Bbo Bbo Bba, which literally translates to "kiss boba." Another cute café among thousands in Seoul.

"Well, you two are technically not done," Yura teases as she gestures to me and Wonjae. "When's your PE physical?"

I look at my phone. "In two hours. Just enough time to digest my bubble tea." AP World History was not as hard as I thought it would be, and Pre-Calc was just as difficult as I anticipated, but New York feels closer than ever and nothing could dampen my mood.

"Hoonee and I are going on a date today, and Kimbeom's joining us later. Text us when you're done with PE?"

Wonjae and I nod, and we spend the next hour celebrating the end of midterms. When the PE exam ends, it's almost 4:00

p.m. It's late October, and the sun is setting earlier and earlier with each passing day. When we walk out together, the sky is a mix of pale blue and yellow.

"How do you feel?" he asks.

I close my eyes. "Like I can taste 99 Cent Express Pizza."

He laughs one of those laughs that make his eyes crinkle. "Your favorite pizza shop in New York?"

I nod. "Hey. Where's your driver?" We're walking down the hill, and Wonjae's driver is nowhere in sight.

"I asked him not to come today. I figured you wouldn't have your driver come, either."

I bite my lips to hide my smile. "You figured correctly."

"Did the PE test make you hungry?"

"*Yes*, like I'm in need of a second lunch."

"There's a great Italian restaurant nearby," he offers.

I make a face. "Let's just go to the pyeonuijum and get cup ramen." I grin at him, poking him in the shoulder. "You know you want to."

"You win. I'm down."

WE POUR THE HOT WATER INTO OUR BOWLS AND take them outside, using our hands to hold down the lid flaps against the wind. My hands feel warm, and after a few minutes, we split our wooden chopsticks apart and slurp down noodles and spicy MSG-filled soup. It's exactly what I needed. "Mmm," I say, satisfied. "This beats Italian, right?"

"Hey, hey, I already said you won." When we're done, Wonjae takes my bowl with his to go toss them and our hands graze each other for just a second, but it's all I need to feel the heat rushing through my body. When he returns, he scoots his plastic chair subtly closer to mine, and soon the sun has set and our friends are asking where we are.

When we get off the bus at the intersection of Hannam O-guri, he pauses in his steps and looks at me. I'm thinking of how Wonjae asked to go on a walk a few days ago. And it's like he reads my mind.

"Want to walk the bridge? It's a great view," he suggests.

Bridge walking after sunset with Wonjae and finished with exams? The best combination. "Definitely."

Instead of walking straight up toward Hannam Towers, we take a left at the intersection where the bus stop is and walk onto Hannam Bridge. It looks long and there are only a few people on the bridge, biking across in both directions. Cars drown out every other noise, and even though our surroundings are loud, everything feels still and silent. As I walk, I look to the view on my left. It's not the New York skyline, but it has the same vibrant, anything-is-possible glow to it, and it's stunning. There are a lot more clusters of buildings and not as many distinctive landmarks like the Empire State Building or the Freedom Tower or the Chrysler Building, but I appreciate this view just the same. I don't think I would have liked this view two months ago.

We walk for another twenty or so minutes, quietly appreciating the city around us. "Look at all those lights," I say, pointing to the stores. "They're so beautiful."

"You're a twinkling lights fan, huh?" he asks.

"A proud one."

Wonjae smiles. "I knew you'd like it."

I stop walking. And maybe it's the reflection of the buildings on the Han River or the breathtaking city skyline, but a surge of confidence rises to the surface and I turn to him. "So that night at Octagon was really fun." I take just a tiny half step closer to him.

Wonjae looks directly at me. "It really was. Any reason you're bringing it up right now?"

I hold his gaze. "I didn't want you to think I regret what happened that night."

He takes a step closer to me, cocking his head. "What happened?" he asks, feigning ignorance.

We've shifted positions, and I'm leaning against the railing and he's directly in front of me. I give him what I hope is a coy smile, shaking my head. "Need a reminder?"

Wonjae puts both hands on the railing so that I'm now in between his arms. He takes a step closer to me.

I lean in, my lips about to touch his, when he pulls back just a bit. "Wait, are you sure?" he asks, his voice barely above a whisper. His face is so close to mine that the air feels warmer now. I can feel his breath on the tip of my lips.

"Are you?" I ask, and our lips meet and I look up at him.

He wraps one arm around my waist, pulling me in tightly, and our bodies press into each other. "Yes," he whispers.

I lean into him again and he cups my face and kisses me, with more urgency this time. It's real and it's happening. I'm not drunk and this isn't a mistake. I let myself fall into him and feel small in the best way possible, like the city is moving around us but we're standing still, in our own little world, surrounded by the beauty of Seoul with the evening moon high above us.

The only thought circling my mind is how right this all feels, how long I've been wanting to do this. His hands go from my cheeks and waist until they find my fingers and he takes them and weaves them with his own. When we finally pull apart, we walk around a little, but we don't let go of each other's hands. He holds mine tighter until we eventually turn back to the entrance of the bridge.

The sun is completely gone now, and it's just black outside. We stop by CU on our walk back and buy two sticks of ice cream. There's no worry of them melting when it's this cold outside. When we make it back to the Hannam Towers, the tips of our noses are pink and my cheeks feel ice cold. We walk to the outdoor playground and do a toast with our ice creams before biting into them. Less than a minute in, we're both shivering but silently and comfortably making our way through our dessert.

"Korean ice creams are so cool," I comment.

He gives me an amused smile. "I guess so."

"No, really. America doesn't have all these flavors. Like corn, soda milk—what even is soda milk? Anyway, it's so good. And it's in a plastic casing. It's ahead of its time; you don't have to worry about sticky fingers and spillage." I press on the plastic to push the creamy ice cream out of its tube.

Wonjae starts laughing, a big open-mouthed guffaw. It always makes me feel successful to make someone laugh this big.

There's an intense sobriety that hits me when I see his face. I've never felt this way before. I've liked guys, I've almost-kissed guys, I've kind of dated guys, but in this moment I know immediately. I've never liked anyone the way I like him. It feels like a soul connection, like we understand each other without having to overexplain anything. It's a gut-wrenching fear and unexplainable happiness at the very same time, and I wonder how that can be. I guess my expression combines both those feelings, because Wonjae frowns.

"Is something wrong?" he asks. He sweeps a strand of hair out of my face and tucks it behind my ear.

I shake my head and push away my rabbit hole of thoughts. "A lot of emotions is all," I answer.

He puts his finished ice cream stick on the slide next to us. "Tell me about it," he says as he wraps his arms around my waist and pulls me into him. The butterflies get bigger, and I turn my head so our lips meet again. It's a different kiss than the one on the bridge, but just as good, if not better. He holds me tighter and I reciprocate. My ice cream falls to the ground, and I wrap my fingers around his shirt before bringing my arms around his neck. He walks over to a swing and sits down, smoothly pulling me down to join him. I swing my leg over him so that we have a spider-swing pose, and it's like our bodies fit perfectly into each other. I used to do this with my girlfriends and compete with others to see who could go higher and faster with two people on one swing, but right now it's just me and Wonjae, kissing as we swing softly back and forth. His fingers press into the arch of my back and then he kisses my cheeks, my nose, my neck, my chin, and my lips again. His lips look extra pink when we pull away, and there's a shyness to us both. The silence between us feels effortless, like we've done this a million times before.

WHEN I'M HOME, I OPEN MY UNREAD MESSAGES IN the HT Chingoos chat.

KIMBEOM

where are wonjae and mel???

YURA

we're at cappo if you wanna join!

let's go eat mandoo after.

Then I read a separate message from Yura in a private chat.

YURA

both you AND wonjae aren't
responding. 😏

i better get an update from you first
thing tomorrow morning!!!!

I smile gleefully to myself and flip my phone over, falling asleep dreaming about our kiss on the bridge.

TWENTY-FIVE

*I*t's the best Saturday morning I've had in a while. Waking up to freedom from midterms, still on a high from my amazing evening with Wonjae, and the bonus of hanging out with Yura last night. A part of me feels guilty that I didn't tell her about the kissing, just that we hung out but that "nothing happened." Like my M&S acceptance, it's one of those things I want to hold on to alone for just a little while longer. The only thing nagging at me is Sophia. Our fight felt like it came from nowhere, and I'm still angry when I remember our conversation and her hurtful words: *poor little rich girl.*

"Good mo-orning," my mom says, bursting open my door in a singsong voice.

"Agh, too early."

"What're you talking about? I could hear you reorganizing your bookshelf from downstairs."

"What's the point of living in a huge home if sound carries so easily?"

"House size doesn't matter when you're dropping encyclopedias from a step stool, honey. Now get ready. We're going to brunch."

I sit up and kick off my satin sheets that I climbed back into after being exhausted from reorganizing and redecorating. "We are? Where? Who else?"

"Just you and me, a mother-daughter date day. Your dad is in Hong Kong for work until Monday, so it's just us girls. What do you want to do?"

"What the? He didn't even tell me!"

"He thought you were asleep, hon."

"Okay. I'll take you somewhere," I say, letting my mischievous smile say more than I share.

Two hours and a clean shower later, we're walking through the narrow alleyways of Ikseon-dong.

"Wow, I'm impressed you found your way here," my mom says, looking at all the stores that surround us. "What is this place?"

I eagerly show her the hanoks and the beautifully tiled roofs and wooden doorways, explaining everything. I detail out our Korean project and how Wonjae introduced me to my now-favorite place in the city. It hits a weird proud spot in me when my mom comments on how she's glad I enjoy hanoks so much. Maybe this is part of what she meant by learning about my culture, appreciating it and its history. We try a different café than the one I went to last time; this one looks a little fancier and less traditional but is packed with people. The smell of soft milk bread easily convinces us to walk in. My mom orders a latte and I order their strawberry-and-apple fruit tea, and we each get a pastry.

I set the thin wooden tray down on the rounded glass tables

and pull the wicker armchair closer in. "I have to tell you something."

My mom looks at me suspiciously. "Go on."

"I had my first kiss. Multiple times. With Wonjae."

Her mouth drops open comically, and she forces more details out of me, and I divulge all the details to her—just like I would have in New York.

"Then what's the little bit of sadness I'm feeling from you?" she asks.

I sigh and take a piece of strawberry out of my teacup. "Soph and I had a fight."

"I figured as much."

"How?"

"You haven't mentioned her at all recently. Or how her dad is doing or anything."

I annoyingly shove a forkful of bread topped with confectioner's sugar in my mouth. "Well, great, that's exactly how she feels. Why don't the two of you go live together?"

"Mel, she probably just misses you."

"If she missed me, she wouldn't just blow up on me out of nowhere. Seriously, she just snapped in the middle of our phone call."

My mom thinks about this for a moment. "Was it really out of nowhere?"

"What?" I look at her, frustrated and confused. Was it not out of nowhere? I sensed tension here and there from our chats, a little distance in our conversations, but I still wouldn't have expected this.

"It was probably building up slowly," she explains.

"Well, I miss her, too, but I'm not going around calling her a 'poor little rich girl,' am I?" I emphasize in air quotes. "She says I've changed."

"Does that bother you?"

"Well, duh."

"Why?" She's sipping on her hot drink and asking questions to draw out all my feelings. Somehow it works every freaking time.

"Because I don't want to believe that I could change so easily just by being forced to move to a different country. I mean, am I that boneless, that I have no sense of identity whatsoever?"

My mom chuckles into her drink. "Oh boy, kiddo. You'll be changing until the day you die, and not just from moving across the globe, but from smaller things—like a new home or growing older—and from bigger things—like having a family of your own one day or losing loved ones. Tell Sophia she's changed, too," she jokes.

I stare at my phone, not feeling that much better from my mom's unhelpful pep talk. "Well, it's one more reason to get back to New York. I need to patch things up with Sophia before we never talk to each other again and forget the other ever existed," I say bitterly.

I WALK INTO AP ENGLISH UNINTENTIONALLY holding my breath. It's Monday morning, which means we're getting our exam results back.

"Most of you did fairly well. This was not an easy test, and I hope you see your grades as an accurate reflection of what you deserve. If you have complaints, you may set up a meeting with me after school today."

I have butterflies in my stomach as Miss Smith walks around the room handing back exam results to students. The clicking of her stiletto heels gets louder as she walks toward me and places an exam facedown on my desk. I continue to hold my breath and flip it over. At the top is a big blue A along with a cursive comment. *Impressed, but not surprised,* it reads, with a checkmark and a smiley face next to it.

I eagerly rush into Mr. Lin's Chemistry class, where my friends are already seated. I slide into a seat and wave around my exam result. "One step closer!" We settle into our respective seats when the teacher walks in, and from behind, Wonjae rubs my neck lightly, and I muffle a giggle.

"Stop!" I hiss at him, but he knows I'm teasing. I turn around for a half second and swat at his hand before the teacher catches us.

Mr. Lin waits until the end of the period before calling up our names one by one to grab our exams on our way out. I have to sit through an agonizing twelve names before mine is called. I rush up and go into the hallway in the corner between a locker and a wall before I flip it over. I'm clutching it to my chest, willing the exam to have an A written at the top. I slowly bring it up to my face: A-.

"YES!" I throw my fist in the air, and other students I don't know well look at me in amusement, but I don't care. Relief pours through me, and I thank all the exam gods for keeping my exam an A- and not a B+. "Too close," I whisper to myself.

New York might really happen. Hope is swelling in my heart as I think more and more about Maison & Saito and about Sophia. Anxiety bubbles inside of me as I walk down the hallway to Mr. Sullivan's classroom. I just need two more A's: AP World History and Pre-Calc, and I'll have my plane ticket home.

Mr. Sullivan has the same annoying method as Mr. Lin and refrains from returning our exams until five minutes before class ends.

"I know the test wasn't easy, but I will admit that I'm a little disappointed in this class," he says to us. He has creases on his forehead when he speaks, and his tall stature feels ominous as he walks in the aisles between our desks.

My palms are sweating as Mr. Sullivan gets closer to my seat. I stare at the exam that's flipped over on my desk, too nervous to see what the exam side says. I hold my breath and turn it over. Then I have to look more closely because I'm hoping what I see is not real. It can't be. But there it is, a B, sitting at the top of the page. I don't even hear the rest of what Mr. Sullivan says, and my entire body feels like rubber. This can't be right. B? I furiously flip through the pages trying to tally up my grade, willing it to be a huge mistake. How did I get so many multiple-choice questions wrong? A note lands on my desk, and I open it up.

are you okay? ☺

I turn to my right and see Wonjae looking at me with a concerned expression. I give him a small fake smile, as if I'm okay, as if New York is still attainable, but I know already that it's not. Not according to my parents, anyway.

When the bell rings, I rush out of the classroom before Wonjae has a chance to catch up to me. I don't feel like talking to anyone right now. I shove whatever I don't need into my locker and speed walk to Mr. Wilson's classroom. Not that it matters at this point, but my incredibly poor score for Pre-Calc worsens my mood. I knew getting an A in Pre-Calc was going to be extremely difficult, but I never imagined I'd get anything lower than a B-. And yet there it is, the ugliest, reddest C+, haphazardly written across the top of the page.

With no appetite and too embarrassed to tell my friends I've failed, I skip lunch and sneak into the library. I stay in there lying on the beige leather sofa bench, feeling hopeless as I stare at the white ceiling. In Korean class, the A we predicted we got on our presentation confirms itself in a smiley face from Mrs. Lee and in-kind praise printed and taped to our project, but I just pass it to Wonjae without uttering a word. For the rest of the class, I face forward and sit in my chair, numbly wondering when the rest of my emotions will kick in. My eyes are on the bell that marks the end of the worst day I've had at SIA to date, and the second it rings, I sling my backpack on and rush down the stairs and out the school entrance.

I walk alone up the hill to HT and avoid my mom, going straight upstairs to my room. I'm not ready to let go of New York, and talking about it will force me to reckon with something I don't want to accept. There must be another way, but I don't see one. I open my phone to a lot of texts from Yura, Kimbeom, Wonjae, and Junghoon. Everyone's trying to cheer me up, but it's not working. I put my phone on silent and flip it over so I can't see or hear any more messages.

By dinner, which my dad made it home in time for, I'm dreading going downstairs, but my mom's already called my name twice.

"So," my appa says, putting his chopsticks down, "do you have a stack of papers you want to show us?"

I shake my head without looking at him. "I don't have an

appetite. Can I go back to my room, please?"

My mom says absolutely not and places my dinner in front of me. Everything looks unappealing to me because I know now the chance of my flying to New York is zero. The proof is in my hands—pages of A4-size paper that now prevent me from returning home. I hate how much academia is prioritized in Korea, like anything less than an A is unacceptable, like I don't deserve to chase my dream because my grades aren't at the top.

"What's that you're holding, then?"

The deal was to hand over my test scores to my dad, who is annoyingly in the know at school because he believes the path to a good university is connections and involved parents, so there's no getting out of it. I silently give him the stack of papers and poke at my rice with my chopsticks.

My mom peers over his shoulder and lets out a surprised gasp. It provokes me to want to throw non-glass tableware at her.

"Melody," she says in a shocked tone, "a C?"

I sit in silence.

My appa sighs. "Solmi, I know you did your best." And for a moment, a short moment, it seems like he might be willing to send me anyway.

My mom jumps in before he has a chance to finish. "But a deal's a deal," she says. "I'm sorry, honey. We're still proud of you for trying."

"Please," I say. "Please let me go."

I look at my mom pleadingly, but when our eyes meet, she shakes her head.

"I'll even pay you back," I promise. My voice comes out like a whimper. The dream that was slowly becoming reality crumbles into my rice bowl.

My mom gives me a tight smile. "A deal is a deal, and for better or for worse, we meant what we said. I'm sorry, but you're not going to New York for the competition."

My dad, for once, is quiet. I look at him, hoping to maybe wring some sort of pity from him. "Appa? Please? You saw me working hard, you saw me trying, you even said you know I'm doing my best. On the sofa in the den, remember?"

He looks at my mom, and she gives him a Look. "I'm sorry, Solmi. I need to stick to my word." He stands up and takes his all-too-quickly-emptied bowl to the sink.

I don't know how he managed to finish his food while watching his only daughter beg and plead, but he did. And that's that.

I'M BALANCING MY PHONE BETWEEN MY SHOULDER and ear as I sketch a drawing of the roller coasters at Coney Island. "I don't feel like going anywhere, though," I say to Yura, who's convinced I need to get some fresh air and away from the temptation to throw plates at my family.

"Meet me out front in five minutes. Or else I'll freeze to death." She hangs up, and I know I need to go outside. Yura is the type of person who will actually wait for hours because that's just who she is. I throw a coat on, tie my hair back, and go outside.

When I see Yura, she's holding a black plastic bag; I can't see what's inside, but it's the kind convenience stores give you.

"When'd you have time to buy all that? You called me five minutes ago," I say.

"You didn't show up for lunch, and you've been ignoring our messages. I bought these a while ago." Yura doesn't say this as if she's trying to be praised for her good deed or complimented on her selflessness. She says it like it's just the normal thing to do. I want to hug her, but I stand there silently instead.

She doesn't say anything else. She just comes over and hooks her arms in mine and drags me out of the courtyard. We reach the same bridge I walked on with Wonjae, but she leads me down a set of cement stairs, and we descend to the bottom and keep walking until we find a flat patch of dry grass. Then she places the black plastic bag on the ground and pulls out the goods she bought: squid chips, two bottles of soju, one bottle of makgeolli, onion ring chips, water, Sprite, coffee, and oranges.

"Oranges?" I ask, picking one up.

She shrugs. "Didn't know what you'd be craving."

The soju drinks aren't hard liquor; they're flavored. Apple soju and peach soju. They taste like juice, and Yura tells me the alcohol content isn't high, so I feel a little better about drinking them. One drunken experience is more than enough for me.

She raises her paper cup to me, filled with a shot of apple soju. "To you," she says, firmly upbeat. "You'll find a way somehow to get back to New York. But I hope you come back to Seoul. Eventually." She smiles and we take the shots.

"You're the best thing that's happened to me in Seoul, Yura," I tell her, learning my head on her shoulder. I sigh as I think of Sophia.

"Another sigh for the second exam you bombed, or is this something else?"

"Sophia and I had a huge fight and I feel like a shitty friend," I admit. I explain our unexpected argument and how I hung up on her.

Yura shakes her head sympathetically. "Sorry. That sucks."

We finish the second bottle of soju. The peach one tastes better.

"I admire that you're so relentless, Mel," Yura says as she opens the makgeolli.

We're lying on the dry grass in the cold with our coats over our bodies to form a sort of shared sleeping bag. "So are you."

She turns her head toward me, removing her gaze from the black sky. "No, I'm really not." She sounds sad and reminiscent. "Remember when I snapped at you about the poster you picked out?"

I wrinkle my nose, trying to remember what she's talking about. "Oh, at Kyobo? When I wanted the ballerina and the winter paintings?"

She nods. "I was training to be a professional figure skater."

I sit up, wide-eyed. "What? What happened?"

Yura's still lying down and turns her face skyward again. "I broke my knee during a competition when I fell wrong. I could have continued, but by the time I healed, I was so far behind."

"Well . . . did you try to get back out there?"

"Yeah. Of course. I could have caught up, probably, but the post-trauma was too much for me, and I had horrible performance anxiety. I ended up giving it up. My mom was relieved, though. To her it just meant I could focus on preparing to run Dynasty."

I exhale slowly, trying to take in this part of Yura I never knew. "Wow . . . I'm so sorry, Yura. When did you start skating?"

"When I was four. I still miss it so much, and it was the only thing I ever really cared that much about." She shrugs. "Now I've accepted that I'm going to be running my mom's department store one day, and it is what it is."

"Can't you try and go back? Slowly start again?"

Yura shakes her head. "It's definitely too late now. Kim Yuna got the gold medal at the Olympics basically around my age now. There's no way I could catch up at this stage." She smiles at me and sits up to fill our cups with makgeolli, but I can see the sadness in her eyes, from having to give up on her childhood dream and accepting that it's gone forever. It makes sense now—the way Yura doesn't care much about school, her upbeat attitude about taking over her mom's company. She doesn't expect anything more. "Ugh, now I'm the one that needs a distraction." She says this lightly, but I know she means it.

"Okay," I say, pulling the edges of my coat closer to my body. "Wonjae and I made out."

"At Octagon, right?"

I look at her slyly. "And last week, when we ditched you, Junghoon, and Beom."

She gasps dramatically and props her knees up, allowing a gust of air to rush into the lifted coat. "You said nothing happened!"

I clasp my hands together in a penitent stance. "I know, I know. Sorry, I felt bad about lying! I was just selfishly holding on to it by myself because it was *so* good."

Yura looks at me like she's deciding whether to forgive me or not. "Fine, then you need to tell me *all* the details."

So, despite the cold, despite the shitty reality that still lies ahead of me, and despite the heaviness I feel hearing about Yura's lost dreams, I indulge her. I share everything. The hand-holding at Gangneung, kissing at the club, the eye contact, the flirting, more details of the makeout on the bridge and the playground after. His secret whispers in my ears during school and in between classes.

"Wow, I knew you were into each other, but didn't know it was a full-fledged secret relationship," she says, still in shock but clearly thrilled.

"I don't know what we are, to be honest," I say.

"What do you mean? It sounds like he's crazy about you. Do you like him?"

"I do. I definitely do. I've never felt this way before. It's kind of terrifying, but when I think about senior year and where I might be . . . I mean, well, now I guess I'll be stuck here." I shrug. "I don't know."

"I feel like you're making this more complicated for yourself, Mel. Just give it a shot," Yura says.

I want to agree. And I want to just go for it, but I'd be giving up on New York if I just accept my life in Korea now. And becoming Wonjae's girlfriend, if that's even what he wants, is an express train to a destination I'm not sure I'm ready for. Then, whether it's due to the cold winter air combined with the soothing sounds of the Han River, or the sobriety that hits you after alcohol's left your system, it all becomes crystal clear to me. I know who I need to talk to. The person who'll understand me better than my own mom.

TWENTY-SIX

*T*hree hours later, I look at myself in the mirror. I put on extra eyeliner to make me look a little older and a sparkling sequined top with leather pants and gold hoops. If anyone could be related to a singer, it's me. I wonder if this is how my mom looked when she was younger and performing.

I take a deep breath and Naver-map my way to the upscale-looking lounge listed on my aunt's website and wait for the show to begin. At 8:00 p.m. sharp, I see a familiar figure come onto the stage, the spotlight shining on her brightly.

Reba Eemo is wearing a navy suede dress, and she's rocking black boots that go halfway up her calves with super high heels. She's also wearing an ivory feather boa around her neck for dramatic flair. She starts singing and my jaw drops. I hear her clearer this time, maybe because the last time, I was focused on my mom. It's not just that she's good—she is—but if I close my eyes, it's like I can hear my mom. But it's better. There's more emotion to her singing, more pain, more emphasis, more everything.

The entire time Rebecca Eemo is performing, it's like witnessing someone's passion come alive. I recognize that fire because I have it, too. As she sings, we make eye contact, and she winks at me. After the performance ends, I wait close to the stage door and play mindlessly with my phone.

"Kid, you really need to stop sneaking away to see me," she says, ruffling my hair.

"Eemo, I need to talk to you, it's urgent." The words tumble out in desperation. It's Tuesday night, which means the competition is in six days. "You were in my shoes once. A long time ago. Maybe even now."

She looks at me keenly. "Okay. What's up?" As I spill, she guides us to a small fast-food restaurant and quickly orders a few dishes off the menu for the both of us.

I don't know how long it takes, but I try to summarize everything. It doesn't really work because being verbose is a curse I can't escape, but my aunt nods at all the right moments and patiently listens as I tell her everything, about design, the internship, the grades, my failure. When I'm done, I pick up a small mandoo filled with meat and vegetables with my silver chopsticks. The steam rises from the Styrofoam plate as I ungracefully eat the dumpling in one big bite.

"I see . . ." she says slowly. She sighs. "How important is this to you, Melody? Because it wasn't easy, following my own dreams. It came at a steep cost."

"But aren't you happy?"

She gives a wistful smile. "Happiness is relative. I'm happy because I sing. And I have to be okay with that for now. Whether I have other things or not."

"Well, this is the most important thing to me right now. Do you regret pursuing this path, knowing how everything turned out?"

Without hesitating, she shakes her head. "No. Because I can't imagine my life without it."

"Exactly. That's how I feel, Eemo. It's not just about wanting to win the competition; it's the fact that I need the chance to at least try."

She nods thoughtfully before speaking again. "Then you need to show them how much it means to you." My eemo picks up a piece of tuna kimchi kimbap with her fingers and pops one into her mouth.

"I was hoping more for advice on how to sneak my way to New York for the competition," I say, partly in earnest.

Aunt Reba laughs and shakes her head. "My biggest regret is that I never helped my mom understand me better. She never approved and never would have, but maybe we could have reached an understanding if I'd tried a bit more. Try a little harder, Melody."

"How, though?" If I sound helpless, it's only because that's how I feel.

She smiles wryly. "I can't tell you that, sweetie. Think about it more. Figure out a way to show your parents—who don't understand your passion—to see it from your perspective. Why do you love interior design? How can they know how you feel? How can they see? That's the best advice I have for you. And I didn't succeed in doing this myself, but I really hope you do."

As she ushers me homeward, I thank her and promise to think about this some more. I'm about to walk down the gray stairs into the subway stop when she stops me. "Sol," she says with a look that tells me a lecture is forthcoming, "this really needs to be the last time you come to see me without Lily's

knowing, okay? Just call me next time. I promise I'll pick up."
I respond with a wave of both my hands before I head back home—a gesture I realize I never did or knew about until Korea.

At home, I lie on my bed for an hour and irritably stare up at my high ceiling, still waiting for an idea to kick in. But no great artist achieves their dreams by idly awaiting inspiration, so I head downstairs where my parents are both sitting in the den. It's a strangely comforting sight, and I join them mid-conversation.

"I don't think moving is the solution," my mom says in Korean. "This place is plenty spacious." They're sipping on tea together, and my dad has a different but equally thick law book by his side.

"Renovations, maybe?"

I sit down across from them, not saying anything as I try to figure out their conversation.

"Yeah, maybe combining the guest room and the reading room."

My dad nods a few times in thought. "We could transform the living room into a longer space."

Then it clicks. They're talking about redoing the house. The design gods have given me a chance, a teeny-tiny window that I will find a way to crawl through. I know exactly what I need to do. I tune them out—not that it matters much since they aren't paying attention to me anyway—and turn to my phone. Ten minutes later, I rush out of the villa and am inside Yura's living room.

"I have all the options here," she says, handing me a stack of artwork. "I even added stuff from our living room."

"Living room? Won't your parents be like, ''Scuse me, where's my art'?"

"It's just for one night. It's fine, just take it."

I grin and hug her tightly. "Thanks, I'll bring it back tomorrow."

"Don't come unless you have good news," she yells at me as I take the stairs two at a time. Yura's like my fairy godmother. I'll have to find a way to pay her back somehow. Maybe I can find her something unique and vintage from New York. She'd like that.

My parents have retired to their room for the night, and I'm in mine. I'm grateful that my room is spacious enough for me to be able to turn it into a workspace. It all feels very DIY, but I try to make everything seem as professional as possible without drilling holes into walls. I gather my materials, my 2D renderings and my mood board, and tiptoe downstairs and turn on a dim lamp, careful to not let light escape into any of the hallways in case my parents step out of their bedroom. I look at the space: The living room that once felt so foreign to me now feels familiar. The sofas and glass table, the velvet otto-man, the large TV that slides out of a cabinet, and the oversized dining table. They don't feel quite like home to me, but it's not a stranger's home anymore, either. It's ours. The Lee family's villa in Hannam-dong. But I know what to change. I put on my headphones and blast music to keep me awake, and then I get to work. I even put a bandana around my head so I can feel like I'm really in the zone.

For hours, I use stepladders and hang up colorful artwork above the sofas; I rearrange the seating so instead of being pointed to the TV, it's now in a semicircle space that feels inviting and open; I put a throw on the sofa to liven it up and change out the pillows for the vibrant ones in my room that complement the accent walls and help the semicircle space stand out. The trick with neutral colors is that you need that pop of color. Otherwise, your home feels like it has no personality, like a page out of a magazine or a showroom. But every home, including this villa I used to hate, has a personality, and the owners need to bring that out. Moving the sofa takes half an hour because it's so freaking heavy, but the new layout is worth the energy. I bring things from my room, too: the crystal vase, a few funky coffee table books, and then the finishing touch: photographs from New York.

Polaroids of my sixteen years in New York hang on a string across one wall. My mom and I are eating at a diner in one, and in another, Soph and I are laughing with our hair covering half our faces thanks to the wind; the picture manages to simultaneously anger and sadden me. There's one of me and Umma, a selfie of us sitting on the stoop of our building. After digging through the family album, I find one that instantly becomes my new favorite. I smile at the image as I hang it up. It's me as a little kid, my mom, my dad, and we're in Times Square. I have no memory of it, so I must've been really young. I pull out one final picture, which I'm unsure of, but I hang it up anyway. It's a little faded with age. My umma and eemo are dolled up, holding each other's waists. I imagine it must have been right before a performance in New York. I can see an entrance to the 7 subway train in the background, so I think it would have been in Flushing somewhere. I close my eyes and pray my parents don't get angry with me for doing this, but the butterflies in my stomach are stronger than the worry. It's the same feeling

I got when I redid Yura's bedroom. I love what I've done, and this is my last hope . . . I think of Rebecca Eemo's words. *How can they see?*

This. This is how they can see.

I FALL ASLEEP ON THE SOFA, WAITING FOR MY parents. A few hours later, I hear the alarm go off as usual. My dad is awake. I hear the shower turn on and, twenty minutes later, footsteps come down the stairs. I'm sitting cross-legged on the rearranged sofa.

I think it takes a moment for him to adjust and see how different the living room and den look. He orients himself before he speaks. "What on—"

"Morning, Appa," I say to him in my most polite and professional voice. "Can I pour you some coffee?"

He looks at me with an amused expression. "What did you do here?"

"I'll bring coffee, but I also need Umma to wake up and join before I start. I have a presentation for you both."

My dad sighs. "Solmi, I know you really—"

But I cut him off. "Appa, please. Just let me share something with you. You can say no after, if you still want to."

Without a word, he turns around and heads back upstairs. I bring two cups of coffee and place them neatly on the side table and listen carefully. I can hear him waking up my mom. She sounds irritated, but after a few minutes, they're both sitting across from me.

"Melody, what's going on?" she asks me in a drowsy voice.

I gesture to the coffee cups. "You can drink your coffee while you listen to my presentation. All I need is five minutes."

"Mel—" my mom says, rubbing her eyes.

"Please?" I ask. "Three minutes, then."

Neither of them say anything, so I take a deep breath and begin.

"As you can see, I rearranged our furniture. Before you get upset, I promise to move it back to its original layout." I turn to my mom, who still looks drowsy and is taking generous sips of her coffee. "Umma, since coming here, I've learned a lot of things I wish you would have told me earlier. I wish I'd known the full story of you and Dad. I wish I got to grow up knowing Eemo better. More than anything, I wish I'd known that you wanted to be a singer. I've learned so much about you in the last two months; it's more than I've learned in the sixteen years we've lived together."

I turn just slightly toward my dad. "Appa." I pause. There's so much I wish I could say to him, and even more I want to ask him. *Was everything you say you did for us, was it really for us?* I want to challenge him, and I want him to admit that he chose himself in the end. I want to ask if he regrets leaving New York and not coming back, though he promised he would. I want to ask if he was reminded of the life he hated, the life he left, whenever he visited us. But I can't and I won't. Not right now. I can't because I don't think we're quite ready for a raw heart-to-heart like that. Not yet anyway, but maybe one day, we'll get there. I won't, because I know he ultimately did what he thought was best, driven by the desperate desire to see his family thrive. I don't know if I agree or not, but that's the truth in all its messiness.

I look squarely at my dad, who is watching me with a puzzled expression from my long pause. "Appa," I repeat, "I wish you'd visited us more often. But I guess if you came back for good, I would never have moved to Korea and experienced this other half of my home and culture."

I gesture at the living room. "I rearranged the furniture because I wanted to show you why I love interior design. Mom, just try, for one moment, to put aside your preconceptions and worries about me pursuing design. Pursuing something creative doesn't always mean I won't find stability and I'm on a path to failure. The competition I got accepted into is run by the best design firm in New York, one of the top firms in the world. There's a bright and practical future in this. This villa didn't feel like a home at all to me for a long time. Even saying the word *villa* was weird and foreign. I still miss New York every day, but I didn't realize I'd feel the way I do here. It's kind of cool to live together like this, all three of us. And Korean food is the best."

I don't know how to explain the look in my dad's eyes when I say this, but they look full of regret and full of love. He nods at me, encouraging me to continue.

"I had the furniture face each other to create a more welcoming space. I didn't really feel like I could talk to you—either of you—when we first moved here. Everything felt off and distant. Interior design can help change all that and make physical places feel warmer and more inviting. I hung up artwork to inspire creativity and conversation. It's more than just throwing nice furniture into a nice space; good design helps make a house feel like a home, to all of us, to people who didn't live here before."

I pause and wait to see if they want to try and stop my speech. But they don't say anything. "Less than three months ago, Appa, you felt like a really distant father figure in my life. But now, you feel more personal than that. And it's taken sixteen years, but hey, I'm still young, and you're, well, you're not that old, so this is when people say things like 'better late than never,' right? And, Umma, I thought our lives were perfect in New York. I didn't understand why you forced me to come to Korea, and I stopped trusting you when I found out how much of yourself you'd kept from me. And frankly, I still don't know if I'd willingly choose to live in Korea for the long term, but I definitely don't mind it for now. I feel like I've gained a new family somehow."

They turn to each other and smile, and I get the sense they are both trying not to laugh at me. I exhale and look at them sternly. "Shall I continue?"

My mom laughs. "You have even more to add?"

"I mean . . ."

My dad puts one hand in the air, motioning for me to stop. "We understand, Solmi."

I smile when he says my Korean name. The name I always heard spoken in a tone of disappointment now sounds more comfortable to me. It finally feels like *my* name.

"I don't want you to end up giving up on your dreams," my mom says.

"But you told me you don't regret giving up on yours," I say.

"Of course I don't. Because I got you," she says. "And raising you became my new dream."

My mom smiles at me in a way that makes me feel both proud and shy. "I don't want to give up on my dream, Mom."

She nods and nudges my dad.

He shakes his head, but he's grinning, and he gives me a thumbs-up. I wonder if that's where I got my habit from. "You can go to New York," he says.

I don't know how to describe the joy I feel when he says that. I'm acutely aware that I've never hugged my dad as tightly as I do just then, but the excitement exceeds the awkwardness.

"Thank you, thank you, thank you," I squeal into their ears.

"Well, I'm coming with you, of course," my mom says.

My dad looks at her. "What? Why? She'll only go for the competition and come right back."

"That's still a few days! And I'll see my friends, too, and check up on my mom."

"She's not four. She can travel alone, Yeobo," he insists.

"New York isn't Korea. Kids don't travel alone."

"Kids in Korea walk to school alone starting in first grade. She'll be fine."

She pretends to flick his forehead. "Am I not getting through to you? I just said New York isn't Korea."

"Fine, then I'm coming, too."

Then we both look at him; it's so out of character for my dad to invite himself on a trip with us, and for a few seconds, no one says anything.

I'm the first to respond. "That sounds fun." And I mean it.

"Wait, Solmi, isn't the competition on Monday?" my mom asks.

I nod. "I get the prompt on Saturday."

My dad furrows his brows. "That's in three days." I see him piecing things together in his head.

I cheese sheepishly. "So it's a good thing I didn't tell the internship director and panel that I was backing out." I shoot finger guns at them as I say this, hoping for comedic relief.

It works. My parents both laugh; it's a big, head-thrown-back type of laugh, and I soon join in.

When we recompose ourselves, my mom taps on her chin. "Where should we stay?"

"I'll make reservations at the Baccarat Hotel," my dad says.

My mom and I exchange glances. "That sounds way fancy," I tell him.

"I bet you'll enjoy it," he responds.

I pucker out my lips in thought. "Fine, then, no first-class seats. It's too costly for all three of us, and we're going for my thing, and I don't want us spending so much when there's no need for it." From the corner of my eye, I see my mom smiling at me.

He groans. "Business?"

"Economy?" I say daringly.

He shakes his head. "Business. But I'll take the subway almost everywhere once I get there. How's that?"

I laugh again at our entire negotiation and give my dad a thumbs-up back. "Family trip!"

TWENTY-SEVEN

"You actually did it," Kimbeom says, sipping on his royal milk bubble tea.

We—the HT Chingoos—are walking around Garosugil so I can hit up my favorite design stores and find something to gift Sophia. I'm practically skipping, and the others have to constantly catch up to me.

"I *know*," I say gleefully. My dad got us flights for Friday morning, which means we'll also arrive Friday morning New York time. It still feels surreal that it's all happening. *I'm going back to New York!*

"What do you want to do most badly?" Wonjae asks.

I tap my chin while browsing a row of stationery. "Probably ice skate at Rockefeller Center. I've only done it once before, and it just seems touristy and local enough for me to partake in this time around."

I spend the rest of the late afternoon curating Soph's gift basket and make it home in time for dinner. Yura makes me promise that I'll keep everyone updated in the chat room. I hug myself in the elevator. My plan worked. It really, really worked, and in less than twelve hours, I'll be leaving Hannam Towers for five days (only missing three days of school) to be home again.

At dinner, everyone talks all at once about what we need to pack and what we'll be doing once we land. Before I start eating, I quickly send a text message to Reba Eemo.

> I'M GOING TO NEW YORK
> TOMORROW!!!!

"I need to go see Soph as soon as I land," I tell my parents.

"You can see her on Saturday, after you rest," my dad answers.

"Friday after I wash up and rest for a few hours," I plead.

"Fine, deal. Have your rendezvous with your friend and meet us back at the hotel for dinner."

"You know," my mom says, reaching over for the jangjorim side dish, "we never actually discussed what would happen if you got the internship."

I clench my teeth. "Don't say it out loud; I don't want to jinx it."

My dad ponders this. "Well, if you get it, will it be the whole summer?"

"You *guys*," I plead, but I know it's no use. "It's twelve weeks, so yeah, basically. But please, *please* can we not talk about this right now? I really don't want to jinx anything."

EEMO
I heard! I'm so proud.

Go get that internship.

○ ○ ○

I'M CLUTCHING THE CARE PACKAGE I ASSEMBLED since it didn't fit inside my suitcase.

I stand up from my seat and gesture to get my mom's attention, who's seated diagonal from me. Business class seems just as lavish as first. I was shocked again when we were ushered on board immediately without having to stand in the very long line that I'd normally wait in. "Mom, Reba Eemo actually gave me the idea to redo our living room," I confess to her.

Mom takes off her headphones like she's waiting for me to continue.

"I went to go see her," I say. I slide out of my seat and go squish into hers. "I'm sorry I didn't tell you. I wasn't sure if you'd let me go. And I wanted to see her without you so we could start to form our own relationship, you know?"

"About time you told me," she says jokingly.

I can't hide my indignation. "She told on me?"

My mom shakes her head. "No, no. Relayed information between sisters," she says, winking. "But I get it. Now shush, the movie's almost over, and I have two more I want to watch before we land." She puts her headphones back on and ignores me. I go back to me seat, satisfied. In recent weeks, I've noticed my mom and Reba Eemo talking more on the phone, and I've definitely noticed more afternoons my mom wasn't home when I got back from school. It gives me hope for their relationship. She's even gone to see a few more of my aunt's singing gigs.

I peer into my dad's compartment and see that he is fast

asleep, tucked in with his blanket, sleep mask and all, so I go back to my seat, bored, and study my care package. I put together a bag full of Korean things that reminded me of Soph. Or things I thought she'd appreciate, like a T-shirt that says in bold black letters PIZZA IS APPROPRIATE and LIFE ORDINARY. It makes zero sense, like a lot of the T-shirts sold by Korean vendors, but I think it'll really speak to her.

I hope.

EVEN THOUGH I'VE LIVED IN NEW YORK MY ENTIRE life—except for these last two months—I have never set foot inside the Baccarat Hotel. The shimmering exterior, the grand high ceilings, giant bouquets of dark red roses, and the Baccarat crystals displayed in every direction make it feel like Christmastime. I'm awed by the beautifully sleek design and even more so when we enter our suite. The marble slab bathrooms, the ginormous four-poster beds, and the crystal chandeliers are a different New York than the one I'm familiar with, but still so good.

"*Wow*," I breathe. "This room."

"Rooms," my dad corrects. "Your mom and I are here, next to the bathroom with double sinks. You can take the other one."

"Thanks, Appa." I know once the prompt lands in my inbox I'm not going to be able to think of anything else, so today's the day I need to mend things with Soph. I grab my Strand Bookstore tote and promise to meet my parents back at the hotel for dinner.

Taking the E train over to Eighth Avenue feels surreal, like

I'm in a dream, or like my entire two months in Korea were a dream. I soak in the familiarity of Hell's Kitchen, walk past Blue Dog, past 99 Cent Express Pizza, past the gross gentlemen's clubs and past corner bodegas, and soon find myself in front of Soph's building. I ring the doorbell and head up to her apartment when she (or maybe Mr. Taye) buzzes me in. I covered the screen with my hand, so I don't think she knows it's me.

"Who is it?" Sophia asks through the closed door.

"Your best friend," I say in response.

The door opens immediately.

"I hope," I add.

I know in an instant that Soph is just as happy to see me as I am her, but she refrains from wrapping me in a hug. I know because her arms go up a fraction then immediately go back down to her sides.

"What are you doing here?" she says. I can see the shock on her face.

I smile just a little. "I didn't get all A's, but I convinced my parents anyway. I'm here till Tuesday."

She closes the door behind her, and we walk back downstairs to the building stoop. Even though it's only been two months, I'm comforted to see Soph looks the same. Except she dyed her hair a deep reddish brown, which I notice right away. She looks more intimidating, but in a chic way.

"I'm sorry, for everything," I say. I sit down on the third step, putting my tote on my lap and the gift basket next to me.

Soph sits there quietly at first. "Me too," she finally says. "It wasn't easy, you suddenly leaving like that, you know?"

"Yeah, but it wasn't easy to go, either." Both of us are staring at our feet, or the steps. "A lot happened in Korea, Soph. Things I just didn't expect. I learned things about my family, about my parents, my grandparents, and I feel like things were kind of awkward with us and it just wasn't the same, sharing everything through the phone. Almost felt like I was in a K-drama of my own."

She looks at me with an expression acknowledging the same sentiment. "And the longer we didn't update each other as often, the more awkward it became, huh."

I look at her sadly. "Yeah."

We sit there silently for a few moments, before I turn toward her. "Soph?" I thought about this on the plane, about the growing distance in our relationship, about what might have added to it. "No one could ever replace you as my best friend, no matter where we are. You know that, right?"

She looks at me then looks up and to the side to try and stop her tears from falling. "Not even—" and I cut her off.

"Not even Yura. She's been a godsend to me in Korea. If it weren't for her, I'd be so miserable there. But I'm not replacing you. I need you."

She leans in to put her head on my shoulder, but I hug her tightly instead, and this is as good as it gets with best friends.

"Hey, Soph?"

"Yeah?"

"I love your red hair. You look a little unapproachable, though," I tease.

"Good, that's what I'm going for. Had to intimidate my dad's girlfriend, you know?" she jokes back.

We spend the next five hours catching up on every detail of each other's lives, just like always. There's no rhyme or reason to the flow of our conversation; one minute we're talking about Mr. Taye's new girlfriend and Reba Eemo and Wonjae, and the next we're talking about street food in Korea and Clinton gossip.

"Oh! Shoot, I almost forgot." I hold up the assembled gift basket.

"For me? Hand it over!" Soph demands gleefully.

She sits across from me, cross-legged, and unwraps the gift gently. As I watch her, it feels like no time has passed, and yet so much has changed. Sophia opens each individual gift I put into the package and laughs at most of them.

Sophia hugs me again. "I missed you. And I love these, Mel. And I saved the best piece of news for last."

That's all she needs to say before I know. "YOU GOT THE PART AS THE FRIEND SLASH LITTLE SISTER!" I yell.

She's grinning so big that even her large eyes become small half-moons. I throw my bag aside and squeeze Soph again in the biggest bear hug.

"You absolutely deserve it," I tell her.

I don't know how long this goes on for, but soon, my parents are messaging me to meet them for dinner at a restaurant on the Lower East Side instead of at the hotel. When I get there, I feel underdressed. I'm escorted to an intimate bar table, with only a few others and a chef, and raise my eyebrows at my mom.

"A woman took my coat and told me to follow her into the dining area for the tasting," I say. "What are we tasting?"

My mom puts her arm around me. "Just roll with it. Your dad wanted to come here; apparently it's a fine-dining Asian fusion tasting menu."

The tasting menu ends up being more than ten courses. The servers hand out all sorts of dishes in bite-sized portions, one by one. They bring out foie gras (nope from me), duck (amazing), and caviar (way too salty, never eating again), and I sneak sips from my mom's drinks (too strong for me) and get myself a mocktail. When we're finally finished eating three hours later, I'm exhausted. I take a selfie with my parents and send it to the HT Chingoos, with the accompanying text: *doing what my dad does in Seoul but in NYC.*

"That was amazing," my dad says, stretching as we head outside. "It lived up to its reputation. That David Chang is a smart man." He's about to hail a cab when I reach out a hand to stop him.

"Wait. We ate in some fancy tasting place that I didn't even know existed, for you. So now it's my turn."

"What do you mean?" he asks.

I grin. "Prince Street Pizza is right around the corner from here. Let's go." Before he has a chance to protest, I drag both my parents down the street. A few minutes later, we're sprinkling pepper flakes and garlic powder on our fat rectangular Sicilian pizza. I missed the sight of the oil pooling in the small pepperoni slices. I watch my dad intently as he takes his first bite.

He chews for a minute and then nods his approval. "This is pretty great, too," he says.

"It's perfection," I say to him.

When we're all too full to even look at more food, we hop into a cab and head to the hotel. Exhausted, I don't bother suggesting the subway. I'm still marveling at the grandeur of our hotel. Seeing the city from this high up makes it feel distant, almost, but before I can get carried away in cinematic visions in my head, my phone dings—with the sound for email, not a text or Kakao message. Heart racing, I rush to my bed where my phone is charging. It's the M&S competition prompt.

The presentation will take place on Monday at 9:00 a.m. I look at the digital clock on the nightstand. It's 11:28 p.m on Friday. The email also talks about how M&S values minimalism and making sure a space feels welcoming without too many distractions. My eyes scan the email slowly, waiting to read about the assigned task.

Then I see it. The task is to create a home with M&S's values in mind. Otherwise, there are no other limits. The presentation has to fit on a regular-sized poster board.

"That's it? What kind of prompt is that?" I say out loud.

"What's the prompt?" my dad asks. He's reclining on the sofa and scrolling through his phone but puts it down to hear my answer.

"Create a 'home,'" I say in air quotes.

"Sounds deep," my mom chimes in from the bathroom, where she's drying her hair.

"Sounds cheesy. What are you doing tomorrow? I think I'm going to go back to our old neighborhood and walk around. Hopefully it'll spark my creativity."

"Your dad has a bunch of things he wants to do that he claims are not touristy, so we'll see. And visiting Grandma for lunch," my mom says.

My dad loves to try a million new restaurants and places each time he visits New York. It's exhausting, so I'm glad I don't have to join him for it tomorrow. I miss my halmoni a lot, but I have to focus on this prompt and somehow manage to conceptualize something as vague and broad but personal as a "home" in less than sixty hours on a 22-by-28-inch piece of paper. My mind races with too many ideas at once: a townhome? A loft? A barn? A skyscraper for one household?

THE NEXT MORNING, I'M WAITING FOR SOPH WITH two cups of coffee from the cart down the block by my old apartment.

"It felt so good to buy these," I say when she arrives, handing her one.

"Like old times?"

I nod, smelling the fragrant coffee from the little opening in the cup. "I missed this diner," I say, pointing at the yellow-and-red signage. My mom and I once came here at three in the morning when I woke up in the middle of the night with the most unexpected craving for pancakes. I remember not being able to sleep because of my desire for a good fluffy stack. Finally, she caved and we went out. It's one of the things I love so much about New York. There's always something open right around the corner.

"Do you like Korea more now?" Soph asks.

"A lot more than when I first got there. I mean, I missed New York all the time, though. I don't know how to explain it, really."

"You love both places," Sophia says matter-of-factly.

"I guess so. Is that weird?"

She shakes her head. "I don't think so. Are you fluent in Korean yet?"

I crack up at that. "Not even close."

"But I bet it's nice to be with both your parents."

"It is," I say, a new kind of warmth filling me up. "It's weird, too."

"Definitely weird. But good-weird, right?"

"Right."

After two hours of walking around and finding no inspiration, we part ways and I head to a café to focus, trying not to feel too disappointed or panicked. On my way to Frisson Espresso, I stop at an art supply store for a poster board, colored markers and pens, and extra notecards, just in case. You can never have too many blank index cards. The wooden tables, the small space, and the kind baristas make this place one of my favorite hidden gems in the city. It's not a place I went to often since I prefer not to spend over four dollars on a small cup of coffee, but I splurged occasionally. I order a cappuccino (in the spirit of self-indulgence) and pull out my sketchbook. I'll stay here until closing if I have to.

It's late in the afternoon now, and I only have three more hours until the café closes. I have sixteen drawings of homes, from farms and castles to funky-shaped studios and homes made only with glass. I even have a stone home, but none of them satisfy me or give me that "I'm finished" feeling. I try to recreate our home in Hell's Kitchen and our home in Seoul, but they don't mesh together well. Nothing feels complementary or cohesive. I look through my phone and the HT Chingoos chat to see all the pictures we took over the last two months; I draw out imaginary spaces and streets, and then I draw things I've seen in Korea, both from my mind and from my phone: coffee shops, Ikseon-dong, Gangneung, Lotte World, street vendors, bookstores, even SIA.

It's half past six, which means the café will be closing soon.

I put my art supplies away and pack up my bag. As I review my sketches one by one, my attention goes to one specific drawing; I copied it from my phone, so I pull out my phone again and take a closer look at the original photo. Finally, it clicks, and I know what my project is missing. I order a ham and cheese croissant to tide me over until dinner, unpack my bag, and get to work on a fresh sheet of paper.

TWENTY-EIGHT

On Sunday morning, we head downstairs to the Grand Salon for breakfast then decide to go to Central Park. Throughout the day, my parents take turns telling me I need to take my mind off the presentation. I think it's ridiculous that they think I can actually do anything without thinking about the one thing my entire future hinges on.

"Oh, please, it does not *hinge* on this one internship, Mel." My mom looks for her lipstick while we wait for the crosswalk sign to change.

"It *does*. Getting this internship with Maison & Saito would open doors to a lot more design firms for my next internship."

"You know, when I was your age, I wasn't even thinking about internships or college. You sure you're my kid?" she teases.

My dad pats my back a few times, and it's not as awkward as it used to be. "She's just like me," he says. I can hear the pride in his voice.

"Listen, this is all very flattering, but I officially have less than twenty-four hours before the competition. Can I go back to the hotel room and do more prep? I still have more to do."

"Solmi, what you need is a mental clearing. What's a place that soothes and inspires you?" Look who's suddenly a meditation expert! At my confused expression, he explains. "It's what I do before every important business meeting or deal I have. It's critical to having good blood-flow, too."

I sigh. "Okay. Um, I guess Blue Dog."

He looks at my mom, nonplussed, and she explains. "It's basically an upscale diner."

"Aigo, Solmi, I meant an outdoor place."

"Why? I find Blue Dog very soothing. They have the best coffee, it's where Mom and I spent a lot of our time, and I love their white truffle fries. I'm answering your question."

"Okay, okay," my dad says, "let's all go to Blue Dog."

My eyes widen with unexpected excitement. In all these years, I never thought to take my dad there; it was never the type of place I thought he'd enjoy. I was more used to Googling "Top 10 New Michelin Guide Restaurants" or "Business Meeting Restaurants" whenever he visited us. That was just what he expected and wanted—clean, new, fancy. He never once asked where I personally wanted to go, and every time he came, he already had a list of places he'd chosen himself. When we settle into the cushioned seats at Blue Dog, a deep satisfaction spreads through me at finally being able to let my dad into *my* New York. First Prince Street Pizza, now this.

"These are really good truffle fries," my dad says, taking three at a time.

When he goes to the bathroom, my mom taps my arm. "Hey, you. What do you say we walk by the old apartment after? We're right there."

"Just us? What about Dad?"

"I think he wants to go check out an exhibition in Chelsea."

I beam. "Yes. Definitely."

It's not that I don't want my dad there, not at all like that. But there's something special about going there with just my mom, to our little home that we lived in, just the two of us. An hour later, we're standing at the foot of the building steps with our coffees, and she has one arm around me. The dark red bricks and the large brown door still bring me comfort. "I wonder who's living there now," I say aloud. "Does this building still feel like home to you?"

"A little."

"Then what's Korea?"

"Also home," she answers. "Isn't that how you feel?"

I look at the facade of the building and nod. "Yeah. I guess it is. Was Halmoni sad I didn't visit yesterday?"

"She understands; she'll join us in the evening after your interview." She ruffles my hair, which is her way of moving me onto a different topic. "Let's go find your dad," she says, pulling me away again from our old apartment. I sneak a glance at her and notice her smiling. I think she feels it, too: the difference it makes coming to New York *with* my dad and not having him come to visit us. And she's happier, I can tell. I am, too.

WHEN I OPEN MY EYES, IT'S BECAUSE MY MOM IS waving a white porcelain cup filled with coffee in a circular motion under my nose. "Mmm," I say, still half asleep. "Why?"

"You told me to wake you up at six thirty a.m. It's six twenty-five, so I wanted to give you a head start."

I get up too fast, which makes my head spin, and almost knock the coffee over. It's lack of sleep, not a hangover.

"When'd you go to bed, honey?"

"Don't know, around four, I think," I say. I'm barely functioning, so I take a sip of the coffee before heading into the bathroom. By the time I'm out of the shower, I'm alert and my nerves have fully kicked into gear.

"I'm freaking out," I say as my feet tap a frenetic staccato on the ground, and I brush my teeth a little too aggressively.

My panic wakes my dad, who rolls over and throws his arm in the air with a thumbs-up.

"Great, thank you for that thumb," I shout back sarcastically. Today is the day. It is The Day. The first Monday of November.

My HT Chingoos have sent me a slew of excited and encouraging messages cheering me on, and I can't help but smile. Wonjae sends me another message in our own private thread, and my nerves kick up another notch.

My parents keep saying they want to come with me, but I argue with them over the gold-and-crystal room service cart bearing our fresh fruit and coffee.

I clench my fists in frustration. "Okay, you have literally never been this involved in my design life, and today is not the day to start," I say as I swallow some pineapple and butter my bread. "I promise, when I get into college, you can come with me to my dorm and do all that first-day parent stuff. I'm too nervous and I know this city. So just let me go alone. Please?"

I throw my dad's business meeting logic at him and tell him I need to take the MTA by myself to be prepared. They sigh but give in. I slip into my carefully curated power outfit: a pair of boxy, high-waisted bright red pants with drawstrings and a cropped white button-down with pearls lining the collar. My hair is braided to one side, accessorized with a mustard yellow plaid headband and small gold studs. I step into my beige booties and smile at myself in the floor-length mirror. "MELODY SOLMI LEE YOU ARE A DESIGNER," I say loudly to myself. "YOU CAN DO THIS."

My mom surprises me from behind and squeezes my shoulders. "I hope you know how proud of you I am," she says, kissing the top of my head. It's just the encouragement I needed, and my heart swells with pride when she says this.

The subway ride is quick and I get off one stop early, at Spring Street, and walk the rest of the way to try and calm my nerves. My poster board is wrapped in case of unexpected weather, which wouldn't be out of character for New York, and I'm careful not to step in any dirt or random puddles.

When I arrive, I hold my breath as I take in the building. It's mid-rise, with glass doors, like any corporate company, but there are brightly colored furniture pieces in the lobby and a massive canvas painting with the words:

DESIGN WHAT HASN'T BEEN DESIGNED
DESIGN FROM THE PAST
DESIGN FOR THE FUTURE
CREATE TIMELESS BEAUTY

It feels cliché but is also inspiring. That must be why it's a company mantra, I guess.

"Can I help you, miss?" the security guard asks.

"I'm here for the design competition?" The question comes out in an abnormally high pitch.

He asks for my ID and gives me a visitor pass. I smile for the camera, but the grainy black-and-white photo makes it look like my eyes are closed. Oh well. I'm still going to put this into my keepsake box. I take a deep breath and head into the elevator he sends me to. It dings on the sixth floor, and I step out and sit on a sofa. No one's at the receptionist's desk, so I just wait and rehearse my notes.

Minutes tick by slowly and feel like an eternity, but four minutes later, someone comes to get me and offers me coffee, which I decline since I can't possibly get any more jittery than I already am, then ushers me into a room. There are four chairs for the candidates and a long table for the judging panel. Two candidates are already there. We wave and smile at each other uncomfortably before redirecting our attention to our own projects.

The fourth candidate arrives dressed like she's applying for a modeling gig, with super high heels, a fitted dress, and big luscious curls. Admittedly, she pulls it off very well. The judges arrive shortly after, introducing themselves and explaining the process to us.

"I'm sure it feels intimidating to be in this office building at such a young age. You four were selected for a myriad of reasons. Your unique styles, your personal statement, your passion, and, of course, your portfolios. We don't look to hire just the best designers or the most technically skilled. We look at the individual person and their story. What do they have to share? Why is design the path for them? We'll begin by asking each of you a series of questions; some might be the same, some might be different. Afterward, each of you will have a chance to present your completed project. Now, we don't expect you to have all the answers, so just answer to the best of your ability. Any questions?"

The competition begins. My palms are sweating and my adrenaline levels are off the charts. They don't want any of us copying someone else's answers, so they'll give us each one minute to write our responses on a piece of paper, and then we'll read them aloud when it's our turn.

"When designing a room, what do you consider the most important factor?" asks a judge dressed in wide olive-green corduroy pants and an ivory blouse. She looks like such a designer icon, and I am determined to impress her.

"The natural light," I answer. "It's really one of the only things you can't control or change. The sun rises where it rises and sets where it sets. Other things can be maneuvered, replaced, or renovated. And personally, natural light makes me feel more positive and adds a level of brightness to my day that no amount of artificial light can do, so that's a big reason, too."

She scribbles something down. "Very good point about the control factor," she says without looking up.

The next few questions are ones I had predicted and therefore are easier to answer. Then they ask us all the same question.

"What is the most important thing to consider before you begin a new project?"

I scribble my answer on my notecard. I had thought about this, too. One candidate says "budget," because that will inform what our options are and determine the end result. Another candidate says "the space," as in, making sure the furniture and all the products will be complementary to the space. I feel like these are all very practical and smart answers, so I'm nervous when it's my turn, but there's no turning back since I already wrote it down.

"The person you're designing for," I answer.

"You mean the client? Or your boss at your firm?" a panelist asks me.

I swallow nervously. "Oh, sorry, the client."

He nods. "Go on," he says.

"I think the client is the most important aspect to consider before you start designing because he or she is the one who will be living in the space you create. My work on a space is not for me, so ultimately, though I have my own preferred aesthetic, it's more important to consider my client's desires and be able to align them with my expertise and the eye that I have for a room. For example, if my client says, 'I hate oak floors,' it wouldn't be right to ignore their preferences and do whatever I want to do just because I'm the expert, even if oak floors would be my preferred style for the room. Half of being an interior designer is nurturing a positive relationship with your client and understanding what they want. Or learning how to read what they want."

I'd been feeling so-so about my other answers, like they were all pretty similar to what the other candidates said, but after seeing the encouraging expressions on the judges' faces, I feel particularly good about this one.

There's a long pause as the judges deliberate.

One of the candidates leans over to me. "How do you know so much about design?" she asks.

"What do you mean?"

"Did you like, stay up all night researching or studying or something?"

I nod, like it's obvious. "Didn't you?"

She scoffs. "You're so extra."

Before I have a chance to throw a snappy retort in her face, the judges turn their attention back to us.

"Okay, candidates, please get ready for the prompt presentations. For this, we'll be calling each of you into the room one by one. Sarah Gessler, please remain in the room and prepare for your presentation. The rest of you, there are chairs right outside this room where you can wait for your turn."

We file out of the room and sit awkwardly outside. The girl who made the sassy comment is next to me, and I want to say something now, but I try to focus on my presentation instead. Sarah comes out of the room smiling and looking satisfied. This makes me nervous, but I'm also somewhat relieved. This must mean they weren't totally harsh and likely won't rip me into pieces. I hope.

Then I hear my name. I stand up too eagerly and open up my poster to the panelists once I'm inside. I take a deep breath and silently pray for peace.

"This is my hanok-inspired home in New York, which is a traditional home in Korea that first started getting built around the fourteenth century. It's entirely conceptual because nothing like this has been done in America yet. From my research, this style of home is not compliant with modern building codes, but there's definitely interest from architects in bringing this style of construction and design into the US. It's not actually the most accurate depiction of a hanok, but it's a modernized version. I've spent the last two months living in Korea and learning about another side of my cultural heritage—I learned about Korean homes, culture, and food, all for the first time in my life. I tried new things and visited places I never even knew about while I was growing up in New York.

"What stood out to me the most was how Korea as a country works to preserve its historical buildings and architecture, that they'll convert old traditional hanoks into commercial stores so they can be seamlessly integrated into a society and economy that are constantly evolving." I gesture to the photos from Ikseon-dong. "My imagined home strays from the original definitions of what constitutes a hanok, but I've kept the core characteristics of minimal furniture and inclusive spaces the same."

I point to my poster board and walk the panelists through the design of my home. I've managed to draw a hanok in Hell's Kitchen, surrounded by other typical New York buildings. I can't possibly imagine that ever happening in real life, but I can dream about it. And I can draw it. I reconcile it with the modernity of New York apartments by incorporating glass windows, clean layouts, and more whites into my home, as opposed to the entirely light brown and yellow hues that most hanoks usually consist of. It's a hybrid between an apartment and a hanok, and almost has a loft-like feel, without the second floor. I explain the roofs and the tiles of the home, the heated wood floors, the extra courtyard space in the middle that the rooms surround instead of a traditional backyard or patio space. I think about the sign I saw in this building's lobby, the same quote that's on their website. Their mantra.

"M&S Interiors prides themselves on their motto of designing from the past, for the future, and to make living beautiful.

In line with M&S's vision, we can take inspiration from the Korean hanok, a building style from centuries ago, to create a home today and for our future, while preserving and honoring the culture of the past and remembering its beauty."

The panelists walk over to study the poster board a little more closely. They ask a few questions, mostly specifics about the roof material (giwa), floor heating (ondol), and the practicality of the courtyard-style structure. "Courtyards would only be implemented when it's more of an apartment complex as opposed to just one home," I explain. Even though this is an imagined space, I don't want them thinking I'm totally impractical.

"Last question," says the judge in corduroy. "Why do you want to go into interior design?"

I think of our small one-bedroom apartment in Hell's Kitchen, how often I've wished for a bigger room, or how many changes our living room went through in those small quarters. "It's how you make a house your home," I answer honestly. I think of our five-bedroom villa in one of Seoul's most luxurious neighborhoods. "No matter where you are, no matter what apartment or house you move into, you can make any place a haven with proper design. Even when it seems impossible. And eventually, one day, the space really does begin to feel like yours."

They smile and shake my hand.

I stand up and smile back. "Thank you."

"So you're living in Korea now?" one of the judges asks. He's peering at a file, presumably mine.

"Well, I moved there a little over two months ago," I say slowly, hoping this won't ruin my chances. "I actually flew in just for a few days for this competition. I'll be returning tomorrow morning."

"Well, that's dedication," the judge says, visibly impressed. I beam, hoping I just earned some bonus points.

"So would you come back to New York if you got the internship? It's for a whole summer, you know," another judge says.

"I'd be here for the summer, and I don't actually know if I'll continue my senior year in New York or in Korea." If I had a choice, where would I want to spend my senior year? It feels so far away, with first semester of junior year only halfway done. Actually, all of this feels like an out-of-body experience. My parents and I here together in New York, enjoying our time together as a family in the fanciest hotel I've ever set foot in. I'm part of the final round of internship candidates for my dream company. I'm reunited with my best friend. Just months ago, I thought my world was falling apart, and the life I knew, the life I loved, felt like it was being pulled from under me, but now it feels like the opposite. Like everything is coming together the way it's meant to be.

"Ah. I see," is all she says.

The judges all say goodbye and congratulate me on completing the final round. Then they tell me the selected candidate will be notified before the end of the week.

The butterflies that have been flying around in my stomach all day finally give way to something else. Hope. I know it's not realistic to hold on to a hope that feels so overwhelming and all-consuming, but I can't help it. Internship or not, I'm in New York, I completed the final round, and I got to work on the greatest portfolio piece of my life so far.

That evening, my dad books tickets for us and my halmoni

to watch *Mamma Mia*, mostly at my mom's wheedling. After a lot of cheek pinching and hair patting, we're all seated next to each other, and we smile with our respective plastic wine cups (mine filled with soda) and take a selfie.

"*Wicked* is a classic, you know," he says to my mom inside the theater.

"Shush, you've already seen *Wicked*, Yeobo."

I pull out a Twizzler and hand one to my grandma, who's sitting on my other side. "Both of you shush, it's starting soon."

The curtains open and the music begins. Finally, I let the stress of this whole competition wash away as I settle more comfortably into the red velvet chairs of the theater.

Tomorrow morning, I leave for Korea again, and I actually don't mind the prospect.

TWENTY-NINE

WONJAE
did ice skating happen?

> nope. family decided to watch a
> musical instead but issok
> still enjoyed my last night 🙂

korea's excited for your return.

    Soph joins us for breakfast the next morning, and we're seated together inside the Grand Salon. "I can't believe this is where you stayed," Soph says, in awe the same way I was. "Such a different location for the same goodbye."

    "That was very poetic of you, Soph."

    "Oh, yes, well, I'm considering it for a career."

"I'd support you."

"I know you would."

"When I get to Korea, I'll be in touch more, I promise. And no more shitty-friend behavior, double promise."

She grins at me. "Me too," she promises back. "I wish we could spend more time here, though."

I make a sad face. "Same, but my dad has to get back to work, and I've already missed three days of school."

"What a private-school-girl thing to say."

If I get the internship, maybe I could stay with Sophia for the summer. The thought makes the distance between us feel much smaller.

Inside the plane, I pull out Michelle Obama's book *Becoming*. I find it an appropriate word for me right now. Michelle Obama talks about the stark but peaceful transition from the White House to her new home, all the changes and the newness of ordinary life—like pulling a plate out of a cabinet or toasting bread. Sophia has always been a pivotal part of my life, and I hope she continues to be, but I know it'll look different. It has to, because we've been drawn apart physically, and that's going to be the new norm. Well, it already has been the new norm for two months, I guess, but it feels like I've only just accepted it now.

TIME FLEW BY SO FAST IN NEW YORK THAT I PINCH myself to make sure it was all real once we're at Incheon International Airport. "It just feels like a blur, you know?" I tell my mom.

"But so much happened," she says, "and I have a good feeling about this internship." My mom, who once told me this was just a hobby, is now telling me she thinks I won. I shake my head, grinning in disbelief, too tired to be overly sentimental but so grateful. I watch her as she walks closer to my dad, and he casually grabs her hand. Unlike on our family hike, the sight of them together makes me smile a little, almost like I can see the love from many years ago slowly blossoming again.

I walk a few steps behind them and text my aunt on how the presentation went, and she makes me leave out no little detail. When we get back to our villa, I barely make it back to my room and throw my suitcase next to my sofa before I pass out on my bed. I'm not sure what time it is, but when I wake up, it's Wednesday night. I sit bolt upright in my bed, panic flooding through me. I told my parents I'd only miss three days of school—Friday, Monday, and Tuesday. But it's Wednesday night. It's almost 11:00 p.m., and I rush down the stairs and find my parents eating dinner.

I rub my eyes, suddenly wide awake. "It's almost midnight, right?" I stare at them, confused. A bottle of wine, two glasses, steak, and of course, jjigae.

"You were so jet-lagged, honey," my mom says, taking another sip of her wine. "We are, too, obviously. We just started eating a few minutes ago. Want to join?"

"I think I calculated wrong." I grab a spoon and pull up a chair. "I said I'd be back at school by Wednesday, but we landed Wednesday."

They both start laughing. "We know," my dad explains. "But the time difference between Korea and the States is confusing for most people who aren't used to it. We knew, don't worry."

Before I can panic, my mom points to the foyer area. "Yura

and Junghoon dropped off all the materials you missed. It's a pretty hefty stack."

Back inside my room after a full midnight dinner, I group text my HT Chingoos and let them know I'm back. Almost immediately after I send that message, Wonjae calls me.

I sit up, just in case my voice comes out weird if I'm horizontal on my sofa, and clear my throat. "Hello?" I say, trying to sound casual and not at all succeeding.

"Hey, stranger. Welcome back. I'm guessing you slept a lot. I called you a few times." I can tell from his voice that he's smiling.

"Hi," I say again. "Did you miss me?"

"Find out for yourself. Are you free tomorrow, or will you be too tired?"

"Nope, not tired at all. Definitely free. What'd you have in mind?"

"So you're free?"

"Yeah, definitely." There's a pause on the phone, and I realize he's laughing to himself.

"You're making fun of me," I say with a pout in my voice.

"I'm glad you're free," he says. "I won't be at school tomorrow because I have a ton of meetings my grandfather is dragging me to, but want to meet for dinner?"

"Sounds good," I answer.

"Dress warmly," he says, and we hang up.

The next day, I barely survive in school, what with the exhaustion of traveling so far for such a short period of time and staying up late to prepare for the presentation, and then trying to pay attention in lectures that are now extra hard to follow due to four days of missed work.

"Did it make you want to go back?" Yura asks me as we walk through the entrance of Hannam Towers.

I tilt my head to the side, pondering her question. "Surprisingly, no."

"Correct answer," she jokes. "And soon, your first official date!"

When I'm home, my head hits the pillow the second I'm upstairs in my room. When I wake up, it's just past 6:00 p.m., which means I only have thirty minutes to get ready before our first date.

"OH NO!" I shout, scrambling out of my bed and throwing open my closet. "MO-OM," I yell, and I run down the stairs. "I have twenty-nine minutes to get ready for my first—" I stop at the unexpected sight of my mom and Reba Eemo drinking tea in the den. "What the?"

"Hi to you, too, sweetie. Congrats again on getting accepted into the competition!" Rebecca Eemo says to me.

"Hi!" I say, hugging her. "Sorry. Jet-lagged, surprised, and panicking. What are you doing here? Mom, you should've woken me up!"

"Just having tea, Mel," my mom answers.

My aunt looks at me with a bemused expression. "Actually, I don't really know what I'm doing here. Your mom said she'll tell me after this cup." She shows my mom the empty cup with raised eyebrows, waiting for an answer.

I look at my mom for an explanation.

"Mel, go get ready," my mom urges.

I shake my head. "No way. Whatever this is, I'm here for it."

She sucks in a breath and reaches for something in her bag. "Here," she says to my aunt, sliding over a thin piece of paper.

My aunt picks it up, and I strain my neck to get a closer look. "What is this?" she asks.

"It's . . . a job application."

"A what?"

"For the position you're hiring? I'd like to be your manager. Or assistant. Whatever it was you're looking for. A jack-of-all-trades, you said?"

My mouth drops open and I know time is ticking, but I can't leave this conversation. I look at my aunt, impatiently waiting for a reaction.

"You . . . you want to be my manager?" she finally manages to say.

My mom pulls my aunt's hand toward her. "I want to be supportive." She pauses. "And I'm sorry. For everything. I'm here for it now, though, if that matters."

My aunt's eyes get misty and she looks down at the piece of paper again, her eyes wandering through each bullet point listing my mom's qualifications. She nods, unable to verbalize any words.

I let out a happy sigh of relief and look at the clock. "OH MY GOSH, twenty-one minutes now. Both of you, please help me," I yelp, running back up the stairs, expecting them to follow.

My aunt has a younger, cooler style than my mom, so she helps me pick my outfit while my mom picks my accessories. Fifteen minutes later, I'm wearing wide, high-waisted velvet maroon pants and a cropped black turtleneck with oversized sleeves, paired with my gold hoops. "How do I look?" I ask my mom nervously, who helps me adjust my headband. It's the one I bought with Wonjae at Ikseon-dong.

She smooths my hair in front of the mirror. "Like you're ready for your first date with Wonjae."

I smile at both of them and grab my small square neon yellow purse, then run to pull on my high-tops. "Bye!"

Her voice reaches me from the living room. "Don't be late and no funny business!" she shouts.

"Oh my God, Mom," I shout back.

Wonjae's already in the courtyard, and he's wearing a chunky knit sweater that I am positive I would have thought was "too Korean" two months ago, but I really love it on him. His hair is parted to one side and he looks clean and handsome. I'm standing still, admiring the view, when he looks up from his phone, and his grin is enough to make me run to him. I jump-hug him in excitement, and he spins me around once and hugs me tightly back. "Hey, you," he murmurs, kissing my temple.

Inside the cab, I ask him three times where we're going, but he won't answer. It takes over twenty minutes by car with traffic to arrive, so for a moment I wonder if we're in Cheongdam-dong.

"Wonjae," I say slowly, "it's not that I don't love Cheongdam-dong, but I'm not really in a fancy-dinner mood tonight. Can we go somewhere more casual?"

He points at the window. "We're here."

We get out of the car and I stand still, understanding immediately what he did.

"It's the ice rink by City Hall," he explains. "It's not the Rockefeller Center ice rink, but it's cool in its own way. We can go get some street food after."

I love how well he knows me. "It's perfect," I say, grinning at him. The assorted smells wafting over from the street food carts lined up along the ice rink make me realize how hungry I am.

"Maybe for our second date, I can take you somewhere nice for dinner."

I'm glad the wind is sharp so he can't tell if I'm cold or blushing. Only I know it's the latter. I look at him coyly. "Second date, huh?" But I already can't wait.

"And third and fourth and fifth," he says, reaching for his wallet with one hand and hugging my waist with the other. He pays for the tickets, and we get our skates and head over to the rink.

"I suck at skating, by the way," I say.

He extends his hand to me.

"That wasn't an excuse to hold your hand!" I say, pretending to be indignant.

"Tell me more about New York," he says as we skate in wobbly circles around the rink.

"It was amazing," I say with a blissful sigh. "I think I—" And before I have the grace and foresight to stop myself, my skates get caught in a deep scratch in the rink and I fall hard on my butt and pull Wonjae down with me. "I'm so sorry, oh my gosh. I told you I suck at skating," I say, mortified.

He puts his arm around me and helps me sit up and bursts out laughing. "My bad for asking you a question while skating."

"I can multitask!" People skate around us as I try to cross my legs in skates. "What was I saying? For the competition, I think I answered all the questions pretty well. My presentation was good, too, but I don't know how the other candidates did on that part, so I have no frame of reference for how objectively good mine was. I made up with Soph, which was the best part of the trip." An employee comes by with a whistle, ushering us to get up and not sit there like idiots in the middle of the ice rink. I look at him and giggle. "Guess we should skate instead of being ice sculptures here?"

Wonjae gets up first and pulls me up, gently holding my waist as we get into a skating rhythm again. "If you get it, will you accept it?"

I look at him, unsure if he's trying to send me some other message between the lines.

"It's just for the summer," I say.

"You should definitely accept it," he says. "Summer in New York sounds really fun."

"It is, but I think we're getting ahead of ourselves. I only have a twenty-five percent chance of getting this internship."

"Think positively," he says.

"I'd want to come back here for senior year, I think."

"I'd like that," he answers, reaching down and holding my hand.

We don't last that long on the ice rink, mostly because I keep falling and it's getting colder and colder. But the hanging lights above the rink add to the magical evening, despite the fact that I'm pretty sure my butt is bruised in multiple places. There's a little tented indoor space, so we take off our skates and warm ourselves up inside. Wonjae brings us hot chocolate, and we eat fish cakes and more ddukbokki.

"I think ddukbokki has been my second-favorite thing about Korea so far, after jjin bbang," I say to him, wiping the spicy red pepper sauce from the edges of my lips.

"That's high praise considering how much you've experienced in the last two months," he says while gently wiping some sauce from my lips I missed.

I stop breathing with his hand so delicately close on my face and exhale. "Guess so."

"Which reminds me, see, now you need to admit that *you* were the one that was wrong, blabbing about how New York has *much* more to do and eat and explore than Korea."

"What? When'd I say that?"

"At Cappo, before we went to Ikseon-dong. You said all Korea had were cafés, shops, and bars. And that's a straight lie." He grins. "Come on, admit it."

I hold up my finger and continue chewing on my dduk very slowly. "Fine," I admit as I swallow. "Korea's pretty great." It's true.

Wonjae looks pleased with his win. "Hey, so actually, will there be a second date?"

"Do you want there to be?" I say, already knowing what my answer would be.

"Definitely. I want this to be the first of many, many dates." He pulls another skewer of odeng from the hot soup and hands it to me. "I have something for you." Wonjae grabs a small jewelry box out from his pocket and opens it up to reveal a simple gold band. "I know it's cheesy, but lots of couples in Korea wear couple rings. I was hoping, well, I wanted to ask you out. Officially. You know, boyfriend-girlfriend stuff."

The ring is so delicate and simple. I've never been given such a beautiful gift from a boy, and it's not that I am entirely surprised by his question, but I'm also never that elegant, either, so of course, I start choking on my fish cake.

"That was definitely not because of your question," I say when I clear my airway.

He laughs and waits for my response.

I beat my chest to clear my coughing. "Okay, one more time. Let's try to be elegant, Melody. Can you ask me again?"

Wonjae dramatically opens his arms wide and lifts his head up like he's going to shout into the sky. "Melody Solmi Lee, will you do me the honor of being my girlfriend?"

I burst into laughter and lean my full body into his open arms. "ABSOLUTELY. Ah! On one condition."

He looks at me, puzzled.

"Are you over Saeha?"

It's his turn to choke.

"One quick lesson? Girls know everything." I make a sly face at him.

He shakes his head. "I was never into her. We met once because my dad forced me to. She goes to a different school, and we don't talk anymore."

"Well, didn't you go over to her place after Lotte World?"

"Wow, you really do know everything."

"So you did!" I accuse.

"No way! We met at a coffee shop nearby. I just went to tell her in person that I wasn't interested in her and to apologize if I had led her on, though I honestly don't think I did. She came on very strongly, though."

"Well," I say, pausing, "good. I'm glad. My *boyfriend* is mine only."

He grins when he hears me say "boyfriend" and slips the ring on my finger. It's official and I love it. We finish eating in comfortable silence and contemplate going back onto the rink, but we grab some more hot chocolate instead before heading back to Hannam Towers.

In front of my building, I don't want to part ways until we have to, so we linger outside.

"You'll find out soon about the internship, right?" he asks.

"Before the weekend is over, according to the judges."

We're swaying again, on the swings, when he nudges me with a knowing look. "You look cute in that headband," he says.

"Needed a memento of one of the best days I had in Korea."

He leans in like he's about to kiss me, I can tell, so I close my eyes and lean in, too, but then he stops. "Can I?" he whispers.

I pull him closer to me and press my lips against his. "Yes, you can," I whisper back.

He grins then kisses me again. And again and again and again. I'm not sure how long this goes on for, but both our noses and cheeks are bright red after it all.

FRIDAY AFTER SCHOOL, I FINALLY FEEL LIKE THE jet lag is starting to wear off. I finish my homework and read up on more lecture notes from the days I missed at the start of this week and spend a few minutes video calling with Sophia before dinner.

"Dinner!" my dad shouts from the hallway.

"Coming," I answer, and put my highlighter down. Closing my AP World History book, I look up and see the rice paddy painting I never bothered to switch out. I like it now and it fits the room well, which has begun feeling very me ever since I got back from New York. I remember thinking on the plane back that I missed my room, my room with this funny-looking rice paddy painting and satin sheets and colorful bookshelf. I walk into the kitchen a few minutes later to heated voices.

"No, *you* picked Melody, and I picked Solmi," my dad is saying to my mom.

My mom shakes her head while she sets down bowls of oxtail soup at the table. "No, *I* picked Solmi, because *sol* and *mi* were my favorite 'Do-Re-Mi' notes. I distinctly remember. *You* picked Melody because you wanted to copy my 'singing-related' name." He's following her around the kitchen as she scoops food into bowls. My mom hands him the rice bowls, and he sets them on the table.

"No, no, no, you have the memory of a goldfish, Yeobo," he says.

"I never realized my name was so musical," I say to them, grinning. It makes perfect sense, and I love it.

My parents look at me, like children caught fighting over a toy. My dad recovers first.

"Well, it didn't do any good since your voice sounds nothing like your mother's. You got that from my side of the family, unfortunately."

"Yeah, I do blame you for that."

"I just don't want you to take credit for my creativity in naming our only offspring," my mom says to him.

"Fine. We can say that I picked Melody, then. She prefers that name anyway, right, Solmi?" my dad asks me.

I shrug instead. "Actually, I kind of like Solmi now."

I watch as my mom bickers with my dad comfortably, with the awkwardness of the past forgotten. My parents, who once felt so distant and secretive, are having a gloriously normal argument, and I'm enjoying listening to them, so I silently dig into my rice and banchan.

I almost don't notice when my phone buzzes in my pocket. It's a longer buzz—the one that signals a new email. My breath catches in my throat. I put my chopsticks down and pull out my phone.

I tap on the email icon.

SUBJECT: Welcome to Maison & Saito Interiors!

My mouth drops open, and a grain of rice falls out. My parents are now bantering about something else, so they have no idea what I'm about to tell them. A surge of affection soars through me as I watch them. In these few short months, amid fights and misunderstandings, unraveled secrets and regrets realized, we fought for each other, and we became a family. We're still figuring it out and it's a mess, but it's ours.

I let them finish bicker-flirting while I pull apart the oxtail meat in my bowl and slurp my soup contentedly.

I'm glad to be home.

ACKNOWLEDGMENTS

I just had a baby. Eight weeks and one day ago, to be exact. And it took all the closest people in my life to keep me grounded, caffeinated, and joy-filled. I understand a little better now why authors call their books their babies. The book you are holding would not have been born into existence without some very special people:

Jim McCarthy, my wonderful agent. I still remember walking out of Sondheim Theatre and seeing a missed call from an unknown number. The voicemail that followed and the phone call we had shortly after is forever emblazoned into my mind. Thank you for sitting with me through long rambling phone calls, for sharing your brilliant mind, and for all the smiles and kindness. Here's to more taco outings in the future.

Jenny Bak, I still can't believe I get to call you my editor. Working with you has been a literal dream come true. Your investment in me and my stories and your excitement for my step into motherhood have been such gifts during these pandemic times. To the entire team at Viking who worked on this book, thank you for your time and dedication. This entire experience could not have happened without you all.

To Kelsey Rodkey and Rachel Lynn Solomon, for choosing me, and for being the mentors and friends I never knew I needed. In my next book, I hope my heroine isn't a crybaby, but if she is, I know you'll let me know. Love ya, PW moms.

During long nights in my former job as a PR professional, I joined Gotham Writers Workshop and it was the best decision I made in my twenties. My biggest hugs go to my first writing teacher, Kody Keplinger, and to our group: Cindy Sullivan, Melissa Chai, Jen Augustinas, Jesse James Keitel, Shannon O'Grady, Jenna Geiser, and Richard Gianotti. Thank you for reading multiple versions of this book, including the very first draft! I still can't believe how insanely talented you all are and how lucky I am to read your words. Our Zoom meetings these last two years have filled up my writing well and were a balm to my days during 'rona. I look forward to all our books being together one day. To Kelly Caldwell, for the kindness you've shown us and the unlimited wine.

If you are an aspiring author, apply to Pitch Wars. Thais Vitorelli, Kaitlyn Hill, Elora Ditton, I love us. And Korean baby hearts to Susan Lee, my PW unni. To the entire team running the program, my deepest gratitude to you all. To the mentee class of 2019, I love all your stories.

So much love for my people: Jackie Oh, Philia Aramaki, Gabrielle Tang, Paul Choi, Annica Ma, Saemee Chung, Sophia Feleke, Josh Hwang, Jiwon Kim, Michelle Huang, Jimin Lee, Rebecca Yang, Josh Chae. Your delight for my book, our long walks, the wine, our FaceTimes kept me going.

Yurieo, my dear Yurieo. Can anyone match your unwavering enthusiasm for my book? I think you may need to be my unofficial editor forever, thank you very much.

To my Mels, for always surprising me with the best little pick-me-ups. I'll never find someone with a chunkier heart than yours, my L.

Linds, for your dedication and love in this friendship. Wo ai ni for freakin' forever, Chandler.

Jennif Shin, for being the dreamiest hypewoman I've ever known. What did I do to deserve you? How you keep track of all my deadlines and what chapter I'm on will always amaze me. My icon.

To all my relatives, especially my halmonis and harabeojis, for being the OG storytellers in my life.

Appa, for demonstrating intense work ethic and for showing me what passion looks like.

My golden sister and my confidante. You believed in me when I was so often on the cusp of giving up. Multiple times. Your love is one of the best gifts in my life, and I couldn't have done this without you, Unni.

For making me snacks after school every day, for staying up with me as I tried to finish class projects, for endless sacrifices for me and Unni, for teaching me to have all-too-high standards, for pushing me to be authentic, for showing up, I am everything I am because of you, Umma. This book is for you.

My Ella. You are the biggest light in my life now. Presently, I'm obsessed with your toes.

And finally, my husband. Daniel Chaka Kim, I love being your wife. Your insistence on celebrating every milestone is ridiculous, but you make me feel so incredibly loved. This life and every day is much better because of you. Promise to always have heart eyes for you, hot stuff.